frenzship

RAY GLICKMAN

for my old friend & mentor

John Aylward Simmons

Also by Ray Glickman

Reality

The ultimate game of manipulation.

Bored with his easy success in life, the unnamed narrator selects
six people at random and makes their worlds collide.

But the choices they make within the relationships he constructs
are theirs.

In the end, who is to blame for their actions -
their deceit, infidelity and crime?

The evergreens stood proud and tall as I hovered above them. I remember vividly the grey-brown bark, the waxy green leaves and the large spiney cones before I crashed and everything went black.

They say I might never walk again. They also said hang-gliding was safe. But it's no wonder I don't know what to think.

Cassidy is so like me. She is in denial about my permanent invalidity. It could be the pregnancy talking. It is weighing on her literally and metaphorically. Suffice to say, she is distant from me when I need her most. Lorna, despite her tender years, is much more attentive. She has absolute confidence in my full recovery as long as I don't indulge in the negative energy of self-pity. She tells me I can't just lie here in this hospital bed. She insists I must do something.

I know she's right. Under sufferance, I am preparing to write this book. It will be about friendship. It will be called frenzship.

The perverse nature of friendship fascinates me. It defies explanation. To do this subject justice, I must find a friendsmith. I need someone with such a deep understanding of the building blocks of friendship that they can deconstruct it and reassemble it for me afresh.

Is it anything more than basic chemistry? Can friendship be reduced to a series of chemical responses or electrical impulses? Is it just a physiological reaction? Do we positively choose our friends or is friending purely involuntary?

I've looked at it from every angle. The f word, 'friendship', is part of a tribe. It has kinship ties with 'forgive' and 'forget'. But is it also related to 'forever'? Is there a use-by date on friendship or does it abide no matter what?

What's the difference between friendship and love? I get that one. Friendship is chronic; love is acute. Friendship is a dull ache; love is a sharp pain.

I've searched for the meaning in popular songs:
Winter, spring, summer or fall,
All you have to do is call,
And I'll be there, yes I will,
You've got a friend.
A friend is there for you. I get that. Is that all there is to it?
Maybe this will help more?
You told me boy look the other way,
You told me boy bite your tongue,
Yes, that's not the way,
Yeah, that's not the way,
That's not the way that friends behave,
That's just not the way that friends behave.

Lorna is making faces at me in that annoying way of hers. I know what that expression means. She's telling me to make a start. She's plumped up my pillows, procured my MacBook and has improvised a desk out of the meals tray that swings over my hospital bed.

Cassidy hasn't fronted today. Her text explained she had a round of meetings to attend and a doctor's appointment.

Lorna's voice slices through my jumbled thoughts. Well?

You can't just write a book, I protest. It doesn't work that way

She pins me with that sideways stare of hers. Sometimes she looks so impossibly young.

You've never written a book so you don't know, Lorna observes dismissively.

I can't do this. My voice is whiney. How can I write about friendship when I don't understand why Ewan and I are even friends?

Write that then, Lorna urges me in that odd blended accent of hers.

How do I do it?

Start at the beginning. Tell them how you two became friends.

That seems sensible. It's just factual, after all.

OK, just to shut you up, I say, so there's no ambiguity. I'm doing this under duress. Just so long as we're clear about that.

How a friendship starts

Opposite sides

It's hard to explain why Ewan and I are friends. There's been a lot of conflict between us over the years. I don't think he understands it either.

This reminds me of some politicians I used to know. They argued like spoiled brats in the playground known as the House. They abused and vilified each other to the embarrassment of the nation. Yet, in the corridors of power, away from the public gaze, I saw the Minister comforting his Shadow in the face of his wife's cancer.

Ewan and I were educated (if that is the right word) in London. We attended what's euphemistically called a public school. Private schools are called public schools there to deceive the great unwashed. This fools no one. Still, you can't blame the establishment for trying.

We were pupils at the same school, but Ewan and I were from opposite sides of the tracks. Not literally. We were born on opposite sides of the famous Abbey Road. I was born on the good side. The one towards which John, Paul, George and Ringo were crossing. Ewan hailed from the dark side.

He was born and raised in the council flats down the hill. Ewan's father was a black cabbie. He wasn't Jamaican. He had done the Knowledge. Ewan's mother died soon after I met him.

The disparity in status was enormous. Yet we were equal in one respect. He was jealous of me and I was jealous of him. He felt guilty about his envy. I accepted mine.

He secretly coveted my posh home, my pedigree dog, my expensive gadgets, my holidays abroad and all my money-dripping paraphernalia. I was jealous of him for just one thing. It wasn't for his mutt. They weren't trusted to look after pets in the tower blocks. As a working class boy, he had something I could never truly have. Ewan was common. He was one of Jarvis Cocker's common people.

Let me tell you about my family. My mother, Jane, was one of the first female surgeons out of the blocks. My father, Leonard, merely jogged along with the male stockbroker pack. I wanted for nothing and so I wanted everything. My parents were cultured and intelligent people. They were bons vivants, connoisseurs of collectables and patrons of the arts. Their life was civilised and comfortable. Refinement and good manners seeped from their pores. Never a cross word passed their lips in public. I'm betting none was exchanged in private either.

Privilege came naturally to my parents. They wore it well. Mind you, we did come from hardy stock back in the day. Our family tree boasts miners and steelworkers. Education and good fortune rounded off our rough genetic edges over time. New qualities of graciousness and gentility surfaced in my parents' generation. The moral fibre of our lineage is now firmly in decline.

They say that opposites attract. In my parents' case, the polarity of human chemistry was reversed. Their backgrounds and personalities were so similar that, if incest were possible between unrelated people, they would have been hauled before a judge.

My parents were spoilt as children and they indulged me, their younger child, in similar fashion. I emerged from my mother's womb an engaging but arrogant sod. Ready access to the expensive trinkets of childhood did nothing to quell those traits. I lacked the dignified restraint of my parents. They were wealthy but not ostentatious. I flaunted it. My parents considered themselves fortunate. I considered myself entitled.

My brother, Tom, will get scant coverage here. Not because of any enmity between us. He is but a shadowy figure in my life. His presence is like a wraith in a haunted house. I catch a glimpse of him in my thoughts and then he is gone. He experimented with drugs at an early age and then disappeared. My parents bore it with the customary stiff upper lip. If it quivered, I never noticed.

Meanwhile, at the foot of the ominously named Shoot-Up Hill, Ewan's family lived a frugal life. They rented a maisonette - a two-level flat. It stood on the fifteenth floor of a grey, dystopian sixteen-storey block. They had a balcony to enjoy such fresh air as pea-souping London allowed. Unfortunately, it faced west. It overlooked the monotonous concrete landscape of the neighbouring council tenements. If it had faced east, it would have enjoyed the inspiring vista of the leafy suburbs. It would have revelled in the visual spectacle of our Georgian-style home, *The Hollyhocks,* where my father would joke that we had put down roots.

Ewan's home and castle was called Cardiff House. For some reason best known to the good bureaucrats of the Greater London Council, all of the buildings on Ewan's estate were named after places in Wales. This was odd. Nobody from this working class suburb of London had ever ventured that far. Undeterred by their ignorance of the land of coalmines and choirs, these council-estate dwellers held disparaging views about that part of Britain's industrial landscape. They slagged it off, so to speak, along Alexei Sayle's lines that, 'They have rainbows in black and white over there'.

Just different

My reflection is Ewan always felt different. Not in a bad way. Not in a good way, either. Just different.

Ewan resisted going to that school. He watched his parents agonise over the decision. His father cringed at the thought. He blushed red as his revered flag at his prospective defrocking as a covert apologist for the public school system. Ewan's selfless mum didn't want her baby boy to take the tube and then change onto another line to get to school and back when there was a perfectly good comprehensive just up the road. Ewan's main objection was that the school didn't play football. The elite preferred rugger. He would drop this concern into the debating pond from time to time. It generated barely a ripple. He occasioned a tiny splash when he confided in his parents that playing rugby scared him. This confidence moved what was left of his mother's body and soul. His father maintained his zealous scorn for those soft of hands and heart.

Ewan didn't fit in. It didn't worry him that much as he hadn't expected to. He was amongst the brightest in his class. This endeared him to the more academic of the teachers. He secretly enjoyed the study - Latin, history, geography and politics. He kept these esoteric tastes from the other kids on his estate, who were busting to make it to sixteen so they could give the two-finger salute to schooling and go look for a job.

The boys at school associated on class lines. The rich ones all knew each other. Their families met socially for a game of tennis at the club or a round of golf. The working class boys gravitated together too. They focused on study rather than social climbing.

We would visit each other's houses after school. To Ewan, a house as grand as The Hollyhocks, was something straight out of the movies. Our mansion had rooms on three levels. He was incredulous that we had five toilets. He loved watching our colour television. The vivid green grass of centre court at Wimbledon held him spellbound.

Thanks to his dad's working class pride regime, Ewan was unembarrassed about his modest flat. I enjoyed the contrast in hanging out with him on his council estate. We poured scorn on the GLC place names committee's lack of imagination. It played safe, opting for the easily spelled locations like Cardiff and Swansea. It clearly lacked the guts to venture out there. Didn't Abergavenny or Rhyl deserve a turn? Ewan and I raised a petition to have the new tower block under construction afforded more challenging nomenclature. We wanted something that would keep the post office on its toes. Llanfairpwllgwyngyllgogerychwyrndrobwllllantysiliogogogoch House.

Thirty-two feet

To my pampered eyes and refined sensibilities, Cardiff House was a dreary and depressing place. It wasn't just the look of it. The behaviour of the tenants left something to be desired. To that point, I'd wondered why toilets were called 'conveniences'. In Cardiff House, the reason sank in. Some of the residents found it convenient to treat the lift as a mobile urinal. I would squelch out of the elevator to feel my way along Ewan's dimly lit corridor. I liked pressing his doorbell. It would flash and play the *Marseillaise*. While I waited to be greeted, I would stare at the decoration on the doorpost. We discovered one revelatory day that the ornament left by the previous occupants was called a *mezuzzah*.

I hesitate to misrepresent the inhabitants of Cardiff House. Back then I thought those people deserved their lot in life, as I did mine. Over time I came to realise that it mostly housed people down on their luck. For some that lack of fortune 'befell' them to the end. This was fatally true for one unfortunate spinster. She'd been perched on a rickety kitchen chair to do a spot of outdoor window cleaning. She reached a little too far to gouge out some ingrained guano only to plummet from her thirteenth-floor balcony. If it was any consolation, she had a wonderful view to the east from her side of the tower.

That stroke of self-imposed misfortune fascinated and horrified us. Ewan wondered whether the luckless Miss Appleby cursed her penchant for the pristine as she counted down the thirteen floors accelerating at thirty-two feet per second per second. I was no better. I was convinced that she'd taken the leap of death to avoid another trip to the ground floor ankle deep in piss.

No Rob Roy

My suspicion is that Ewan felt at odds with the world because everything about his life was, frankly, odd.

With a name like Ewan Mackenzie, he would stoically endure the standard greeting that went, 'Och aye the noo'. He would sheepishly explain that his father, Jamie Mackenzie, despite his Caledonian name, was no Scotch-swilling, wild-eyed, red-bearded Rob Roy. His dad was in fact a politically rabid, but otherwise mild-mannered London boy. So pervasive were the north of the border trappings in his life that Ewan would check his public hair now and again to make sure there was no nascent strand of orange. Once he passed that test, he would check out his adolescent features in the mirror. He had inherited his dad's mane of unruly black hair, the aquiline nose and his pointy ears. Ewan was disappointed to find such an average-looking guy peering back at him. He wasn't ugly, but he was no oil painting either.

Ewan had heard the story countless times. His grandparents, Jamie's mother and father, were Lithuanian immigrants. Their family name was Wachensee. Courtesy of British immigration, which was neither welcoming of foreigners nor tolerant of their inability to speak the King's English, Wachensee was transcribed to a name much more familiar. Mackenzie.

Ewan's grandparents were quick to seize upon the unexpected opportunity to assimilate their imposed identity afforded them. They revelled in its familiarity. They milked it by calling their firstborn, James. Ewan's dad would joke, 'Naming me like an Orkney didn't stop me speaking like a cockney, did it, my son?' In turn, Jamie persuaded his own wife, to call their first-, and ultimately only-born child, Ewan.

So the Mackenzie clan was born. Ewan became an impostor Bonnie Prince Charlie. He would amuse himself by designing his own faux-Mackenzie tartan. When we had had nothing to keep the boredom at bay in the school holidays, we would create the entire merchandise range, including tie, kilt, tam o' shanter, sporran and everything required for that Hogmanay to remember.

The elections

The elections came around to take our minds off what the local rag called the 'horror plunge'. The polls were manna from heaven for me. While Ewan was a reluctant conscript into his dad's fighting force, I was a willing volunteer. I would sign up for a further tour of duty whenever the democratic cycle required Labour Councillor, Jamie Mackenzie, to defend his seat. I loved every second of it. I dismissed with contempt my parents' less than subtle jibes about collaborating with the political enemy.

The elections made me feel important. Ewan and I, at our tender ages, ran campaign HQ. We got the rare opportunity to tell adults what to do. We were convinced that Cllr. Mackenzie's political career hinged on us.

As I didn't give a toss about the politics and didn't want to acknowledge my real motives, I convinced myself that I was helping Jamie out of respect. Deep down I knew that wasn't it. The real reason for loving the elections was simple. I got to be common. For two or three weeks, I hung out at Cardiff House amongst the proletariat. I looked and sounded different, but to all intents and purposes, I was one of them.

Ewan and I fought bare-knuckle, last man standing election campaigns for Jamie. We took nothing for granted. Jamie's historic popularity with the electors did not disabuse us of our conviction that the quality of our campaign organisation would decide the result.

Jamie was a rare breed amongst the unprincipled scum that passes for practitioners of the political arts, particularly amongst the inglorious ranks of local councillors. Jamie cared about his constituents. He didn't see those people as a conglomerate group like that. To him, they were his fellow tenants in the serried ranks of council flats in his neighbourhood. He spent such spare time as he had, when he wasn't driving the cab, doing what the Labour Party used to stand for - helping the workers. That was before the party was hijacked by political advisors and union officials who have never done a real day's work in their lives.

Candlestick

I remember when Ewan's mother died. Fleetingly, I paid some attention to my own mum. My mother found the sudden solicitousness disconcerting. I assured myself that she looked hale and hearty. It's appalling, I know, but I thought that for my mum to be fine and for Ewan's to die was the natural order of things.

Ewan told me his mother looked like a bird when he was allowed past the curtains to see her lying inert and lifeless. He fancied she'd fallen from her nest, perched high on one of London's tallest plain trees, and had drifted to earth precisely where she lay - dead in St Thomas's Hospital.

The sparrow wasn't really his mother. She had long departed. Similarly his dad had taken himself off somewhere to sob in peace. Ewan didn't feel like crying, although he suspected he should. He imagined himself in the Colosseum he had been studying in ancient history. If he failed to shed a tear, he fancied the assembled uncles, aunties and family friends would shrug and sigh but have no option but to thrust their juddering thumbs groundwards. That judgment would have been harsh. Ewan couldn't associate the lifeless artefact on display in this museum of sterilisation with the centre of his world that had once been his mother.

He was sorry he'd shouted at her a good twelve months before when she'd asked him to get the candlestick and then insisted when he brought it that he was to get the candlestick. He hadn't heard of a brain tumour. He wouldn't have got angry with her if he'd known.

His mum stayed in bed a lot. After a while she camped in the living room because it was getting too tough to manhandle her up the narrow staircase to the bedroom. She rarely spoke. Perhaps from the fear or shame of mixing up basic things. His dad, a loquacious man at heart, found the strain of doing all the talking at home too much to bear. He saved his words for his taxi passengers and his impassioned oratory in the council chamber.

Apparently, on the night of Ewan's mother's funeral, one of Jamie's constituents came calling for help with an eviction notice. At such a time, most people would have ignored the persistent ringing of the bell and the repeated rendition of the French call to arms. Ewan looked at his dad, assuming he would leave well alone.

I remember Ewan describing to me the despondent figure Jamie cut shuffling his way to the door. Ewan's dad invited the distraught woman in. He took careful notes so he could follow it up the next morning.

We ignored them

Everyone knew Jamie in his council ward. Those that hadn't encountered him in person, knew of him by reputation. That made no difference to Jamie's fervour at election time. He would browbeat voters in the travelling toilets. At the local shops, he would berate those who hadn't bothered to vote last time round.

Jamie was the high profile candidate in this low-rent universe. Ewan and I were the back-room party machine - the faceless boys. For the duration of the campaign, Jamie's cramped flat was submerged beneath a sea of propaganda – electoral rolls, voter supporter lists, leaflets, posters and banners screaming the message, 'Send Jamie Back Where He Belongs'.

I immersed myself for this brief interlude in plebeian society, relishing the contrast to my normal social milieu. Before I met Ewan at senior school, I'd never met a boy from a working class family. My parents weren't snobs. It's just that the social classes in the UK never mixed. It was normal for the middle-classes to feel superior and for the working classes to know their place. We instinctively looked down our noses at people we'd never met. We were like those racists and homophobes so determined to hate people they don't know. We didn't so much despise working class people. We ignored them.

Guildhall

Our senior school, Guildhall, was named after the symbolic seat of power of the merchant classes nestled in the heart of the City of London.

Guildhall was a melting pot. I got to meet boys from all walks of life. The majority were fee-paying pupils. Their education cost their parents plenty. We shared our classes with scholarship boys, whose tuition was paid for by their local authority.

Ewan was a scholarship boy (a 'freebie' as they were called). To gain this free tuition, he had to prove himself a gifted and talented pupil worthy of the financial assistance of the local ratepayers. I was not a scholarship boy. I was as talented and gifted as him. More so I was convinced. But my parents could afford to pay. That meant I was unfairly deprived of the opportunity to compete on academic merit. To me, that was an egregious example of life not being fair.

Despite the school's best efforts to be terribly jolly and get the boys from all backgrounds to mix, the ingrained teaching of the British class system saw to it that the oil of the wealthy rarely mixed with the water of the poor. Ewan and I were the exception.

We became unlikely soul mates thanks to the exigencies of the school's cadet corps. We shared the excruciating embarrassment of travelling once a week on the London Underground, dressed in full army uniform. This adolescent torture gave us common cause. The other boys believed the jingoistic crap peddled by the school or lacked the intestinal fortitude to protest. Ewan and I dared to be different.

The teachers, masquerading as army officers for cadet corps purposes, labelled us Trotsky and Lenin. They were half right. They had Ewan down to a tee. He had been indoctrinated by comrade Jamie's lefty rhetoric and could parrot it down pat. He railed against the multinationals and the imperialist running dogs. He was a sworn enemy of the British army. He saw it as an instrument of oppression. For him, to playact as a junior British soldier was frolicking with the fascists.

I went along with the teachers' branding of me as Lenin, or was it Trotsky? This helped me cultivate the common touch. But I knew they had me wrong. I didn't believe Ewan's socialist twaddle any more than the school's bullshit about the glorious history of the British Empire. I didn't fight the good fight against the cadet corps and against many establishment institutions since because I'm a revolutionary. I'm anti-authoritarian. It's as simple as that.

Ewan and I became blood brothers. As Groucho Marx would have said about us, 'Whatever it was, we were against it.'

Push Back

At the pointy end of school, when the dreaded A-levels were looming, Ewan would insist on recounting his recurring nightmare to me. He would file into the school gym with his jittery classmates to take his first final school exam. He would lay his pens neatly in a row pointing away from him (he really did that OCD stuff, BTW). He would wait for the crusty old teacher to look over his half-moon glasses and pompously intone, 'You may now turn over your examination paper'. Then the horror would set in. He had forgotten to revise.

I refused to sanction this nonsense. I would hurl the nearest available object at him. Often it was a cricket ball. Ewan had honed his evasive skills from so frequently ducking out of the way. He would look dolefully at the accumulation of nasty dents in his bedroom wall before covering them with another poster extolling the heroism of the Soviet working class.

His exam angst defied logic. Ewan was spending countless hours with his head over the books in that cramped bedroom of his. Rightfully, that was my nightmare. I was barely studying at all.

Ewan was snaky with me around that time. Although we were friends, I think Ewan realised he didn't like me much. That's what's so weird about friendship.

Deep down, Ewan was like his father. Jamie put on an act in his public life to mask his reserved nature. Ewan was also the quiet type. He thought deeply but mostly kept his opinions to himself.

I was the exact opposite. I had no qualms about speaking up. I'd say the first thing that came into my head. I wouldn't hesitate to unleash my acid tongue on anyone or anything. Ewan was often the one on the receiving end.

My reflection is that Ewan was attracted by my self-confidence and repelled by it at the same time. Now and then he would teeter on the brink of retaliation. He would start to push back and then hesitate and withdraw.

I can see now that these behaviours reflected our social status. I could afford to mouth off and snub my nose at convention. I had nothing riding on my school results. Ewan, on the other hand, had nothing to fall back on. More importantly, he had something to prove.

In the end, I think he accepted me for what I was - a jerk. But, sub-consciously at least, he recognised that I was of value to him. I was good fun to be with. Without me around, I think Ewan realised that his serious side would dominate too much. Secretly, he feared he would become the revolting bookworm I said he was.

From my standpoint now, I realise that there is yin and yang in friend-ship. There is some indefinable interconnectedness between things that are opposed.

Dirty Dorothea

While Ewan was immersed in tedious study, I had better things to do. Thanks to the unstinting generosity of my parents, I had the wherewithal to otherwise distract myself. My hopeless brother, Tom, procured dope for me. I had the choice of shit or grass. I chose both. Although not on the official syllabus, I developed a deep interest in comparative pharmacology.

As absorbing as these narcotic diversions were, I found time to hang out with Dirty Dorothea. She was the long-haired, almond-eyed, super-hot offspring of my dad's best friend, Richard, and his wife, Frances. Dirty Dorothea and I would race off in the BMW her parents gave her for her eighteenth birthday and find a quiet place to do what she called joint honours. I'd roll a joint and she'd do me the honour of removing her knickers.

After the deed was done, we'd giggle like halfwits in the back seat. I remember the day Dorothea literally wet herself when I shouted to a passer-by dog walker on Hampstead Heath, 'Excuse me, madam, do you happen to know the whereabouts of this young lady's underwear?'

Never mix politics with pussy. That was my recommendation to Ewan. Unfortunately, he was too deeply indoctrinated by Jamie to follow such sage advice. To explain it in modern terms, his father had downloaded Indoctrination 101 so firmly onto his mental hard drive that poor Ewan didn't realise that what we now call his profile page was his own to populate.

Consequently, Ewan eschewed my wise counsel on where to meet girls. Instead he joined the Young Socialists. Van Gogh suffered for his sanity. Ewan suffered for his socialism. His virginity remained safely intact.

Trust me, I said to him, scraping the tobacco and the dope into the Rizla from the top of a Fleetwood Mac album cover, it's a merciful release you're not getting any comrade cunt. If you were poking one of those Trotskyite tarts, you'd be rummaging around the dustbin in the morning looking for your balls.

Those were the days, my friend, we thought they'd never end. Apparently, memories have the same effect on the neurons in the brain as the original experience. That means that cogitating about doing the dog with Dirty Dorothea is as pleasurable as doing it. No wonder I think about her so often and with such abiding affection.

The silly things school friends do

Safe Word

I must tell you about the day we invented the so-called safe word.

We were twelve, maybe thirteen at the time. We were on our way to Ewan's house after school. We were dressed in the cadet corps uniform that identified us as fair game for the skinheads. As we turned into a laneway en route to Ewan's tower block, we walked slap bang into a bevy of bovver boys.

As Ewan eyed the neo-Nazi hoard, I could see the fear in his eyes. Most of us at school didn't mind a barney in the playground, but physical violence filled Ewan with dread. Ewan was a committed pacifist. Beyond that, he lacked physical courage. I didn't mind laying or receiving a crunching tackle or two on the rugby field. Ewan watched from the safety of the touchline. Ewan hated the sight of blood, particularly his own.

Reluctantly Ewan clenched his fists alongside me in the appropriate manner. His pseudo-threatening pose lacked conviction. It generated mirth rather than mayhem. The skinheads sniggered. Then the bovver boys circled us. At that point, I was scared too.

I pondered the likely length of my hospital stay. An idea came to me in the nick of time. I unleashed a bloodcurdling scream and then, out of the blue, tackled Ewan violently to the ground. I pinned him judo-style against the crumbling asphalt. I called him every vile name under the sun. The Neanderthals were enjoying the show. They overcame the nagging thought that victims thumping each other could put them out of business.

Once over his shock, Ewan surprised me by fighting back. The adrenaline rush took over. It was like some schoolboy movie on the tele. He swung some impressive haymakers for a peace activist and sank the slipper like one of the Kray twins. We went at it hammer and tongs to the delight of the local morons.

The skinheads chanted, 'Fight, fight' in total delight. Then the ugliest of them swiped his mate's jacket and ran off with it. Their short attention span kicked in and the rest followed, distracted from their blood lust by the thrill of the chase.

What the fuck is wrong with you? Ewan snivelled.

Nothing you dimwit, I said. Who would you rather fight – me or them?

The penny dropped. Ewan wiped his bloody lip. A smile of recognition played on his face.

Am I a genius or what?

You could've warned me, Ewan whined.

How could I with the Hitler youth bearing down on us?

We need a safe word, Ewan said, brushing himself down.

I don't think you mean a 'safe word', I corrected him. You mean a code word.

It doesn't matter what it's called, Ewan protested. We just need a word that means, 'For fuck's sake, help me'.

We continued our journey up the laneway. Cardiff House reared up in front of us like an angry dinosaur.

Skinhead, I said.

What do you mean?

Skinhead will be our safe word as you insist on calling it.

And what will skinhead mean? Ewan asked to be sure he understood.

If one of us says 'skinhead' to the other, I explained, it means 'help me'.

And we come running? Ewan asked.

We come running, I agreed.

Ewan stopped dead in his tracks. I turned back to find him bent and dejected.

It's OK, they've gone, I ventured.

It's not that.

What then?

I can't trust you really will come running, Ewan said sadly.

I will come running, I insisted. That's our promise. If one of us cries skinhead, we come running.

How friendships inevitably evolve and change

Oxbridge

When our A-level results came in, I outperformed Ewan. To my intense gratification, I won the coveted Godwin Johns prize for academic excellence. This came as a shock. I thought Ewan's relentless swatting might have paid off.

As Gore Vidal puts it, 'Whenever a friend succeeds, a little something in me dies.' That was Ewan's story. *Schadenfreude* was mine and I enjoyed Ewan's obvious pain. I'd been vindicated. Having been barred from proving myself against the freebies in the entrance exams, I was fully entitled to the thrill of success when it counted most. That is when the fat school dinner lady sang.

Ewan and I stayed on at school to sit the exclusively named Oxbridge exams. In my youthful arrogance, I considered the wheat had been sorted from the chaff. Those destined to do real work had left school and those attending the inferior 'redbrick' universities were girding their loins for the adrenaline thrill of studying science in Sheffield or maths at Manchester.

Those that stayed on were the elite. Some were the social elite, who would go through the motions because a place at Oxford or Cambridge, at the college attended by their fathers and grandfathers, was already assured. The others were the intelligentsia. Most of them were freebies. They had the smarts to blast through the class system to gain a place on merit. I straddled both camps, resigned to an uncertain fate - never knowing whether I'd got there via route one or two.

We both got the places we wanted at Oxford. Mine was at Christ Church – the most aristocratic of the places of learning. Ewan got into Wadham, an upstart college founded as an afterthought in the early seventeenth century.

Our rooms at the respective colleges reflected in an uncanny fashion the accommodation we'd left behind in the big smoke. Mine were grand and spacious with a charming view beyond the majestic chapel to the daisy-dotted Christ Church Meadow that sloped gently towards the lazy river Isis. I discovered that my rooms were once occupied by a duke of the realm.

Ewan's college digs were more suited to priests than princes. His lodging was a glorified shared cell. He and his roommate had a small cupboard each that served as a bedroom and a tiny living room with a one-bar heater that kept one toe warm if you sat right on top of it.

To my constant amusement, Ewan and his room-mate could not have been more incompatible if they'd been paired by a malicious psychological profiler. As much as Ewan was a studious, serious socialist, so

Desmond was a lazy, lecherous libertarian. After a hard day's study at the library, Ewan would return home to the unedifying sight of Des sprawled on the sofa ploughing the back passage of a barmaid from Cowley.

Ewan and I saw little of each other during our first year at Oxford. We studied different subjects and mixed in diverse social circles. Ewan embraced student politics while I spent my time indulging in, what we term these days, networking. Ewan was forever sitting-in at some symbol of oppression or marching and chanting around town. I would stand on the sidelines enjoying the spectacle. The long-haired, scruffy lefties would saunter along, bristling with effete middle-class menace. On the side of the road, the upper-class twits in their tweed jackets and ties would proffer gentlemanly insults.

To me it was great sport. I remember one occasion when I was watching the latest march process through town. Rent-a-crowd was occupying the examination schools to fight increases in student union fees. I assumed a vantage point on a high stone wall, joint secreted behind my back, to observe the passing parade. It was fun watching the privileged fight the absurdly privileged.

A clean-shaven face with multiple chins poked itself out of an overlooking first floor window.

'Occupy the ex-am schools! Occupy the ex-am schools!' The unwashed protesters chanted.

'Occupy the bath-room! Occupy the bath-room!' Fat face shouted down at them.

I moved into a flat share with a motley student crew for my second year. Ewan secured a single room in the newer part of his college by impersonating another student who'd won a place in the room ballot but had decided at the last minute to move out.

One day, I raced out of the front of my college in a hurry to meet my dope dealer. I ran straight into Ewan. To my amazement, he had a girl in tow.

You're a dark horse, I said.

This is Sally, Ewan said with obvious pride, pointing to an elfin blonde girl who was struggling to propel her bicycle over the cobblestones.

Hi Sally, I said, nice to meet you.

Ewan and I embraced. We'd missed each other.

Sally

Ewan met Sally at a rally. 'Sally at a rally', they would joke. It was the only pick-up joint likely to work for Ewan.

Sally was pretty from some angles, but from others she looked quite plain. The piercing sky blue of her eyes distracted your attention from her chin that was a little too square and her forehead a fraction too imposing.

Ewan was an activist leader. He was the convenor of his student union. Politics came naturally to him, having learned campaigning on his father's knee. Like his dad, Ewan shook off his inhibitions in the political arena. He had the courage of his convictions and the restrained eloquence to enlist others to the causes he pursued with infectious passion.

I recall how he and Sally met. He was catching his breath after a rousing speech on Apartheid or some such evil, when he fancied he caught sight of a girl eyeing him from the sidelines. Ewan had no confidence around women, particularly the pretty ones. However, to his credit, he plucked up the courage when he spied her again to sprint after her as she plied her bike through the lunchtime crowd.

I imagine him like a precursor to Hugh Grant, bumbling and stumbling his way through a tortuous request for a date. How romantic is it that he asked her out under the Bridge of Sighs?

Ewan and Sally got on well. Ewan made Sally laugh. Sally helped Ewan relax. They held hands and kissed. At long last, they made love. Typical Ewan, the first time was a fiasco. Ewan's single college bed collapsed. The crash brought Desmond rushing, pants round his knees, to catch the nervous couple in a similar state of undress.

After the chance meeting outside Christ Church, Sally tagged along with Ewan to visit me in my share house in Fairacres Road, a few miles out of town. I can imagine Ewan would have warned her about me. Could the words, 'arrogant', 'opinionated', 'sarcastic' and 'selfish' have been used?

Sally must have asked Ewan why he was even friends with such a person. That's the point, isn't it? That's what I'm trying to get at writing this, lying here, finding something to do under Lorna's orders. Why the hell are Ewan and I friends?

My household back in those days could have been a police line-up. It included the pushy Bernie, who was grooming himself for a political career with any party that would have him. I also lived with the blond and handsome Donald, who split his time between working out at the gym and preening in front of the mirror. And there was Sebastian, the compulsory stoner. He would only leave his room for one of two things -

a bag of dope or a chicken vindaloo.

Then there was my final housemate, Pete. He was another kettle of fish. As I showed Ewan and Sally around, we found him lying in the bath dressed in a full dinner suit, cummerbund and all. Banknotes dripped on him from the string over the bath that served as a washing line.

No big deal, he said in response to the visitors' audible double-take.

It's no big deal, Pete insisted. I swam across the river to crash the Brasenose Ball. The security guards took exception. Lord knows why.

I spirited Ewan and Sally away before they could ask Pete why he was taking a bath fully clothed. I did my best to explain that a reasonable question like that would seem obtuse to Pete. His brain was wired differently from everyone else's. From his point of view, a river crashing was the natural thing to do if you couldn't score a free ticket to the gig. And then, with his clothes in a smelly state from the silt and the weeds, it was efficient to wash the formal clobber while he bathed. Don't try to go there, I begged them, life's too short.

I could tell Ewan was wary that I would chat Sally up. She was a bit too prim and proper to be my type, but I wouldn't have kicked her out of bed if I correctly recall my thought processes from a less PC era.

Sally had been sitting quietly, taking the circus in. I thought I should include her, but I couldn't help myself but provoke her.

Are you a bolshie too?

After a moment, Sally realised I was talking to her. No, I'm not, Sally insisted in an offended tone. But I do want to live in a world where those with plenty share a little with those less fortunate. That's what Ewan wants too.

But, Ewan's a card-carrying commie.

Labels are unimportant, Sally chided me. Values matter.

All these years later, I see that she had a point.

Comfort zone

I remember slumming it with Ewan in his student union for a pie and a pint one lunchtime.

He waxed lyrical about Sally. He said she was the best thing that had ever happened to him. I thought he was talking through his dick.

She was from one of those historic towns in Hampshire, Winchester or Dorchester. Her father was a Church of England rector and her mother the local schoolteacher. She had an older sister who was married with kids and a younger sister away at boarding school.

Ewan told me he envied Sally her family life. That makes sense to me now. As an only child, and then a motherless adolescent, he missed out on a so-called normal family life. In Sally's company, the pain of his loss must have hit home.

Ewan and Sally seemed happy together. Most people would have celebrated with their friend, observing such a match made in heaven. That wasn't me, I'm afraid. I actually felt sorry for him. If that was a match made in heaven, I thought, heaven must be a fucking boring place.

Perhaps I was jealous of their premature, cosy domesticity. I'll leave that to the analysts amongst you. I challenged Ewan about it when I got in a second pint.

I thought you reds didn't believe in marriage, I said to get things rolling.

What do you mean?

I mean you and Sally.

Sally and I aren't married, Ewan said.

You're as good as married. If you ask me, she's got you by the short and curlies already.

Nobody's asking you.

Don't try to shut me up, I said. There's an important issue here. It's about you lefties.

Not this again, he observed in a world-weary tone.

Explain this to me, I continued unabashed. How come all you children of the revolution, all you freedom fighters, all you starvelings from your slumber or however that stupid anthem goes, basically all you people who hate the system and the establishment and want to change everything are the most conservative bastards I know and are shit-scared of trying anything dangerous or new?

What a load of crap!

No, hear me out, comrade. You're so scared of playing the field that you hitch up with the first chick desperate enough to let you poke her.

You talk such bollocks, he said,

It's the sad truth. You're scared to take even the slightest risk. You won't even venture a toe out of your comfort zone.

Ewan sat silently for a while. He was weighing up whether to dignify my remarks with a response. Bob Dylan comes to mind here, he said. Don't criticise what you can't understand.

I understand it all right, I protested. I'm trying to help you, that's all.

You're not, actually, Ewan replied firmly. You're trying to help yourself. It's always that way with you. You lash out at things that don't fit into your narrow worldview.

To be honest, that sounds more like you, I pointed out.

Let's say it's true of both of us then, Ewan persisted in that annoyingly measured manner of his. I know you won't want to hear this, but Sally and I have something beyond your comprehension. We love each other. We care for each other. We care about more than just ourselves.

Ewan looked at me. I'm not like you, he continued. I don't feel the need to screw around and chalk up conquests. Sally is enough for me. More than enough.

My old mate was getting very serious. I was after some sport, not something so d and m.

If I needed advice from anyone, he added, it certainly wouldn't be from you.

That comment was designed to hurt. Its impact was like being savaged by a sheep. I spluttered into the froth of my beer. You know how to hurt a guy!

Ewan could but see the funny side. We laughed long and loud. Our ribs hurt. Despite all the jousting and the banter, we were glad to have found each other again. This was the first of many such exchanges during that year. I would accuse him of being an appalling conservative at heart. He would pity me for the superficiality of my life.

We were both right.

Mega-streak

I did manage to prise the fake Scottish laddie from his domestic routine for a memorable soiree. I collected him from his college room and escorted him next door to the King's Arms.

We found Pete there in full flight. He was obsessed with streaking at the time. He thought of little else. We would go to great lengths (fully clothed) to derail his thinking before it would inevitably lock back onto the track of naked athletics. He had all but abandoned his official studies in the law, but his education was not being wasted. He applied academic rigour to this new pursuit. He was meticulous in his planning of an escalating program of streaking. This was to culminate one day in what he referred to in hushed tones as the apotheosis of streakdom - the Mega-Streak.

The Mega-Streak involved running naked through the historic Bodleian Library. I suggested to Pete that he might as well keep running once he'd done it. The chances of him not being sent down after such an escapade were so close to zero as to be incalculable.

At the time we inveigled Ewan into streaking, Pete's program remained within the bounds of rational behaviour. It was humorous rather than humiliating. It was risqué rather than rash. It was daring rather than deranged. It was an activity undertaken for recreation rather than retribution.

Those of us privy to the plan for naked nonsense pre-loaded to dull the inhibitions. I omitted to let Ewan in on the streaking plan. He would have run a mile rather than amok, particularly as the event involved streaking through his own college. Having got him to the pub under false pretences, the next challenge was to get him legless so that he'd acquiesce.

We showed him uncharacteristic generosity, setting up sufficient pints on the bar so as to render him laid back, but not laid out. Once Ewan was deemed appropriately mellow, Pete roused us Henry V style to embrace the Papal Peregrination, his code name for the night's operation.

We advanced next door en masse, where old George, the scout, was waiting for us. The staff-cum-servants at Oxford are called 'scouts' for some arcane reason. For once, this title was apt. It was George's role, thanks to the ten-pound note he had gratefully palmed to keep a look out for representatives of authority and to ferry our clothes back to the gents' toilet at the King's Arms.

Pete had planned this event with military precision as he did every fast flash. A chair had been placed strategically outside the function room window, which had been unlocked by our co-conspirator George some hours before.

Charge! Pete cried.

The six of us, including Ewan, who by now was too blotto to back out, burst through the window. We ran at full pace, foreskins a'flapping and balls a'bouncing, through the hall occupied by the Mary Magdalene Young Catholic Ladies' Dinner Dance, out the front door, round the corner and hot foot into the gents' bogs round the back of Ye Olde King's Arms.

Ewan crashed the night at our house. He could barely raise his head as the rising of the sun gave birth to a new day. He felt like shit and he looked worse. He could barely speak.

I drove a bunch of us into town, dropping Ewan off into Sally's care and protection.

What were you boys up to last night? Sally asked.

We were running round Oxford with no clothes on, Pete said helpfully out of the rolled-down window.

I could sense Ewan's relief that it was Pete who said that. Sally didn't believe a word he said.

The Joni Mitchell

When you leave Oxford, you 'go down'. It isn't as much fun as the other sense of that phrase, but it is still meaningful. The concept is imperious.

It signifies that nothing will rival your halcyon student days. It asserts that learning and breeding is everything. It means, as Sinead O'Connor sang, 'Nothing compares to you'.

It was a beautiful summer evening when Ewan and I first ran into each other after we'd gone down. After our flurry of contact in the second year at Oxford, Ewan and I drifted apart again in the final year.

We chatted for hours in the garden of a delightful London pub. The inn was later demolished to put up a parking lot. I think of it now as the Joni Mitchell.

Ewan didn't strike the first blow. Understandably, he was biding his time.

How did you do? I asked, once the first round of drinks was in.

Pretty well.

I didn't like the quiet confidence behind that remark. I focused on my real ale.

How did *you* do then? Ewan inquired.

Ewan's smile told me that I shouldn't answer the question.

You didn't, you little creep? I accused.

I might have, Ewan responded, smug as a dog with his balls intact.

So you got a first did you? You slimy, swatty, nerdy fucker!

I certainly did, Ewan said.

I confessed my upper second.

At least you didn't get a Desmond! Ewan said.

A what?

A two-two! Ewan said, lapping this up.

I hated the way Ewan was savouring the moment. What could I do but beat a tactical retreat to the bar? I didn't hurry back. I returned some minutes later spilling the majority of the round.

What are you going to do now, Mr. fucking academic genius? I asked. Please don't tell me you're going to prostitute yourself and become a fucking don?

No, Ewan responded calmly. Sally and I are going to Botswana to help build an orphanage.

His reply stunned even me - the person most familiar with Ewan's history of conscience-salving acts of martyrdom.

You're not joking, are you?

No, I'm not joking, Ewan said.

At that moment, Ewan could just as easily have been an alien from a distant planet. The world was our oyster and to my way of thinking back then, I was going after the pearl.

Don't you think those poor parentless fuckers have enough problems without *you* going over there as their fucking builder? I appealed to him.

Your toolkit consists of a hammer and a screwdriver and you're going all the way to Africa on the strength of that.

Ewan sipped on his beer, looking down his nose at me.

I was building up steam. What are they going to say over there when they realise the stupid British do-gooders have sent them Big Ears instead of Noddy?

Ewan's manner was assured. I didn't like that. I did my best to bait him. He explained that he and Sally wanted to use their education and their advantages to give something back to society. He said they'd be away for a year and then they were going to live in Leeds, where Sally had a place to study social work.

Leeds! I said, pulling out onto Disbelief Drive. After a week in Leeds, you'll be wishing you were back in beautiful Botswana.

Ewan sought solace at the bar. He returned laden with beers and foil packets of peanuts.

I'm serious, I said, taking a surreptitious drag on a joint I'd lit while he was away. I can't see why you worked your arse off for a first class degree if you were going to waste it in some outpost in darkest Africa.

Helping people in desperate need is hardly wasting education, Ewan said calmly.

His equanimity was annoying me.

That's where you're wrong, I continued. I paused to exhale a massive cloud of fragrant smoke. Even *I* am not so heartless that I don't have sympathy for deprived kids in Africa. I think it's a great thing that an orphanage will be built for those poor bastards. But, why you? That's my point. Why would someone as smart as you do something the average vandal could accomplish in his time off from defacing National Trust monuments?

Ewan peered at me with pity on his face. It's OK, Ewan said in a patronising tone that impressed me. I wouldn't expect you to understand.

I was far from finished. If you must make some contribution to world peace and happiness, why don't you become the head of the UN or Save the Children Fund or the PM, rather than show yourself up with your two tools and your ten thumbs, and then do more fucking penance in the arsehole of the universe, Leeds?

Have you read any Brecht? Ewan asked, changing tack.

I've had bad Brecht, I answered.

Ewan ignored my pathetic attempt at humour. Unglücklich das Land das Helden nötig hat.

OK, I'll play along with you just this once. What does that mean?

Unhappy the land that needs heroes, Ewan said.

I think you've taken leave of your senses, I protested.

Not at all, Ewan insisted. Brecht was saying that justice can only be achieved by the collective action of us all, not via a few heroic acts by the prominent and celebrated.

So?

So, I don't need to become the PM. That's not the point. Doing what one can is what really counts.

Ewan refused the joint I was trying to slip him under the table.

For someone so intelligent, I said, you are incredibly stupid.

I didn't say it, but I know I must have thought it. I love this idiot regardless.

Lorna has set up my writing table again. Her expressive unlined face is wordlessly asking the question. Unlike Gerald Ford, she can do this and chew gum at the same time.

How's the book going, old man? She asks, now focused on her hopeless little screen.

Terrible.

I bet it's not, Lorna says without breaking thumbstride.

I don't know how the next bit goes. My whiney voice is back.

What's it about?

Your mum and dad.

Best make that chapter short.

Don't be so rude. I need to write about them back in the day.

BC was it?

How do I write this when I wasn't there?

Make it up. That's what I would do.

She always gets me with that cheeky grin. Fair enough. That's what paraplegics do, right?

Huh?

They lie.

How friends invariably drift apart

Procrastination

Sally called Ewan on his procrastination. He's got a right to know, she told him.

Ewan's reasons for not informing his father were many and varied. It was complicated. But Sally was right. He couldn't put it off any longer.

Ewan was negotiating the short stroll from the Maida Vale tube station to Cardiff House. He recalled the famous encounter with the skinheads as he forced his way up the now gentrified alleyway into the teeth of the familiar man-made gale that howled between the tower blocks. The rustic wheelbarrows and colourful planter boxes looked guilty sporting their nasturtiums and African violets, having displaced the grime and graffiti that had been the traditional owners of this thoroughfare.

Ewan's dad was an exceptionally busy man with a hectic life of public engagements. Yet deep down, Ewan knew that Jamie was a shy and private individual. His father never talked about such things, but Ewan realised that his dad must have been very lonely since his wife died all those years ago.

Jamie had coped when Ewan went up to university, leaving him a lonely man in an empty house. Young people spreading their wings and flying the coup was a normal part of life. They all did it. Ewan leaving the country was another thing altogether. His dad always put aside his personal feelings for a good cause. That was the core of his nature. Heading off to Africa to do Voluntary Service Overseas was not an endeavour of which comrade Jamie would approve.

Finally, and this was the hardest part for Ewan to admit to himself, the problem was that he was going with Sally. When Ewan first told his father he had a girlfriend, Jamie responded with a perfunctory nod. This three wise monkeys act – hear no evil, see no evil, speak no evil – was his dad's reaction of choice to news he found unpalatable. It riled Ewan so. Why couldn't he be happy for his own son just for once? Was he a cold fish or plain simple jealous?

One night when Ewan was weaving his way through the hustle-bustle of the theatre crowd in Covent Garden, his attention was drawn to a car horn's persistent tooting. He recognised his dad's cab. Ewan stuck his head through the driver's window of the taxi, acknowledging the fare in the back as he did so. Sally came running up, shouting to Ewan that she wanted to walk. Ewan corralled Sally and introduced her to his father. His dad nodded and then spoke to Ewan as if Sally wasn't there.

The lift to the fifteenth floor was much cleaner than he remembered from his childhood. It's my life, Ewan muttered to psych himself up for the task ahead. I have to forge my own path.

Ewan negotiated the dark corridor extra slowly. The truth is he left *me* long ago. His politics and his council meetings were more important to him than his son.

The *Marseillaise* rang out. As he waited, Ewan fought to bridle his resentment. His father was a respected man and a great community leader. He mustn't forget that. Jamie just hadn't been a great dad.

You can't be good at everything, Ewan said more loudly than he intended as his dad's face appeared in the doorway.

What's that?

Nothing, Dad. How are you?

I'll write

Much to Ewan's surprise, Jamie insisted on driving the young couple to Heathrow in the cab to see them on their way. Sally's parents travelled up from the West Country, allowing plenty of time to negotiate the traffic in the big city.

Ewan should have been excited. Instead he felt nervous. His session with his father a few weeks earlier had drawn the expected condemnation of do-gooders assuaging the colonial guilt. Ewan held his end up in the argument fairly well given that his heart wasn't in it. Fundamentally, he agreed with his dad, but, as he explained, he was allowing himself the opportunity to experience international service first hand. Sally believed in it. For now that was enough.

He was anxious at the prospect of the two sets of parents meeting. Sally's folks would be unfailingly polite. Jamie was a different proposition. Ewan didn't want a scene. Surely Jamie could keep his opinions to himself just this once?

The taxi chugged its way through the milling cars and cabs jostling for position to disembark their passengers. Heathrow was chaotic even on a Sunday. Sally was eyeing the time anxiously, particularly as her parents would have arrived at some ridiculously early hour. Just to be sure.

Ewan patted Sally's arm to calm her. Her skin was so soft to the touch. The gridlock failed to clear. Ewan could feel Sally tense again.

I'll drop you off here, Jamie called through the hatch, flipping his blinkers on as he wrenched the cab towards the kerb.

Sally gratefully clambered from the back while Ewan bundled their rucksacks from the front luggage compartment onto the pavement.

I'll look out for you, Ewan called through the window to his dad.

I won't come in, Jamie called back, avoiding eye contact.

Ewan was relieved, but Sally looked upset.

What's the matter? Ewan asked her.

Your dad has to wave us off! We're going for a year.

But, it's frantic. He'd have to park the cab.

So?

Dad, can't you put the cab in the car park and come and see us off? Ewan pleaded with him.

I can't, son. I wish I could. I've got an address for you. I'll write.

Jamie waved to Ewan and acknowledged Sally with a dart of the eyes.

Sally watched the taxi drive away. Ewan could tell she was confused.

We need to hurry, Ewan said, lifting Sally's bag so she could thread her arms through the straps and carry it on her back. Ewan swung his own backpack over his shoulder.

They trotted off towards the rows of thronging check-in counters.

He couldn't face it, Ewan said breathlessly to Sally.

I don't get it, she replied. I wanted him to meet my parents.

He's a public figure but a private man.

What has that got to do with it? Sally snapped, steering Ewan towards the British Airways counter.

It means he couldn't face the emotion of saying goodbye.

Dust, heat and flies

Ewan's bum hurt before the rickety truck had even left the township.

The flight to Salisbury had been little better. He'd never been in such a tiny plane before. It reminded him of the balsa wood models he played with as a kid. The sudden drops in altitude left his lunch as well as his heart in his mouth.

Ewan and Sally were the only passengers. The pilots were within touching distance. The white guy was the chief pilot, judging by the bars on his lapel. He was a scrawny, middle-aged man with a number one buzz cut. Hidden behind his reflective aviators, he dozed throughout the flight. He snored like a dog in the sun until his head succumbed to gravity, waking him with a start. The whole flying thing, like the craggy rocks and parched fields below, seemed beneath him.

The black co-pilot was a dead ringer for Idi Amin. He chatted amiably across the crackly intercom with his mate in the control tower. They concentrated on the banter rather than their respective jobs at hand. Idi was further distracted by his cramped bucket seat, which was several sizes too small for a man of his generous proportions. Sweat cascaded down his face like the overflow of the Victoria Falls.

The truck clattered its way over potholes. It swerved disarmingly around the under-nourished livestock and braked violently in front of skittering children. Ewan didn't dare look at Sally. He could see from the corner of his eye that she was clinging white-knuckled to the metal seat in front of her. With her free hand, she held onto her hat as the torn green tarpaulin shade flapped around her face. As perilous and uncomfortable as this journey was, he sensed she was in her element.

Prior to their departure, Sally's excitement had reached fever pitch. The missionary zeal of her upbringing shone from her. She was at last on the verge of serving humanity. Right now, she would be taking masochistic pleasure from travelling cattle class.

Ewan sat in sullen silence. There was nowhere in the world he less wanted to be. He felt demoralised and powerless. He was defenceless in the face of the relentless aggression of the dust, heat and flies.

Mubuwe

They say you can get used to anything, given time. After a month in Mubuwe, Ewan could sense the truth in that. The sun still burned like flame. Dust penetrated every orifice. The flies were purgatorial. Yet he was starting to feel at home.

The smiles of the tent-dwelling orphans shone like the omnipresent sun overhead. Rather than to 'dusty death', their countenances 'lighted' the way to pristine life. Having nothing, the people found something in everything. They drew inspiration from a tree branch tumbling to earth in the wind. They played football kicking a tin can to each other in the dirt. They amused themselves watching a captive fly thrash around in a glass jar. These were the ragged people from Robert Tressell's book Ewan had so voraciously devoured as a boy. In contrast to those victims of the industrial revolution, these people could maintain their human dignity in blessed ignorance of the sources of their oppression.

Ewan wanted to adjust, for Sally's sake. Surprisingly, the building project energised him. Despite the jibes at his lack of handyman prowess, he tapped into a vein of competence he didn't know he had. He found himself enjoying the simplicity of manual labour.

Sally worked close by. Her responsibilities were to run the affairs of the village and organise the women to wash, cook and clean. Her role in reinforcing such gender stereotypes irritated her like a pebble in her shoe, but not so much as to hobble her enthusiasm.

Sally acclimatised like the proverbial duck to water, although both were rare commodities in those parts. Inner zeal insulated her from the rigours of the harsh environment. She seemed instantly fulfilled. She lived in the moment of the toil, shutting out all memory of an easier life.

Ewan envied her that. *He* could never forget that the first world had so much and the third world so little. Despite his decision to do VSO, he was outraged by the necessity for it. The imperialist nations should be making reparations to the lands they'd pillaged by building and funding the schools, hospitals and orphanages that were so desperately needed. Volunteerism was an indictment of the capitalist system.

Ewan and Sally made a go of it. He was happy that she was happy. She was grateful for his forbearance and proud of his accomplishments on the project. Milton, the missionary priest, was the only source of friction between them. His balding pate, encircled by outcrops of frizzy grey hair, gave the appearance of a lake in the forest. It was line ball whether his face or his clothes were more crumpled. Overall, he resembled an unmade bed. He reminded Sally fondly of her father. Milton rubbed Ewan up the wrong way.

Milton was the head of the village. There was an octogenarian elder who nominally held that title, but Milton pulled the strings. He'd spent the best part of his life in Mubuwe. Somehow he'd retained the air of a middle-class vicar from the Chilterns. He would amble through the village, every inch the local rector taking his morning constitutional to the general store to pick up the morning newspaper.

Milton was in charge of the project. Ewan therefore took directions from him. The rest of the work crew comprised a local 'builder' (whose largest construction to that point had been a mud hut) and four or five youths, who would report for duty irregularly and do some work occasionally.

Ewan, son of Jamie, had no tolerance for God-botherers. He had moderated his behaviour around them in deference to Sally's father. But, in this harsh environment, surrounded by the trappings of missionary colonialism, Ewan felt disinclined to cut Milton any slack. In fact, he detested Milton. Everything about him raised his hackles. His conversational style annoyed him most. It was as circuitous as the racetrack in the closest township, which was a good hundred miles away.

Ewan suffered Milton's shambolic project management in silence. He made it his own mission to encourage the boys to turn up for work and do something while they were there. Kenneth, Muzungu, Robert and Mangwe reminded him of a favourite song. Young and black, they may have been. Gifted they were not.

Kenneth and Mangwe looked very much alike. Ewan was embarrassed at his inability to tell them apart. He'd invariably call them by the wrong name.

Bravely, he confided in Sally. I know it's a horrible cliché, but Mangwe and Kenneth look the same to me.

Sally laughed uncontrollably. Her reaction was a pleasant surprise. He'd expected her to lecture him about his racist slur.

What's so funny? Ewan asked.

Nothing, Sally said, trying to recover.

Nothing can't be this funny, Ewan said, folding his arms.

I'm sorry, Sally said. It really *is* funny. They happen to be identical twins.

Ewan learned some useful words in the local patois to help him whip the boys into shape. He kept one step ahead like a novice schoolteacher. He would demonstrate to the boys how to saw a plank safely and hammer nails instead of thumbs. The boys would stare into space. Ewan would snap his fingers and parrot the lingo for, 'This is important, so pay attention'. The boys would smile roundly and nod vigorously to show that they understood. Then they would wield the axe and swing the hammer as dangerously as they did before.

Milton stopped by Ewan and Sally's hut one night, as he was wont to do when the loneliness got the better of him. Ewan rolled his eyes when he saw the pastor making a beeline for them.

A young girl had died in childbirth in the village the previous day. There were complications with the umbilical cord. As there was no qualified nurse for hundreds of miles, the local women with Sally in support had tried to no avail to manoeuvre the infant's position and untangle the cord.

Ewan poured three rotgut whiskeys. Life is cheap in Mubuwe, isn't it? He said. How can a black life be worth less than a white one?

Sally hoped Milton would recognise one of Ewan's provocations by this time and leave his rhetorical question well alone. He didn't.

God truly does work in mysterious ways, he said.

You don't really believe that claptrap, Ewan snapped.

I grant you that many things in this world are hard to understand, Milton said. Above all, the suffering and the injustice. But I have dedicated my life to showing these wretched people that they are made in God's image and that they are loved by the Lord forever.

Knock it off you two, Sally said. Let's be respectful of that poor young girl.

The trio sat in silence for a while. The insects were tuning up.

Sally tried changing the subject. Are you still worried about the boys? She asked.

As Ewan didn't answer, she continued. They will injure themselves on the project if they don't pay more attention. That's if the twins don't kill each other first. They have fiery tempers and they fight like cats and dogs.

Sally had tried her best, but Ewan could never let things be.

By believing in your God, you oppress the masses, he said, looking Milton squarely in the eye. You'll get pie in the sky when you die!

A day at the races

Thus life in Mubuwe went on. In due course, the makeshift orphanage took shape. Ewan and Milton goaded each other incessantly. Sally did her best to keep the peace.

Time passed in a familiar rhythm. Up before dawn, a cold water wash under a barely-there bush shower, a simple breakfast of maize and cow peas, work on the project, supervising washing and cleaning. Time crept in its petty pace from day to day.

The exception to this established regimen came in the shape of the Ulugatu race day. Horseracing was the only subject that came close to uniting Ewan and Milton. They shared an abhorrence of any form of gambling, albeit for very different reasons.

Milton would quote 1Timothy, 'For the love of money is a root of all kinds of evil. Some people, eager for money, have wandered from the faith and pierced themselves with many griefs'.

Ewan, who could never bring himself to concur wholeheartedly with Milton, would half-agree with a sting in the tail. Karl Marx grouped gambling with religion as an opiate of the people, he said.

Sally kept her own counsel. She took comfort from the fragile peace breaking out between the prelate and the zealot. Further afield, she could sense the wave of excitement that was building amongst the villagers about the imminent race day.

To imagine the Ulugatu race day, picture Royal Ascot, Longchamp or Melbourne Cup Day. Then jettison those images to the trashcan of your memory. In the place of manicured lawns and gracious grandstands, there was bare earth and rusty tin sheds. The going on the course was crumbling and dusty rather than good or soft. The horses were mules and their condition was skin and bone, not sheen and muscle. The only common denominator between the first and third world experience was the riotous colour. The hues of the dresses and the 'fascinators' of the native women were every bit as vibrant as the gaudy garb worn by the jockeys and the finery of the fillies on the courses of the western world.

Work on the building project ground to a standstill as preparations for race day took over. Ewan was grateful for the down time. The hard physical work of those early months had toned his body from flab to fab, but his newly developed musculature needed a break to refresh. He sat under a tree and read a book. He felt at peace. Even Sally took some time out from her duties. They held hands and made love. They reconnected. Ewan felt comfortable in this alien world.

Race day arrived. Until that morning, Ewan and Sally had remained sceptical that the entire village could be transported the hundred miles to Ulugatu. Milton's old banger was the only vehicle around.

Without warning, clouds of dust filled the sky. A convoy comprised of trucks, vans and clapped-out buses emerged through the fog, bumping and clattering over the rough terrain. Ewan raised his eyes from his book. It was an incredible sight. He felt like Sir Francis Drake looking up from his game of bowls to behold the menacing majesty of the Spanish Armada rounding the heads.

The well-behaved villagers, who had gathered quietly around the well that passed for the centre of the hamlet, transformed themselves into an unruly mob. Skirmishes broke out as people pushed and shoved their neighbours aside for pride of place on the transport. Ewan and Sally stood back and watched. Milton appeared shortly afterwards. He gestured for them to follow. The front bench on the leading bus had, by some silent convention, been reserved for them. They squeezed in. Ewan felt guilty. Sally had the presence of mind to sit between the men.

No police force

The journey was interminable. The vehicles were unserviceable. The seats were uncomfortable. The roads were impassable. The flies were unbelievable. The heat was unbearable. Milton's snoring was abominable. The poverty of the shanty towns was indescribable. Yet the spirit of the villagers was irrepressible.

They gossiped, laughed and sang the whole way. Only at the outskirts of the township, did the song, noise and chattering abate. A hush enveloped the bus like a blanket of low cloud. We had just arrived at the centre of Rome, St Petersburg or Prague. The scale and majesty of the surroundings took their breath away. And yet, seen through the eyes of Ewan and Sally, the bus was driving through the mother of all slums. It was Brick Lane not Park Lane.

The Mubuwe cavalcade pulled into a makeshift, ungraded parking lot. It was jam packed with transport well passed its use-by date. The bus came to life again. The passengers jostled and jockeyed to be the first to step down. They laughed and cursed as they went. Unsure which emotions to entertain, Ewan and Sally sat in silence.

Ewan cracked first. Look on the bright side, he said. We can wake the old bastard now and give our eardrums a break.

Just as the most terrible songs are often the most enjoyable, so the races at Ulugatu proved thoroughly memorable. The rampant joyfulness of the crowd was infectious. Sally got into the swing of things, defying Ewan's disapproval of the track. She wagered the equivalent of a few British pence on a nag that probably didn't exist and almost certainly couldn't run. She frolicked like a girl at a playground, snapping reels of photographs on her father's Pentax.

The occasional dispute broke out over beer that tasted like petrol or a bet gone wrong. Otherwise the crowd remained good-natured. There were no police in evidence. The only security was a posse of gangly youths patrolling the perimeter of the concourse. They were kitted out in grubby singlets and outsize shorts. They were armed with pointed sticks that they trailed distractedly behind them in the dirt. They put Ewan in mind of a schoolboy production of Dad's Army.

The afternoon sun was descending at a viciously fiery angle. Sally was feeling faint. Dr. Ewan diagnosed the malady as dehydration and set off in search of an overpriced cup of well water. He squeezed his way through the massed ranks of gesticulating, staggering men near the hooch shed. His progress was halted by a crowd of chanting youths, formed into a circle like in the school playground. His instincts proved correct. Through the billowing dust, he could make out three or four shirtless boys wrestling and punching each other in a writhing mass.

To his horror, Ewan recognised Kenneth and Mangwe as two of the combatants. Mangwe had his exhausted opponent pinned beneath him. Kenneth, on the other hand, was in deep strife, fending off a relentless salvo of blows. Ewan wanted to intervene and knew he should. Yet he found himself rooted to the spot, yelling ineffectually for them to stop in a language the fighters barely understood.

A roar went up from the crowd, silhouetted against the setting sun. The human circle exploded. Men and boys hurled themselves out of the path of a speeding truck. The onlookers melted away, content to leave the offenders to the tender mercies of the police.

The police presence was like an earthquake sending a tidal wave of panic crashing through the race day crowd. A human tide ebbed towards the carpark, sucking all before it. Ewan tried to swim his way back to Sally, but resigned himself to floating helplessly in the rip.

A disorderly mob ran helter-skelter away from the police. Despite the shemozzle, people somehow located their buses. The human cargo was loaded and dispatched. Over time, the crowd thinned and the dust abated. Ewan caught sight of Sally in the distance. He muscled his way to her.

Are you OK? He shouted.

Yes, I'm OK. What on earth is going on? She asked

I don't know. There was a fight and the police came.

Did you see it?

Never mind that now. Where's our bus?

I recognise that tree with the red ribbons, Sally shouted, pointing towards a group of buses parked parallel to the road.

Ewan took Sally's hand and guided her through the melee. There's Milton! Ewan cried.

On this occasion, Ewan was pleased to see him. He and Sally clambered aboard the rickety bus. It seemed more packed than before. Dozens of youths were perched atop, clinging to the luggage racks. Milton ushered the passengers on board and then waved to the driver to get going.

At that moment, a jeep closely followed by three police trucks screeched to a halt in front of the bus. Armed men jumped to the ground to surround it. They screamed at the passengers, grabbing at people through the windows. They somehow forced a passage through the impenetrable aisles. Batons were swung. Arms were bruised. Heads were smacked.

The penny dropped for Ewan. Shit!

What's the matter? Sally asked.

They're after Kenneth and Mangwe.

What for?

There was a fight… Ewan said, his voice tapering away as he saw a twin he was pretty sure was Mangwe tumble down the front steps to be swept up by the guards. The police sergeant, seated some distance away in the jeep, pointed to Mangwe, barking instructions.

Sally's cries of protest went unheard. At that moment, Milton emerged from behind the bus. Bible in hand, he placed himself defiantly in front of the jeep. The scene reminded Ewan of those illuminated icons featuring the pious and heroic acts of martyred saints. Milton spoke calmly but firmly to the captors. They responded by allowing Mangwe to stand up. The guards restrained him, awaiting further instructions.

Milton approached the jeep, leaning in to address the leader. Voices were raised. The commander spat on the floor before jumping down. Milton stood his ground, toe to toe with the menacing giant of a man. Ewan could hear Milton shouting the word 'Kenneth', 'Kenneth'. The stand-off ended with the captain motioning to the guards to release Mangwe. The troops returned to their trucks in disgust and sped away.

Milton ushered everyone back on the bus, shouting at them to hurry. The engine spluttered to life and the grating clutch was noisily engaged.

Once the bus was bumping along faster than walking pace and no police appeared in pursuit, Ewan mopped his sweating brow. He was embarrassed at his own cowardice in the face of such abuse of power.

How did you get them to let Mangwe go? Ewan asked Milton, bamboozled by the turn of events

I told a little white lie, Milton said, with a guilty smirk on his face.

You told a lie, Ewan said, feeling some of the tension drain away.

A little one.

What did you say?

I told them they had the wrong man.

How so? Ewan looked puzzled.

I told them they had his twin brother, Kenneth.

Ewan laughed. At that moment, he didn't hate Milton quite so much. Some sort of fascist police force they have here, don't they! Ewan exclaimed.

That wasn't the police force, Milton explained in a quiet voice. In these parts there is no police force, fascist or otherwise.

Orphanage

The opening of the orphanage reminded Ewan of that fateful race day. The scene was festive. The villagers were dressed proudly in their Sunday best, strutting their stuff in their least threadbare outfits. Bunting made from plastic bottles and scraps of material festooned the new structure. The children were excited. They chased each other round the building. The adults, who had scrubbed them clean moments before, were stoic in the face of them tumbling around in the dirt.

Ewan admired the happy-go-lucky nature of the villagers. People had told him that Africans were lazy. He wasn't so sure. They did go about things slowly, but then again they had no reason to hurry. The locals had learned to be content. Sure the villagers had just given the little children a lick and a promise so they were squeaky clean. And now they were grubby again. So what?

Sweat ran from his temples. It was stinking hot by eight in the morning. Ewan swayed in his hammock to create a breeze while he watched the heat haze shimmer from the shiny new tin roof.

Around midday, a convoy of trucks and buses drew up. The strangers bunked in with the locals to make best use of the limited shade. Soon the village was bursting at the seams. It was time for Milton to strike up his rag-tag school band before consecrating the orphanage with a prayer.

Ewan was relieved that the building was complete. While he had valued the experience and learned useful skills, he hankered for some creature comforts. If Sally wanted out, she wasn't letting on. She sometimes spoke of missing family and friends. She never intimated any desire to return home. Nevertheless, their stint in Mubuwe was nearing its end.

Milton sauntered over. Keep a weather eye out, won't you? Milton said.

Ewan didn't understand. He pulled himself upright, swinging his legs onto the dried mud. An eye out for what?

Oh, nothing really, Milton said in a distracted tone before wandering off.

Then why say it? Ewan muttered to himself.

As Ewan cast his now trained eye over the buildings, he was conscious that the workmanship was second rate. But, given the circumstances, taking into account the resources, the equipment and the available talent, he was satisfied that they'd done a reasonable job.

At the same time, disappointment tugged at Ewan's sleeve. Beyond the serviceable physical structure, he'd accomplished very little. He'd hoped to leave a more imposing legacy. It disturbed him that he'd failed to motivate and galvanise the efforts of the boys. That cultural divide had proved a bridge too far.

Sally considered Ewan too hard on himself. But, by his own reckoning, he had neither passed nor failed. The trouble was that these youths were a law unto themselves. They operated according to statutes that he couldn't begin to understand. Mzungu was the only one with the temperament to knuckle down. Robert and the twins were temperamental to say the least. They would disappear more often than they stayed to work.

The events of race day nagged at Ewan. He realised he knew nothing of these boys' lives. They weren't just underprivileged. They faced ever-present dangers he didn't comprehend. He kept pumping Milton to gain some understanding. Milton either didn't know or was unwilling to enlighten him.

Milton signalled for the school choir to come forward. While the musicianship on the triangle and flute left something to be desired, the voices of the children were angelic. The hymns, beautifully sung in English and the local dialect, would surely please the most capricious Lord.

Once the rapturous applause subsided, Milton said more than the few words the occasion demanded. He read a passage from the Bible that had scant relevance, in Ewan's estimation, to the job at hand. At last, Milton cut the ceremonial ribbon Ewan and Sally had been commissioned to hold. The crowd thronged inside to inspect the new lodgings.

Earlier, Milton had instructed the team not to put anything out that could easily be 'recruited'. Ewan, Sally and the crew looked at each other confused. Milton attempted an explanation, but it was expressed in his habitual riddles.

As Eve tempted Adam in the Garden of Eden, Milton explained solemnly, so the anonymity of a crowd might extend the forbidden apple to our community.

Responding to the puzzled looks on the faces of the group, Milton expanded on the theme. Let us not encourage those whose faith may be weak to break the fifth commandment, he said.

At sunset, the crowd of strangers drifted away. The villagers then set to work, making the beds and laying out the 'valuables' Milton had kept hidden. The dormitory and its accoutrements were basic to say the least, but they served their purpose.

By nine o'clock that night, Ewan and Sally were in bed and fast asleep. So exhausted were they, that the clanking and grating of the antiquated fan and the voracious biting of the mosquitoes through the holes in their net could not rouse them.

They slept through the noise of the trucks swerving on the gravel. They were oblivious to the screams of the terrified children when the armed men in uniform burst through their flimsy, homemade doors. Ewan and Sally were woken only by the acrid smell of smoke.

They fumbled into their clothes and ran headlong to the orphanage, or what was left of it. They found Milton and Nurse Millie (who wasn't really a nurse) comforting the frightened, sobbing children.

Praise be to God, Milton intoned, the little ones survived the fires of hell.

At first light, Ewan and Sally joined the chastened locals in sifting through the charred remains. Of the five boys, only Robert was to be found. He stared fixedly at the ground, fiddling with a piece of charred wood. He could not bring himself to speak.

Milton prayed for greater understanding of the ways of the Lord. Sally comforted the villagers through the veil of her own tears. Ewan drew abstract pictures in the dust with a stick. With a year's hard labour literally gone up in smoke, he had no spirit left to argue with the priest. His report card now emphatically read FAIL. He was devastated but at the same time felt thoroughly vindicated. Volunteerism truly was an inadequate response to the vile injustice of the world.

Ewan searched the veldt for the missing boys. He did so without strategy or enthusiasm. It was pointless and fruitless. He was a stranger with no idea where to look. He lay down in the dirt and cried. He had fought the good fight for Sally's sake. But his dad, Jamie, had been right all along.

Ewan composed himself, wiping away the tears with his grubby sleeve. He had been fooling himself, but would do so no more. The system had to change. He would re-dedicate himself to exposing its nefarious machinery. He would find a way to tell the world the awful truth. How the politicians, business proprietors and ruthless militiamen conspire to make themselves wealthy at the expense of the poor. He would expose their corruption for all to see. Then perhaps justice could be done. All children would have a proper home and care. All people would be equal under the law. Might and the power of the gun would not be right.

****

The bridge

Leeds confounded Ewan's expectations. Was it an outpouring of relief on returning to civilisation? Or was Leeds more interesting and cultured than southern snobbery had allowed him to believe?

His time in Mubuwe had changed him. He recognised that. Maybe, by the end, it had un-changed him again.

Ewan wasn't stupid. He did realise that his dad had force-fed him opinions from babyhood. Ewan hadn't wanted to go to Africa – to become a virtual missionary. He had succumbed to the experience. He had acquiesced for Sally's sake.

Once he'd recovered from the culture shock that was Africa, the shock of the new, he had embraced it. It was an opportunity to let go of childish things. His routines. His favourite haunts. His familiar friends. His father? If not his father, then his father's all-pervading influence.

Africa represented freedom to him. Freedom to find himself. Freedom to love Sally. Freedom to meet her halfway. He thought of it as a bridge from the kingdom of socialism, where he lived, to the sympathetic but different principality of social democracy.

The bridge was built from both sides. It fitted together imprecisely in the middle. It was sound enough to be serviceable, but the imperfect construction was clear for all to see. From Ewan's end, the piers were made of dogma; from Sally's side, the struts rough-hewn from religion.

Ewan walked onto the bridge with as open a mind as someone from his background could. He met Sally halfway, ignoring the botched woodwork beneath his feet. He then walked hand-in-hand with Sally towards the other bank. He dedicated himself to the project. He accepted that it was for him as much as Sally. But, as the planks on her side creaked, barely supporting their weight, the orphanage burst into flames. The embers slowly but surely ignited the bridge. Ewan turned instinctively towards the sanctuary of his own land and his reinforced values.

As he sprinted, his outstretched hand beckoned to Sally. Come with me now. Seek refuge there with me. Join me where the belief systems are founded on changing the system, not propping it up.

All Leeds path to roam

Ewan was at ease with Leeds, and not just because Sally seemed content.

Leeds was an unpretentious city. It reminded him of his history teacher at school. Mr. Marsh, Swampy, was the only chalkie Ewan respected. Despite his impeccable grooming and deportment that spoke of rectitude, he was a downcast man, coated in the dandruff of his own disappointment. He spoke *sotto voce*. The morons in the back row couldn't hear him, but they weren't listening anyway.

Ewan did pay attention. His dad, Jamie, had warned him never to judge a book by its cover. So it was with Mr. Marsh. He spoke with intelligence and sensitivity. His observations were insightful. He was a man many ignored. That was their mistake. It was the same with Leeds.

Sally settled comfortably into her social work course. It provided a ready-made circle of friends in the strange city. Her fellow students were mixed in age, ranging from a career-change potter in her sixties to green, new grads. But for the diversity in age, they were like cards of the same suit in every other respect. A passion for social justice united them. They would disagree on some of the detail but were rock solid in their shared beliefs.

Ewan was relieved to see Sally stable again. The orphanage fire had rocked her. She'd struggled to cope. Having been sheltered from the harsher realities of life by her protective parents, the brutality and violence unnerved her.

Ewan observed Sally with her new friends. He was concerned that she was glossing over the horror of what happened. She portrayed their time in Mubuwe as a priceless adventure. Ewan conceded all of that. But Sally omitted the balancing aspects of the deprivation and the ugliness. As a budding social worker, it troubled him that she did so. In her company, he'd picked up plenty of the jargon. He was unhappy that she was repressing her true feelings.

Ewan recognised that he wasn't behaving that differently himself. He was reluctant to speak about what occurred. His own motivation was transparent. He had compromised his principles by volunteering overseas. The ghastly outcome should have been totally predictable. To make his naïveté public would expose him as a fool.

Just as Sally felt empowered by her purposeful studies, Ewan was energised by his born again mission. He now felt a strong calling to journalism. The prospect inspired him. He devoured the articles in The Times by John Pilger. One day, his pen would be mightier than the sword. He fantasised about headlines that would oust Watergate from the history books and expunge the names of Woodward and Bernstein from the annals of investigative journalism. It would be a hard climb to such lofty heights. He was grateful to his father for instilling in him an appreciation for those who perform the basic tasks in life. He embraced the need to start at the bottom. This meant finding work as a cadet journalist.

Sally was immersed in her studies. This gave Ewan the freedom and opportunity to look for a job. He cast his net far and wide. He applied to the Morley Observer and Chronicle, the Yorkshire Evening Post and the Sheffield Morning Telegraph. He caught nothing. He trawled further afield. He wrote to every journal within a hundred miles. He petitioned publications with dubious politics.

Ewan received a postbag full of rejections. He pinned them on his notice board. He saw an ad for the role of manager of the England football team. He applied for that for a laugh. That generated another thanks but no thanks letter. He assigned that one pride of place on his dishonour board.

Ewan's frustration must have been evident to Sally. A cursory glance at his forest of failure would have sufficed. But she was cocooned in her own captivating world. Sally's indifference irked Ewan. He didn't let it show. He rationalised his failure. There was an upside. How egalitarian had the system in Britain become that a graduate with a first-class degree from Oxford couldn't land a writing job even as a stringer? There was nothing for it. He would find other work to keep him going.

Very bad people

Ewan applied for jobs as a waiter. He was offered two positions in a short space of time.

The first was in a café frequented by cab drivers. Given his familiarity with his father's noble profession, that would have been a breeze. However, the second job offer intrigued him more. It was at the Himalaya restaurant just round the corner. During what passed for an interview, Ewan found himself inspired by the murals depicting Everest and K2.

Ewan was a crap waiter. He mixed up the orders or forgot them completely. He had an annoying habit of removing the ashtrays from people who were smoking. The irate customers would gesticulate violently at him and harangue management to hire some decent staff. Dev, the owner, was an ornery sort of guy. Despite his challenged command of English, he had proudly labelled his marketing initiative for the quietest trading night of the week, Tight-Arse Tuesday. The more his customers complained about Ewan, the more staunchly Dev defended him.

Dev was preoccupied with a running feud he was having with the Indian restaurant five doors down. Ewan practised his would-be investigative skills to uncover the source of this ill feeling. Dev would furrow his brow and teeter on the brink of explanation. Then he would think better of it, shrug his shoulders and walk away.

From time to time, Ewan would pester his boss for an answer. Under pressure, Dev would wag his finger. Moti Mahal people, very bad people, was all he would say. Very bad people, he would repeat, rolling his Rs and shaking his head to underline the point.

Ewan got home as usual after midnight from what he called 'the late shift with the Sherpas'. Sally was waiting up for him. Her pretty face was all smiles. He was eager to hear her good news.

Look, she said, holding up a crumpled white envelope.

What is it? Ewan asked.

It's an envelope, Sally replied, hiding it behind her back, encouraging him to come and get it.

Ewan chased her round the living room until he could tackle her onto the sofa. He tickled her to get hold of it. It was a letter from the Leicester Mercury. It had been so long since his interview with them that he was primed for another rejection.

On securing the envelope, he could see it had been opened.

You're opening my mail?

Sorry.

Is it good news?

Maybe.

Don't. Please. Is it?

Yes. You got the job.

Ewan was elated, but immediately depressed. What are we going to do? He asked. I can't leave you here in Leeds.

You have to take it, Sally said firmly. If you're going to change the world, you have to start somewhere.

Even in Leicester?

Especially in Leicester.

Ewan was grateful for Sally's understanding. And disappointed that she didn't protest.

Emergency brace position

The several years Ewan and Sally spent largely apart sped by. The days motored along like the police cars on the M1 every Friday evening and Monday morning when Ewan went 'home' for the weekend and back to Leicester again.

From time to time, Ewan would wonder why he was always the one to travel for the weekend reunions. Was it because he was the one who'd left home? Was Leeds actually 'home' to them in any true sense of the word? Did Sally's refusal to travel signify she held the whip hand in their relationship? She probably did. Did that matter? Did that have anything to do with why she never entertained the prospect of spending the weekend with *him* in Leicester?

Sally was making a go of things in Leeds. She did seem genuinely pleased to see him when Ewan lumbered up the three flights to their flat of a Friday evening and repeated his Jack Nicholson impression from the Shining with a malicious, 'Sally, I'm home', called around the door.

Ewan felt lonely during the week. He was something of a misfit in Leicester. This experience took him back to school. He was ridiculously over-aged and over-qualified to be a cadet journalist. Not knowing how to relate to him, his colleagues at the Mercury left him well alone.

His problem, if you can call it that, was compounded by the fact that he couldn't be bothered to make friends. He didn't really 'live' in Leicester. Nor was Leeds home. He felt displaced like the nomadic peoples in Africa who would drift into Mubuwe from time to time and then melt away in the night like grains of sand reuniting with the Kalahari Desert.

Ewan's editor, Stuart, made an effort to befriend him. Stuart was a decent enough bloke. He hailed from Birmingham and spoke with that Brummy nasal accent that Ewan couldn't bear. Worse than that, he was a car enthusiast – an interest Ewan found impossible to understand.

Stuart would take Ewan to a country pub some evenings after work. He would zip home on the way in his classy old Daimler to pick up his dogs. They extended the 'D' theme of his car. The dalmatian was called Dora and the dachshund, Douglas. The dogs would pile into the back of the car. One dog was tall and thin and the other short and fat. They reminded Ewan of the comic duos of the day, Morecambe and Wise and the Two Ronnies. Not to mention, Laurel and Hardy from a previous era.

Stuart was a crazy driver. Ewan clung on for dear life in the passenger seat. Douglas and Dora had learned from experience how to survive country driving with their motorhead master. When they heard the sound of a gear change from third to second, the dogs would respond in

Pavlovian fashion to what they knew would be a hairy bend. They would assume the emergency brace position until the car eased up a gear and the canine captain, that only dogs can hear, announced that he was switching off the fasten seatbelts sign.

Doesn't ring a bell

Ewan was happy to have a job, any job, as a journalist. He'd almost given up hope. Prior to receiving that acceptance letter, he'd feared his most prestigious investigative assignment might have been to uncover why the proprietors of the Moti Mahal were very bad people.

The work itself depressed him. His dad's advice about starting at the bottom was all very well, but he found himself in an extremely deep well and he was scraping the bedrock. How was he going to make a difference? All he did was report on fetes, lost dogs and tedious parish council meetings.

As a cadet, Ewan reported to Tim and Annie, the qualified journalists on the paper. They were middle-aged, middle-class and middle of the road in every way. He'd given up on persuading them to let him cover stories that didn't feature a cat stuck in a tree. They'd made it in journalism the hard way. They had no intention of letting Ewan climb the journalistic ladder any faster than one rickety rung at a time.

Stuart remained his best hope of accessing something more exciting. After a couple of pints at the pub, Stuart's tongue would loosen. Ewan was careful to remain sober so he could recall any information that might prove useful.

Stuart had mentioned a company called Midlands Developments more than once. It was owned by wealthy locals, backed by interests out of Eastern Europe. Stuart would complain about their Managing Director, George Braithwaite, who was forever in his ear. Tim and Annie's coverage of his affairs was always anodyne. George wanted Stuart to make it glowing.

Ewan dug into George's affairs in his spare time. He pored over the corporate information that was publicly available and did background searches into the company, its subsidiaries and its directors. Alas, everything seemed above board.

Ewan lost interest until his ears pricked up in a country pub on one of his outings with Stuart. He was minding Stuart's dogs while he went for a snake's. A young man approached, holding the hand of a cautious toddler.

Can my son pat your dogs? The father asked. He doesn't bite.

Ewan told Stuart the funny story then headed off to get a round.

While mooching at the bar, Ewan overheard a snippet of conversation about a certain Tom Braithwaite. He couldn't hear everything, but the gist of it was that Tom was harassing some guy's relative to get him to move out of his rent-controlled house.

Does the name Tom Braithwaite mean anything to you? Ewan asked Stuart on his return.

Can't say it does, Stuart said.

He's not related to George?

Not that I know of, Stuart responded tentatively, still wracking his brains. No, that name doesn't ring a bell.

A journalist

Stuart seemed to be telling the truth so Ewan left it at that. Still curious, he insisted on buying one more round so he could return to the bar.

He waited for a lull in the barflies' conversation. Sorry to intrude, he said. But I couldn't help overhearing the name Tom Braithwaite.

Who the fuck are you? Came the response from a leathery old drinker in a trilby hat.

I'm a journalist with the Mercury.

Are you now? The old boy said, raising his head this time to get Ewan's measure.

I'm writing a story about Braithwaite, Ewan lied.

Well, fucking print this. Tom Braithwaite and his toe rag of a brother, George, can go fuck themselves as far as I'm concerned.

Ewan left the conversation there. He didn't mention anything further to Stuart. Instead he did more research. He discovered that, while George kept his nose clean, his brother Tom was a slum landlord in London who was now turning his attention to other parts of the UK. Where better to branch out than where he had family?

Ewan's career in journalism took off one rainy Tuesday. It was a drab and depressing winter's day. The sun had a rostered day off. He took the risk of bypassing Tim and Annie. He handed his well researched and hopefully sharply written piece direct to Stuart.

Stuart thanked Ewan and dropped it onto his in-tray. Ewan assumed, like a gangland victim, it would drift to the bottom never to see the light of day. He was wrong. Stuart summoned him a couple of hours later. Stuart checked the facts with Ewan. He could cover all of the bases.

George Braithwaite won't like this, Stuart said.

Ewan did not respond. Stuart was weighing the consequences. He took his time in deep reflection. Ewan mused that the story would be buried. He assumed this was how big business ultimately controlled the news.

Stuart took a deep breath. This is good. It's actually very good. We'll run it and wait for the shit to hit the fan.

Do you mean it? Ewan asked tentatively.

Yes. That's what we do here. We print stories.

Fantastic! Thanks so much, Ewan said on his way out.

By the way, Stuart, called to him.

Yes?

I've got a job for you.

Great. What do you want me do?

Some real work, Stuart said. You're a journalist from now on and not a bloody cub.

Standing there

Ewan was dreading Sally's graduation. Since their return from Africa, there'd been a falling out between him and her parents. Thanks to his re-awakening, Ewan was finding their sanctimonious preachifying intolerable. For their part, Sally's parents were showing increasing concern that Sally's relationship with Ewan might become permanent. They wanted grandchildren, but not his.

It was obvious that Sally was angry with him. She was playing piggy in the middle again, just as she had between him and Milton. She searched for a compromise that would smooth things over for her graduation day. The best she could do was to invite her parents to the ceremony at the university rather than stay the night with them, as had once been their custom.

The doorbell sounded that Saturday morning. Ewan reluctantly abandoned the warmth of his bed. He trotted down the stairs in response to the persistent ringing. He was dressed in nothing but his underpants - his costume of choice to deter the Witnesses from returning to save his soul. He prepared his devastating repartee as he descended the three flights. He avoided the missing stair rod that was a death trap for young players.

Ewan opened the heavy wooden front door with a flourish to maximise the shock of the jocks. He was horrified to find Sally's parents standing there.

Ewan and the unexpected parents eyed each other up and down warily. Nobody knew what to say. Ewan broke the silence, calling to Sally in a theatrical manner to warn her that her parents were at the door. Ewan reluctantly stepped aside so they could enter. He hoped the delay had given Sally sufficient time to ditch the freshly used condom.

Ewan made himself scarce. Even from the next room, he could sense the simmering tension around the kitchen table. It didn't take Sally's mother long, putting it in her husband's terms, to cast the first stone. She made some gratuitous comment to Sally about the state of the carpet. As ever, Sally's father sat on the sidelines. In more cordial times, he'd moaned to Ewan about the way the women in his life carried on together. Neither of them is entirely without sin, he would remark with a pointed raising of the eyebrow.

After the graduation, the students and their families milled around in celebration. Introductions were made and congratulations exchanged. All was forgotten between Sally and her mother. They hugged warmly. Her father kissed Sally stiffly on the cheek. Ewan and the parents shook hands.

Ewan and Sally walked the parents to their car. Standing a little to the side, Ewan noticed the suitcases on the back seat. They had obviously planned to stay. He felt sorry for them, but couldn't face the prospect of them sticking around for longer. He said nothing to Sally. It was best that way.

Once they were safely back in their flat alone, Ewan cuddled Sally and congratulated her. He told her he was proud of her. Sally kissed him, snuggling up against him. Sally told him she had some other news.

Do tell, he said.

It's big news.

Try me.

Are you ready?

Go for it.

I've been offered a job in Western Australia.

Is that all? Ewan said, hiding the intense churning in his stomach.

No, it's not, Sally said.

This one had better be more significant then.

It is.

Ewan felt sick.

I'm pregnant, Sally said, looking into the distance.

Ewan's mind went blank, except to wonder momentarily why they'd been bothering to use durex

Today my mood is dark. It's darker than that. It's black. It's black as coal. It's hole of Calcutta black.

Cassidy is mooching around in the lounge chair opposite my bed. Her mood is sullen. I can feel the brooding tension as she stares fixedly at the clouds scudding across the smudged blue sky.

I feel like we are in some weird depression contest. I resent her participation in it. Isn't pregnancy a natural part of life? As hard as hers seems to be, I can't accept that it can match up to paraplegia.

Every morning I try to give up on my writing. Then slavedriver Lorna always appears. She hasn't arrived yet. Today I can't face her enthusiasm and her absurd optimism. Maybe she will skip her daily visit and I can be left in peace?

No such luck. Is she oblivious to the murderous atmosphere in this room or does she choose to ignore it?

The preparations are now made. I can but acquiesce. This absurd show must go on.

How friends go their own way over time

James James Morrison Morrison Wetherby George Dupree

If Ewan had been a true Scottish laddie, I could have said that he took the low road after university while I took the high.

I hadn't bothered busting my balls to get a first class degree. The universities and government departments were chock-a-block with professors, scientists and bureaucrats with first class honours degrees and subsequent PhDs. Not one of them even made extra in the feature film of life.

Let's face it. The purpose of Ivy League universities is not pedagogic. They exist to perpetuate power and wealth. And they were, and still are, damn good at it.

While Ewan spent his time toiling under the searchlight of his Anglepoise lamp or linking arms with Sally chanting, 'When do we want it? Now!' I was busy courting influence. I was a natural. When you have a stockbroker for a father and a surgeon for a mother, you find schmoozing just oozing from your pores.

On this score, I owe Dad's mate, 'Uncle' Richard, big time. He helped me a lot. He was an older man with a lot to give. I was a younger guy with a lot to take. We were made for each other.

Uncle Richard inherited the auspicious City-based accounting firm, Morrison Morrison, in extraordinary circumstances. His old man shuffled off his mortal coil in unique fashion. Life imitated the lyrics of a classic country & western song. Uncle Richard's dad popped out to the corner store for cigarettes and never returned.

He left behind a grieving widow and three sons. He deserted a burgeoning accountancy powerhouse that was spreading its influence to the far-flung reaches of the Empire. Its accruals had penetrated every corner of the globe that was then coloured red.

His widow and his older brother and business partner, Sir Ernest, could not accept what was supposed to have happened. The distraught Mrs Morrison was at a loss to explain her husband's disappearance. She told the police that he was a loving husband and a doting father. Sir Ernest was equally dumbfounded. He couldn't credit it that a decent chap like his brother would leave the firm in the lurch when the operations in Colombo were hitting their straps.

No one could find the hapless hubby. The family 'invested' heavily in 'gratuities' for the Metropolitan Police and shelled out exorbitant fees for private detectives. Nothing concrete emerged. Salacious rumours abounded about the businessman's shenanigans and whereabouts. Some had him absconding with millions from the accounts of WW1 widows and living the high life on the beaches of the Costa del Sol. Others had him shacked up with his secret man-lover in an apartment block in Beyoglou, just the other side of the Golden Hind in Constantinople.

Sadly, as is usually the case with such titillating tales, the truth turned out to be much less strange than fiction. How mundane is this? It transpired ten years later, when his skeleton was found lodged upside down in a manhole over the Marylebone sewer, that he'd tripped and fallen not fifty yards from the Baker Street tobacconists. This denouement has implications that reverberate beyond the family tragedy. Clearly, the lyrics of country & western songs are not to be believed and drain maintenance in London once left a lot to be desired.

The firm passed into the incompetent hands of the genial Sir Ernest. He was a jolly good chap and all that but couldn't organise his way out of a paper bag. Some time later, Sir Ernest succumbed to a deep bout of melancholy, literally wasting away for all to see. Being queer as a coot, Sir Ernest had no offspring. The next in line to take over the company was my dad's best friend.

Richard was a trendsetter when it came to commercial nomenclature. In those days, there were no spin-doctors or marketing gurus providing high-priced advice on partner appointments or on mergers and acquisitions that would deliver the most market-friendly brand name. Richard understood this stuff instinctively. His company rejoiced in the successive identities of Morrison, Morrison & Carrington; Morrison, Morrison, Carrington and Hatch; Morrison, Carrington, Hatch and Singh. Alas, none delivered the spike in sales and profit that had been projected. Disenchanted, Richard bought out his partners and reverted to plain Morrison & Morrison. In a nod to modernity, Richard later dropped the ampersand. Thus the company became Morrison Morrison.

To this day, I wish Uncle Dickie had been a TS Eliot fan. He could have elevated to partner Stephen James, his brother Richard James, Charles Wetherby, Marcus George and Alphonse Dupree. Then the company could have been called James James Morrison Morrison Wetherby George Dupree.

Uncle Richard had a soft spot for me. He put in a good word at Christ Church. He gave me a job in my school holidays that proved invaluable through my university career.

For me, Morrison Morrison became the hub around which my networks and contacts revolved. MM was the accountancy firm of choice for my parents' friends and relatives. It served as the link to the City of London that gave our college's alumni the leg up to which birth and breeding entitled them. Thanks to my time at Morrison Morrison, and my finishing school at Oxford, I also had the luck to meet Johnny.

Loo Jin Pao was my tutorial partner for economics. His Chinese accent was hard to understand. I found macro-economics difficult enough without having to hurdle a language barrier. Fortunately, Loo compensated for his unintelligibility in other ways. His father was a director of Jardine Mathieson, the Asian trading juggernaut.

We dubbed Loo Jin Pao, Johnny. It was fashionable for young Chinese people to adopt a western first name. The yanks on our course insisted that Loo be called John. Loo loved the name. We were never sure whether he got the joke.

Uncle Richard did so much for me. He launched my career and was kind enough to employ his delightful daughter to help out with the accounts.

Dorothea was seriously good at double entry.

The life of Riley

After loonyversity, I was footloose and fancy-free. I lived the life of Riley. Who knows, he might have lived mine?

I spent five reckless years at MM and twice as long playing the field all over the world. As a young buck, 'privilege' was my middle name. I had precious few responsibilities counterbalanced by many precious possessions. I had money to burn. Unencumbered by conscience or constraint, I lit a raging conflagration of bank notes and credit cards. I had my fill of wine, women, song, and coke.

Parents tell their kids to look after their teeth as they only get one set. When I wasn't coked-up, I extrapolated this message to my nose. I drew the line under too many lines. I figured the odds were better, having more than one kidney. I ripped into the booze instead.

Wheeling and dealing came naturally to me. Thanks to my dad's broking contacts and my invaluable networks from MM, I was in pole position to lead the race for market tips. I sourced them from the legitimate analysts and sniffed out the tittle-tattle from the hush-hush, you-didn't-get-this-from-me insider traders. The stock market is the racetrack of the middle-class. It was invented by the born to rule to provide a heady rush for their cashed-up, fucked-up progeny. I found myself addicted to share trading as surely as a junkie lives to fill his arm.

Wheeling and dealing

My twenties are a blur. I catch a glimpse of scenes from that era like scratchy sepia stills from silent movies. These memory jogs tell me that my lost years took me far and wide. They say if you remember the sixties, you weren't really there. In my twenties, I was there, at least somewhere.

When the prodigal son of my consciousness returned, I relished the speculative mining and resources start-ups as a source of fast bucks. From a safe distance at first, I relished the gritty, real man's world of digging stuff up and pumping it out. The resources sector was fertile ground for a namby-pamby Oxbridge graduate to hit pay dirt without dirtying his hands.

I dabbled in the 'penny dreadful' mining stocks. You could pick them up for a penny or a cent depending on your market of choice. These were the equities that dreams were made of. If they came to nought (literally), as most of them did, it was no big deal. But when they did come good, and the share price climbed from a cent to a dollar, and you happened to have five million of the little beauties, the seething mass of selfishness that was then me truly understood why the working classes had a monopoly over hard labour.

Dig dirt and pay dirt

I based myself in Southern Africa to get close to the resources action. Maybe you can't win them all, but I had, in my relative youth, achieved a win-loss ratio coaches would die for. Gains short of a million left me cold. Cooking a straightforward deal, without adding a pinch of perfidy or a soupcon of skulduggery, failed to get my taste buds firing.

As time went by, my record started to fade. Whether it was the law of averages or some imperceptible and insidious loss of form catching up with me, I couldn't say. Some of my risk-taker, filthy rich mates were in the same boat. They explained it away by reference to factors beyond their control. The problem was 'deteriorating global market conditions' or 'a worldwide tightening of liquidity'.

Ewan would have blamed it on global warming. But the inconvenient truth in this case was that I was suffering from *commcussion* - a condition contracted by taking one too many serious blows to the bank balance in too short a time thanks to failed commercial transactions.

To keep our spirits up, my coke-forth-and-multiply mates formed a club. It was members only for those with a serious jerk ethic. It was for thrillseekers still stupid enough to risk obscene amounts of money on preposterous projects that would never work. In theory, we would meet for dinner and drinks on the fourth Wednesday of the month. In practice most of us forgot the arrangement or couldn't be bothered to turn up. But we still had a club. It was called 'Barking Mad'.

I suffered a momentary bout of sober reflection. I went on retreat. Retreat in my case from the spirits and the whores. Deprivation fuelled inspiration. It was obvious. My problems stemmed from a lack of hands-on experience. The Safari Club must give way to the safari suit. I determined to travel to far-flung outposts to revive my flagging fortunes. I took myself off to Mozambique like a latter-day Dr. Stanley, looking for liquidity, not Livingstone.

Over there, I had some adrenaline junkie white mates who'd sourced a huge deposit of nickel. The local black farm owners didn't know it was there. We were excited. There were bundles of cash to be made in legitimate currencies or an entire bank vault to be filled with the attractive but worthless local bills.

Between dig dirt and pay dirt, there were one or two tight turns to be negotiated. We had to acquire the land at a price that didn't reflect its underlying mineral deposits. We needed to access equity or debt to fund the plant, equipment and transportation. We also had to undertake the entire operation on the QT. If the government found out about it, they would impose humungous royalties on us or steal/confiscate the mine, depending on your point of view. And, aggregating the challenges above, we had to pull this off without getting our throats cut.

The inherent challenges were sufficient to daunt and deter the vast majority of the population. But that's how shit-kickers earned their name. *We* were Wall Street masters of the universe and still gung-ho enough to have a crack.

Our primary problem was lack of readies. We secured a dodgy line of credit from the Soviet black market, but this required us to add the blindfold to our high-wire act, as they insisted that the ultimate debt be repaid in US dollars.

The project started with a bang. We were more than pleased with ourselves. We 'negotiated' a wonderful price for rights over the land - something in the order of a string of beads. The first tranches of funding flowed smoothly out of Russia and the mining equipment was quickly sourced and transported over from Namibia and Angola. Things were going swimmingly and the adrenaline high was matching anything extreme sport could offer.

Which one?

I recall that I was consuming what passed for the buffet breakfast at the Maputo Grand Hotel. The eggs and bacon were served cold and congealed in bains-marie (note the plural, you Attorneys-General). A very black waiter, dressed in a very white uniform, brought me the antiquated house phone. I'd been anticipating a sexy little call from a conquest I'd made at the country club the night before.

Hello cherie, I cooed down the phone.

Johan, our South African site manager (nicknamed Hardman Johan BTW) didn't whisper sweet nothings in my ear. Instead, with a catching sob in his voice that chills me to this day, he said almost inaudibly, I've been shot twice in the fucking leg by Frelimo militia, you stupid little prick.

I'm not proud of how I responded.

Which one? I asked.

Palestinian Hijacker

I recalled the only other time in my life I'd been truly scared. I was raking in some easy money at university by flogging cheap kibbutz holidays via ads in the Oxford Mail. I thought it a clever marketing pitch for my copy to read, 'Palestinian hijacker requires hostages; fly to the Ein Gedi kibbutz for only 50 pounds'. I still think it was clever. However, I'd overlooked one simple fact. Stateless freedom fighters seldom see the funny side of life.

I staggered home from the pub one night to find a note pushed under my door. It read in letters pointedly cut from the same publication, 'You will be made to suffer as Eichmann suffered'. The prospect of being crushed alive under a speedboat didn't greatly appeal. I determined to withdraw from the travel agency profession forthwith.

Similarly, I left my daredevil southern African mates in no doubt that Hardman Johan blubbering down the phone was persuasive enough for me also to wish to retire from the mining and exploration sector. Surprisingly, my colleagues agreed. We took a monumental hit, but here I am alive to tell the tale.

Honkers

I pulled my head in after that. I was no longer a kid. On the positive side, I'd learned a thing or two from my escapades and misadventures. I'd dabbled in an impressive array of fields and financial settings across all of the continents. I had a good education and even better contacts. I touted myself around as a consultant. My dubious talents proved surprisingly popular. I spent several years in Sydney, living down by the Rocks, and then I passed a similar time in Cape Town in an uncannily similar neighbourhood.

I deliberately picked a fight with my MD at Cape Minerals and Mining. I took advantage of the broadcast capacity of those new-fangled emails to tell all and sundry that my boss was a stupid, lazy cunt. He took exception to my note. To which part of it, I'm not sure.

My old mate, Johnny, found me a lurk in Hong Kong that sounded much more my style. I enjoyed my sojourn in Honkers. I didn't mind the rivulets of sweat streaming from my armpits or the stench of refuse bobbing defiantly in the swirling harbour.

It was another time for reflection. In a setting where life assaults your every sense from every angle at every moment, you can't help but seek refuge inside yourself. This was no safe haven for me.

Similarly, reconnecting with Johnny challenged me to peer into the mirror of my own life. Loo had everything, but he had nothing. His time on earth was slipping away like the coke residue seeping from his nostrils.

I saw myself in him and, for maybe the first time in my life, I didn't like what I saw. I determined to escape Hong Kong before it got me too.

Loveliness

As soon as the role was secured, I got the hell out of HK to take up my shiny new position in the futures room for the French bank, Société Générale.

I arrived tired and hung-over after a six-hour delay in Frankfurt while our plane got fixed. The firm had a quaint way of welcoming high-priced contractors in those days. The directors put them up initially in their own homes instead of at an apartment or a hotel.

I was collected from Orly airport by a uniformed flunky driving a black Merc with tinted windows. I was uneasy throughout the drive, conscious that cars like this were the preferred conveyance of the mafia. I kept my wits about me. If a car backfired that day in the suburban traffic jam, I would've hit the deck faster than a toned housewife watching a workout video.

Thankfully, we evaded the hitmen and arrived unscathed at M. Le Maître's humble abode. I thanked the chauffeur for opening the door for me. I alighted to a sight that took my breath away. It was clear that, while SG's share price had been plummeting of late, René Le Maître's personal stocks had not. This place made the Palais de Versailles look like a kit home.

After *le lacke*y escorted me along the gravel driveway, up the stone steps, into the vestibule, up the sweeping marble staircase, along several corridors, through an ornately carved dark wood anteroom and into my suite, I felt like begging him to stick with me so I wouldn't be doomed to wander the maze of corridors like the lost tribes of Israel for the duration of my stay.

Dinner was at seven. I had time to settle in. This was a style of living to which I could easily become accustomed. I had a few drinks and a spa. I would've taken a turn around the orchard, if I'd had the guts to try to find my way. I checked in the mirror that my bowtie was straight and set out at six-thirty precisely so I wouldn't be late.

When I found the dining room, I was greeted by Rene and introduced to Jacques, my new boss at SG. We exchanged pleasantries. Jacques looked quintessentially French. He had short, tightly curled hair that was chestnut on top and greying at the sides. He had smooth, tanned skin and was dressed in fashionably pastel polo shirt and cream linen pants.

I was jerked from my appraisal of Jacques by a vision of loveliness glimpsed out of the corner of my eye.

It was Nina.

Can I read it? Lorna is trying it on again, bouncing onto the corner of the bed.

I'm desperate to fool myself. The ugly truth is that I didn't feel the slightest tremor below the waist.

No reading it! I sound mean even to myself.

Why not? Screwed up face.

Because it was my one and only condition for starting this godforsaken enterprise in the first place. I don't want to inflict this dross on the world.

I'm not the world, Lorna replies calmly, ignoring my bad temper.

She reminds me so much of her father at times like this

Am I in it yet? Lorna persists.

That's a typical question from the selfie generation. Thankfully my tone is now lighter.

Well? Am I?

You're about to be born.

Cool.

Not for your mum and dad.

Tongue poked out as she leaps off the bed.

No sensation again. No surprise in that.

How friendship tends to be neglected when real life takes over

Fremantle

As unfamiliar as the scenery was, the sense of déjà-vu for Ewan was overwhelming. The blinding light of Western Australia reminded him of that first day in Africa. Sally was clinging doggedly to the seat in front of her just as he remembered her in the cattle truck.

They clambered down from the airport bus in Fremantle. He surveyed the scene. This wasn't Africa. There was heat and there were flies. But there was no dust.

Ewan helped Sally haul her bags away from the tourists and the shoppers criss-crossing King's Square. Sally looked dreadful. She was ashen-faced and drawn. Sally spent the flight throwing up. As soon as the fasten seatbelts sign was switched off, Sally would run to the aeroplane toilet.

Thanks to the deadly duo of fatigue and culture shock, Ewan hallucinated as the cab rattled its way along and beyond the Cappuccino Strip to South Fremantle. He registered a blur of café umbrellas, busking hippies, delicatessens, historic buildings, concrete monstrosities, plaster lions and ocean glimpses. Most of all, he was struck by the clarity of the light and the bright blue sky, cloudless as far as the eye could see.

Ewan and Sally settled into the two-storey, mud brick and weatherboard house they'd rented. It belonged to a famous yachtsman, a grinder, who'd starred in Australia's celebrated victory in the America's Cup. The neighbours were friendly, but kept their distance. They were a close-knit group that had lived together for years in that little street two blocks back from the beach.

The transition to their new life was challenging. Sally battled her symptoms from day one. The relentless bombardment from morning sickness broke her spirit. She bunkered down in bed most of the time. She understood why pregnancy was once called confinement.

Ewan escaped from tending Sally whenever he decently could. He explored the neighbourhood and investigated the local culture with journalistic zeal. He was fascinated by Fremantle's short but dramatic history. He tramped around the port city, noting the architecture, the maritime relics and the eclectic mix of artists and fisherfolk. He found the laid-back environment refreshing compared to the formality of society back home.

The day loomed when Sally needed to report to the Fremantle Community Legal Centre to start her job as the welfare rights officer. Ewan knew Sally wasn't physically up to it, but he didn't dare voice his concerns. They'd ventured to Australia to foster Sally's career. It was cruel fate that she had fallen pregnant and doubly so that it had laid her so low.

Ewan awoke one morning to find Sally in an unusually cheerful mood.

Shall we walk on the beach before it gets too hot? She asked.

Yes, great, Ewan responded enthusiastically, leaping out of bed.

They strolled hand in hand along the grassy mound, inspecting the flat early morning waves off South Beach. They stopped at the toilet block that passed for a café. Ewan ordered two flat whites with his favourite blueberry muffin.

I rate this muffin a 2.5, Ewan said.

Not so good?

It's acceptably moist but lacks fruit intensity in the opinion of the judges.

Sally smiled. Ewan loved the way her nose turned up.

What are you thinking? Ewan asked.

You know that I can't take up the job.

Ewan took Sally's hand. They sat silently for a while.

I could go to the community legal centre for you, Ewan suggested. If that would help.

Sally was silent for a moment. No, not that, she said.

Then what?

Come with me. Can you do that?

I can do that, Ewan said.

That's settled then, Sally said, kissing Ewan on the cheek.

Yes it is, he said

It is, isn't it?

Yes, but what was it?

I can't remember, Sally said.

They laughed. It was their first Australian laugh.

Haroldic labours

Ewan loved the oddball locals. Everyone made the time to chat. Was it the relaxed pace of life compared to the rat race of the big cities? Maybe it was the climate that afforded people the old-fashioned luxury of hanging around on street corners yakking to the neighbours?

He took an immediate shine to Harold, who lived a few doors up the road. Ewan placed Harold as being well into his eighties. He passed the time perched on a rickety bench on his front veranda. He watched the world go by with his brown and white spotted dog. Judging by the moth-eaten look of his dog-eared coat, he was as old as his master in dog years at least. The pooch slumbered, snored and farted at his owner's feet.

The mongrel would prick up its ears at the sound of a passing stranger and occasionally raise his head an inch or two from the ground. One bright morning, Ewan took the dog's response as an invitation to join them.

The man eyed Ewan up and down a couple of times. Then he proffered a wrinkly hand. Harold, he said, introducing himself.

Ewan reciprocated. What's your dog's name? He asked.

Harold.

No, I meant your *dog's* name.

That's Harold too, the old man said without a hint of amusement.

Harold 2, Ewan laughed. That's brilliant!

Not Harold 2, he corrected him gruffly, Harold, as well.

Ewan took an instant liking to someone so arrogant or devoid of imagination as to name his dog after himself. They became firm friends. In those early days, Ewan had time on his hands. Once Sally succumbed to her afternoon nap, he would take Harold a beer. They would nudge the flies away from the horizontal hound below. Sometimes they would chat away. Other times they were comfortable with the view, the company and the silence.

Harold had lived in the same house for the last forty years. He'd bought it for four thousand dollars. That was a lot of money in those days, Harold would point out each time he told Ewan the story.

A journalist, Harold would hiss at Ewan from time to time. What kind of job is that? It's just preying on human misery, if you ask me. Harold would muse with a lengthy sigh.

Harold had an old codger mate, Clarrie, who lived two doors from him. When Harold had come to trust Ewan, he confided his four decade long Clarrie-quest to him.

No way! Ewan declared.

Harold sighed. I'll have to show you then.

He didn't move for ages. Ewan wondered whether Alzheimer's had ambushed him. In the fullness of time, Harold nudged the comatose canine with his foot.

Clarrie on, old boy, he said to his dog, laughing out loud.

Ewan smiled at the joyful scene.

That's a clarrie-on call, Harold said, marooned to the spot, unable to laugh and move at the same time.

Come on, old timer, Harold encouraged his dog, willing their respective atrophied muscles and arthritic joints to rise again to the challenge of motion.

Ewan set off to join them. Human Harold wagged his finger, motioning him to stay put.

I don't want you putting him off his game, the old man admonished Ewan. Harold can be temperamental with an audience.

The Harolds shuffled painfully along the garden path. They emerged onto the gentle downhill gradient of the footpath. Ewan sipped at his beer. The pace of the action was glacial. Ewan wondered what on earth could have taken this man and his best friend half a lifetime to perfect.

In due course, the fruits of their *Haroldic* endeavours were revealed in all their glory. The twelve labours of Hercules were a challenge unworthy of the name as compared with such achievements of man and dog.

Once outside old Clarrie's place, two-legged Harold whispered un-heard words of encouragement to the Harold with four. Harold the latter set off, scratching his way along a slightly worn track to the middle of Clarrie's front lawn. Then he made two tight three hundred and sixty degree turns, hunkered down and did his business on top of the mental bull's eye long imprinted on his brain.

Harold the human looked triumphantly back at Ewan, brandishing his walking stick in celebration. Ewan formed a solitary guard of honour to salute his heroes as they shambled back up the path. A Compton or a Bradman received no finer standing ovation for a home-town hundred.

Ewan let them catch their breath. Don't you like Clarrie? He asked.

Whatever gives you that idea?

Why did you get Harold to crap on *his* lawn then?

Because I can, Harold responded, beaming proudly down at his dog. Or rather, because *he* can, he added.

Barefoot & pregnant

Months had passed. Sally's belly was swollen and her ankles the size of footballs. She insisted on seeing Ewan off on this special day.

Ewan glanced back at her from the driver's seat. This was a classic movie scene. Sally stood there, literally barefoot and pregnant. With one hand, she shielded her eyes from the slope of the early morning sun. With the other she waved limply like the women in the newsreels farewelling the heaving troopships in WW1.

He was off to work, not to war. He didn't know whether to laugh or cry. He could see the funny side of Sally's set piece, but for him the send-off was poignant. What was Sally thinking behind those blinking, blue eyes? This should've been me?

Ewan accompanied Sally when she fronted the community legal centre to break the bad news. They stopped for a coffee opposite the council offices. The entry, with its metal notice board and rusting canopy, reminded him of the soviet realist architecture that dominated the posters on his dad's living room wall. By the time they'd negotiated the busy traffic to cross the road to the prefabricated building, Sally had changed her mind. She asked Ewan to let her do the deed alone.

You asked me to come with you that day at the beach, he protested

This is not about you! Sally rebuked him, negotiating the ramp alone.

Ewan demurred. He was trying his best to be supportive. Sally's fate was nobody's fault. Sometimes she seemed determined to apportion blame

Not sure how to respond back in the present, Ewan acknowledged Sally's fey farewell with a nod of the head and pulled away. Five minutes later, he was regretting his lazy decision to drive to work. There was nowhere to park in Fremantle. He did another tour of the one-way system, jagging a parking space in an inadequate two-hour zone.

Ewan settled for it, hoping he would remember to move the car later. He groped around in his pocket for coins, finding three fifty-cent pieces. The meter took every coin but. Ewan negotiated a change exchange with an old lady. She fished deep into her oceanic handbag. Her purse was a bottom feeder. Appropriate coinage was eventually trawled. Ewan purchased the maximum period allowed and slotted the ticket on his dashboard. He then sprinted to Cliff Street, finally bounding up the stairs to the office of the Fremantle Herald.

Ewan was late on his first day and fluster-faced to prove it. He leant on the jarrah door with the opaque glass centrepiece. It didn't budge. He tried again with the same result. He collapsed onto the wooden steps, relieved and amused. He laughed out loud. What was he thinking? Had it been that long since the Mercury? Hard-bitten, hard-living journalists don't rock up to work at eight-thirty. They don't wake up until ten.

He trotted down the stairs to seek a coffee hit. He was confronted by a silhouette in the doorway.

Do you work here, mate?

This is a newspaper office, Ewan responded jovially. Nobody actually works here.

The Herald

Ewan took to the Fremantle Herald and it took to him.

This was one local newspaper that lived up to its name. It was local. It sought to represent the opinions and aspirations of the local people.

Freo was a real community, with strong values. Ewan loved that. His job at the paper placed him in the thick of things. Compared to his work for the middle of the road Mercury, he relished the opportunity to write for a paper that championed the cause of the disadvantaged.

While the hearts of the owner and the journos were in the right place, Ewan found the standards of journalism sloppy. So keen were they to expose the local council's disregard of heritage and its CEO's profligacy with the ratepayers' revenue that their coverage frequently lacked balance. Worse than that, Ewan deplored the way their zeal to support a cause undermined their enthusiasm to look for the cause. As committed as Ewan was to right wrongs, he was equally motivated to write stories.

He came to appreciate the value of Stuart's mentorship from his time at the Leicester Mercury. He recalled Stuart's incessant repetition of his journalistic mantra in that accent so inclement to Ewan's ears. ABC, son, he would say, ABC. Ask questions. Believe nothing. Check everything.

Despite the prosaic nature of much of the work, and his reservations about the quality of some of his colleagues' craft, Ewan was content to be there. He kept his opinions to himself. That was another thing Stuart taught him. Ewan followed up the same stories as his colleagues, but with much greater rigour. By this time, Ewan's nose for political cant and bureaucratic bullshit was finely honed. Like the police trying to hook a drug-dealer, he would eschew the small fry to search for the bigger fish.

He still championed the underdog as the Herald's owner-editor demanded. Ewan wrote sympathetically about the plight of the street trees threatened by the chainsaw and the cultural heritage value of another old waterside workers' pub succumbing to the relentless juggernaut of the all-consuming Catholic university, but he checked his facts carefully and balanced his articles with official comment. Once the editor took to his copy, Ewan accepted that the egregious behaviour, real, imagined or fabricated of the local powerbrokers would dominate the story, but Ewan took comfort from the professionalism of his own work.

Occasionally a Herald article would achieve a re-run in the West Australian or snag coverage on the local ABC news. Ewan worked diligently towards making the next article to be so elevated one of his.

Ewan was fulfilling his mission, in baby steps at least. He made sure that the views of the silent and powerless were fairly heard in the Australian media landscape dominated by the rich and powerful.

Ewan found himself on the other side of the fence when he got home. He was the privileged elite - a person with a body that didn't disgust him and a life enriched by meaningful work. Sally's aggrieved mood and sullen expression mirrored perfectly the photographs the Herald printed of groups of surly neighbours.

Sally would give birth any day. The simplest task for her now demanded a super-human effort. Ewan forgave and forgot. The twist of circumstances had been tough for Sally. He hoped against hope that the birth of the baby would turn things around.

Ruining his life

Ewan was engrossed in the feature he was writing. It was an amazing story about an elderly man whose neighbour, thanks to various planning and building stuff-ups, was allowed to build a house in front of him a finger's width higher than was strictly allowed. The man's sense of injustice was so strong that he daubed his house with slogans alleging corruption by all and sundry and drove around town with a coffin tied to the top of his station wagon.

Ewan was a method actor in character. He found himself assuming the persona of that man who was ruining his life. As hard as he tried to identify with the fellow, he couldn't understand why someone, even if he was Dutch, would obsess to the point of self-destruction about a structure built a fraction too high and lose his wife, family and fortune in the process.

The office was relatively peaceful. He could concentrate sitting at his desk. He cursed when the phone rang. It was Sally.

My waters just broke, Sally yelled down the phone

How do you know?

Because the floor's a fucking swimming pool!

Don't panic, Ewan said in a panicky voice.

Get yourself home. Sally ordered. Fast!

Ewan leapt to his feet, knocking the desk chair over. He set it upright, gathered his case and got going. He backtracked to shut down his computer. The insomniac machine took its time going to sleep. Once the last spec of light had vanished at the end of the tunnel, Ewan sped off, leaping down the stairs two at a time.

He blinked into the late afternoon light, disoriented as to where he'd parked his car. He remembered he'd walked. Cursing, he jogged in the direction of South Fremantle. He was unfit and breathing heavily by the time he reached the Esplanade Hotel. He remembered that the hotel had a taxi rank. He was in luck. There were taxis waiting.

He climbed into the front seat of the cab at the head of the queue. Ewan caught his breath, relaxing back into the passenger seat.

Are we going anywhere, mate? The driver asked impatiently.

Sorry, Ewan bumbled. South Freo.

You're kidding, right?

What do you mean?

South Fremantle starts two streets away.

Oh no, Ewan reassured him. The other end near Douro Road.

Very funny, the driver said. It's taken me an hour to get to the front of this fucking line and I am not, repeat not, going one k down the road for five fucking bucks.

You've got to take me, Ewan responded. My dad's a London cabbie. I know my rights.

I don't care if your dad is Prince Fucking Charles. Get out of my cab.

My wife's gone into labour, Ewan wailed.

Piss off out of my fucking taxi, the driver snarled. I've heard them all before and from much better liars than you.

Hard labour

The labour was long and hard. Sally toughed it out for sixteen hours without the dilation required to reveal even the baby's fontanel. She clung doggedly to her principles about natural childbirth. She had resentfully conceded that a home birth would be too risky. She would not succumb to the lax seduction of drugs to dull the pain.

Ewan stayed dutifully by Sally's bedside. He held her hand, massaged her shoulders and played her favourite music. Between contractions, he begged her to accept an epidural. He asked her in a pathetic tone to do it for him. That suggestion got the lack of response he expected.

As hard as Ewan tried to fight it, sleep eventually got the better of him. A bossy Italian nurse dispatched him to the hospital cafeteria. It was closed at that hour of the morning. He resorted to the vending machine. He selected a murky hot liquid that was impersonating a coffee and a snack wrapped in plastic that had been a ham and cheese sandwich in a former life.

Ewan slumped onto a green plastic chair. He allowed his head to fall onto the matching laminex table. He took a sip of caffeinated liquid and a bite of rubbery dough. The soft, white bread, moulded itself into his upper jaw. The experience reminded him of many a service station pit stop between Leicester and Leeds.

He lapsed into a semi-sleep stream of consciousness. What joy was there in childbirth? Why did God condone such suffering? I should've phoned my dad to let him know. What a bastard that cabdriver was. Why ruin your life for a view? Why am I ruining my life? For all this pain and the endless responsibility of parenthood?

Ewan fought to rouse himself. He was aware of his situation, but couldn't haul himself back into consciousness. Why would someone ruin his life for something so inconsequential and then go so far as to rope a coffin to the roof of his car? A coffin that I might as well climb into now that I've ruined my life and my wife and child are dead.

He fought to come around. He still couldn't make it. Sally's dying in childbirth. For what? To propagate the human race? What's the point? Everything's ruined. My life is ruined. Sally's dead.

Ewan woke with a start. He looked around. Where the fuck am I? Has Sally died in childbirth? Oh my God. Why wasn't I with her? No, that can't be right. I've got to get back. I must eat this. How did I get here? Where's the maternity ward? It's on the third floor. I think. Is it?

Lorna Bonnie

Lorna Bonnie arrived after a twenty-eight hour nightmare of a labour. She was delivered via a c-section. Sally had passed the point of all resistance. Ewan was devastated for Sally but consented in a heartbeat. He clutched Sally's limp hand as she was wheeled away.

Prior to that, a medical SWAT team arrived. The masked men and women applied themselves to the baby extraction task with impersonal professionalism. They conversed in brusque robotic speech. To Ewan's untrained eye they passed everyday household items to each other from the sanitised stainless steel trolley. The sink plunger was produced to suck the baby out. No result. The salad servers were deployed to lever the recalcitrant infant free. No luck there. There was nothing for it, Ewan speculated. They would unleash the tear gas to flush the baby out. Instead they opted for surgery.

Once Lorna squawked to announce her arrival to the world, the tragedy that was this birthing did not abate. Sally, wan and listless, was granted the most fleeting of opportunities to bond with her bub before Lorna was whisked away to the neonatal intensive care unit. Ewan, like an airline passenger on a plummeting plane, searched the faces of the automaton nurses in this case for reassurance. He found none.

Lorna's birth trauma was profound. She needed assistance to breathe. She slept fitfully. She couldn't feed. Sally was a spectator when she should have been a player. She was present for everything but participated in nothing. As for Ewan, he was consigned to watching the match on TV.

Ewan worked at the newspaper as best he could during Lorna's three-month hospital stay. Sally lived at the clinic, rarely making it home. She devoted herself to the thankless task of bonding with an infant through the reinforced plastic of a crib. Ewan lived a lonely life, devoid of human affection. Meanwhile the coffin man was ever-present in his thoughts. There were many ways to ruin your own life.

Lorna eventually made it home. Ewan arranged a small welcoming party. Sally nodded to the guests before proceeding to the bedroom with

Lorna. She didn't re-emerge. The well-wishers were extremely understanding. Once they'd gone, Ewan ventured warily into the bedroom. Mother and baby were asleep.

Ewan poured himself a generous red wine. The coffin man's circumstances no longer seemed insane. He at least was a victim, albeit of a trivial crime. In Ewan and Sally's case, the pain was entirely self-inflicted. Their life would never be the same. His daughter was a runt. His wife might be lost to him forever.

The West

Time slowly healed. For Ewan, his world was no longer ruined. His life was a delicate sweater left too long in the drier. It had shrunk. It didn't fit him as well as it used to. But it was still a life.

Lorna was a sickly baby and then a fractious toddler. She was thin and pale like an abused child living in the cupboard under the stairs. Her behaviour was sullen and withdrawn. Mother and daughter spent most of their lives at the hospital, the doctor's surgery or sitting around in the maternal and child health centre.

Life did not return to normal in any sense. Ewan could hardly remember life BL (Before Lorna). Everything unfolded to a new rhythm and routine. Ewan joked when Sally was not around that they didn't have Lorna, she had them. Ewan was a lodger in his own home. He was a renter In his own life for that matter. He understood his banishment from the inner sanctum. He could accept it, but he refused to fool himself that he liked things that way.

Work was his salvation and fortunately for him it was going well. His incisive article about the coffin man had put his name up in lights. It was featured by the West Australian and inspired a provocative and moving TV episode on Australian Story. Other poignant features and hard-hitting exposes followed over the next couple of years. The editor of the Herald now looked at him sideways. It was a matter of time before Ewan would move on. They all did - the ones who were any good.

It was no surprise when Ewan asked to see him one late afternoon when no one was around.

Which job are you going to? He asked. Spit it out.

How did you know? Ewan asked.

I'm telepathic, he replied in a world-weary tone.

Ewan laughed. I'm sorry to do this to you, he said.

The West is it? His editor asked.

You're a clairvoyant.

Guessing the bleeding obvious doesn't require psychic powers, he observed sarcastically,

On the features team, Ewan explained, working hard to contain his excitement.

His editor did not find Ewan's enthusiasm infectious.

Too Unfair

Breaking the news about his new job to Sally wasn't going to be easy. Ewan needed to think it through. Most journalists would seek inspiration from the bottle. Ewan chose a bracing walk instead.

He didn't doubt that Sally would be pleased for him. It was just that the contrast between their respective fortunes was growing wider by the day. He was already free to work and escape from the drudgery of caring for a sickly child. Soon he would have made it in Australia in his chosen field. They'd emigrated in the first place to advance Sally's career. Everything had been turned upside down.

Ewan set off towards the beach. Fremantle was littered with bikes. They whirred past him on the footpath. They loitered untidily against street-lamps. They teetered precariously against heritage shopfronts, balancing with their handlebars like tightrope walkers against the buffeting Fremantle Doctor.

In this town, cycling was a statement not a conveyance. Peddling was political not positional. Even Sally had a bike. How alluring she'd been trundling over the cobblestones in Oxford! She hardly used it these days in the PL, Post Lorna, era.

Ewan rarely got on one these days. He was still traumatised from a nasty accident years ago when he was an exchange student in France. He'd stayed for a month with the baker's family in a tiny village in the south. He lost his virginity there but also his dignity when he pulled out of a steep descent and literally gate-crashed into an old lady's living room.

Ewan arrived at the Seaview pub. He resisted the temptation to seek inspiration there. How was he going to break this news to Sally? He would focus on the matter once he reached the beach. He crossed the road and skirted around Sealanes. He turned the corner into a mighty onshore breeze. The salty blast overpowered the rank odour of the seafood rotting in the waste bins out the back.

As hard as he tried to focus, Ewan found mental distraction every-where. Life was uncomplicated back in Leicester and Leeds. Sally was relaxed then. He smiled at the playact she put on when he got the acceptance letter from the Mercury. Perhaps he should hold the letter from the West behind his back and make Sally guess what he was hiding?

Ewan plodded south past the controversial new seawall and the lime-stone groynes he'd covered frequently for the Herald. How would Sally react to him making a joke out of it? She seemed happier now she was finally working at the community legal centre one day a week. But the approach seemed too frivolous given the comparative slavery of her everyday life.

Ewan turned for home. Walking in the sand was effortless with the wind at his back. He faced facts. Sally would not respond well to his wonderful opportunity with the West Australian. She would hate herself for it. But life would seem just too unfair.

They were out

Ewan strode towards home. For some reason, his schoolboy studies of Macbeth came to mind. If it were done when 'tis done, then t'were well it were done quickly.

None of this was anybody's fault. Not his. Not Sally's. Not Lorna's. Landing an exciting job with the metropolitan daily would create opportunities for Ewan to bring about social change. It had been his dream since Africa. Sally wanted this as much as he did.

Ewan slowed as his front yard came into view. His courage faltered momentarily. He lashed himself on. He had no reason to feel guilty. He had always supported Sally. He had made sacrifices for her over the years. He had acquiesced to the volunteering stint in Mubuwe. He had moved to Leeds so Sally could pursue her social work studies. He had commuted every weekend from Leicester back to Leeds. He crossed to the other side of the world for Sally's career. And he was sporting the scar tissue of their parenting experience.

Ewan quickened his step again, walking on past his own house. He waved to the Harolds. He could sense their disappointment at his curt greeting. He couldn't stop now. His mood had changed again. Out of nowhere, he found himself consumed by a savage anger. He was incandescent with rage. He had sacrificed himself for Sally all the way. He had subjugated himself to her wishes all along. It was up to her now to accommodate him.

He turned on his heel. He hurried back past the Harolds. This time he waved. He would make his peace with them when the time was right. The rusty hinges grated before his front gate swung shut. His cheap plastic key struggled to turn the lock. He was a proud messenger with glad tidings.

You'll never guess what I've got here behind my back, he shouted down the corridor. He repeated the words as he opened the double doors to the garden. He rustled the hidden envelope to add to the excitement.

Sally and Lorna were out.

It Can Wait

The best laid plans. Ewan was on the toilet when Sally and Lorna returned. He finished the business. He took his time washing his hands. He slipped into his home office to grab the letter. It was best to stick to the plan.

As Ewan emerged into the corridor, he was bowled over by a malicious demon charging at him full pelt. He managed to break his fall. Look at you! He said, recovering some composure.

Ewan scooped Lorna into his arms. You're a wicked little devil!

Ewan scanned the house to find Sally. Where's Mummy? He asked.

Lorna pointed to the garden. Ewan carried Lorna outside. Sally was seated at the outdoor setting. She looked happy. Ewan smiled back.

Tell Daddy your news, Sally said.

No, don't want to, Lorna refused, squirming in Ewan's arms to be put down. Don't want to! She repeated, racing off in the direction of the sand pit at the bottom of the garden.

Ewan and Sally exchanged glances. Ewan wanted this tension over. He took Sally's hand. I've got news too, he said.

Sally looked deflated.

Mine can wait, Ewan said cheerfully. I had a lovely welcome from Lorna. From the ghoul, anyway, he added.

Won't you tell Daddy your news? Sally called out to Lorna.

I don't want to! Lorna insisted, compacting the freshly watered sand into her plastic bucket.

Sally shook her head. Our news is, she said, taking up Ewan's other hand as well, I've signed Lorna up for school.

Ewan was nonplussed. She's not old enough to start school.

It's a Montessori school. It's beautiful. You know the one, right beside the beach near Cottesloe.

I didn't know they took kids so young.

It's an alternative school, Sally explained.

Sally was excited. Her smile was broad. She was more animated than she had been for God knows how long. Ewan focused himself on this news and away from the other.

Sounds great, Ewan said. Tell me more.

We have an interview, Sally said. Next week. We can all go there together and ask our questions.

It's not a Satanist school, is it? Ewan asked, raising an eyebrow.

Sally shot him a look. Then she figured it out. No, the Halloween gear was a value for money bribe at the Two Dollar Shop.

Sally got up. Lorna, let's go inside now, she called out.

No, Mum, I'm building a castle, Lorna shouted back.

What do you think? Sally asked, heading out to fetch Lorna.

About the school?

No, about Satanism, Sally replied sarcastically.

It's great, Ewan said. But, isn't she a bit young? You know, given her behaviour.

She's not too young, Sally insisted. She has to learn to mix.

OK. It's great then, Ewan concluded.

What was the other news?

Oh, nothing. It can wait.

Beehive

As weird as the school and everyone connected to it seemed to a boy brought up in a tower block in central London, Ewan came to see the Montessori school as a lifesaver. If it hadn't saved his life exactly, he credited it with rescuing him and keeping him afloat.

The location of the incongruously named Beehive school was a country mile from the nearest apiary. The school comprised a ramshackle collection of buildings with a schoolyard too small to kick a ball around. It had a rag and bone outlook to the back over the shunting yards and million dollar views from the front over the sparkling Indian Ocean.

Beehive had an unconventional approach to education. The different age groups were blended in multi-age classes. The school encouraged the boys and girls to choose activities according to their personal passions rather than have them follow a set curriculum. Learning was experiential rather than instructional. The Montessori goal was to produce independent, confident children, not necessarily well-educated ones in a conventional sense.

Sally found the alternative approach inspiring. Ewan found it confronting. They argued frequently about the virtues and vices of the school.

Wasn't that wonderful? Sally said to Ewan as they walked to their cars after attending a classroom event for the parents.

Ewan had found the Show and Tell bewildering. The children had brought in a motley collection of artefacts, ranging from a Rolex watch to a self-portrait of a child with the sun for its head. The teachers watched on as the children failed to organise a sensible roster to display their wares. Meanwhile, the proud parents, formed in a wide circle round the children, warmed the earth with their beaming admiration.

Weird, maybe, Ewan replied.

The kids were so confident and creative, Sally cooed.

Off their faces might be more accurate.

That school is perfect for Lorna, Sally insisted.

I agree, Ewan conceded, remorseful at having opened his mouth in the first place.

You do?

Yes, I do.

Why are you always so negative about it?

I don't add the halo, that's all.

Ewan regretted having needled Sally. It's the right choice, Ewan said, putting his hand on Sally's through the rolled-down driver's window.

I'm glad you think so, Sally said, escaping from Ewan's grasp.

It is right for Lorna, Ewan added, weighing his words carefully. Because she is different.

Exactly.

Lorna is precocious. She is demanding. She is self-indulgent, Ewan said.

She is odd.

It was better for Sally to say it.

So the school is perfect! Ewan concluded.

Sally smiled at him. Peace had broken through again.

Outcast

Ewan remained an outcast in the make-believe Montessori world. He came home early from work one day to find after-school playgroup in full swing out in the garden. Boys and girls alike were dressed as fairies. The mothers, seated in a circle on the grass like a middle-class coven, were blowing bubbles over the children and sprinkling them with fairy dust.

It was a steamy day thanks to a cyclone camped off the northwest coast. Ewan gulped water straight from the tap as he watched the pantomime through the French doors. He felt something brush against his hand. He made to pull away. Then he saw a cherubic, blond-haired boy with full gossamer wings staring up at him.

Hello, Ewan said.

I'm Lunar Solstice, the boy replied.

You're what?

I'm Lunar Solstice, he insisted, I'm named after the moon, the boy said, slipping silently away.

Ewan spied on the proceedings. It was crazy stuff. His eyes followed Lorna. At home, she spent time alone. With her school friends, she was at least connected to the group, if not part of it. He and Sally might find Lorna fickle, moody and unpredictable, but her school friends found her normal. More or less, insofar as normality had any application in this unusual environment.

The routine around school afforded Ewan breathing space to embrace his calling. At the same time, it provided Sally with a peer group of parents. Now freed up significantly from her surveillance duties, Sally had quit the community legal centre to undertake private family counselling.

Sally was right. If Montessori hadn't exactly saved Ewan's life, it had salvaged it. He forgave it its idiosyncrasies. He blessed it for embracing Lorna and releasing Sally to pursue something of the lifestyle she had coveted since leaving Africa.

Stamping your feet

Once he'd tendered his resignation to the Fremantle Herald, Ewan found himself wracked by guilt about selling out to the right-wing media. As much as he justified his career progression to himself as enhancing his opportunities to create change, he recognised his own personal ambition. It sat uneasily with him.

Ewan had prepared himself for a difficult adjustment from a local paper to the Perth metropolitan daily. It turned out tougher than he'd expected. He hadn't realised that everything in his working life would change. Instead of a lazy stroll into work, he had to sit in traffic slogging his way to an office complex on the far side of the city. The Fremantle Herald's tiny staff group worked from three upstairs rooms in an iconic building surrounded by heritage splendour. The West's huge personnel was accommodated in a soulless new commercial precinct surrounded by showrooms and carparks.

Ewan was glad of the relative stability at home as he embarked on his new work challenge. The West was a big break and he didn't want to squander his opportunity. He was thrilled to be heading for the features desk, covering the big stories in depth, but stood nervously at the foot of a very steep learning curve.

The features editor, Samantha, greeted him on his first day. She was thirty-five tops. Ewan thought her very young to hold such a senior position. Ewan noticed a Scottish lilt to her voice. It jarred with her dark hair and olive complexion. He'd better not confess his fake background.

She took him to the open plan cubicles that were home to the feature writers.

It was a tough morning, Ewan confided in Samantha to make conversation. I was a bag of nerves and my daughter was throwing a tantrum about going to school.

Samantha pointed to where he should put his things. Your daughter should come and work for us, she said. Stamping your feet is the only way you get anyone to listen round here.

Sassenach

Ewan discovered that the West Australian had more personalities than a patient with a dissociative disease.

Despite the dictatorial nature of the capitalist ownership, the editorial management at the West was fiercely independent. At the same time, they were sticklers for the rules, forever summoning the corporate lawyers for advice on defamation. In complete contrast, they could be cavalier at times when presented with a banner headline far too good to miss.

Amongst the hard-drinking, hard-done-by, hard-core journalists, the work ethic was seriously lacking. Yet there was a younger crop of ambitious reporters who were hungry for success.

Ewan was impressed with Samantha. She was intelligent and creative. Still wet behind the ears, she lacked the experience and confidence to stand up to the greybeards in senior positions. Despite these shortcomings managing up, Ewan found her very attentive and supportive managing down. She gave him wise counsel in his own dealings with management. She politely suggested he toe the line until he had proven himself at the journalistic coalface.

Restraint didn't come easily to Ewan. But, he had learned over the years to hasten slowly and to trust in his own ability. He exuded a quiet confidence that in the fullness of time his keyboard would do the talking for him.

While his investigative skills and writing ability were now well honed, he still had much to learn about the newspaper business. Digital technology was burning through the hallowed temples of the print media like wildfire. The sacred cows were turning to overcooked steak. The heat was on the journalists to master the new software and electronic production of their copy. The old-fashioned printing presses would soon be consigned to the flames of hell.

Ewan was happy spending time with Samantha. Her eyes entranced him. They were blacker than black. Such feelings for another woman unsettled him. Never more so than when she unfrocked him as a fake highland priest.

Laddie, you have the accent of a regular Sassenach, Samantha accused him

Ach, stop dribbling on just now, woman, Ewan replied bunging on the brogue.

Fess up, Ewan Mackenzie, Samantha said.

Having been so resoundingly outed, Ewan recounted to Sam the exotic family history of the Mackenzie clan. He left nothing out.

Samantha was fascinated at first. Then she was incredulous. By the time Ewan described the merchandise range, she was struggling to contain herself. Finally the dam wall burst and hilarity flowed over the spillway.

Ewan took it well. He picked at his fingernails to hide his embarrassment. He held back from laughing with her.

I'm sorry. I'm really sorry, Samantha said, trying to suppress her giggles.

It's OK. It is pretty funny.

I'm sorry. I really am.

Anyway, Ewan countered. What about you?

What about me?

If you're a true braveheart, what are you doing here on the other side of the world?

My mother is Spanish.

That explained why Samantha looked like the beautiful actress who played Carmen in the movie, but it was a poor defence against the charge.

Dinna avoid the question, lassie, Ewan persevered

Samantha looked shamefaced. I hate Scotland! She confessed.

Ewan lost it at that point and they rolled around together in laughter.

It's so fucking wet and cold, Samantha added.

They were uncontrollable.

And the men wear skirts! Ewan embellished, slapping his thigh.

Bugging Me

Ewan and Samantha were enjoying an after work drink in Leederville, the closest cool suburb to their office complex. Ewan was finishing his light beer while Samantha sipped away at her sparkling wine. They looked at each other for a moment.

You're a nice guy, Ewan, she said.

You're beyond nice, Ewan gabbled inaudibly so he could maintain plausible deniability.

Ewan could tell Samantha had heard him nevertheless. He regretted being so rash. Sometimes it was better not to speak the truth. There was an awkward silence. Ewan changed the subject to cover his embarrassment.

CCTV, he said.

What about it?

Are you OK with it?

I'm not sure, Samantha said. I don't really have a problem with it.

Not even the civil liberties aspects?

I suppose…Samantha pondered the issue.

What are you two lovebirds up to?

Ewan and Samantha looked up to see Marcus, the senior crime writer and official office creep, standing over them.

Fuck off, Marcus, Ewan said. Go and join your bikie friends over there.

I'd be delighted, he said, walking away with three pints balanced precariously. Wouldn't want to crash the love nest.

What a wanker! Samantha said.

Ewan refocused. What about a world where big brother spies on you all day, every day?

It's hardly like that, Sam protested. Don't you want to catch muggers in the Hay Street mall?

Ewan rearranged his keys and notebook to help him assemble his thoughts. What if I told you all the new cameras were networked?

What does that mean?

It means they're all linked and centrally controlled.

Same again? Sam asked, sliding out from the booth seat.

I've got to get home soon. Just a midi.

Ewan watched Sam make her way to the bar. She was a black beauty. She was the sexiest woman he'd ever met. He forced himself to look elsewhere.

Samantha woke him from his daydreaming. Where are you going with this, Mr. Mackenzie? She asked, depositing the drinks onto the beer-stained coasters graffitied with doodles and phone numbers.

There's something about the roll out of cameras in Perth that's bugging me.

The pun was intentional. Ewan enjoyed making Samantha laugh. They caught each other's eye again.

It does make sense to link the cameras and monitor them centrally…Ewan continued.

…Precisely. So where's the problem?

I barely understand the technology involved. I admit that. But, once all this data is collected and stored centrally, I can't help wondering what happens to it.

They say it's only kept for a short time unless it's needed for evidence.

That's what they say.

You lefties see conspiracies in everything.

Granted. But just because I'm paranoid doesn't mean they're not trying to get me.

Samantha laughed again. Touché, she acknowledged with her glass.

I was chatting to the guys installing the cameras around the city, Ewan resumed. I'd seen them several times around the place. And you know how pride gets the better of people sometimes?

Yes. They tell journalists things they shouldn't.

Exactly. This guy banged on about the sophistication of the cameras and the overall set-up, including the storage, data exchange, and all that stuff.

How do workmen know about that?

Ewan paused to get on with his drink. He was eyeing the time nervously. This guy wasn't one of the workers. He wore a suit - a smart Italian number. I reckon he works for the technology company rather than the City.

Where are you going with this? Sam was in editor mode. Businesslike. Professional.

I've lined up a visit to the City of Perth control centre.

O-kay. Do they know who you are?

Yes. I told them I was doing a human-interest piece. You know, a positive feature on keeping the streets of Perth safe.

It hardly sounds like the CIA if they're inviting you to tea.

I agree.

So, where are you really heading with this?

Nowhere, boss. I just thought I should keep you informed. In case you had any problem with it.

Are you asking my permission?

Yes, boss.

There's a first time for everything!

Got to go, Ewan announced, snatching up his things.

Do you *have* to go? Sam asked, sliding her delicate hand onto his.

Ewan felt the jolt of electricity, recoiling instinctively. I have to, he insisted. I don't want to, he added, looking into those deep, dark eyes. But I have to, he concluded, extracting his hand from danger.

ASIO

Kevin, the Manager of the City Safety team, guided Ewan proudly around the surveillance facility. Kevin screamed ex-cop. He was in his forties but seemed a lot older with his old-fashioned slicked back hair, his trimmed moustache and his cautious pattern of speech that was reminiscent of someone choosing his words carefully in the witness box.

The operations room fascinated Ewan. There was action aplenty on the streets. This Saturday Night Fever featured drunks, hookers, graffiti artists and muggers.

The ops team kept a wary eye out for what they called 'crimes against the person'. With so much activity out there, it was important to remain focused. They ignored the street drinkers and the tarts to concentrate on higher priority issues, particularly violent crime.

I don't get how these cameras prevent crime, Ewan said in an affable tone. Isn't it too late by the time you pick something up?

Sometimes it isn't, Kevin said. We can be lucky with the police on patrol just round the corner. And it won't surprise you to know, he added, slurping down his instant coffee from a badly chipped mug, that some crims aren't that smart.

What do they do?

They snatch someone's purse and then they loiter around in the malls for a smoke.

But, if you're not lucky and the muggers aren't stupid, I still don't see what the cameras do to help.

To be honest, Kevin said, the main purpose is not to apprehend the criminals. The cameras provide us with evidence once some of these mongrels are arrested. They also have a deterrent effect.

Because people know they're being watched?

Precisely. With this modern technology, you can't get away with anything.

Ewan accepted a council issue Arnott's cream biscuit. Kevin's remark had opened a door for him. He needed to walk through it, but step with caution.

I guess it's the same with the new stop and search powers, Ewan mused aloud. That also makes the hoodlums think.

Certainly does. The more forms of detection we have to disrupt the bad guys, the better we can all sleep at night.

What about terrorists? Ewan asked, making his play. I guess these cameras help to track suspicious characters too.

Kevin said nothing. Ewan could see him weighing up the wisdom of imparting a confidence.

This is strictly off the record, Ewan reassured him. My piece is just about the safety angle on the streets. I was curious that's all.

Kevin responded cautiously, back in the witness box. You didn't hear this from me, but we know what some of the real bad guys are up to.

Ewan controlled his facial expression. Great, he said. There's no point in investing in this amazing technology if we don't use its full power.

Let me show you something, Kevin whispered. He took Ewan to a second control room. This area was clearly restricted access. Ewan eyed off the bank of controls reminiscent of the cockpit of a jumbo jet.

Kevin sat on a swivel chair in front of a screen. He entered a password and pressed a series of keys. The screen came to life revealing a swathe of red lights pulsing on a map of central Perth.

That's impressive, Ewan responded.

Do you know what you're looking at?

I haven't the foggiest.

Those are the whereabouts of persons of interest.

Persons of interest?

People under suspicion, I guess you'd call them.

That's brilliant, Ewan said. He wasn't a good liar. He kept his comments in check. It's good to know that we have everything so well under control.

Too right, Kevin said, shutting down the console.

They walked back to the central ops room. Kevin motioned for Ewan to wait before they joined the surveillance team.

You're not printing any of this, are you?

Of course not! Ewan's outraged tone convinced even himself. This is strictly off the record.

Fantastic, Kevin responded, visibly relieved.

By the way, Kevin, Ewan said, holding him back by placing his hand on the door handle to the ops room. I meant to ask you something.

What's that?

I'm guessing that you're an ex-detective. Ewan calculated that would sound better than 'cop'.

Close, Kevin said.

What then?

Kevin paused for effect. ASIO - the Australian Security and Intelligence Organisation.

Right to know

The suit was late.

Ewan had been agonising over the article for days. Sally had tried her best to be supportive, but he could tell she had qualms about the ethics. Ewan rationalised his intentions based on the public's right to know. Sally didn't buy it. Sally didn't properly understand the environment he worked in. Ewan appealed to Samantha for help.

What should I do? Ewan asked, having laid out his moral dilemma.

I'm your editor, Samantha responded.

Meaning?

Meaning, I'm hardly going to tell you to pass on a great story.

I feel for those guys, Ewan moaned.

I know you do. You're a nice guy, Ewan. But we don't pay you for that.

Andrew Chadwick from ESD Technologies, alias the suit, arrived hot and flustered. He offered to buy the drinks. Ewan thought it odd in the circumstances but deferred to his generosity.

Chadwick placed two Belgian beers down on the table. He checked his phone for messages. He was a guy who wanted to be wanted. There were no messages. He looked up at Ewan.

I'm not attacking you, Ewan said in a reassuring tone. I won't even mention your name.

As Perth city is my project, it won't be hard to put two and two together.

I can't pretend not to know what I know.

Andrew was struggling to contain his emotions.

Ewan sat there, troubled and conflicted. Andrew was right. The proverbial ton of bricks would fall on him. A similar prospect awaited Kevin from the city surveillance team. Ewan didn't need to name names. How else could he have found out what was going on?

This story would have come out sometime, Ewan said in a final attempt to placate Andrew. At least with me, you know I will cover the issues. It won't be an attack piece.

Andrew looked at Ewan. Do you know why I bought the drinks?

Because you're a generous guy?

Very funny, Andrew shot back. No one will be able to accuse me of taking anything.

I'm not out to screw you, Ewan said. I promise.

Andrew thought better of saying whatever had entered his head.

I asked you to come so that there would be no surprises. You deserve that.

Andrew smiled. That's very magnanimous of you.

I didn't mean it like that, Ewan said apologetically. Forewarned is forearmed.

Andrew checked his phone. Still no messages.

The story explores a range of different perspectives. I assure you it will be balanced.

Andrew shot him a cynical look.

It *is* balanced, Ewan insisted. As I said, there are pros and cons. You can argue it both ways. You can take the view that protection of the public is paramount. So snooping by the state is justified. Or, you can see things from the civil liberties standpoint. My article puts both sides.

I'm just a technician, Andrew protested. I don't decide where the cameras go or what they record or who gets to see the tapes.

I know.

If you're out to catch a crook, it's best not to ring him up and warn him the law is on its way.

I don't get you.

It's pretty simple. If you publish this article, you'll tip off the stando-ver merchants and the jihadis that they're being tracked.

They have a right to know.

Andrew snorted into his beer. Get real!

We all have a right to know, Ewan insisted.

Andrew's phone rang. He seemed relieved. He nodded to Ewan on his way out. Ewan could relax a little bit. Andrew was gone. The nagging feeling wasn't.

Ewan felt terrible as he trudged towards his car. On impulse, he punched in Samantha's number. She seemed reluctant, but agreed to meet him at the Leederville Hotel in an hour.

Ewan felt pathetic spilling his guts on his guilt yet again.

Samantha took Ewan's hand. He felt the spark. Tell me why you came to talk to me rather than unburden yourself to your wife.

Because I wanted validation.

Is that the only reason?

Ewan took his time to answer. I also wanted to see you.

My flat's just round the corner, Samantha said, gathering up her belongings. If you're coming with me, I'd like to go now.

Amazingly enough, Cassidy is lying in a hospital bed two floors up, a few hundred metres east and yet a million miles away. We chat briefly over the in-house video network. She can hardly raise her head from the pillow. I can see her fears about the baby etching deep lines into her beautiful face. The doctors say she has an infection. Cassidy does not sound reassured.

Cass can sense my indifference. Under the pressure of my invalidity, my callous ways are returning. How can I care so little about the fate of my own child?

Lorna arrives to organise for me to get outside for some fresh air. Who are they kidding – this is LA! As it happens, there is a decent breeze blowing away the smog today. The sun feels fierce on my pale skin. I put on a brave face for Lorna's sake. I must try to pull myself together.

We sit in silence for a while. Then Lorna breaks it. Am I born yet? Lorna asks

Funny question. I smile to show I'm not grouchy.

Don't be smart, old man. In your book.

Yes.

Can I read it now? You promised.

I did not.

Did so. Tongue-poking out again in that special way of hers.

Lorna kicks free the brakes of my chair. Time to get back to it, she announces, seeing that you won't let me read it.

Slavedriver!

Who's in it today? Lorna asks as we reach my room and she presses the buzzer for assistance to lift me into bed.

I'm writing about Nina today.

Don't get yourself all sad, Lorna says with such kindness and sincerity that it makes me feel ashamed.

How some friends turn into lovers

Un peu

That was it. There was no doubt about it. Her question had been, 'Do you speak French?' There is something axiomatic about asking someone in a particular language whether they speak that language because, ipso facto, if they didn't, they couldn't respond. But, never mind, that's what she asked me, *en Français*, what's more.

I didn't reply. I had forgotten how. Nina's ravishing beauty had compelled me to prioritise sight over the other senses. Yet, at some level, I was conscious that a question had been directed at me. My lips formed a reply, but no sound was forthcoming.

The human brain is a wonderful thing. Even mine. Did you know that we only use one per cent of its capacity? Imagine if we used a tad more. We could cure cancer, reverse climate change and work out why anyone watches Rugby League or listens to Christmas carols sung by geriatric crooners.

Irrespective of all that, the human brain remains a thing of wonder. Accordingly, from some dusty basement records department within my hippocampus, a retired army officer, dressed in a brown attendant's jacket, managed to retrieve the question Nina asked me at that fateful dinner on my first night in Paris, blow off the cobwebs and send a message up to me about it.

I did speak a little French. So, when I stationed myself at the lecture theatre exit at the Sorbonne ParisV to bump into the gorgeous Nina on purpose but by accident, I was happy to be able to answer her question, albeit a little belatedly.

Oui un peu! I said triumphantly.

You know how in life someone says something to you that you never forget? Sometimes it's a throwaway line like, 'What could be more agreeable?' That phrase captures to perfection a resonant interlude in your life when you were gazing down at a gorgeous rose garden with a spectacular wine on the palate in the company of a great friend. For some reason that expression strikes a chord with you and you adopt it and use it whenever the occasion befits. Then later in life, when you see that person again, you say, "I still love that phrase of yours, 'What could be more agreeable?'" And they look at you blankly. I call that the theory of emotional relativity. Events have relative worth in people's lives. An event, a word, a glance that becomes a priceless antiquity for me is for you but a mere bagatelle.

Nina looked right through me when I spoke those three little words in French that already meant so much to me. In place of the radiant smile of recognition that had illuminated my fantasies, her response was go wither rather than come hither. Thankfully, I had approached her with the light behind me. Once I had drawn alongside her *sans silhouette*, to my great relief, she recognised me.

Oh, pardon, c'est vous, I mean, it's you!

It's me, I confirmed, cursing my ongoing inability to say anything to Nina that didn't identify me as a babbling fool.

I thought I should explain why I'd uttered those three little words, but she spoke first, striding purposefully away from me.

Walk with me, she said. I have to take another class.

We chatted for the few glorious, fleeting moments it took to cross from one historic quadrangle into another. I used every ounce of my vital energy to force myself to concentrate on what she was saying. I stifled the urge to stem the flow of words by covering her lips with my own. The temptation to connect my Mills with her Boon was almost irresistible.

I held it together sufficiently to tell her that I was settling in well, had found a great little apartment in the VIth, just around the corner, and that SG seemed happy with me. We arrived at a steep stone staircase. Nina skipped two steps at a time. Then she scuttled back down, stumbling as she rummaged inside her bulging leather shoulder bag.

She produced a business card and then, with an enchanting smile that will remain forever filed in my brain alongside 'Oui un peu', she said, call or email me sometime.

Two o'clock on Sunday

I was perched on a barstool at Heathrow Airport waiting for my flight back to Paris after visiting my parents. A fierce electrical storm was battering the south of England. A forked lightning *son et lumière* show lit the runways. I was ignoring the British Airways announcements about my flight as they had already lied three times about our imminent departure.

I absent-mindedly stirred my tea, re-screening my own movie, "When should you call a girl, who said 'Call me'?" I didn't want to seem desperate. On the other hand, I didn't want to appear aloof. I could chicken out. She probably gave me her card out of pity.

I was on the twentieth re-run when my brick of a mobile phone vibrated into life. It waltzed across the bar. As it plummeted towards the concrete floor, I took a neat slips' catch. I resisted the temptation to toss it into the air in triumph. I was sure it was my mother calling. It was Nina!

She'd put me out of my misery. It was on the tip of my tongue to ask her, thanks to that terrible death wish streak of mine, how long she thought a guy should wait before calling her so as not to appear desperate or aloof. Fortunately, she foreclosed on my opportunity to further humiliate myself.

I've invited some friends over on Sunday, she said. Why don't you come along?

I was considering when and how to answer so as not to appear desperate or aloof.

She interrupted my rumination. I have to go, she said. It's two o'clock on Sunday at the address on my card.

By the time I'd worked out my response, the line had gone dead.

Insouciance

I debated with myself what time I should arrive on the Sunday so as not to appear desperate or aloof. I settled upon fashionably late.

I struggled to find the door to Nina's apartment. Her flat was upstairs from an old-fashioned butcher's shop located on the corner of a picture postcard winding laneway. The macabre trappings of animal slaughter adorned the store. There was a marble slab as cold as death itself, an ancient chopping stand hollowed from countless acts of dismemberment and meat hooks sharp as any instruments of torture. The shop was closed on a Sunday as was clear from the sign that read 'Fermé'. It was emblazoned, ironically enough, with the face of a smiling pig. That vignette was living proof that ignorance is bliss.

I found a red-painted door some distance up the lane. There was no name on it nor any bell or knocker to attract attention. I assumed it was the right place. A hubbub of cool jazz and warm conversation drifted from an upstairs window like the aroma of freshly baked pie that attracts a tomcat thief in the old cartoons.

I was poised to ring Nina's mobile when a young couple rocked up on a Vespa. They knew the lay of the land. They retrieved a key that dangled from elastic inside the front door and let us all in. There was no hallway. We mounted the steep flight of stairs to emerge like blinking badgers in a light-filled loft apartment.

I'd been expecting an intimate gathering. It was no such thing. There would have been fifty people there. They chatted, drank and smoked in groups. There was a tight huddle on the Persian rug. They spoke intimately, like old friends. Others lounged decadently on the bright red leather sofas. They laughed lustily, draped across each other like lovers.

It's disarming when everyone around you speaks another tongue. I didn't feel excluded. I just felt like one of Camus' outsiders. I was a distant acquaintance at a family wedding. For them, the endless flow of words, syllables and sentences was finely nuanced. I could grasp many of the words, but not necessarily the meaning.

Nina neither welcomed nor snubbed me. She greeted me with a kiss on both cheeks then slipped away. Cast in the role of observer, I strove to assemble the cues to the real Nina that were coming at me thick and fast. Her apartment was a tableau of studied indifference. Every piece of furniture, ornament and artwork spoke of casual placement. The total assembly screamed of organisation.

The appointments in Nina's apartment were melodies in counterpoint. The extravagant paint colours on the doors should have clashed with the old-fashioned flock wallpaper. The minimalist modern furniture should have grated with the crusty antique vases. The post-modern canvasses screaming *merde* and *con* had no business sharing walls with works in the style of Monet and Cezanne. And yet the lion and the lamb of interior design lay down together in peace.

When Nina returned into view, I studied her with the same attention to detail. Her presence in this gathering was no less a representation of nonchalance. Or was it insouciance? She floated from person to person, from group to group, cuddling the adoring men and the envious women alike. She flirted her way around the room like an amorous butterfly. Yet I could trace her eyes, wandering from those she was with to those that might constitute a better offer.

Jacques sidled up to me with a bottle of *vin rouge* in hand.

You seem deep in thought, he said.

I am.

Care to share it with me?

Actually I was wondering whether the right word was nonchalance or insouciance, I said. Do those words have the same meaning in French?

They do or at least they can. It really depends on what you are trying to say.

I was trying to make Nina out.

Op, you're trying to understand Nina, he said, amused at the prospect. He shook his head and wagged his finger as if to say, 'Don't even try!'

I think she's an insouciant trying to be nonchalant, I persisted.

Good luck with that, my friend, Jacques said.

He refilled my glass and set off to resume his waiter duties. He thought better of leaving me and returned to place his free hand on my shoulder.

You're trying to comprehend a beautiful, intelligent, crazy French-woman, he said with a wistful shake of his head. May I offer some advice?

I nodded,

You know the phrase about mad dogs and Englishmen, of course? Jacques said accompanied by his broad, handsome smile. Nina is the midday sun, Jacques observed, withdrawing with bottle in hand.

Not tonight

My Nina reconnaissance mission was interrupted by a group of colleagues I'd seen somewhere at SG. They insisted that I not hang out alone. They painstakingly introduced themselves to me. Then they told me I couldn't possibly remember all their names. I've never understood the point of this introduction ritual. In those days, I forgot people's names as a matter of principle.

A manicured hand was sent by God to save me. It appeared from the heavens, raising me up and parting the Red Sea of my name-forsaken colleagues. Nina guided me up a winding metal staircase. We found ourselves in a tiny roof garden. There were plant pots everywhere, save for standing room for two next to a rusty railing. Nina steered me in and around the flowerpots and parked us in the confined viewing area.

Wow! I exclaimed at the sight of the Eiffel Tower so close up.

C'est beau, hein? Nina said.

Oui un peu!

She was set to chide me for downplaying such a wonderful view. Then she caught on to my little joke and smiled.

I looked at her. I would never undersell *that* view. Barbara Cartland assumed control of my brain anew. My bosom heaved. My bodice begged to be ripped. I yearned to be upswept in her manly arms.

Then Nina spoke without averting her gaze from the vista below. Her delivery was matter of fact, like a reminder to pay the gas bill. I suppose you want to fuck me, she said.

My double-take was audible. In the manner of a drowning man, the entire gamut of possible responses flashed before my eyes. My head was full of everything and nothing. Was it a rhetorical question? Was there a right answer? Had I stopped beating my wife? How long should I wait before answering so as not to appear desperate or aloof?

Is it such a hard question? Nina teased, still scanning the sprawling city below.

She was obviously resigned to my not answering her questions. Come, she said, dragging me back through the plant pots.

She stopped at the top of the staircase and looked at me. I had to say something. I was a mere wasp's penis from an apt response when she kissed me gently on the lips. She pulled away and led me clanking down the stairs.

At the bottom, she pulled me close and whispered in my ear. Don't worry about it. We will fuck.

As she disappeared into the crowd, I gestured for her to stay.

But not tonight, she called, turning her head towards me, but still slipping away.

Walls have ears

Apparently walls have ears. In the case of my apartment in Paris, I could have sworn they had legs. Somehow the spacious, light and airy penthouse apartment I'd fallen in love with at the inspection had remodelled itself into a pokey closet by the time I moved in.

Maybe the fat and greasy real estate agent, Ghislain, had distracted me like some overfed magician with his calculated warning that the lift often shuddered to a stop mid-floor. I shrugged this negative off, intoxicated as I was with the romance of this historic apartment building in gay *Par-ee* on that beautiful, crisp and sunny winter's day.

The apartment was indeed small, or as Ghislain's profession put it, compact. It was pleasant enough though. It fitted my self-image to be within spitting distance of the Seine. The décor was serious and dark, with a heavy dining table, leather armchairs, wrought iron and fading rugs. The furnishing was aspirational. The tables, chairs and sofas, merely old-fashioned at that point in time, harboured pretensions one day to be considered antique.

The apartment had been furnished by an interior decorator with a permanent stoop. Sadly unable to raise her head, she had given no thought to adorning the walls. They were baby's bottom bare. There were no pictures, tapestries or even mirrors. It presented a learning opportunity. I discovered how blind men comb their hair.

I have exaggerated slightly. A solitary work of art did grace the walls. As the apartment was a short walk across the river from the Louvre, it was fitting that the Mona Lisa gazed benevolently down from the living room wall. It was a pathetic copy of the great lady, acquired from one of the cheap and trashy tourists stalls down on the Left Bank. She certainly didn't look herself.

Absinthe-induced paranoia got to me one night soon after I moved in. The elderly elevator had turned in for the night. 'Call yourself a lift?' I mocked. Even ridicule failed to get a rise out of it. Resentfully, I trudged up the six flights of stairs. I fiddled with my key in the lock in the manner approved for drunks. I flopped gratefully onto the no longer well-sprung armchair. I found myself looking up at that dreadful caricature of the most famous face in the world.

Why are you there? I mumbled out loud.

Had I, in asking that question, succumbed to the existentialist spirit of Jean-Paul Sartre's hometown or was my question more realist than that? Why place that one object on the wall right there with nothing else on the walls anywhere else?

Eureka! I shouted, confused in my cups as to my whereabouts in Europe.

I realised with limpid clarity that the incongruous so-called painting had been placed precisely there to cover up two eye-level spy holes drilled into the wall. The more I looked at the iconic face with the crooked smile, the more certain I became that those dark eyes, in this case real human eyes, were watching me. I rose clumsily from the depths of my sunken seat like a hippopotamus emerging from thick river mud. I staggered across the room. I removed the offending travesty of art from the wall.

There, hey presto, in all its glory, was a nasty patch of crumbling plaster the owner had been too lazy to fill.

Instruments of torture

I loved my charming apartment, but soon found myself no longer in love with it.

Despite the glamour of the bohemian life in Paris and the mouth-watering trading opportunities SG had laid out before me like a banquet in a brothel, I found myself broody and irritable. Although devoid of an artistic bone in my body, I took on the pain and angst of a penniless painter holed up in an airless garret.

The human psyche can be an instrument of torture. If I'd never set eyes on Nina, I would have been perfectly happy in my new life in Paris. But I had been unfortunate enough to encounter her. And not just in a momentary fleeting fashion across a crowded room or opposite me on the metro, causing my heart to skip a beat and my mouth to form the words of the chorus of 'You're Beautiful'.

Her presence would form and fade like the myriad images in a kalei-doscope. She would invade my consciousness like a ghost at the bedside. She was as elusive as the eleventh commandment. I tried the standard remedies for the lovelorn. Excessive drinking and masturbation came naturally. Others, like throwing myself into work and going to the gym, took more effort.

Amidst all the wishing and hoping, and mooning and moping, my mother's words of warning rang loudly in my ears. She was right, as mothers customarily are. Even if this un-requited love were somehow 'quited' and the impossible dream somehow became possible, this *would* end in tears. And, like the ever-present anti-hero in a Woody Allen film, I would walk away a bitter and lonely man.

Like endless night

Nina hit my apartment like a tornado. It was some unearthly hour on a Sunday morning that my life was blown apart.

I forced myself out of bed to answer the door. I struggled into a t-shirt and shorts. I dragged myself along the hallway like the pink panther on Valium. I trudged slower than Serena Williams between points when she's losing.

My neighbour, the ancient Madame Dupigny, had miscast me in the role of nice boy next door. She was forever calling upon me at insomniac hours to un-stick her window or reach up to the top shelf to retrieve her husband's ashes.

Fuck! I said on seeing who was there.

That's the idea, Nina responded, brushing past me.

What happened next remains a blur. Nina assumed control of me. That's the only way I can describe it. Rather than mistress-servant with all the shades of grey that might conjure up, it was more like doctor-patient. I complied with her silent instructions because I implicitly accepted they were for my own good.

Wordlessly, she undressed in my living room as I looked on in awe. For all she knew, I could already have had company in my bedroom. Oblivious to all that, she pulled off her black leather boots and dropped them to the floor. She shimmied out of her blue denim jeans and abandoned them like some shapeless life form. They had a button-through fly like men's Levi's 501. My gaze locked onto her taut brown tummy and her tight, perfect arse. I noted her sensible floral knickers. They were more Marks & Spencer than Victoria's Secret.

Nina removed her top, discarding it followed by her matching floral bra. She had a firm boyish body. Her tits were small and unassuming. But her brown bullet nipples boasted attitude.

She held out her hand and led me to the bedroom. Fleetingly, I wondered how she knew where to go. The thought did not linger as you can well imagine. Methodically she removed my clothes. She did it like a mother, not a lover. I half expected her to send me to wash my hands.

She spoke at last. Lie down, she commanded.

She knelt between my legs. Slender manicured hands took hold of me. My poor penis was in shock. Excited and anxious in equal measure, it dribbled in dick dissonance. Despite her manual dexterity, it remained half-cocked. Like the share market when the news is mixed, it was undecided which way to go. Reduced to the role of interested bystander, I distracted myself by marvelling at the softness of her long brown hair.

They say men think with their appendages. Regrettably I was all brain. I willed myself to dispel the mental image of humiliating non-performance. Then I was literally roused to action by the magical warmth of soft lips. As she tongued the sensitive tip and drew me by turns inside, alarms screeched in my brain and my anxiety drive thrust into reverse. Vivid images of embarrassing prematurity haunted my thoughts.

At times like these a guy needs a friend. Nina was mine. We were as one in our desire to avert disaster. All too conscious of the imminent danger, she pulled away and slid herself up my body. Before I could tune into what was happening, she lowered herself adroitly onto me.

These are passing moments that you never forget. My rapturous incarceration in the vault of her cunt will forever hold pride of place in my highlight reel. I recall the scent of frangipani on her neck. How could I forget her delicate sigh as my longing flowed into her like endless night?

There was joy

Nina disappeared as fast as I came. She dismounted with the elegance of an Olympic equestrian and cantered off to the bathroom. How did she know where to go? I was horrified she'd find my dirty washing in the bidet. She appeared briefly in the tiny hallway and then set about retrieving her clothes from the living room.

What are you doing? I said plaintively

I have to go

Why?

Because I have to.

What if I cooked you breakfast?

Can you cook?

No.

I heard a distant snigger. OK, what if I *buy* you breakfast?

No.

Don't be so negative.

I'm not negative, she said, gliding now fully dressed into the bed-room, I'm busy.

OK then, I conceded in a defeated tone.

Don't pout, she mocked pinching my chin to open my mouth for a kiss.

Arrivederci, she called on her way out.

A bientôt, I corrected her, but she was gone.

I lay on my sweaty bed, a transformed man. I wished I still smoked. There was much to process. I felt great. At some level, Nina must like me. I felt anxious. I worried that my rating on the FTSE (the Financial Times Sexual Evaluation) index would be underperform.

I resolved to look on the bright side. I would be unfuckwithable. Nothing would faze me. The hills would be alive with the sound of music. My body would be a wonderland. I would sing to myself what a wonderful world.

I felt different and it felt different. I wouldn't dither. I would call her the next day and we would date each other. I was clear-headed. I knew this whole affair would end in tears and that I'd get hurt. The pain would be all the worse now that I had tasted what I'd be losing. But there would also be joy. I felt powerful at that moment and more than ready to endure the pain to attain the pleasure.

And there *was* joy. I fell head over heels in love with her. Like a girl. And she loved me back, for a while, like a boy. I fucked her with passion. She fucked me back with more. I took her to cool places. She showed me cooler ones. I introduced her to rich and famous people. She'd known them for years.

All or nothing girl

Nina was an all or nothing girl. She'd grapple me tightly to her. Then she'd cut me adrift. One day she'd demand to know everything about me. The next day she'd call me a narcissist. At times, she would demand my absolute attention. I was expected to drop everything for her. Later she'd accuse me of cramping her style. Sometimes she would demand despicably dirty sex. The next morning she'd call me a pervert.

I was under the sway of a control freak. I'd been brainwashed by a cult. But I didn't care. The highs were so high that they obliterated all memory of the lows. The interminable rejections were worth it for a second of intimacy. The carnality of the physical fucking vitiated the insidious way she fucked with my mind.

There were periods of calm between the storms. We talked and talked. I admired her intellect. I drank deeply from the cup of her teaching at the Sorbonne.

I recall the night of our first anniversary.

Tomorrow night we have to celebrate, I insisted, as I dropped her off at her apartment.

Celebrate what?

Our one month anniversary.

Pif! she snorted. Anniversary of what?

Our first fuck.

Tu n'est pas fou?

No, I'm not mad. Maybe madly in love, I said with a pathetic smile.

It worked. She leant over to kiss me.

I've booked a table at the 7th Ciel, I lied.

On the terrace with the view?

Bien sûr!

OK, you win, she conceded. I will see you there at nine, but I'm only staying if we're truly on the terrace.

I raced to contact Jacques. If anyone could pull this off, it would be him.

He got back to me minutes later. All done, my friend.

Really? You're a lifesaver.

It's nothing.

Nothing! I said, punching the air. It sure is something to me.

I will cry

She was typically late. I was fretting about losing the table. Then the sublime Nina appeared. She was wearing that delicious strappy dress from the first night I saw her. She told me mid-kiss that she was impressed that I'd secured a table on the terrace. I told her not to doubt me so.

A waiter appeared as if from nowhere. He poured us both a perfectly beaded champagne. I admired the professionalism of a man who could do that while looking down Nina's dress. As we sipped away, I felt the eyes of the diners turn to us and the entire terrace submit to Nina's gravitational sway.

Tell me about yourself, I implored her.

I have. Too much already, she said.

You've thrown me little tit-bits, that's all.

She sipped approvingly from her flute, assessing her options. OK, then, you want chapter and verse?

I do. I really do.

There's not much to tell. I am an only child. My father was a diplomat. My mother is a dressmaker, and, as a matter of fact, she is a Jewess.

She paused. That makes me Jewish you know.

I know. Some of my best friends are Jewish, I said.

She looked perplexed.

Don't worry, it's an expression in English, it's not important, I said.

OK, she continued, concentrating on what to say next. I felt she was being guarded and was censoring herself. I didn't then understand why.

I loved my father with a passion. I suppose most little girls do. He was forever travelling because of his work as a diplomat. Alas, he was never posted abroad. I dreamed of living in the exotic Far East, at least for a while.

I nodded that I understood.

So Papa was away a lot. My mother had a strict upbringing and was highly principled. My father sometimes went away two or three times a week. Even then, my mother would insist on collecting him from the airport. To her it was the right thing to do. So, from the age of three or four, I would accompany my mother on these exciting outings. I looked forward to them a lot.

Because your father was coming home?

Partly, yes. But mostly, because my mother would buy me a special hot chocolate at the airport. Does that make me a bad person?

Not of itself.

Anyway, she continued, I'm getting round to something I haven't told you. I warn you. I will cry.

Playing with my doll

I told you that my father died when I was young, Nina said, eyes downcast. But I didn't tell you the circumstances.

We went to meet his plane. He had been to Tunisia – it's funny the irrelevant details you remember. Everything was normal. I had my hot chocolate. The arrivals board showed that his aircraft had landed. My mother and I went to the barrier as we always did. The passengers spilled out. We waited and waited but he never came.

Maman led me by the hand to the Air France desk. We stood there for what seemed to a little girl like an eternity. The pretty ladies in their smart blue uniforms made phone calls and buzzed around my mother attentively. I sat on a stool next to the desk, singing my favourite nursery rhymes. I played imaginary games with Eva, my doll that I carried everywhere.

Then my mother knelt down next to me and told me very sternly that I should stay right there with the nice ladies while she went away for a little while. A man in a uniform came to meet her. She went off with him, ignoring my question about how long she would be.

Nina pulled her hand from my grip and left the table. I made to follow her, but she motioned for me to stay put. With her face buried in her hands, she ran into the restaurant. The Maître D pointed to the back of the restaurant. I watched Nina slalom through the rows of tables, each adorned with a centrepiece depicting a different planet.

In time, she returned with a strained smile on her face. The oysters had arrived and she began to slide the first down her throat.

I'm sorry for upsetting you, I stammered.

She waved my apology away. It's OK. I want to tell you. Alors, she said summoning up the courage, my father had a heart attack on his way through customs.

My God!

Yes, I know it's terrible. She looked up, wiping away a tear and breaking into a giggle at the same time. I suppose it would be funny if it weren't true.

Poor you. Your poor mother.

Yes, it is my mother I feel sorry for. She has never recovered. The horror of it haunts her to this day. The love of her life died a few metres away and she did nothing.

But she didn't know. What could she have done?

I know. There was nothing she could have done. She still blames herself. And, thanks to the burden of her guilt and her crazy sense of principle, she has virtually given up on life.

That's very sad, I said, fiddling with an empty oyster shell.

Yes, it's sad and a shocking waste. But she doesn't see it that way. She married her husband for better or worse. So she has never re-married.

Really?

Nina gave me a reproving look. No, she hasn't remarried. As far as I know, she hasn't even seen another man.

I motioned to the waiter that he could clear the plates. How did *you* cope with that?

I was very sad too. I had lost the papa I adored. Over time I lost my mama too. She is a pale shadow of the woman she once was. But the worst of it was, she said, summoning the waiter to get more water, I felt so damned guilty myself. I still do.

Because you didn't help your mother enough?

No, not that. I sat there in the police car when my father had just died, singing and playing with my doll.

You win

For obvious reasons, we lightened the tone from there. We chatted about frivolous things. I joked that I would be taking out a mortgage when the bill arrived. It turned out close to the truth.

We decided on a midnight stroll. We grabbed a cab for a five-minute ride. Then we wandered along the riverbank. I noted the awesome view of Paris from the overpass near where Princess Diana died. Nina was still sad. Vulnerable and fragile, she was even more seductive. She walked with one hand around my waist and the other slung over my shoulder dangling her high heels to the sway of our gait.

She led me to a smoky bar. We found a table in a quiet corner. We sipped on a café noir with a pastis and looked at each other for a while.

Tell me about the Sorbonne.

Ah, more questions, Monsieur l'Anglais.

Yes, more questions, mademoiselle, but hopefully not such personal ones.

The Sorbonne? Let me see. The university itself is very historic. It dates back to the thirteenth century. It's like Oxford, she conceded to me with a nod of recognition, but so much more beautiful!

I let that go.

As you know, she continued, history in such places seeps from the walls.

Yes. Rather like the cold.

That's true. The classic universities are magical, but you find that everything is old. Our equipment is ancient too. I have friends who teach at the Grandes Ecoles that will become the new ParisTech. Everything there is new. Their projectors and sound systems actually work!

But you wouldn't swap with them, right?

No. Not in a million years. Still, the Sorbonne is not my first love.

Is it me? I asked hopefully.

Sorry to disappoint you, she said, screwing up her nose. My first love is my subject.

The next two hours flashed by like the Lyon express. Time was marked by the delivery of a coffee or an anisette. To a man like me who worked to make money, Nina's passion for her vocation was extraordinary. The new digital age excited her. She believed the World Wide Web would democratise information. I recoiled at some of it. Her zeal reminded me too much of my old friend, Ewan. But, for the most part, I was engrossed in her dissertation on the socio-political significance of the media.

To my well-educated but simple brain, media outlets served one of two purposes. They dispersed government propaganda or they sold advertising.

Nina's take on this subject was less jaundiced. She focused on the communications process as opposed to the ownership and means of production. In her utopian view, the impending communications revolution had the power to free the world from tyranny and injustice.

Isn't that rather naïve? I said, taking a typically dystopian position. The powers that be will always find a way to control us in their own interests.

It will be different in the new world of digital communications. The individual citizen will have the freedom and the opportunity to communicate his viewpoint directly to the world without censorship.

I could see the exciting potential in what she was saying. But I doubted that governments would cede their control over communications and information so readily.

That's the critical factor in this whole argument, Nina explained. Thanks to the accessibility of information in the digital age, governments and corporations won't be in a position to manipulate the public so effectively by keeping secrets and covering up the truth.

I pondered that prospect for a while. The waiter cleared our table and replenished our caffeine drips.

Surely governments have to keep some things secret, I mused. I was thinking aloud rather than continuing the debate. This innocent comment struck a raw nerve.

Absolument pas, Nina said, throwing up her hands in exasperation. Absolutely not! So-called secrets are not theirs to keep. The information is ours. It belongs to the people, not our representatives.

I didn't want to antagonise Nina at this delicate point in our relationship, but diplomacy had never been my strong point.

Hang on a minute, I said. Are you suggesting that the allies in the war should have broadcast their troop movement to the Germans?

That's a stupid argument, Nina said dismissively.

It's not so stupid. It's the logical consequence of your position that governments should not keep secrets.

Sheepishly, Nina produced a crumpled pack of cigarettes from her bag. I accused her with my eyes. She claimed only to smoke OPs, other people's. She stared me down, gathering her thoughts, unlit cigarette poised between her lips.

In three seconds flat, a lecherous man from the next table chivalrously offered her a light. Nina inhaled deeply.

As you well know, she said, wafting her smoke deliberately in my direction, your war example is sophistry. In extreme circumstances, normal rules of engagement sometimes need to change.

I nodded. I couldn't disagree.

What happens in everyday life is the thing that matters, Nina said more calmly now. The fact is governments do keep secrets from their own people and the big corporations cover up their exploitation of child labour, their pollution of waterways and so the list goes on.

She was enchanting in full flow like this.

I am excited about living in a world where these activities can be more easily exposed and where ordinary citizens will have the means to publish the truth.

You win, I said, waving a mock white flag to surrender.

At last! Nina said, making a victory salute.

I stood up. It's time, I said, to fuck.

You win too then, she said, stubbing out her cigarette.

****

The cup of life

Paris was cold. The wind cut through my bones. Nina warmed me some of the time and chilled me the rest. I did some decent deals for SG. These were welcome distractions from my ongoing Nina torture.

That winter of my partial discontent turned glorious spring as if overnight. Once the great city arose from its hibernal coma, la Coupe du Monde infected its debilitated host body like a virus.

I was no Ricky Martin fan. I hated George Michael even more. I've never trusted people with two Christian names. They're not as bad as people with three names. It turns them into assassins. Like Lee Harvey Oswald and Mark David Chapman.

'Here we go, Olé! Olé! Olé!' This noise pollution battered the eardrums of Parisians and visitors alike. Was the World Cup football or bullfighting?

It was impossible to avoid that fucking Cup of Life. It was there when you woke up. It drove with you to work. It was piped into the toilets while you pissed. It did your head in at night when you craved some peace. And yet it was so apt. It was so timely for me. I was with Nina. I was drinking from the cup of life.

I pleased Nina well enough and that pleased me. But I lived in a confounding world of qualification. Our relationship, if you could call it that, was provisional. Her feelings for me were conditional. My happiness was transitory. My cup of life teetered precariously on the saucer of Nina. The aroma was sweet jasmine, the stimulation Earl Grey, the taste deep bergamot and the sex was rough as guts, lapsang souchong. I struggled to keep the cup level. I was a hapless diner balancing on a swaying train of emotion. One day my cup would run over. It would surely spill into my lap and burn my balls.

Nina loved the spectacle but detested the game. The primitive tribalism of the fans excited her. The game itself disappointed her. While we agreed to disagree about the merits of the world game, the vibe that enveloped the city was indisputable. Paris lay prostrate on the ground, open-mouthed, gulping from the fountain of life. As spring passed the baton to summer, the world raced to Paris, eating, drinking and partying the day and night away.

SG was first and foremost amongst the commercial institutions determined to cash in. It sprinkled sponsorships like confetti. It snaffled the prime corporate boxes and the coveted front row seats for the prestigious matches. If the Jules Rimet trophy had been a competition for largesse, SG would have won 6-0.

In keeping with its quaint hospitality traditions, SG invited to France a party of movers and shakers from each of the participating countries. One morning, Jacques gathered the senior staff, including contractors such as myself, to what his PA called mysteriously, 'une lotterie'. The ever chic Jacques glided in once we were all assembled. He called for silence, placing a goldfish bowl on the table. It contained plastic toy caricatures of footballers wearing national costume. Jacques averted his eyes in dramatic fashion. He raised his arm with a flourish and then plunged it into the glass container. A footballer wearing a sombrero emerged. Jacques handed it to Gilles, who was standing to his immediate left.

'Gilles, you will host the group from Mexico', Jacques said.

One by one, the figures were drawn to catcalls and a few bars from songs from each nation.

For me, Jacques selected Cameroon. My ballot was received in stony silence. Did my colleagues feel sorry for me or did no one know the first goddamn thing about the place?

Jacques declared la lotterie complete. Everyone had a plastic figure except for him.

Et toi? A voice called out from the back.

Which country did you get? We chimed in.

Moi? Naturellement, I must do my patriotic duty. I will look after our champions from la belle France!

Thin & confidential

Despite the madding crowd at the airport, I couldn't fail to recognise the party from Cameroon. A blaze of colour burst through the grey sliding doors from the customs hall.

The dignitaries led the way. They edged slowly forwards like the trees in Macbeth on the way from Burnham Wood to Dunsinane. The remainder of their retinue emerged in dribs and drabs. The underlings struggled under the weight of outsized Samsonite suitcases and massive metal trunks forced shut by worn leather straps drawn tighter than a fat man's belt. Keen to justify their passage to Europe, the minions swatted away the swarm of predatory porters that descended on them.

If it was good enough for Cassius to have a lean and hungry look, then the same could be said for Henry, the chef de mission for the team from Cameroon. He was a coffee-coloured whippet of a man. His sole non-canine feature was his moustache. That was thin too. It balanced precariously on his upper lip.

Henry was a man after my own heart at that time. He was on the make. His goals for the World Cup were clear. They had nothing to do with hitting the back of the net. I suspected the quick exit predicted for his national team would suit Henry just fine. He would be free from the irksome distraction of attending soccer games and in the clear to devote his full attention to exploiting his pseudo-diplomatic status to bring shady investors to Cameroon to make his fortune.

Henry was a confidential man, but not in the conventional sense. No one in his right mind would take Henry into *his* confidence. Yet he was forever confiding in *you*. His favourite word was 'confidentially'. He would whisper it conspiratorially in his impeccable Etonian diction. He sounded like an African President that was prominent on the TV News. This was the inspirationally named, Dr. Canaan Banana. I will never forget the day the British PM described negotiations with the good doctor as 'fruitful'.

Henry trusted me with his secrets. I was an unlikely priest in his private confessional. He had a mistress, illegitimate children and numerous accounts in Swiss banks, the Cayman Islands and the like. I mentally absolved him of his sins in the hope that he would cease to tell rather than be saved from hell.

I felt for Henry's long-suffering wife back home. Henry was an early adopter for the ring tones becoming popular for mobile phones. One morning our conversation was interrupted by Wagner's Ride of the Valkyries. That would be my dear wife, Henry explained, discreetly covering the mouthpiece.

Jacques tied us up with these international dignitaries tighter than a hog on a spit. I was spending all my time with Henry. It was getting me down. I was at breaking point. One more ridiculous admission and that would be it!

We were seated in the back of the chauffeured Citroën on our way to view Monet's garden in Giverny. I wondered why we were going there as to date Henry had not shown the slightest interest in the cultural or horticultural delights that abounded in this fair city. For the best part of an hour, he'd been staring sullenly out of the window. I couldn't believe my luck. We were just minutes from the destination. My hopes were rising that I could get there without donning the robes.

And then, like the time I was stranded at Heathrow willing the PA not to announce a further delay, my hopes were dashed.

My friend, I have something of a confidential nature to confide in you, Henry said, without looking in my direction.

I'm sure exasperated priests must pull the grille aside every now and again to punch irritating penitents. I was more than prepared to face my time in the sin bin.

Cameroon won't lose

Frankly, I'm not particularly interested in Monet.

I hoped that wasn't the full import of the impending revelation.

I admire the impressionists, of course, and Monet's works are perhaps the finest of the genre…

Our driver slammed on the brakes to avoid an early morning drunk, stopping the car in its tracks and Henry mid-sentence.

Henry took a moment to compose himself. I prayed for further distractions to spare me additional insights on European art. No such luck.

To be candid, I'm visiting the garden today on account of an important assignation.

Really? I said. My habit was getting worse.

Yes, the matter at hand is rather delicate.

The car cruised to a halt on the lawn area roped off for VIP parking for the Cup. Henry paused again to allow the chauffeur to walk round to his side to open his door. I slid out after him.

Walk with me a moment, Henry said, dismissing the driver and beckoning to me in one fluid motion.

Delicate? I said, rather proud at not having said 'really?'

Yes, but it's not a lady friend on this occasion, he said, ever the rake. It is an important business venture.

Ah, I said, impressing myself again. Maybe SG can help? I added, remembering the script Jacques had been hammering into us.

Possibly, but possibly not, Henry said with a knowing smile. How shall I put this?

He lowered himself onto a garden seat. I joined him.

I consider myself a good judge of character, Henry said with an air of deliberation. Perhaps not a judge of good characters…he added, pausing for my amused response.

I smiled so as not to disappoint him.

I have assessed you as a man after my own heart. We are two peas in a pod.

The thought of sharing this confined space with Henry turned my stomach.

I have therefore decided to take you into my confidence on this matter, which requires the greatest discretion.

Here we go, I thought.

In a moment, I will be meeting two gentlemen from the subcontinent. As we promenade around the garden, I expect them to apprise me of the good news that they have arranged things.

Really? I said. Damn!

Yes. Please listen carefully. You will learn something to your significant financial advantage.

SG is not going to like this, I was thinking. What can it be? Insider trading? Short selling? Margin calls? The possibilities were endless. I couldn't have been more wrong.

You see, despite what the pundits say, I am very confident that Cameroon will not lose its first match.

I was surprised. I didn't think Henry cared about the football.

Although the game is in Toulouse, Henry continued with a self-satisfied grin, I am certain our destiny will not be to lose.

Very droll, Henry, I stammered, but…

…Confidentially, and strictly between us, Henry interrupted me, it is a sure thing.

There's no sure thing in…I responded automatically, and then the penny dropped.

Very alone

I made an excuse to hotfoot it from Monet's garden. The bourse is throwing a wobbly, I explained.

What had I done to end up in the confessional box with Henry? Was this the prospective punishment that awaits all unbelievers?

Once my taxi reached familiar territory in Paris, I asked the driver to pull over so I could stroll through the parks. I trudged through the verdant gardens, barely noticing the abundance of sycamores, lindens and ashes. I longed for the halcyon days when Henry restricted himself to confidences, marital and material. Was it only two weeks ago that I was leading the uncomplicated life of the untrustworthy?

I stopped at a kiosk in the park.

Un espresso, s'il vous plaît.

I consoled myself that I could tell this to my grandchildren. That is, in the unlikely circumstance that (a) a woman would (knowingly) give birth to my progeny and (b) our unfortunate offspring would allow me to babysit. And even then, how long would these grandparental visiting rights be extended after I'd vouchsafed to the innocent darlings that I'd been an albeit unwitting party to the fixing of the 1998 World Cup?

Merci, I grunted as the coffee was slid ungraciously in front of me.

The trouble was that the grandkids were the only people I *could* tell about this. I should tell Jacques, but I wasn't going to. I rationalised this. It was unfair on him. What was he to do once I tagged him, passing on my priestly vestments? Turn Henry into the *flics* and risk a public scandal?

Where was Henry headed with this? Having given me the heads-up, could I then keep my head down? Would Henry leave it at that? I doubted it. For sure, he will offer me a piece of the action. He will want to implicate me.

What should I do? It would go against the grain to pass on such a favourably stacked hand. It was all 'arranged'. But what were the chances of getting caught? How likely was it that I'd become an accessory after the fact? Or more accurately, an accessory *before* the fact? But what if I declined Henry's offer? Where would that leave me? How would Henry react to a firm, but diplomatic 'no'?

At that moment, Johan's whimpering voice came back to me. I was frightened. I tried to think happy thoughts. Nina. Yes, Nina. Tell Nina. Ask Nina's advice. How would she react? With horror and disgust.

I felt sorry for myself. I felt very alone.

Yes I do

I kept out of Henry's way as much as I could. I avoided the pest like *la peste*. When I couldn't, I made sure I was never alone with him. I was now behaving less like a priest and more like a teenage girl auditioning for Jimmy Savile.

As the game versus Austria loomed, my anxiety levels elevated. It was against my nature to miss out on a killing, but images of Dreyfus and Napoleon, expelled for lonely decades on rocky outcrops, gave me pause.

I needed the solace of Nina. My nervous malaise was nothing that couldn't be cured by the exchange of bodily fluids.

Nina had also been preoccupied with hosting duties for the Cup. The Sorbonne had its own guests and the lecturers were entertaining academics from around the world. We'd barely spoken in recent times and then only to exchange notes on the people we had in tow.

I gave Nina's phone one last try. Amazingly, she answered.

Can I see you tonight? I asked, doing my best puppy dog imitation.

I can't make it. I'm sorry. I've got these visitors.

All night?

I can't hear you. Say that again, she shouted.

Where the hell are you? I asked.

I'm in a bar. There's music. It's very noisy.

I thought your guests were geriatrics.

Not this one, she said.

Are you trying to make me jealous?

Quoi? Speak up.

Are you trying to make me jealous?

No, not at all. I don't have to try with you.

Very funny. I'm coming anyway.

You can't.

I can.

You can't. You don't know where I am.

Yes I do, I said, hanging up.

Ali Bar Bar

I was relieved to find 'Bertrand Le Bounce' on crowd control duty outside the club. He and Nina went way back. This guy was tough. He'd been a mercenary in Algeria. He once worked for Oakley sunglasses. They tested the strength of their lenses by firing ball bearings at his eyes. Stupid maybe, but tough.

BLB recognised me. He nodded me through with an incline of his head so slight you needed an action replay to see it.

The band was taking a break. The noise from the club still hit me like a blast of hot air. Nina was at her favourite table. I kept out of sight like a cuckold husband spying on his cheating wife. She was talking to a handsome Asian guy dressed in a sharp blue suit. Their conversation was a little too deep for my liking. Their heads were intimately close together across the cramped wooden table.

I observed them for as long as seemed safe. I didn't want to get sprung. Then I bounded up to the table as if I'd bumped into them by chance. Nina shot me an inscrutable glance. I placed it somewhere between annoyance and resignation. The Asian guy stood up. He was surprisingly tall.

Bonjour, he said. Je m'appelle Miki.

This is my friend, Nina explained to Miki in English, nodding at me as I shook his hand.

The answer to this next question wasn't obvious. Do you mind if I join you? I asked.

Bien sûr, of course, Miki said in a soft transatlantic accent.

Nina's expression was more transparent this time. It was resignation. In the hiatus while a seat was found and a drink ordered, I concluded that Nina had worked out how I knew she was there. It wasn't that difficult. She liked to take new acquaintances to the Ali Bar Bar. It was so cool it was freezing. Rocking up like that was a risky strategy. Nina disliked acts of desperation. Desperate people do desperate things. Not always sensible things.

Once the housekeeping had finished, I smiled at the two of them benignly. After a slightly uncomfortable silence, Nina explained that Miki was a guest of the Sorbonne.

Are you an academic? I asked, doubting from his fashionable clothes that he could be.

Oh, no, he laughed politely, I'm not clever enough.

Op, exclaimed Nina. Miki must be the smartest guy I know.

How long *have* you two known each other? I asked. That was a dumb and dangerous question.

Nina narrowed her eyes.

Oh, we've only just met, Miki explained affably. I have the honour to represent the Sony Corporation here in Paris for the World Cup.

Sony. Really, I said.

Miki is their head of research and innovation, Nina explained. That's the tie-up with the Sorbonne.

I see, I said with a smile, glad that Nina seemed to be forgiving me.

What do *you* do? Miki asked me.

I'm a consultant with SG.

You must be very rich then, Miki joked.

Not compared with a senior executive at Sony, I'll be bound.

An impatient frown was etched on Nina's face. She wanted the jousting over.

Don't let me interrupt, I said, doing my best to placate her.

I was just hearing Miki's views on the future of communications. It was enthralling, Nina added. That comment stung.

Oh, it's nothing really, just my views.

Don't be silly, Nina chided him, it's fascinating. I insist on learning more.

Miki resumed talking about the technology scene in Japan. Despite hating that handsome, smooth Jap bastard more by the second, I couldn't help myself. I was interested too. This *was* fascinating. I could see some new commercial possibilities.

Then the band started a new set. Miki might as well have been speaking in his native tongue for all I could understand of what he was saying.

Let's go somewhere quieter, I shouted.

What's that? Miki asked

I can't hear you, Nina said.

There's another bar over the road, I screamed, forming a megaphone with my hands. Shall we go there?

Miki hesitated. Nina held out her hand to pull him up.

That was not a good sign at any decibel level.

Clever Boy

We decamped to the seedy but quiet joint across the road. I reached for Nina's hand as we crossed the busy street. I quickly thought better of it.

As it was a pleasant evening, we decided to sit outside. The traffic was noisy, but compared to the ABB, the sound was muffled like whispering in a library.

The pink neon Ali Bar Bar sign, featuring a stereotypical Arab man resplendent with scimitar but lonely without his forty shonky mates, blinked at us from across the street. I remembered that I'd forgotten my Henry troubles for a while. Anxiety stalked abroad. If a trouble shared was a trouble halved, a trouble bottled up like this might turn out to be double trouble. I decided to take the risk a little longer.

Miki, correct me if I'm wrong, I said, but you don't seem that confident about Sony.

Are you trying to get me sacked? Miki asked in mock outrage.

Yes I am! I said forcefully.

Nina laughed, tossing back her head in that way that made me want to throw her immediately onto the bed.

Between friends here, Miki continued, I'm not confident about Sony at all. The company has now reached a tipping point. As one of the technology giants, it has the size and scale required to deliver the grunt and capital backing to spend big on R&D. I head that up for them. They also have the critical mass to hire top executives, manufacture to the highest quality, etc. etc. In short, they have the capability to create best of breed products.

He checked we were following him. Nina was making doe eyes at him. No wonder Bambi got shot.

Miki continued. This is the thing. The Sony brand and the company itself have reached the mature stage of the life cycle. The sheer bulk of the juggernaut is now a millstone. As I was telling beautiful Nina here, it will sink it.

Miki lit a cigarette. Nina bit into her croque monsieur. She recoiled as the melting cheese burned her luscious lips.

Why is Sony any different from Hitachi, Panasonic or NEC? I asked.

Miki stubbed his barely lit cigarette, knocking his wine glass over in the process. He paused to mop up the wine with a serviette.

There's no difference. All the Japanese technology companies are in the same boat. They're all going down together. They are not Sony's threat.

I considered the implications of this. I knew the high labour cost in Japan was exposing its manufacturing base to competition from lower cost countries.

I thought the threat to market share would come from Korea, I said.

It will, Miki confirmed. But...

... You're saying something else? I interjected.

Correct. Irrespective of cost, Japan will stagnate.

In that case, who will sail ahead while the Japs, sorry Miki, sink to the ocean floor?

Can't you guess? Miki teased.

The States? I ventured cautiously.

Exactly. Innovation will be the key.

But you head that up for Sony? I don't get you.

Miki leaned back like a guy who'd laid down a full house. I was missing something. I needed to understand this stuff. It was the way all business was heading. Then I put two and two together. Not for the main equation, but at least something was adding up.

I'm guessing you studied in the States, I said.

I did.

Berkeley maybe? I guessed

Clever boy! Miki said.

Miniaturisation

Miki expanded on his fascinating thesis. I was trying to concentrate, but my head was spinning.

I was desperate to get Nina into bed. Or was it out of Miki's clutches? I wanted to share my Henry problem with her. At the same time, I didn't want to because of the reaction I expected. I was keen to give Miki the flick, but I wanted to hear him out.

With no clear path forward, I stayed where I was. Miki was expounding on the burgeoning field of digital communications. I struggled with the technical aspects of what he was saying, but the business angle was writ large as the Hollywood sign.

The key concepts here, Miki explained, are miniaturisation and digitisation. Let me explain this in terms of the impacts rather than technology. In ten years from now, these clunky phones we have on the table will be dinosaurs. The cell phone will evolve to become sleeker and smarter. It's hard to believe, but we will carry in our pocket the entire repository of human knowledge.

Miki looked at me to check I was following him. As mind-boggling as that is, Miki added, that is not the most revolutionary aspect of all this.

That's right, Nina agreed, that's what I keep telling the boring profs back at the Sorbonne.

I felt like Rip van Winkle. I'd been asleep for a hundred years and everyone knew about this stuff but me. What is the biggest deal then? I asked, desperate for this sleeper to awake.

Let me put it this way, Miki said. He was warming to the task of explaining the obvious to the ignorant. I think Marshall McLuhan will be proved right. The medium will be the message, but not entirely in the way he meant it. In my view, the medium and the message will merge.

I looked puzzled.

Nina weighed in to help. We are entering what the academics are calling the information age. The impact on society will be as great as the industrial revolution

Really? I said. I'd got away with it once. This time I looked apologetically at Nina.

She smiled in recognition, but kept going. The industrial revolution reshaped nations, societies, work, basically everything. In the information age, work will be transformed but so will the very nature of our relationships.

Really? I said, raising my eyebrows to indicate that this time I'd said it as a joke.

Yes, really, Miki responded. It will be as easy for an American to relate to someone in China as to say howdy to his next door neighbour.

It's a social revolution, Nina said. It's so incredibly exciting, she added, clapping her hands.

I pursued the subject while Nina went looking for the bathroom.

So, Miki, consumer expenditure will migrate from manufactured goods to…I don't know how to describe it.

Virtual goods, Miki said.

Virtual goods, I repeated the phrase, trying it on for size. So, if I'm not mistaken, the commercial opportunities arising from this seismic shift in expenditure patterns will be significant?

Humungous! He said, lighting and stubbing another Gauloises.

In that case, I said, surreptitiously repositioning Nina's chair closer to mine, I would have thought the Sonys and the NECs of the world would find a way to adapt themselves to grab their slice of the action?

Ah, Miki said knowingly. That's where miniaturisation becomes relevant.

Only to myself

Once Nina had returned from the bathroom, Miki stood up to leave.

Nina took him by the arm to detain him. Don't go, Miki, she begged.

Fuck off, Miki, I thought.

I have an early start, Miki explained.

So what? Nina pleaded.

Miki has an early start, I agreed. I was firmly on his side.

I really have to go.

No you don't.

Yes he does.

The matter was settled with a compromise reminiscent of the UN, except that the decision took less than a decade. Miki would stay for one more drink.

I sulked for a while. Miki and Nina chatted about the joint lecture they were giving the next afternoon. It sounded interesting, but I wasn't feeling charitable. My phone rang. It still gave me a childish thrill that phones bought in France had the *Marseillaise* as a ring tone option. I'd sent Ewan a postcard to tell him the good news. It occurred to me that he hadn't replied.

A moment of inattention can wreak havoc. I answered the phone without thinking.

Hello, my friend, the voice said, it's Henry.

I reacted with a start. The conversation around me stopped abruptly. Nina and Miki looked concerned.

I shook my head to reassure my companions. What can I do for you, Henry?

I need to see you, Henry said, as a matter of urgency.

My mind reviewed its extensive catalogue of excuses. Mmm, Henry, I bumbled, playing for time to make a selection...Henry...I'm not in a position...I'm not well placed right now to meet.

Let's talk later, Henry said with the tone of insistence that comes easily to people in authority even when they are being unreasonable.

It's already midnight, I protested.

I have another idea, Henry said. Then the line went dead.

Frustration was written on my face. Nina looked irritated. Miki seemed sympathetic.

Anything I can help you with before I go? Miki asked.

I remembered my original game plan. Don't let me hold you up.

I really have to go, Miki insisted, making a move.

Nina pleaded with her eyes. He smiled. I scowled.

Just one more, Nina entreated him.

Jesus Christ, I said to myself.

No, no, Miki insisted.

I became aware of a presence behind me.

Il y a quelquechose, monsieur? Nina asked the passer-by.

Excusez-moi, madameoiselle, he said. Je cherche mon copain ici.

I turned around to find none other than Henry. His bodyguard was a few paces behind him. Obviously, he'd called me from across the street.

Henry signalled to the waiter to order drinks all round. Miki settled back down. Nina perked up. I slumped forward.

Are you here for the World Cup? Miki asked politely.

You don't want to know, I said under my breath, but not quietly enough.

Of course he does, Henry insisted, completely missing my point. I am the head of the Cameroon delegation, Henry said puffing out his chest, but…he added to forestall any interjection…confidentially…

I've bribed the Austrian players, I chimed in, but only to myself.

The pellet with the poison

Was the pellet with the poison in the vessel with the pestle or was the chalice from the palace the brew that was true?

I could but channel the Court Jester at that point. I briefly wondered how Henry had tracked me down there. It seemed a coincidence after I'd successfully located Nina over the road. Was he having me followed? I didn't put it past him. I was feeling sorry for myself. What had I done to deserve this? I let that thought flash by as I was in no mood to compile such a lengthy list.

Confidentially, Henry continued, football is not my only interest here.

I couldn't let him continue. Henry's here for business too, I added cheerfully.

I've heard so much about you! Nina said provocatively to Henry.

And I of you, Henry responded sleazily, taking Nina's hand tenderly in his.

Well, we've all heard of each other then, I said, trying to shut things down.

But I still haven't had my question answered, Miki protested. Do tell me about your business interests in Paris.

I'm here to fix some things, Henry said in that man of mystery way of his.

This was feeling more like a French farce than the rerun of an old Danny Kaye film. Henry was about to fuck me. I had a mission to fuck Nina. She had her heart set on fucking Miki. Miki just wanted to fuck off. If we'd been on stage, doors would have been opening and closing every few seconds. The audience would have been in hysterics. For me this was no laughing matter. This was a fucking disaster.

Come on, do tell, Nina said, grasping Henry's hand. I was squirming in my seat. Nina was in her element. What is the nature of your business here, cher monsieur?

It's commercial-in-confidence, I jumped in. I don't want to be too boring about it, but SG is looking to help Henry.

Quite so, Henry said, much to my relief. I have identified an urgent need for SG's assistance and that's what brings me to seek out my good friend and host and to inadvertently crash your delightful party.

It can't be *that* secret, Nina said in that seductive manner of hers that inveigles men to confide in her.

Well, chère mademoiselle…Henry stuttered.

…Henry, seriously, I interjected, we need to discuss this in private.

I attempted to dislodge Henry from his chair as I stood up. The body-guard bristled. He relaxed once Henry allowed me to escort him to another table. I selected one within line of sight but out of earshot. It distressed me to leave Nina and Miki alone. But there was nothing else for it.

Henry fussed around, calling the waiter. He dispatched the human guard dog on an errand. I waited head in hands. There was no way I could discuss this mess with Nina now. I would need to bear this white man's burden alone.

It transpires, Henry said, that SG *could* help me out.

Fantastic.

With my deal.

Which deal? I asked.

With the Indian gentlemen.

Henry! Tell me you're joking.

No, Henry said, relieving the waiter of the bottle of champagne, I'm not joking.

You can't seriously believe…

…I'm not talking about the arrangement, as such.

You're not.

No, heaven's no, he said, smiling broadly.

I relaxed a little and drank some of the champagne.

No, not the match fixing...

...Keep your voice down, I begged him.

No, what I need is...

He was interrupted by Nina and Miki hovering over us. We're off, Nina announced, bending to kiss me on the forehead.

So soon, Henry said, standing up to be polite.

Henry engaged Nina in an unctuous conversation, restraining her round the waist.

I know you're tired, I said to Miki. I'll let Nina know you said good-bye.

Best not to, he said with a look of resignation.

Nina freed herself from Henry's grasp.

Just one more bubbly, that's all I ask, Henry pleaded with Nina.

Miki and I need to go, Nina responded firmly.

The devil was now actually swimming in the deep blue sea. I had to make one last stand to stop them leaving together.

Yes, just one more, I begged.

You have to talk to Henry, Nina insisted.

It's not that urgent, I said.

Actually it is, Henry protested.

This was the moment to punch him.

We'll leave you boys to your business deals, Nina said, dragging Miki behind her.

They make a beautiful couple, Henry said cruelly, unable to avert his salacious gaze from Nina's swaying behind.

Henry, I said, slugging the champagne straight from the bottle. This had better be fucking good.

So, confidentially...

...There's only you and me here, Henry, I snapped, checking that the guard dog hadn't returned.

Henry ignored me as usual. In confidence, he continued, I am not as well cashed up at present as I would like to be.

Fiscal distress was not apparent from the rate at which he was slugging the Veuve.

As I say, in order to capitalise on the extraordinary opportunities offered by my arrangement with the gentlemen from the Indian sub-continent, I would very much like a loan from SG.

Henry!

He waved my protest away, pouring the last dregs of the bubbly into my glass. He signalled to the waiter for another bottle in that incredibly fluid Henry fashion that I was coming to admire.

My friend, between you and me, SG need not know the intended purpose of the advance.

Henry, they will ask. There will be forms.

Yes, of course. But, if I may divulge this to you now we are friends, I have been dealing with SG for some time on a similar basis.

What do you mean? I asked, dabbing at the sweat on my brow with a napkin while the waiter refreshed my flute.

What I mean, between you and me, is that I have already accessed loans that have been washed through many legitimate projects operating back home in my country.

I felt faint. I don't want to hear this, I said, putting my fingers in my ears like a child.

Henry lowered my arms to stop the playacting. My esteemed host, relax – this is a confidential discussion between friends.

Despite the dulling intoxication that had enfeebled the rest of my body, my brain was functioning clearly. Henry's revelations about SG had forced my hand. I couldn't risk becoming a conduit between Henry and the bank for a bogus loan, especially for a purpose as spectacularly illegal as this one. Nor could I wash my hands of the whole business. I was caught in a rip-off and there was nothing for it now but to go with the flow.

Confidentially, Henry, I said. He gave me a puzzled look as if to say where have I heard that line before? Henry, let's leave the bank out of it.

But I really need this capital.

I know.

You understand that there is no risk. It has been arranged, he said

It's a safe thing then? I asked.

As safe as houses. As safe as the Bank of England, he replied.

I wasn't sure if the irony in that remark was intended.

In that case, I said in as confident a voice as I could muster, we don't need the bank.

I don't follow, he said, nodding to the guard who had returned but was standing at a discreet distance by the limousine.

I will privately access a loan for you, and…

…And what?

I will take a stake in the action myself.

Splendid, Henry said, beaming. He clapped me on the back while at the same time pouring champagne.

How did he do that?

Fabulous, Henry continued. I feel so much more comfortable having you on board as a partner.

I didn't need to ask why he took comfort in my complicity.

I am truly blessed, Henry continued in his classically obsequious fashion. It is an honour to be able to repay you for your generous hospitality.

We clinked glasses. Henry smiled. I contemplated what the hospitality might be like at the Bastille where I feared I might be staying for some little time if it was still receiving guests.

No shame

The day of reckoning arrived. We flew down to Toulouse on the first flight. I endured Henry's repertoire on the theme of 'Toulouse or not to lose, that is the question'.

Given Henry's position as chef de mission, we had seats in the President's box for the fateful match between Cameroon and Austria.

It was stifling hot.

Very good for the African team, Henry joked over the pre-match drinks.

The heat provided excellent cover for my profuse nervous sweating. Tributaries of perspiration flowed together to form Armpit River.

Il fait chaud, hein? A friendly reveller observed, raising his snout from the corporate hospitality trough.

C'ést ça, I responded. But it wasn't that. I had a bad case of the jitters. When you've shelled out a hundred grand to fix a sporting event, you're entitled to feel a little anxious. I would've given anything at that moment to sweat the match out in the privacy of my little apartment. However, the call of duty required me to parade my perfidy before the innocent.

I slipped out of the corporate box to get some air. I tried to think of other things. Nina came immediately to mind. This wasn't going to help. She'd been conspicuous by her absence of late. Even my jealous scouring of her usual haunts had drawn a blank. Was she turning Japanese? I really thought so.

The crowd's roar snapped me back to the dreadful here and now. I pulled myself together sufficiently to scuttle back into the box and take up my seat next to Henry. He looked serene.

The band struck up. As we took to our feet, I heard Henry confiding in his neighbour on the other side.

I have a good feeling about this game, Henry said.

The Austrian anthem wasn't too bad. It could have been on the B-side of Johan Strauss's first 45. It would have won the 1998 Eurovision Song Contest hands down. The Cameroonian counterpart was execrable. The sound of a tone deaf Henry singing lustily added to my pain. If their soccer team was anywhere near as bad as their conservatory, my hundred big ones were already half way down the drain.

The Russian referee waved ceremoniously and blew his whistle. The big match was underway. Austria settled to its task. The Cameroon side was a Sunday school outfit at best. Fortunately for them, their mountainous goalie pulled off a series of fine saves. For half an hour, the Austrian threat was neutralised

In the thirty-third minute, Austria's silky smooth midfielder shimmied through the Cameroon defence like the proverbial machete through margarine. He evaded two clumsy tackles then slipped a through ball to their number 9 who smashed it past the keeper as if he wasn't there.

The Austrian fans erupted in joy. The Tyrolean band struck up a joyful oompah-oompah number. Henry looked unflustered. His neighbour commiserated with him.

Thank you my friend, Henry replied, but I know we will hit back.

Not only did Henry have no shame. He didn't know the meaning of the word.

Own goal

Half-time and the associated hospitality in the box came and went. I sweated on. Henry schmoozed away. The gathering speculated by how much Austria would win. Quatre zéro, one of my SG colleagues predicted. Henry politely disagreed. They must have thought he was dreaming.

The all-important second half was underway. Austria continued to dominate. They attacked relentlessly, but their timing was just a smidgeon off. Their crosses were a fraction over-cooked and their passes a touch telegraphed.

Cameroon launched the occasional counter-attack, but these were easily repulsed. We were in the last ten minutes. Henry remained unflustered. As for me, I felt as secure as a Buddhist relic in a Taliban takeover. Austria still led 1-0 and Cameroon looked less likely to score than a pothead at a meeting of narcotics anonymous. The excessive acid was burning a hole in my gut. I was suddenly indisposed. I hustled my way out of the seats and high-tailed it to the gents. Henry smiled at me affably as I pushed past him.

I made it to the stall just in time. An avalanche launched itself down the slippery porcelain slope. I was shit-scared. If I survived this trauma, I resolved to wring Henry's neck. He had conned me into dropping a hundred Gs. Maybe this whole match-fixing pantomime had been an elaborate charade to rip me off?

When I emerged ashen-faced from the john, the fans were filing past me. The game was over. I jostled my way against the traffic to clear a path to the corporate box. I was a man on a chef de mission.

A smiling Henry greeted me. Are you OK, old chap? He asked.

Listen here, Henry, I said in no mood for any of his BS.

Bottoms up, he said, handing me a glass of champagne. They all count, he added.

What all count? I said, menacing him with my glass.

Own goals, of course.

Own goals?

Yes, own goals are still goals, aren't they?

What own goal?

The one that unfortunate Austrian fellow scored so close to the final whistle.

Unfinished business

Is 'insufferable' a superlative? If not, Henry was even more insufferable after the drawn football match. Or perhaps he was even less sufferable? Either way, he was more of a pain up the arse.

I lost count of the times he took me aside in avuncular fashion. He beamed at me every inch the proud uncle. Our little secret binds us together, he would say. He was right. If we didn't keep our mouths shut, we would find ourselves bound together in a dark alley somewhere.

While Henry was omnipresent, Nina was omni-absent. I would have reversed this if I'd been omnipotent.

Wherever I turned, wherever I went, Henry was there. He was my constant companion, my Kemo Sabe, for the duration of the Cup. I was grateful for the millions of francs I'd made. I just wanted him out of my life. I longed to put the whole sordid affair behind me. Once Henry was no longer around, I was convinced I'd be able to forget the whole thing.

Nina was another story. I snuck up on her at the Sorbonne. She seemed pleased to see me, but I felt like a brother not a lover

What's going on? I asked her. I instantly knew it was a stupid thing to say.

I'm busy.

You're always busy. But now you're too busy for me, I said.

I don't like dependent men. You know that.

There was a tone of finality in her voice. Perhaps it was a construction I was wanting to put on it. In that fatalist way it has, my mind considered how I should react to being dumped without seeming too desperate or overly aloof. I followed Nina round the corner of the Sociology building, only to bump into Miki. He was reading Le Monde on a bench shaded from the blinding sun.

Salut, he greeted me warmly after kissing Nina on the lips.

I nodded in his direction. I wanted to hate him. I just didn't. I have never forgotten that moment. I looked back at Nina and could see that she was gone. Not to Miki. He would be replaced in time too. Just gone from me. Like the spirit departing the corpse.

We stood in an awkward triangle.

Un café? I proposed to the group in a cheerful manner that surprised them and put them more at ease.

Nina stood between us. She hooked her arms into ours as we set off for the campus cafeteria.

Ewan had accused me all those years back of shallowness in the face of the enemy. As we stepped out as a threesome, I felt myself moving on. I had unfinished business. But it was not with Nina. It was with Miki.

California

SG's Cup after-party was a lavish affair. It was very Jacques. The decor, the catering, the guest list cut a dash. Jacques insisted that the hosts got fully into the spirit of things. He looked resplendent, dressed as the President of the Republic. I had to borrow a gaudy Cameroonian costume from one of Henry's serfs. I looked like a walking Christmas tree.

After weeks of boundless hospitality, I was ready for my bed, even alone. I psyched myself up for this one last trip on the gravy train. The hosts were required to hobnob with their assigned teams. Our covert responsibility was to keep the chefs de mission sober enough to deliver their speeches. The prospect of twenty-four orations in broken French and English from some of the dullest dignitaries on the world stage filled me with dread.

I saw Nina and Miki across a clichéd crowded room. I briefly caught Nina's eye. She was wearing that dress. I felt that pang. I controlled it sufficiently to watch her at work, seducing the latest coterie of admirers.

The speechmakers from the assembled nations were called forward in alphabetical order. Thankfully my waiting time would be short. It was hard to determine Henry's state of sobriety. I'd dutifully tailed him as he worked the room. As a networker of note, I could but admire Henry's technique. To say that he big-noted himself would do him a disservice. He was a huge-noter, at the very least.

The moment for the speech from the chef de mission from the Cameroons arrived. I loosened my red and green tie. Henry insisted that I stand beside him. Henry's monologue was extensive. I strained to concentrate. His next word could land me in jail.

Henry had been in the debating team at university. He adored public speaking. He loved the sound of his own voice. He opened in his habitual hushed tone, bringing the entire group into his zone of confidence. His favourite story was the urinating somnambulist and the squashed chihuahua. I'd heard it a number of times before. Not again, I said to myself.

This reminds me of my golfing friend, the sleepwalker, Henry intoned.

There was no justification for this. Nothing that had happened so far could remotely have reminded him of his apocryphal mate. Like a three-legged dog, this did not deter him from running with it.

My somnambulist friend was staying in a five-star hotel. Unbeknownst to him as he was still asleep, he indulged in an early morning bladder evacuation from his first floor balcony. He returned to bed only to be rudely awoken by ferocious knocking on the door to his suite. Once apprised by the management of the unseasonal shower he had inflicted on a group of Asian tourists below, my friend plucked two bottles of Bollinger from the bar fridge and sought to make amends for his sins. .

The buzz of conversation was rising around the room. Sharp knives were eyed off by the restless.

Henry continued at a higher volume.

I will save my audience the agony his had to endure by summarising the story. Relieved that his peace offering had successfully placated the afflicted holidaymakers, the golfing mate plonked himself down on the sofa to quaff his champers only to squash their pet dog he had mistaken for a furry white cushion

Needless to say, this abridged version of Henry's story has not so much cut a long story short as hacked it into tiny pieces. Henry continued undeterred by the sustained heckling, including the apposite observation from an impatient Kraut that compared to ours the poor dog's suffering was over.

When Henry's soliloquy ground to a halt, the crowd was unsure whether to laugh or cry. Jacques launched himself into thunderous applause. I took my opportunity to hustle Henry off the stage. I ushered him to the nearest drinks waiter. My work here was done.

Scant attention was paid to the Danish dignitary who had the alphabetical misfortune to have to follow Henry. Having regained the will to live, the crowd dived for medicinal relief. Henry was engulfed by the thirsty mob. I took my opportunity to slip away. I caught sight of Miki across the room. He was unsure how to react. I sensed an inclination to avoid me, but a stronger attraction to make fun of my ridiculous garb.

My friendly greeting reassured him. He approached and we shook hands.

I hope you didn't write that speech, Miki said.

That wasn't a speech, I corrected him, that was GBH of the ears.

So it was, he said.

Miki, I said. I need to ask your something.

He stiffened.

It's not about Nina, I reassured him.

O-kay, he said. How can I help?

I steered him to a quieter spot. You remember that night we were with Nina when Henry rocked up?

When I thought about it, it was a stupid question. Accordingly, Miki smiled but didn't respond.

I was interested in what you were saying about the future of telecommunications and the likely fate of the Japanese conglomerates.

You won't tell Sony, will you? Miki said, feigning horror once again.

What you said made a lot of sense and gelled with my own thinking about future business opportunities.

That's great, Miki said.

But there was one thing I didn't understand.

What was that?

I waved to a SG colleague, but turned my face to deter interruption.

It's about miniaturisation.

Right.

I understand the significance of miniaturisation in a technical sense. But I didn't get why you were saying that miniaturisation would prevent the Sonys and the NECs from competing in the future.

Isn't it pretty obvious?

Explain it to me.

It's miniaturisation.

I still don't get it.

Only miniatures will be able to miniaturise.

At that moment, Nina approached me from the rear, kissing me on both cheeks. I resisted the temptation to put my arm around her.

Great to see you two together, Nina said.

Miki and I smiled politely.

Were you talking about me? She asked.

Actually, we weren't, I said with a little too much edge. I have to find Henry now.

For once, I wanted the irrelevant company of Henry. I slipped away. The hide of the man! I found him conversing with team management from Austria. Maybe some of them were counting their good fortune too?

Ah, my great friend, Henry said in greeting, leading me away.

His warmth was genuine. Just between you and me, Henry said, what will you do now that the Cup is over?

Actually, Henry, your timing is impeccable.

Really? He said. I had infected him.

Yes, I have just made up my mind.

May I be the first to know? Henry asked true to form.

You certainly may, Henry, I said. Go west young man!

Henry looked confused.

Henry, I said, confidentially, I'm going to California.

California, California, Henry repeated, moving away.

Then an idea came to him and he stepped back towards me. He sidled up closer.

Do you consider yourself a man of the world? He asked.

Yes, no, I don't know. I replied.

That's a good answer, Henry said with a broad smile. You see, if I may speak candidly, you are like the curate's egg. Sophisticated in parts and naïve in parts.

Really?

Yes. Please don't take offence, Henry added. But in relation to our little match-arranging venture, we are not exactly orphans.

Henry, no offence taken, but I haven't a fucking clue what you're talking about.

Surely you realise that we were not alone.

Are you saying that other matches were fixed?

Henry pulled me so conspiratorially close that his tongue was literally in my ear. The World Cup is the greatest show on earth, he said, pausing for effect. Such events cannot be left to chance.

That's it for me, I announce to the two women idling time away in my hospital cell. I've had it with this stupid book.

I look for some reaction. Cassidy and Lorna are a study in contrasts. Sad Cass is up and about again if you can call her clumsy waddling that. Bright Lorna is indefatigable in her cheerleader role.

My tantrum is in response to the latest diagnosis just delivered by a trio of specialists. They are now of one mind that I need several more surgeries to attempt to kick my spinal chord back into action.

You might die under the knife, Lorna chirps in bizarre encouragement. So you need to get this finished.

Is that supposed to inspire me?

Sure is, Lorna says, organising my writing table like some junior Florence Nightingale in the Crimean War.

Cass and I exchange a wry 'whatever' smile. This is a funny way to make a connection, but it warms me nevertheless.

When everything is plumped and prepared, Lorna moves my hands into the typing position.

I'm not doing it.

Lorna ignores me. Type!

Why?

I told you. You're going to die in surgery so get on with it.

What shall I write next?

It's time to tell your readers about frenzship.

I don't have any readers. Not even you.

You will. You'll have even more if it's check out time under the knife.

I resign myself to my fate. Actually, it's time to write more about Ewan, I announce without enthusiasm.

He can wait, Lorna insists. You're not in the mood.

OK, I concede. She's right. It's easier to write about myself.

How friendship means different strokes for different folks

Gunfire

Gunfire rang out the first time I visited Randy's house.

It wasn't altogether surprising. The tiled roof of the terracotta fortress poked its nose over forbidding walls. His hacienda was convent-style reminiscent of the Camino trail. The landscape was mud brick, red earth and cactuses. I imagined guards stationed in the bell tower. I wondered if they'd seen me loitering.

I was calculating whether to duck or run. Another volley rang out. I floored it. There was no cover. The walls were impenetrable. I eyed off a clump of desert bushes ten yards away. I contemplated rolling into them like some has-been cowboy actor.

I heard another loud crack. Fear paralysed me. Moving was no longer an option. I lay still with my eyes closed for an eternity. An eerie silence descended. Had the fighting stopped?

I heard footsteps approaching. If I'd been religious, I'd have said my prayers. Instead of threats, I heard laughter and backslapping. This was more like a Tarantino movie by the minute.

Can I help you? A deep brown voice inquired.

I looked up, squinting into the sun. I could make out a portly, middle-aged man wearing a checked shirt and baggy striped shorts. He had a golf club in one hand and a cocktail in the other.

Are you OK? He asked.

Yeah, I'm fine, I said, scrambling to an upright position before brushing the gravel from my palms

You gave me a fright lying there in the dirt.

I avoided the obvious riposte. Randy invited me, I explained.

Great day for it, he said, ambling away. By the way, my name's Bill, he shouted back to me.

Dusting myself off, I followed my rescuer.

Hey, Randy, he shouted through an open concertina door.

I followed him inside. I found myself on a different film set. This was an old Peter Sellers movie. Except, where were the bikini-clad girls?

We walked onto the pool deck. Wherever I looked, there were middle-aged guys, tanned, chained and boardied. They lazed on loungers and lolled on lilos. Now I was thinking Boogie Nights, except there were no naked girls.

Bobby, one of the men shouted, your ball's orbiting Mars. I just heard it from NASA.

The guys whooped and cheered.

Randy, you got a visitor, Bill persisted.

A mountain of a man, with a shock of grey-blond hair and a vat of fat round his gut, hauled himself out of the pool. He dripped his way towards me.

It's you, he said.

He looked puzzled. He offered a damp hand.

Hi again, I said, restrained in Randy's vice-like grip.

You picked a hell of a day to come calling, Randy said.

You told me to come today.

Did I? He said, shaking his head. Anyways, we need to get you a drink.

Randy beckoned to a Latino dressed like a lifeguard. He bounded towards us like a puppy dog thrown a squeaky toy. This guy was eager to please.

Fix my buddy here a Birthday Ballbuster, por favor.

Si señor, the lifeguard replied, bowing then easing himself through a narrow gap between the potted ferns to squeeze behind the beach bar.

Randy escorted me to a rainbow-coloured lounger in an area shaded by palm trees.

I thought I was being shot at, I said.

LA is one scary place, my friend.

No, not downtown, I said. Just now when I arrived.

Randy cottoned on. Oh yeah, I get you now, he said.

The lifetender-cum-barguard brought two lurid drinks decorated with the mandatory cocktail umbrellas and maraschino cherries.

Randy lit a cigar. He took a series of short puffs to give it momentum. Best thing ever to come out of Cuba, he remarked, not counting Conchita, our maid.

Randy alternated deep draws on his cigar with noisy sips through his bendable straw. He radiated contentment. Finally, he took time out from his hedonistic pursuits to register my presence. Today's my birthday, he explained.

Happy birthday, I ventured.

Me and my buddies have this kinda ritual.

I nodded encouragement.

For the last twelve years maybe, we've been celebrating the day I checked out of my mommy's womb with a special golf game.

That's great.

My buddies tee off from the surrounding haciendas and the first one to land his ball in my pool is the winner.

Isn't that dangerous? I asked pathetically.

Randy took a deep pull oh his smoke. Damn right it is! He said proudly. It wouldn't be birthday ball if we didn't have some collateral property damage and a trip to the ER, he roared.

I relaxed into sipping at what appeared to be a quadruple tequila sunrise. It was virulent red leeching into dayglow pink. It was the colour of the early morning sky before God perfected creation. Drinking it was unnecessary. Inhaling the fumes was getting me high.

I looked around the pool for a second time. Is it a guys only game? I asked.

Hell no! Randy answered in an offended tone. The gals have their own birthday tradition.

What's that? I asked, falling into his trap.

I slip the pool boys a hundred bucks to slip it to them, he said.

I looked at him narrow-eyed, unsure if I should believe him. Really? I asked.

Sure thing, he said, puffing away. In a few minutes, it'll be dead Indian tribe time.

I looked at him perplexed.

Yeah, you'll hear them coming from a mile away.

It was hard not to like this guy. Abruptly, he hauled himself upright.

We'll have to make this quick, Randy said, with a sudden change of tone. What with it being my birthday and all.

Sure, I said. As I was saying to you on the flight...

At that moment, the guard-tender cruised up to whisper in Randy's ear.

The hell he is! Randy screamed in response.

One moment, Randy said with an apologetic shrug in my direction, striding away with his multi-tasking minion in tow. Can't they leave a guy in peace on his birthday? He appealed to no one in particular.

I waited for the longest time. I wondered if Randy had forgotten about me. He returned, having changed into cheesecloth and chinos.

Let's break bread in the morning, Randy said. I'm a little preoccupied right now, he added in a conspiratorial, Henriesque fashion.

Nothing wrong, I hope.

If there was nothing wrong, Randy said, shaking my hand vigorously, it wouldn't be LA.

All about France

Pitching to Randy was like teaching calculus to delinquents with ADD. To be fair, he had been calmer and more focused on the flight from JFK to LAX on TAA when I first met him.

Once the gargantuan stranger had shoehorned his way past me to sit by the window, he'd proven larger than life as well as larger than seat.

Tough luck getting the big guy, he said in response to my squirming.

I twigged that he was talking to me.

That's OK, I said in that cool, reticent manner I'd perfected to close down conversations with party bores and deter girls shampooing my hair from asking me if I had plans for the weekend.

I maintained my fixed gaze on Time magazine. It was my crucifix to keep the vampire at bay.

It was after sunset and Randy was determined to rise from his coffin. I know that dude, he said, pointing to the picture of Mark Zuckerberg on the cover.

Really? I replied instinctively, but far too open-endedly for a guy intent on getting some peace.

He's a right sonofabitch.

Really? I could no longer resist the bait.

He sure is. We were college buddies. More friends of friends, to be honest. But we moved in the same circles.

Randy looked around. He raised his huge frame like the Loch Ness monster emerging from the deep. He motioned to a hostess. A scotch for me and one for my pal, he said. On the rocks, he added as an after-thought.

There was a whole bunch of guys sniffing around this connective technology stuff. A lot of them were much smarter than him.

Randy drifted off for a moment, clearly reliving the scene in his mind.

Did you lose track of him? I asked to get Randy to continue.

No, nothing so innocent, Randy said, returning to the here and now. The motherfucker double-crossed me. Some day I'm gonna get even.

Really! I said as an exclamation on this occasion and not a question.

Randolph J. Steinbacher Jr., the big man said, holding out his hand.

I nodded as I returned the handshake. As I couldn't measure up in a name-pissing contest, I left it at that.

Randolph… I said.

…Please, Randy, he interrupted. My friends call me Randy. Only my mom called me Randolph, he added with a smile that was becoming infectious, and then only when I set fire to a stray dog or something harmless like that.

Randy, then, I stammered, trying to retrieve my train of thought. I might be the man you've been looking for to sucker Zuckerberg.

Nessie surfaced again from the murky waters. Two more whiskies, he shouted to a stewardess ten rows back. On the rocks, he added a few seconds later, sliding back to the depths.

Randy turned to me, somehow appraising my worth. I'd give anything to pucker that Zucker, he said wistfully, and I've got plenty to give.

A wealthy guy like him was exactly what I was looking for. Are you in banking? I asked.

A venture capitalist, he corrected me.

This was getting interesting. I was glad my rebuff had been snuffed. How to reel this guy in? I've been sniffing around the social media scene myself, I said, gasping as the alcohol burned my throat.

I waited for the captain to finish his announcement that, due to the heavy inbound traffic, we would be flying in circles around LA for thirty minutes when we got there.

Since I've been Stateside, I've been developing a prototype. I have a partner who cut his teeth with the Sony Corporation. I met him when I lived in France

France, Randy said in a reverend tone. I gotta go there, don't I?

The train wreck that was Randy's wayward thought pattern momentarily derailed me. He had this disarming knack of honing in on the information you were imparting that was the least relevant.

I resolved to push on regardless. I've got a concept that might interest you. You might yet get to sock it to Zucker.

Randy poured the lonely ice cubes straight down his throat. Then he looked at me with such a hopeful expression that I felt like the Messiah himself. Come visit me on Friday and tell me all about it.

I'd love to, I said, responding to his invitation to clink our empty glasses.

I'd like to hear all about France, Randy added disconcertingly.

Fuckerberg

Randy kept me waiting at the Blue Jam café on Melrose.

I paced up and down for a while. I'd been living in the Bay Area of San Francisco for some time, but had visited LA frequently. I had my doubts about the place. The whole must be greater than the sum of its parts. Compared to London, Paris or Rome, LA seemed to me just a sprawling mass of mediocrity.

I chilled for a while, opting for a seat at the bar. From there, I had a good view of the bustling café. I ordered pancakes. They were stunning. The coffee was great too. Just as my world was putting itself to rights, my breakfast companion burst in.

Randy is not a relaxing guy. The cool waiters lost their composure. They buzzed around him like flies on a turd. We were relocated. Juice was delivered. Randy's regular breakfast was offered and accepted. Randy looked at me at long last.

Tell me about France, Randy said.

Henry came immediately to mind. Which of these guys was the more irritating? I should have fed Henry the knuckle sandwich. I wanted to snot Randy now. The uppercut or the right cross was the only issue.

Randy's puffy face turned Cheshire cat. He raised the palms of his hands towards me as if to sue for peace. He leant back in his banquette seat. I'm just joshing with you, pal, Randy said. Let's talk Fuckerberg.

You can tell a lot about people from the way they eat. I address the components of my meal one by one. If I had a plate of steak, chips, carrots and broccoli (God forbid), I would eat it in the order of broccoli, carrots, steak and chips. From this, you could infer that I have an orderly mind and that I had no siblings around when I was young to steal the best bits. You might also think me capable of deferring gratification. That's where you would be wrong.

Randy contemplated his serving of waffles, maple syrup, strawberries, mangoes and fruit compote. He studied it like a surgeon weighing up the preferred locus for his first incision. Then, without warning, Randy transformed himself from Dr. Jekyll into Mr. Hyde. He fell upon his innocent breakfast like a famished savage. He struck out like a zombie on crack. As the resulting fluorescent mush took shape, I didn't doubt this was a true reflection of Randy's mind.

Steinbacher would be German, I said.

I was hoping this would subliminally trigger associations with the name, Zuckerberg, and take our conversation forward. It didn't.

It sure is, Randy said, trying to stem the iridescent lava flow dribbling onto his Hawaiian shirt. I am the descendant of Volker Steinbacher, master butcher.

Really? I said. Ooops.

Yep. He emigrated with his wife, Liesel, in 1910.

I told myself to relax and go with the flow. I needed Randy, or someone like him, to bankroll my project. It was clear that he would not be rushed. Information is power, I reminded myself. You might learn something of value from the family history.

They arrived at Ellis Island, Randy continued, to seek their fortune in the land of the brave and the home of the free. They set foot on these fair shores with nothing but a set of butcher's knives and the clothes on their backs.

My mind wandered to Nina's apartment.

Randy regained my attention. Sadly, my granddaddy was a humourless tyrant. He made my grandmom's life a misery. Liesel eventually escaped his clutches in the dead of night, cradling her two rugrats, my daddy and my Aunty Gretchen. They endured many hardships before they made it to California.

Did you ever meet your grandparents? I asked.

No. They both died young.

It's sad not to know your grandparents.

Not in my case, Randy said. My grandmom was a broken woman. My grandpa served time on Rikers Island.

Did he catch up with Liesel?

He never found her. But his violent nature got the better of him in the end.

What happened?

He used his knives on the wrong kind of meat.

Human meat?

You got it. Sliced off some guy's buttock over a gambling debt.

There was no response to that.

Randy fell silent.

I contemplated a life standing up.

Can I ask you something else? I cut in.

Shoot.

He motioned for me to wait. More coffee, Dolores, if you ain't too busy.

I've done some homework on you. Some due diligence, you might say. I discovered that your dad's name wasn't Randolph.

No, it was Ernst, Randy replied. His face lit up. He grinned like a patient whose tumour turned out to be benign. He was playing me. He was going to make me ask the question.

OK, Randy, I acquiesced. If your daddy's name was Ernst, why are you called Randolph J Steinbacher Junior?

Randy cracked his fingers. He was happy now. How long have you got? He asked me.

I'm in no hurry. Although I would like to talk about Zuckerberg.

Sure, sure, we'll get on to Schmuckerberg soon enough.

I sat back to demonstrate my Zen state.

My daddy was a peculiar man, on account of his distressed upbringing. My folks would invite friends and family over to our house now and again when I was a boy. My saintly mom would serve a beautiful meal and would wait on the guests hand and foot. She'd make them really welcome. My dad would do the opposite. He would tell people that he went to bed, come what may, at 10.30. On the dot, he'd say, on the dot.

And then, Randy said, waving his finger in the air to indicate we were getting to the good bit, Daddy would count back from 10.30 to let the guests know how long they could stay.

My amusement was evident. Randy's fat belly jiggled up and down.

How did that work?

The old bastard would say I have to be in bed by 10.30...

…on the dot, I interjected.

On the dot, Randy agreed, and then he'd say 'and it takes me 5 minutes to get undressed, that's 10.25', 'and I need 10 minutes to perform my night time ablutions, that's 10.15', 'and I always listen to the radio for a quarter of an hour to relax, that's 10 o'clock', and so he'd go on until he told them they had to leave by 9 o'clock! Randy could hardly contain himself in the telling.

I shook my head, enjoying the moment with this endearing but frustrating man.

My daddy was a weird guy, Randy reflected.

Weren't you explaining how come you're Randolph junior and your father wasn't a Randolph at all?

So I was, he agreed. My pop was a very strange man, like I said. He was real smart, though. He was forever thumbing through journals in the barber's shop and listening to his serious radio programs. Anyways, he loved a theory. It could be about any subject. He had his own view about how pigeons return to the coop. But to get to the point, he developed this hypothesis about how the land of opportunity worked.

And how did he think it worked? I asked helpfully.

To him, it was simple. The business world loves dynasties.

That's true, isn't it?

Randy nodded. But, to my old man, it was OK for the Hearsts and the Rockefellers because they had that pedigree. But what about Joe Shmo? Randy asked as if it wasn't a rhetorical question.

I shrugged my shoulders. I don't know, I said.

They have to invent one. That was Dad's theory.

So, for you to get on, you had to be Randolph J Steinbacher Jr..

Exactly.

That's bizarre, I said.

He was a weird guy, Randy repeated.

Bring me the check, he shouted to no one in particular. Then he stood and looked directly at me. Let's go back to the hacienda and talk about that shitbag, Blubberberg.

Rich not famous

Randy's limousine drew up outside the Blue Jam.

Randy negotiated his way into the front passenger seat. The multi-talented Latino factotum I'd seen at the hacienda opened the rear door for me. I did a double-dose, quadruple take. I slid in beside a slim blonde wearing a sky blue skirt shorter than a pygmy's loincloth and come-fuck-me heels higher than the Empire State Building.

This is Cassidy, Randy said without turning around.

Pleased to meet you, I said truthfully, accepting a daintily extended hand.

Cass is my assistant, Randy explained.

I assumed she multi-tasked too.

Randy barked instructions to Cassidy as the Chevy negotiated its way through Melrose and up Beverly. Cassidy smiled benevolently at me as we pulled onto Santa Monica Boulevard for the long stretch to the beach. I failed to avert my eyes from those tanned and toned thighs. OK, so I didn't try that hard.

Randy ran out of orders for his staff. I took the opportunity to update myself on other aspects of his past.

Tell me about your surfing days, I said.

Ancient history, buddy.

Please, I urged. I gather you were good.

Better than that, Cassidy enthused.

I know it's hard to believe, looking at my perfect physique, Randy said with a grin that filled the driver's mirror, but, back in the day, I was a physical wreck.

You were a hunk, Cassidy interjected. You've seen the movies? Cassidy asked, looking at me.

I nodded.

I was top ten in the world, surfing the majors in the States, Hawaii, Cape Town, Australia, you name it.

You gave it all away when you were still young, I said. Why did you do that?

I had to choose, Randy said sadly.

Choose? Between what? I asked.

I had to choose whether to be rich or famous.

Really? I asked (and I meant it).

And you ended up both, Cassidy said.

Not exactly, Randy said wistfully. I'm rich. I'm not that famous.

Why choose one or the other? I asked. They usually go together.

Randy sat silent for a while. Unable to see his face, I couldn't tell whether he was considering the answer, choosing his words carefully or nodding off.

Randy turned full around. His eyes were moist. It was the worst decision of my life. Not a single day goes past when I don't regret it.

Cassidy leant forward to comfort him. He waved her away.

I acted out of duty, Randy said. Cassidy knows that. A decision that denies passion can never be right. I was pressured by my father. He was a weird guy like I told you. He also had this tough streak. Mean, you might say. He must have got it from that piece of shit of a pappy of his. Anyways, things were different back then. You didn't argue back. He told me that I would miss the wave if I kept surfing. He literally said that, Randy laughed, kinda clever huh? I listened to him. I felt I had to. I've cursed myself for it ever since.

The car fell silent. We gazed out over the impossibly wide Santa Monica Beach. Soon we pulled into the gravel approach road I'd hugged a few days before. Randy turned around again. The sadness must have grounded him.

When we get inside, I'm listening and you're talking, Randy said.

I don't believe you, I replied.

Nope, it's gospel, my friend, I truly am intrigued about someone who figures he can shove it up the ass of Buggerberg.

Fluction

I searched Randy's features for a clue to the real man. Was I just sport to him? Was he toying with me as a cat does a mouse? Would I ever get to roar?

We were seated on his patio in the shade. The man of many talents had served us frosted Coronas with a twist of lime. Randy was scoffing mixed nuts from a huge ceramic bowl half a handful at a time.

I figured that Randy was sizing me up too. I wasn't fooled by his dumbass behaviour. Sure he loathed the very sound of Zuckerberg's name. But, without a compelling business case, Randy wouldn't be throwing money at some guy he sat next to on the LA flight.

This was my moment. I didn't want it spoiled by any diversions. I took a swig from my beer and waited for an invitation. I needed some assurance that when I pulled out onto the freeway, there wouldn't be some roadblock over the next hill.

Show me what you got, Randy said, relinquishing the empty nut bowl in favour of his beer.

Suddenly, after the rehearsing, I felt nervous being out on the stage. I didn't want to fluff my lines.

I've got something better than Facebook.

Randy laughed. His huge frame convulsed. It did sound like a fanciful claim.

He hadn't interrupted me so I felt inclined to continue. When I was in France…

I looked at him to check for tomfoolery.

…When I was in France, I continued, I met this beautiful girl.

Randy raised an eyebrow. How do you like Cass?

Please, Randy, I said in a firm tone that surprised us both.

Her name was Nina. *Is* Nina, actually. She's a sociology lecturer at the Sorbonne.

Impressive, Randy whistled by way of observation rather then obstruction.

Nina opened my eyes to the impending knowledge revolution, as she called in. I'd heard of digital media, obviously, but I hadn't understood the way the global economy would be reshaped. In particular, I hadn't grasped the way investment would shift from manufacturing, making things, to services. In other words, to supporting lifestyles.

Randy sipped attentively at his beer. This was the most serious I'd seen him.

Nina was an intoxicating cocktail of brains and beauty. I admit I got drunk on it. The trouble was she remained sober.

That's the story of my life, Randy reflected sadly.

I'm only including this personal stuff, I continued, spitting a lime pip out into the palm of my hand, because it introduces the guy in Nina's life who followed me. His name was Miki. He was, rather *is*, Japanese. I think I told you about him on the plane.

Randy nodded. He was fully engaged. It was like sitting with a different person now. He was a schoolboy rather than a playboy.

Miki was a senior exec at Sony. He studied at Berkeley, by the way. Well educated, experienced and smart, he could read the play before most of the others. He wanted out of the rust-bucket factories in Yokohama and into the innovation scene playing out in the bedrooms and garages of Silicon Valley.

Randy raised two fingers to the man of many talents. That's all very well, he said, but Bill Gates, Steve Jobs and Suckmydick are light years and megabucks ahead of you.

They are and they aren't, I responded.

Randy accepted his replacement beer, sitting forward in the process to pay close attention. Go on.

They are household names. They have established products. They are billionaires many times over. That's crystal clear. But…

…Is there a but?

There is actually, I said, pausing for effect. I've been in the States for quite a few years now and have been working on this project night and day. Miki has been here too for most of that time.

So the girl gave him the flick…

…Miki's love life is not the issue. More importantly, he has been head down and ass up recruiting the whiz kid programmers and designers that we need. In this age of disruption, finding the right talent is no easy task.

You can't holler for them on the street corner, can you?

No, you can't. But, beyond all those guys, we have someone else on our team who is our secret weapon. This dude has been developing the point of difference that will make our social media venture unique.

Tell me more, buddy, Randy said, standing up to restore circulation without taking his eyes off me.

Nina had a profound effect on me, I continued. She changed the way I see things and the way I think about people. Before I met her, the world was a simple place. To me things were black and white. There were the rich and the poor, the smart and the dumb, the healthy and the sick and so on.

Randy sat down again, nodding for me to continue.

Nina opened my eyes to the truth that nothing is immutable. Everything and everyone is in perpetual motion.

Isn't that quantum mechanics?

Yes it's like that. But this is my point.

Hit me! Randy said, full of enthusiasm.

Your friend Zuckerberg and his acolytes developed what they called social networks, am I right?

Randy nodded.

It is based on a static premise.

Randy looked perplexed.

A Facebook friend is a friend is a friend.

I don't get you, Randy said with a hint of frustration.

But you'd like to, right?

Right.

Before I expand on this, I need to ask you a question.

Randy inclined his head as a gesture of compliance.

How bad do you want to fuck the Zuck?

Dr. Levine

In response to my question, Randy's persona changed again. He was neither playboy nor schoolboy. He was now ballboy, sitting forward in his chair, with his fingertips to the floor, ready to chase something down.

There you are! A female voice with an exaggerated Southern drawl called out.

I turned around. A larger than life, exquisitely manicured, middle-aged blonde flounced in our direction. She stifled Randy's attempts to introduce me by smothering him in sticky red kisses.

Don't forget the dinner party tonight, she insisted, allowing Randy to come up for air.

The blonde bombsite winked at me in passing and was gone.

Thank God for the pool boy, Randy said.

It took me a while to cotton on.

Otherwise I'd be on wife support, he moaned.

I smiled. So, what would you give to get even? I said, steering Randy back to the matter at hand.

Since you ask, Randy said, I'd give my maiden aunt's left testicle if that would help.

That was good enough for me.

In that case, I said, reaching for my bulging man bag, have a look at this.

I pulled a sheaf of papers from my bro-sack and extracted a magazine.

Do you remember this copy of Time magazine? I asked like a lawyer cross-examining.

Randy saw Mark Zuckerberg's smiling face on the front cover. Sure do, he said. It made me puke the first time you showed it to me.

It's funny how things work out, I said, flicking through to the middle of the magazine and folding it back. Do you know this guy?

You're not LAPD, are you? Randy asked, projecting his infectious smile as he took the magazine from me.

He peered at the face of a swarthy man with grey thinning hair, a black beard and round rimless glasses. Dr. Jeremiah Levine, Randy read his name from the photo's caption.

Nope, I don't know this john, Randy said, flipping the periodical down onto the table that was now messy with escaped peanuts, beer bottles and sucked limes. Should I? He added.

I predict you will very soon, I said, picking up the magazine and returning it to my pile of papers.

Randy signalled to the jack-of-all-trades to source two more beers. How come?

Because I've flown him down to meet you, I said, enjoying this moment where I was wresting some measure of control.

A dish

Jerry was expected in ten minutes' time. I briefed Randy on the good Dr. Levine.

It's funny how things work out, I said. I didn't want to talk to you on the plane.

I may be dumb, but I'm not stupid, Randy said.

In actual fact, I didn't buy the magazine at the airport for the Zuckerberg article at all. I wanted to check out what Jerry had been blabbing to the media about.

So you know Levine well?

We were at Oxford together.

Another Limey?

No, South African.

A distant look played on Randy's face. I guessed he was riding a memory wave off Cape Town. At that moment, the clickety-clack of heels rang out in the distance. Cassidy came into view with Jeremiah a deliberate few paces behind her.

Dr. Levine tells me you are expecting him?

There was a distinct edge to Cassidy's question. Was she pissed that Randy hadn't told her about Jerry?

Randy struggled upright from his padded cane chair. Knowing Jerry's feeble frame from way back, I winced as Randy's handshake crushed his bones and hearty backslap took the wind from his sails. Cassidy organised a drink for Jerry and herself. She joined us without seeking Randy's permission. What role did she play in Randy's affairs? Her presence irritated me. I wasn't ready to share our ideas with anyone more of a stranger than Randy. More so, I didn't want the distraction that she would present for Jerry who was an incorrigible pervert.

Randy's demeanour was worrying me too. In the short wait for Dr. Levine's arrival, he'd been pacing the room. I feared I'd exhausted his attention span in the preliminaries. If this proved the case, I suspected his mind would surf back to Cape Town. Any moment, he would be asking Jerry about the waves these days off the Cape. Randy wouldn't realise how pointless such a question would be. Dr. Jeremiah was an academic. To him the beach was an expanse of silicon dioxide in the form of quartz separating the ocean from the adjacent land formation.

Dr. Jeremiah Levine here, I said, extending the upright palm of my hand in Jerry's direction, is an important member of my team.

I glanced at Cassidy. She was frowning and fidgeting in her seat. She hadn't been included in our earlier conversations so she clearly didn't know what I meant by 'team'. I hesitated a moment to see if she would interject. The thought clearly crossed her mind, but she didn't speak. Cassidy held sway with Randy, but there were limits.

As I explained earlier, my associate Miki, the ex-Sony executive, has successfully recruited a team of tech-savvy screenagers in the nick of time before puberty set in...I paused Henry-style for the amused response...but now it's my pleasure to reveal to you the point of difference, the point of supremacy to be precise, we have over your very good friend.

Randy eyeballed Jeremiah.

I cut Jerry off before he could speak. He was a brains hero and a communications zero.

Dr. Levine is the Professor of Social Psychology at UCLA, I continued. He has helped us to create a new concept for social media that is rooted in the fundamental principles of human psychology. When brought to market, this will be a next generation social network product that that will make Facebook look lame.

Randy's eyes were shining. He was intrigued. But his trademark impatience reared its head again.

You gonna tell me what it is or am I heading to the hot tub where a man should be at this time of day?

We had been called to put up or shut up. Randy and Cassidy surveyed our faces to see if we were playing them. This was Jerry's moment. I motioned to him to take up the reins.

The professor leant forward in his chair. He looked at his feet, interlacing his fingers as he searched for the right approach.

You are familiar, of course, with social media, he said. His accent was a crazy mélange of plummy home counties English, harsh Afrikaans and laid back Californication. His voice was so soft that Randy and Cassidy had to crane their necks forward to hear him.

You are familiar with traditional social media, Jerry whispered, but I doubt that you have yet encountered psychosocial media.

What the hell is that? Randy said in an abrasive tone.

He was clearly not a man to be played for a fool.

All will be revealed in good time, I interjected mischievously.

Tell me already! Randy stormed. Plenty of people have starved reading a cookbook, he wailed, collapsing back into his chair in exasperation.

For you, it is a kind of dish, I said, having calculated the impact of a message that would string him out even further.

A dish? Whaddaya mean a dish?

The kind of dish that's best eaten cold.

Not for me

Cassidy rang me the next day. It was an unknown number. I let it go through to voicemail. It was lucky I lchecked my messages in an idle moment. She'd fixed a follow-up dinner at the Hotel Bel-Air.

The previous day's sales pitch had culminated in a doozy of a jacuzzi experience. Randy excused himself to do some 'housework'. Cassidy showed us to the hot tub deck on the other side of the property. She proudly pointed to the stunning view out over the San Fernando Valley.

Jerry's tongue was hanging out. He looked longingly at the beautiful scenery - Cassidy. I could tell the prospect of a near-naked frolic with this gorgeous girl was getting him all hot and bothered.

Jerry stripped off before invitations. Cassidy handed him a towel, expecting him to cover his privates. Instead he mopped his publics. I took the opportunity to steer Cassidy away from Jerry's mounting expectation.

What did Randy mean by 'housework'? I whispered to her. The prospect of him doing the dusting in a floral pinafore was less than inspiring.

Cassidy laughed, averting her gaze from the sight of Dr. Levine's swollen goods.

'Housework' for Randy is talking to his wife, Sonia, she explained.

Cassidy pronounced the name phonetically in three venom-laced syllables. So-knee-ah. I tucked this reaction behind my ear for later.

Could you do me a massive favour? I pleaded with Cassidy.

She listened, smiled and nodded. Predictably, Jerry's excitement at sharing the hot tub with Cassidy wasn't reciprocal. She beat a tactical retreat. I could breathe again, having contained the risk of her messing with a loaded gun.

'Last one in's a fairy!' Randy sang out, bounding down the stairs and bombing himself into the spa.

Gingerly, Jerry and I joined the naked walrus. I slid below the surface, safe in the knowledge that Dr. Jerry would survive another day without a criminal molestation charge. When I came up for air, I found myself in no state to relax.

Say, Jeremiah, Randy said, wiping the frothing bubbles from his mouth, don't those right-handers down at the Crayfish Factory scare the crap out of you!

I was recalled to the here and now by a slender hand on my shoulder. I looked around to find the beautiful Cassidy. Her gown was as revealing as my wide-eyed reaction.

I was surprised to find her alone. Where's Randy? I asked, scanning the bar.

He asked me to handle this meeting for him, Cassidy said as if that should have been my expectation in the first place.

A marguerita, Sonny, she called to the buffed black barman.

Meeting the gorgeous Cassidy on her own was unsettling me, at various levels. I guessed that was the plan. I wasn't sure what to drink. I needed to stay on my guard.

A beer, I said to Sonny, keeping it simple.

What's going on here? I asked Cassidy.

What do you mean?

I think you know what I mean, I said, adjusting my bar stool so that I could see out into the restaurant. I had a sneaky feeling that Cassidy might be getting a jump on Randy before he showed.

What's going on here is that you and I are having a pleasant drink, she said.

Is that what's happening?

You tell me, she responded playfully, sculling her cocktail and then signalling to Sonny for another round.

OK, you win, I conceded. When is Randy getting here?

He's not, she said, pouring the dregs of her first marguerita into the fresh one.

Fair enough, I said, walking away from the bar to compose myself. I could see Cassidy eyeing me. She was winning this encounter, whatever it was intended to achieve.

I needed to at least break even in the contest. I decided to segue into different territory to gain some measure of control.

How long have you been working for Randy?

About five years, I guess.

I whistled through my teeth. You don't look old enough, I said.

Thank you kind sir, Cassidy replied, lowering her eyes at the compliment.

There was a moment's electricity. We both felt it. What exactly do you do for Randy? I asked.

Is this Twenty Questions?

Can it be?

If you like, Cassidy responded, blowing an air kiss to a young woman whose jet-black hair was pulled so tightly back into a bun that it was crushing her frontal lobe.

May I ask what you do for Randy? Exactly.

Cassidy swizzled her marguerita for a moment. I'm his assistant, she responded calmly, looking me in the eye.

What do you assist him with? I asked. Exactly.

That's two gone, Cassidy said. Pretty much with everything.

I assumed she was implying sexual favours, particularly given her vitriolic comments about Randy's wife.

Run out at two questions, have you? Cassidy teased.

Why did Randy send his assistant tonight and not come himself?

Cassidy pondered her response while sucking her fingertips to taste the salt she'd skimmed from the rim of her glass. Randy is not a detail guy.

I was unhappy with that response. The expression on my face made that clear.

You asked me a question and I'm answering it, Cassidy insisted. Randy is a big picture man. A big everything man actually. She smiled at the thought.

Was she being suggestive? Or was I reading too much into it like a clairvoyant on a slow night?

You'd have me believe, I said much louder than I'd intended, that Randolph J. Steinbacher Jr., one of the premier venture capitalists in California, is considering investing a billion dollars, in round figures...I weighed the wisdom of the words about to emerge from my mouth.

...on my say so. Cassidy completed the sentence for me. Yes, that's right. Exactly, she added with a grin.

Bun-brain lady, who turned out to be the Maître D, appeared beside us. Your table is ready, she announced.

Let's go eat, Cassidy proposed, gathering up her silver sequined handbag as she shot me a triumphant smile.

Cassidy led me directly to what must have been her favourite table. The view of the Hollywood Hills was spectacular. A posse of waiters fussed over us, smoothing napkins into our laps and offering the sparkling rainwater. I was feeling uncomfortable with how things were going. Cassidy was playing me. She was a pro. It's easy to underestimate beautiful women. Yet I'd never done that with Nina.

I pondered why that was. Cassidy snapped me out of it. Tell me about psychosocial media, she said.

I'm not a detail guy, I responded, smugly raising my glass to toast.

Touché, she said. Randy is taken with the idea. That's dangerous as far as I'm concerned. So convince me why he should invest a billion dollars. In round figures.

Isn't revenge enough for Randolph J Steinbacher Jr.?

Maybe for him, Cassidy said. But it isn't for me.

The service at the restaurant Hotel Bel-Air was beyond attentive. The waitstaff were obsequious with a capital O. They busied themselves folding napkins and sweeping malevolent crumbs off the table with a silver brush. As they rarely did anything of importance, I figured they were there to bump up the check.

My name is Ryan, our well-groomed waitperson announced. I will be your waiter tonight, he added.

In that case, who is our waiter now? I asked.

I'm sorry, sir? Ryan responded.

Given that you *will* be our waiter, I explained, I was just asking...

...Don't mind my friend, Cassidy interjected with a radiant smile.

Ryan and I waited for Cassidy to finish her sentence. She didn't.

I tried to get along with Ryan for Cassidy's sake. However, my patience was severely tested when I excused myself for a trip to the little boy's room.

On completing my mission, I found Ryan waiting for me outside the men's. For a second, I thought he might mug me. He followed me back to the table.

Welcome back, sir, he said on the way.

If you missed me so much, I said over my shoulder, you should have come in and held it for me.

I'm sorry, sir? Ryan responded.

With a napkin, I added for good measure.

Cassidy flirted with me over the entrée of asparagus wrapped in prosciutto drizzled with a dill balsamic dressing. I think that was what she was doing. She made small talk with me. She smiled at me a lot. Was she there as a honey trap or was she really Randy's right-hand woman? Would I finish the night in her jar of honey or would I be using my right hand?

The Californian merlot so maligned in that movie was as smooth as Cassidy's perfect skin. I was relaxing far too much. I called the piss time-out to try to refocus.

Are you going to explain psychosocial media to me or shall we just make small talk? Cassidy asked, as Ryan slid my seat forward to meet my rear end.

I forced a neutral smile. It would be my pleasure, I responded.

I was interrupted by the arrival of my doubly-minute steak that was miniscule as well as short cooked. Cassidy chose the langoustine in its shell roasted with artichokes with an infusion of Grand Marnier. For the foodies amongst you, my diminutive steak was served accompanied by a lonely newborn carrot with the stalk still on and a round of parsnip the size of a dime. A midnight excursion to Burger King seemed on the cards.

Are you on Facebook? I asked Cassidy.

Who isn't?

Have you got many friends?

Enough.

Can you have enough? I asked.

What point are you making? Cassidy asked, digging an obstinate mouthful out of her shell.

What is the point of having a Facebook friend? I continued.

There's no point.

But there *is* a point. Facebook has become a popularity contest.

So what? They are making a mint. They monetise the product in a dozen different ways.

Sure they do. They clip the ticket more often than a zealous bus conductor.

Cassidy winked at the ever-attentive Ryan.

Let me ask you a question, I persisted. Why do you think those bastards use the term, 'friend'?

Go on, Cassidy said.

Thanks to his telepathic powers, Ryan produced a finger bowl from thin air like a magician with a rabbit.

It's ironic, I said, beaming in triumph.

Ironic?

Of course. Facebook as good as owns the word 'friend' now. Or at least they will. But this is the thing.

I leant forward and held Cassidy's hand out of instinct. They call the contacts 'friends' because they don't meet any of the accepted criteria for friendship!

Cassidy stroked my hand back and smiled at me. You're quite smart, aren't you?

I like to think so.

Correct me if I'm wrong, Cassidy said, but I get the feeling that you, or most probably that pervert professor friend of yours, has developed an approach to creating another dimension of social media friendship.

You're quite smart, I said.

I like to think so, Cassidy replied.

Psychosocial media

I had a repulsive dream.

Randy sauntered into my bedroom. He stood there towelling his wet hair. He was dressed in an undersized gold bathrobe from which his nether regions protruded. 'Rise and shine', 'Rise and shine', he sang gently like a kindly entertainments officer on a cruise ship. I was burying my head under the pillow to drown out the bonhomie. Nina slept soundly beside me.

I woke up to a repulsive sight. Randy was in my bedroom, dressed in an undersized gold bathrobe, encouraging me out of bed while he dried his wet hair.

I was disoriented. I glanced over to Nina. Only her blonde hair was visible over the covers. I looked back. Blonde hair? It wasn't Nina. Is that? Could it be? Did we? What is Randy doing here?

I stuffed my head back under the pillow. Randy? Cassidy? Not in the same bed? I needed to recall. What happened after we finished dinner?

Memories of loud music and flashing lights crashed the party in my thumping head. Cassidy and I hit a club. I broke out my moves - both of them. What were we drinking? What were we taking? Whatever it was, my pounding headache told me it couldn't have been recommended by the WHO.

And before that? There was still a lot of time unaccounted for. We went for cocktails. Up in the lift. The bar had an amazing view. You could see forever over the twinkling lights of LA rolled out like a carpet of stars beneath those famous Hollywood hills. Cassidy looked great. She kissed me. She dug me. But why?

We were there for ages. We must have moved onto the club pretty late. What were we talking about? It was heavy. Serious. Of course, psychosocial media.

It was coming back to me. I took encouragement that I could remember the important stuff. I was repressing the scary shit. I was giving Cassidy my well-rehearsed pitch - the one that's supposed to sound like I'm making it up as I go along.

Jeremiah is the most brilliant man I have ever met. He was head nerd at university. Most of the guys ran a mile when they saw him. I rather liked his eccentricity. He was harmless really, except when you had a girl with you.

Cassidy was attentive. She let me prattle on.

Jerry was obsessed with the concept of affiliation. He was fascinated with the way human association worked. He did incredible laboratory research mapping the relevant centres of the brain. He wrote brilliant papers on affiliative learning. He developed his approach into a doctorate thesis. It became the seminal academic work on the nature versus nurture debate about the human affiliative drive.

People find this stuff impressive. Cassidy was no exception. She had eyes only for me. I was growing hornier than a priest watching nunny porn.

When Myspace and then Facebook emerged, they transformed the communications landscape. No one had seen the like before. They were revolutionary. Transformative. It was Disruptive Technology 101. Lives were changed. Society was turned on its head.

She was still looking at me with those big blue eyes.

I studied these social networks. I couldn't help thinking that people would eventually get bored with them. To me, they're as shallow as a toddler's swimming pool.

Cassidy kept lining up the shooters.

I couldn't get Jerry out of my mind, wondering where he'd got to with his affiliation research. Once I got to LA, I made a beeline for Jeremiah. I knew he was teaching at UCLA. I tracked him down. He was more eccentric than ever. More like a mad professor. He didn't have a mobile phone. He only used the Internet for research. Yet he understood it as if he'd invented it. Maybe he did work with Tim Berners-Smith, I added, winking at Cassidy.

Those blue saucers were still locked onto me. She rested her chin onto those perfectly manicured hands.

He sat me down at his messy, coffee-stained desk. He launched into a rambling monologue about his latest theorem. I cut him off.

What do you make of Facebook? I asked him. Have you heard of it? I added, just to be sure.

Jeremiah blinked at me. He removed his glasses and rubbed at his beard. He mumbled in that annoying way of his. I asked him to speak up.

I find the concept of Facebook interesting, he said. The phenomenon of social media is fascinating, don't you think?

I nodded.

I see Facebook as a prototype. A first foray, if you like, into the digitisation of affiliation. Like all first efforts, it can be improved upon.

I smiled at him. He had not disappointed me. Could *you* improve on it? I asked.

He shot me his 'do bears shit in the woods?' look.

What do you need? I entreated him. Tell me what you need.

Money. Lots of it.

I'll get it for you, I promised, jumping to my feet in excitement. Tell me what you're going to do with it.

With a lot of cash, I could re-invent affiliation, Jerry said solemnly.

Reinvent it? How would you do that?

I would transform social media to serve that purpose.

What purpose exactly? I begged him. Explain.

In lay terms, it would generate true online friendships, Dr. Levine said as if the answer was obvious.

Does this thing have a name?

Yes. Psychosocial media.

Psychosocial media?

It is in essence psychological social media. It is the marriage of psychology with digital communications.

What does it do? I asked.

It makes Facebook look like Space Invaders.

How?

It adds psychological testing, personality profiling, psychosocial measurement to the process of electronic communications.

But how does it outdo Facebook? I begged impatiently.

Simple. A psychosocial media friend is, by definition, a friend.

I needed to understand this. Do you mean a psychosocial media friend is better than a real-life friend? I stammered.

I mean that a psychosocial friend is the only real friend. There are no other friends worthy of that description.

Don't live in the past

Reality was becoming grosser by the second.

Randy sat right beside me on the bed. The whale's penis was winking at me. Moby Dick? I prodded Cassidy. She groaned. Surely to God, I didn't. Not with Randy. He's not my type.

Cassidy came to. She registered Randy's huge presence. She climbed out of bed, wrapping a sheet around her.

Put that thing away, Randy, she said, padding towards the bathroom.

Cassidy returned immediately, wrapped in nothing bigger than a hand towel. I didn't want Randy seeing her like that. I wanted him out of my bedroom. To be precise, I wanted him out of this bedroom because I had absolutely no idea where I was.

The trouble was Randy seemed more than comfortable, perched there next to me, rubbing his hair, playing dick-a-boo out of his robe.

So far from covering her modesty, Cassidy walked round to Randy's side of the bed. She tousled his hair and styled it back in the Elvis-ian manner that he wore it.

You OK, sweetie? She asked solicitously.

I guess, Randy replied like a pouting schoolboy.

He reminded me of Fred Flintstone. That line of thought wasn't helping. What the hell was going on? I had more questions than a three-year-old quizmaster.

Randy stood up, tossing his fluffy white bath towel into the corner. I need to understand more of how this psychosocial media actually works, Randy said, slumping down on the bed to lie down beside me.

I turned my head to avoid the direct line of sight to Randy-Fred's blubbery face. What's going on here, Randy? I replied. Why are you in my bedroom for starters?

Randy stood up and moved away. That was a victory of sorts. He looked offended though.

It's *my* bedroom, if it's anyone's, he said. I own this suite, he said sniffily.

But what are you doing here, with us? I said, turning to Cassidy, who was naked except for her panties. Modesty clearly wasn't her strong suit.

Cass gave me a very positive report before she turned in. I'm excited.

I want to get down to business.

How could she have done that? We were both wasted. Or maybe she really was playing me?

Why don't you meet us in the lobby for breakfast? Cassidy suggested.

I could have them bring something up, Randy countered with an expectant look.

I scowled at Cassidy.

Be a sweet boy, Cass said, snapping closed her bra.

Very well, Randy said in a defeated tone. But I got a busy day today and I wanna be loaded up with the lowdown before I head out in an hour.

Randy took off his robe as he left the room. It was a fuck-you gesture I admired. Once the door was opened, I could just see past Randy's wobbling buttocks. Beyond his Grand Canyon I could see an apartment suite pretty much the size of the real thing.

What's going on, Cass? I asked, climbing gingerly from the bed.

Cassidy put her arms around me. She had shimmied herself into skintight aquamarine jeans. She pecked me on the lips.

No, seriously, I whined.

This could be your billion-dollar day, she said, squirming from my grip. In round figures, she teased.

I scanned the room for my clothes. What about last night? I insisted.

Don't live in the past, Cassidy scolded me.

She blew me a kiss on her way out. See you in the lobby, she called back.

Like a Navajo tracker, I followed the scent of my undies. The perfume led me to the trail of my abandoned clothes. I found them scattered at regular intervals between the living room and the bedroom. The apartment was something else. The artwork alone could have graced a self-respecting palace.

I needed to focus. I pictured my dead paternal grandmother. It was a blank frame with no face in it. I had never met her. I tried my mother's mother. Same result. What did I take last night? How to concentrate?

I imagined how much space a billion bucks (in round figures) in one-dollar bills might occupy. I found that thought inspiring. If only I could stop the sound of AC/DC playing Wembley Stadium inside my head. I returned to my boxers. Then I retraced the path to the entry hall, donning trousers, shirt, socks and shoes along the way

I looked around for a mirror. I remembered there was a grotesque gold-trimmed looking glass in the bedroom. I positioned myself in front of it. Still summoning the courage to look within it, I studied the frame. It was elaborately decorated with overblown figures from Greek mythology. The big-breasted lion with snakes for hair did nothing to settle my stomach. I dared to take a peek at myself. I looked away again. I was a sight with sore eyes. I licked my fingers. I impersonated a long-suffering mother prising dirt from a grubby child's face with her fingers. I looked dreadful but my mother would love me, if I ever remembered to ring her.

After blundering into bedrooms, bathrooms and a closet or two, I found the front door. I summoned the elevator. The lift operator was dressed like an extra on the set of Charlie and the Chocolate Factory. He looked me up and down. The elevator followed the same trajectory.

Sorry, sir, Willy Wonka apologised. It has a mind of its own.

That was more than I could say for myself. This joyride was doing my insides no good. I was relieved to make it to the ground floor before I threw up.

Where's the breakfast buffet? I inquired of a second Oompa-Loompa standing by the lift.

Could that very attractive woman be waving to you? The bellboy speculated.

I smiled politely. I circumnavigated the plush leather sofas that ringed the circular lobby like a wagon train. Cassidy took me by the arm to escort me in the direction of the Wipe-Out restaurant.

What *did* happen last night? I asked.

You're quite the historian, aren't you? Cassidy replied, placing me next to Randy at his reserved table.

All-in

Thankfully, Randy was eating grapefruit like a normal human being. My tender stomach could not have borne one of his food deconstruction extravaganzas.

Sonia's got us both on the new grapefruit diet, Randy explained. It's a game of patience, he added, scraping the last sinews of fruit out of the husk before picking up his grapefruit juice.

My body is a temple, Randy muttered like a mantra.

I looked to Cassidy for clarification.

Normally it's a crack house, Randy added with a guilty smirk.

It's Sonia, Cassidy hissed. If he waits a couple of days, this nonsense will be consigned to the bin of history along with the Atkins diet, the soup thing, that regime where you can only eat food picked or killed the same day and all of Sonia's other get-thin-quick schemes.

Grapefruit-free dishes were placed on our side of the table.

Is there such a thing as a disengagement ring? Randy asked in a dejected voice as he eyed our eggs, smoked salmon, oysters and hash browns enviously.

I know time is tight today, Cassidy said to Randy, so why don't you fire away with your questions?

Randy sucked noisily on his straw like a naughty schoolboy. Cassidy has given the prospect the once over. She thinks there could be a return on investment, even at venture capital levels. So, run over the target with me now. Tell me how your concept ranks against Facebook?

Sure, I said, mopping at the Kilpatrick escaping from the corner of my mouth. 'Frenzy', that's our working title, will be a psychosocial version of Facebook. We will leverage off its popularity, but ours will be a quantum leap forward. It will capture the public's imagination by virtue of its absolute point of difference. When you are hooked into Frenzy, you can't choose or accept friends. The system will determine who can and should be your friends. Based on the various psychometric testing modules developed by Dr. Jeremiah, you will be matched according to your deep personality with people with whom a friendship would be meaningful and rewarding.

Why Frenzy? Randy asked.

It's a play on *Friend-sy*.

I don't like it.

It's a working title, Cassidy reassured him.

There will be no video, I continued. The relationships will be conducted through typed messages. Dr. Levine is insistent on this point. What Dr. Levine calls 'intense friendship' has nothing to do with sexuality or physical attraction. It is not some shallow form of online dating.

Couldn't I just send a photo or arrange to meet this friend?

No, you couldn't, I explained. We have now perfected the platform so that any attempt to identify yourself gets scrambled.

Randy ordered another grapefruit. He was pensive. What did you mean by 'should'? You said candidates or whatever they're called will be matched with people who 'should' be their friends.

That's right. When we make friends in what was once called the real world, we do so for all sorts of reasons. And, being imperfect creatures, human beings make friends with many of the wrong people.

The 'wrong' people, huh? Randy muttered

Dr. Levine will provide chapter and verse and can answer any further questions you might have. Suffice to say for now, that people will make kick-ass friendships thanks to the science, the Internet and the sheer numbers of people around the globe ready, willing and able to be a true friend should they be fundamentally compatible with them.

I checked their faces. Randy seemed satisfied. Cassidy was smiling at me again.

Run the business model past me again, Randy said.

Let me put it this way. Frenzy will generate a feeding frenzy for its investors. We will have all of the monetising capability of Facebook, Google and the rest, but our targeting of the advertising push will be pinpoint.

What does that mean? Randy asked, picking more pith from his teeth. 'Pinpoint'?

Facebook is like throwing a dart blindfold, I explained.

Yes, It's only as good as the underlying algorithms, Cassidy agreed.

Correct, and they are amazing, I conceded. But we will have deep psychometric testing to work with. No other social media program has that.

So we won't be blindfolded? Randy considered the proposition.

Quite the reverse, I said. We will be aiming at the bull's eye with laser guidance.

Fuckerbum's bull's eye! Randy chipped in excitedly.

Exactly. Randy, we've cut the numbers multiple times with a full range of sensitivities. If you don't make a hundred percent every year, I'll go on the grapefruit diet...for life.

Careful what you wish for, pal, Randy said with a smile. If I'm kicking in a small fortune, Randy continued, I want to know that other folks have some bare skin in the game.

I get that, I said reassuringly. I have some serious Asian finance to bring to the table.

The Chinese can be mighty hard to do business with, Randy mused.

Not all of them, Cassidy said.

Do you remember those Taiwanese jackasses? Randy said to Cassidy.

That was different, Cassidy reassured him. We learned from that, remember? Play at home by our rules, not theirs.

Do I know these dudes? Randy asked me.

Possibly, I said.

Are you gonna identify them?

I hesitated.

Cassidy intervened. Randy, I suggest an all-in.

An all-in? Randy pondered the proposition.

Like a bad cricket team, I felt all-out. What's an all-in? I asked cautiously.

Cassidy explained. Let's get the whole shooting match in the same room.

Every single motherfucker, Randy confirmed.

Yes. We get everyone who is going to be involved to come here to the

Bel-Air. We'll lock ourselves in and we'll walk out with a deal or we won't, Cassidy explained.

What does 'every motherfucker' mean? I asked

It means what it says, Cassidy said.

So, you mean the twelve year olds writing the code before their moms put them to bed? Them too? I asked.

Yep, Randy said. These are my terms. That's how we do business. Isn't that so, Cass?

Yep.

Are you in? Randy asked. All-in?

I'm in, I agreed. All-in.

The days of Frenzy

I surveyed the group seated at the sumptuous Oregon board table in the business wing of Randy's suite at the Bel-Air. It was a weird bunch. They reminded me of the intergalactic creatures gathered round the bar in that famous scene from Star Wars.

I was nervous but relieved at the same time. Herding cats had nothing on assembling this motley crew. I played spot the loony while we waited to get underway. There were too many to choose from between the outrageous venture capitalists, the geeky programmers and the loser academics. Fortunately the slick PR guys and the pretentious designers hadn't joined us yet.

The techos were putting the final touches to the multimedia presentation. Loo Jin Pao sniffed and scratched. I'd collected him from the airport the night before. The white snow now controlled him. He had trouble concentrating. He rarely made eye contact anymore.

By contrast, Yukio, an old family friend of Miki's parents, sat upright and dignified. He was a man of few words and they were all in Japanese. Randy rounded off the capitalist team. He needs no introduction.

The geeks – Axel, Marco, Lexi, Zapper, Konrad and Angel - passed the time watching videos and playing games, each in a world of their own.

Jeremiah sat there with his UCLA research assistants on either side. No need to tell you what he was doing. His eyes were locked onto Cassidy, who was seated at a safe distance from Jerry's wandering hands.

I'd come to understand why Randy relied so heavily upon her. Randy had a head for business. He had a sixth sense for an opportunity. He could unearth one if it was lined in a lead box and buried in ice. But, for all his business nous, Randy was flaky. He blew hot and cold. He would react with his heart not his head. Cassidy was the opposite. She was analytical, constant and level headed. She provided sage advice backed by relevant data.

Miki sat with me at the head of the table. He and I shared executive responsibilities. Every day, I thanked a God I didn't believe in for Miki. He was deeply strategic. Beyond that, I prized the fact that he was dependable. He and I were minor investors in money but the principal underwriters of the project in terms of leadership and management. This was our creation. We had been working on it for years. If it failed, the cost to the others would be in dollars and days. Failure to us would be the end of the world.

The presentation was loaded and ready. I called the meeting to order.

Welcome one and all to the all-in, to the Frenzy all-in to be precise. We are the privileged few. We are the people lucky enough to be in on this amazing project from the very beginning. From the ground up as it were. We are here for different reasons. We bring different resources to this incredible enterprise. But we are united in our drive to succeed.

I looked around the table. Miki nodded encouragement. The others were looking at me. They were paying attention. This was a miracle in itself. I felt emboldened to make the big call. The one Miki and I were relying upon.

Facebook is the Roman Empire. It is ubiquitous. It is all-powerful. It is invincible. It is the zenith of human aspiration. It is the peak of human achievement. It will endure. Forever.

Facebook is the Third Reich. It has conquered the world. The weak have perished and the master race has prevailed.

The Romans and the Nazis were deluded. Mark Zuckerberg similarly so. No empire lasts forever. We are the barbarian hordes. We are the allied forces. The days of Facebook are numbered. If we commit, truly commit our skills and resources, we will herald the fall of Facebook…

My pause was beyond pregnant. It birthed.

…and the rise of the days of Frenzy.

Striking a deal

The presentations were done and dusted.

Jeremiah outlined the base concept behind Frenzy. Miki ran through the business plan, laying out the risks and returns, the market and competitor analysis and the cashflow sensitivities. The geeks explained the gobbledygook of the code, the algorithms and the logic of the graphical interface.

I caught Cassidy's eye. We were straining to read the body language of the investors. Johnny was a cat on a hot tin roof, excusing himself several times to go to the bathroom. Randy rode the slides like a rollercoaster, exhilarated at times, depressed at others. Yukio? There was no way of telling how he was reacting or what he was thinking. Miki probably understood, but I couldn't ask him there in front of a room full of people.

A feast was laid out on the expansive patio. Calls of nature were answered in the affirmative. Plates were piled fat and high or diet low. At another time, an analysis of the dietary habits would have been instructive.

After the comfort stop, I called the meeting back to order. It was time to strike a deal. The questions about the concept, the code and the capital-raising were answered to a level of satisfaction. Miki and I responded to the questions. The adolescents looked bored for the most part. Loo Jin Pao sniffed and scratched like a man with the flu in a swamp full of midges.

Yukio, who'd been mute for two hours, weighed into the debate in spectacular fashion. The detail is in the devil, he said.

Miki turned to Yukio, whispering in Japanese. There was a lot of smiling and nodding.

Yukio cleared his throat. The devil is in the detail, he announced proudly.

Miki smiled at his protégé. Our lawyers should be here by now, he said, motioning to Cassidy to let them in.

A baseball team of guys entered the room. They fussed around, assembling spare seats and removing coats and ties. They laid out the contents of their archive boxes, piling draft contracts higher than the Rocky Mountains. A short, elderly man with thick glasses commenced proceedings from a legal perspective. At the end of each sentence, a thin, bespectacled oriental gentleman translated the presentation into Japanese.

The schoolkids switched off at the first mention of conditions precedent. By contrast Loo perked up at this point. He interrupted the legal speak flow.

The most important clause in any contract is how you get out of it, he pronounced.

I thought we were trying to get into it, Randy responded sarcastically.

It's like a dark tunnel, Loo persisted. Don't go in if you're not sure how to get out.

Miki diffused the issue. Gentlemen, I assure you there are robust safeguards for all parties in the draft contract. Mr. Loo, I promise that this particular cave has a neon exit sign.

As no one commented further, the legal eagles returned to their task, expounding on the relative risks and responsibilities, the prevailing commercial and taxation law and notably the mediation, dispute and exit arrangements.

A brooding silence descended. Everything had been clarified and yet nothing was clear. Unease lurked in the corners of the room. I needed to venture into the area that I felt to be the most contentious. As it involved the investment, profit share and board governance arrangements, I asked the attorneys and the non-essential members of our team to leave. The academics seemed reluctant to miss Showtime. The programmers didn't need to be asked twice.

Cassidy got up, but didn't leave. Instead she took up a vacant place next to Randy. Both Loo and Yukio were classically inscrutable. I guessed they would resent both a woman being present and Randy having an adviser with him when they were on their Jack Jones. I didn't want Cassidy's presence to become an elephant in the room. Nor did I wish to force the issue of her presence for fear of how Randy might react.

Ms. Regan is Mr. Steinbacher's principal assistant and adviser, I explained. I suggest, in this phase of the negotiations, that Cassidy be granted observer status.

Loo gave a motion of acquiescence. Miki translated my proposal to Yukio. He responded at great length.

Miki smiled. Yukio-san says that this is not an appropriate role for a young lady. However, he does not wish to deprive us of the only thing of beauty in the room.

I pleaded with Cassidy silently to let that remark go.

We all smiled. The tension dissipated. The likely stumbling block remained. It was time to jump rather than trip over it.

Gentlemen, Randy has explained to me privately that he is reluctant to enter into significant business dealings without holding a controlling share.

I had sanitised this position in deference to the delicacy of Asian ears and sensibilities. Randy had expressed his distrust of oriental business-men in a more straightforward manner. 'It's like a fucking magic show with them. They distract you with all that bowing, scraping and business card mumbo-jumbo and before you know it, you've fallen for the three card trick'.

I'd protested that these guys were different.

They could have plastic surgery to straighten their eyes for all I care, an animated Randy responded, 51% with those bastards is my bottom line.

Loo stroked his stubbly chin, considering the right play. Yukio and Miki conversed in Japanese.

Out of the blue, Cassidy spoke next. She'd just broken the agreement. No one knew how to respond.

She picked up on the unspoken disapproval. Mr. Steinbacher has authorised me to outline a proposal. In effect, this is Randy speaking.

Cassidy circulated copies of a one-page document, passing two copies in Japanese to Miki. I will let you absorb the content first and then, with your permission, I will speak to it.

I scanned the content superfast, anxious at losing control. Miki exchanged glances with me. We nodded to each other. The Randy-Cassidy team was impressive. They were trading off profit share and appointment of the executive management team for a controlling interest at board level.

Cassidy took the group through the key points of Randy's proposal. Any questions? She asked.

Doubtless there were many, but Asian business etiquette was bound to prevent any further negotiation at that point. Loo folded the sheet of paper in half and tucked into his jacket pocket. Yukio made a brief note with his Mont Blanc fountain pen.

Let me sleep on your proposal, Loo said. It was an ironic choice of words from a man I knew to be a rampant insomniac.

Hai, Yukio nodded in agreement.

Cassidy explained the dinner arrangements on showing the men out. No business talk, she stressed.

Miki ushered the team members back into the room. He briefed them on the progress so far. Jeremiah wanted to know how the business negotiations were proceeding. Miki gave a typically diplomatic response. They were progressing satisfactorily at this point.

The group dispersed prior to returning for dinner. Once the room was empty, I raided Randy's drinks cabinet to produce two Suntory whiskies. Miki and I collapsed next to each other on a yellow leather sofa.

That was close, Miki said, loosening his tie.

Was it ever?

Thank God for Cassidy's trade-off.

Cassidy's or Randy's? I asked.

I don't know, Miki said, swilling his whisky. Those two are a team.

They are, I acknowledged mournfully.

I didn't mean it like that, Miki said sympathetically.

What *is* their relationship? I asked.

I wasn't expecting that

The group reassembled the next morning in Randy's boardroom at times determined by the team members' socio-cultural backgrounds.

Yukio was ten minutes early. Loo Jin Pao arrived on time. Randy appeared two minutes late. Jeremiah and his sidekicks showed up fifteen minutes after the appointed time, muttering about the traffic. The gum-chewers rocked up once they'd got out of bed.

After my recap of the progress made on the previous day, I confirmed that the all-in needed to revert to half-out to allow the investors to continue their negotiations. Jerry and his team shuffled resentfully out, muttering that they'd only just arrived. The programmers didn't need to be ejected. They were still asleep.

Miki informed the group that Yukio had asked him to put certain points of negotiation on the table. Loo, jittery again, stumbled through a couple of incoherent questions. Cassidy conferred with Randy, who nodded.

We can live with those, Cassidy announced.

Loo was non-committal. Distracted.

You're still not comfortable, Mr. Loo? Miki inquired.

I can accept Yukio-san's balloon payment proposal, Loo said wiping at his brow, but I'll need more edge on this whole deal if I'm ceding board control to Steinbacher.

The edge is razor sharp, my friend, Randy responded. You guys can choose the executive team and bag most of the profit.

If it makes a profit, Loo said.

Yukio nodded.

It will make a profit, Miki intervened. There will be more than enough for everyone. What changes do you want, Loo?

Another ten split between Yukio and me.

Ten? You're kidding, Randy scoffed.

Ten, above the Scenario 1 profit projection. Not all of them.

And otherwise? Cassidy asked.

As is.

Randy pursed his lips. Cassidy whispered in his ear.

You got a deal, Randy said. But my boy here, Randy said, pointing to me, will be the inaugural CEO.

You gave away the executive appointment right, Loo huffed.

Just the inaugural CEO, Randy clarified. We'll add a clause that you guys alone can hire and fire the CEO, including giving him the bullet if he doesn't perform.

There was a long silence. Randy stood up to his colossal height. Loo and Yukio stood too. Randy dwarfed them.

Shake or don't, Randy said. It's time.

Yukio bowed instead. Loo reluctantly extended his palm. Miki and I avoided the triumphalism of a victory grin.

Celebrations were in order. The partygoers eventually drifted away. Miki hugged me before he turned in.

Cassidy called up the limousine. I've got to show you Malibu.

Now?

Now.

Moet? Veuve? I asked delving into the car fridge.

Bolly! Cassidy replied emphatically.

I served and slopped us a couple of flutes.

I have some questions, I said, passing the bubbly to Cass.

You must have used them all by now.

Just two more.

Not your usual history shit?

Of course. One modern history and one ancient.

If you must, Cassidy said, gulping at her bubbly as if to fortify herself.

Modern first, I said.

OK.

Was that your idea or Randy's?

Which one?

You know.

Randy's.

You liar.

I'm not lying.

You are so.

Well, maybe a little, Cassidy conceded.

Now ancient.

If you must.

It's a little personal.

I knew it.

What is it between you and Randy?

Are you jealous?

I'm asking the questions.

Don't be jealous, Cassidy said, moving close to smooch with me.

Don't avoid the question, I scolded her. What is your relationship with Randy?

You really want to know?

Yes.

Really?
Yes. Yes. Yes.
OK. Are you ready?
For fuck's sake.
He's my brother.
Like the song I just heard on the radio, I wasn't expecting that.

We're all smiles today, even Cassidy despite her swollen ankles, back pain and relative incontinence.

The three wise men of surgery just arrived to deliver their verdict. They are cautiously optimistic that I will walk again. In the modern world of lawsuits and medical defence, this highly qualified prognosis is better than gold, frankincense and myrrh to me.

My long lost friend, optimism, is coursing through my veins. I swear I can feel the itsy-bitsiest sensation in my toes.

Told you, Lorna says, helping herself to my lunch.

I've been out of it for weeks. Cassidy is updating me on world affairs, business performance and the local gossip. She nods in Lorna's direction. I get the impression she's got something to tell me about Lorna. I feel anxious, but it's obviously something Cass needs to say when we're alone. I let it pass. The world looks good today even to a potential paraplegic and a glamour puss inflated like a balloon.

Prepare my writing table, young lady, I command.

Right away, sir, Lorna replies in the spirit of things, buoyed by my rare good humour.

Back to your mum and dad today.

Bor-ing. I'm out of here.

How friendship is like an undrained swamp when you're up to your neck in alligators

The greater good

Ewan's CCTV feature didn't so much ruffle feathers as blow the birds out of the trees.

Ewan insisted on taking Lorna to school that morning. He ignored her protests about leaving so early. He was instantly forgiven when he stopped off at the pocket park with the playground equipment she loved. On the way, he snuck into the deli to pick up his copy of the West. He deliberately dragged out the anticipation. He studiously avoided looking at the front page.

Ewan watched Lorna on the swings. She was too big for this playground really. She flew above him then plummeted back. His daughter's trajectory was a metaphor for his career. Would he soar like a bird or would his wings melt from flying too close to the sun? He forced these fears and speculations from his mind. He abandoned himself to the rhythm of the playground equipment. He wanted to savour the expectation and the hope.

Ewan's defining moment arrived. He sat on the bench where he could keep an eye on Lorna. He flattened out the newspaper. He glanced at the back page, registering the Fremantle Dockers' belting by Carlton. He took a deep breath. This was it. He closed his eyes and flipped the paper to the front page.

Dad, watch!

In a minute, Lorna, he shouted.

He opened his eyes. CARNAGE ON WA ROADS. His heart stopped. They hadn't run it. Ewan looked more carefully. To his great relief, the banner read, 'Secret State - Ewan Mackenzie reveals big brother's surveillance of us all'. Ewan flicked to the centre spread. He didn't so much read the words as recall them one by one.

That's fabulous Lorna. Try not to kill yourself going headfirst.

Ewan assessed the content. It didn't name names. It was balanced. He felt guilty about the individuals. There was a price to pay. But, there was a higher order purpose.

He called his father, Jamie, to mind. He was forever preaching on the need to serve the greater good.

I'm famous

Roll over Woodward and Bernstein, Sally toasted.

Lorna was growing up, but she had this uncanny ability to act out with every babysitter. Sally and Ewan would choose restaurants within walking distance so they could respond faster than the emergency services to any 000 call.

The celebration dinner had been Sally's idea. It symbolised her brighter mood now that Lorna was established at Montessori and was forming some relationships at school. Ewan kept hoping that one day Sally might truly lift her head and focus on the world beyond Lorna.

As much as he appreciated the gesture, Ewan had been dreading the event. Guilt was his ever-present companion. It was suffocating him. He'd been on the point of confessing his infidelity several times. He'd bottled out at the moment of truth. There was no excuse for his behaviour or for his cowardice for that matter. At the same time, he didn't want to knock Sally down when she could be on the verge of getting up.

The Middle Eastern food was delicious. There was lamb falling off the bone, couscous, harissa and roasted vegetables.

Isn't it delightful to go out together, just the two of us? Sally cooed.

Ewan nodded and smiled. To respond wordlessly felt less hypocritical.

I'm proud of you, Sally said, taking Ewan's hand.

The impulse to admit guilt stabbed Ewan like a shooting pain. Deceit dug its sharp nails into his back. Sally noticed him wince. This time, he had to say something. I'm proud of you too, he bumbled.

I can't think why.

Are you fishing for compliments?

No. I'm not sure I'm doing anything for you to be proud of.

Lorna?

Well, there's Lorna.

Listen, Ewan said, grabbing Sally's wrist to make her look at him. What you're achieving with Lorna is incredible.

It's not exactly changing the world.

It might change *our* world, Ewan said, instantly regretting a remark so open to interpretation.

Before Sally could respond, the waiter arrived to clear the cutlery and the spotless dishes they'd licked clean.

Delicious! Ewan enthused.

I'm glad you enjoyed it, the young Turkish waiter said. He turned to leave and then swivelled back. A compliment from someone famous is especially welcome, he added.

Famous? Ewan asked.

Of course, sir, the young man replied. I have seen your face in the newspapers and on television.

That doesn't make me famous.

He *is* famous! Sally interjected.

Indeed, madam, the young man concluded, making his way towards the kitchen. By the way, he added, I am in my final year of journalism so you are something of an idol for me.

It seems I'm famous, Ewan conceded to Sally.

To confess

Ewan committed relationship suicide on a Saturday afternoon.

He'd lived the past twelve months in an escapist fantasy. Whenever his own world became that much too real, he would flee to another that oozed hedonistic freedom. Sam's only condition was that there were no strings attached. The irregular hours of the newspaper business provided perfect cover for their illicit fumbling in the night.

While the sun shone perennially at Samantha's, the prevailing forecast was far gloomier back home. Lorna was growing up. She bristled with attitude. She was more than a handful. An armful? She was wilful. She was occasionally spiteful. She was exhilarating, frustrating, ingenious, devious and even imperious.

Sally's life was a permanent busy bee. She was working close to full-time in her counselling practice. On top of work, she spent her time exhorting and exporting Lorna here, there and everywhere.

Ewan justified his infidelity on the basis that Sally remained oblivious. If she paid him such little attention that she failed to detect the telltale signs of a passionate affair, he could resort with impunity to the old 'my wife doesn't understand me' defence.

Yet guilt was a thief in the night. It was a thought stalker. Without warning, it would mug him, balaclava-clad. It was murderously efficient. His conscience would parade before his eyes a heart-rending tableau of family life - meeting Sally, courtship, limerence, Africa, Leeds, Australia and of course Lorna. He was forced to watch his entire guiltworks in all its shameful glory.

Ewan would determine to put things to right. He would end it with Samantha. Sam was not the type to cry and beg him to change his mind. Yet sadness would be written on her face. He might falter but his resolve would return and he would be resolute. He would be a man. Then he would face the court of Sally for his sins and take his punishment.

Ewan's fantasy was willing but his flesh was weak. He found greater sympathy for those with addictions. Like them, he would see Samantha, smell her scent and he would crave that one more hit.

Things changed the day Lorna cut Dylan's arm with the scissors. Ironically, she managed to carve him with the blunt ones the risk-averse school issued with safety in mind. Ewan had put his copy and then his editor to bed. He showered the evidence and guilt down the plughole. He checked his mobile while dressing. He found an angry message from Sally.

When he got home, Sally and Lorna were breathing fire at each other. Lorna had decorated Dylan's forearm with a pretty picture. Dylan was a peculiar creature. He had come to their house to play several times. Ewan thought he looked like Gollum from Lord of the Rings.

Where the hell have you been? Sally screamed at him.

I've got a job, he responded defensively.

Not that your colleagues would know. None of them have seen you all day.

It's not that sort of job. Anyway, would you like to tell me what's going on?

Lorna will tell you, Sally shouted, leaving him to take up the cross-examination.

Lorna's explanation disturbed him. She hid nothing. She showed no remorse. Dylan asked me to, she said. That was her matter of fact explanation. She stuck to it even after Ewan had challenged her to admit that what she had done was wrong.

Ewan returned to Samantha's that evening.

Hello big boy, she teased him. Can't get enough, eh?

It wasn't like that. He told her calmly what had happened. His family needed him. As he set off on the classic speech for such occasions, Sam interrupted him.

Go, Ewan. No strings attached, remember?

On the drive home, anger evicted guilt from the house of Ewan's emotions. Throughout his relationship with Sally, he had sacrificed pleasure for duty. Come to think of it, this had been the story of his life. His father preached some weird form of secular evangelism, requiring sacrifice over individuality.

Frustration got the better of him. Ewan crunched his fist into the dashboard. Soon the tenancy of his resentment expired. Contrition moved in. What he'd done was wrong. To hurt Sally when she needed him most was a treacherous act. Purification was his only viable course.

That Saturday, at one in the afternoon, he sat Sally down. It was time to confess.

Get out of my sight

Ewan discovered how difficult it is to break momentous news to someone living in ignorance.

For goodness sake, Sally said, I'm trying to finish these casenotes before Lorna gets back from Daisy's.

It's important, Ewan said in a defeated tone.

It had better be, Sally said, sitting down and glaring at him.

Ewan had prepared his speech a hundred times, but had no idea how to start. Sally's impatience wasn't helping. Maybe he should regroup and try another time? What else could he tell her now that would be a plausible reason for all this song and dance? Nothing came to mind. He couldn't even bail on it.

Enough, Sally said, standing up. I don't know what's wrong with you lately, she added, heading for the study.

I'm having an affair.

What? She said, turning to face him once the words had sunk in.

I've been having an affair, he said sotto voce. But it's over now.

Sally sat back down. She wouldn't look at him. He stumbled his way through it. She asked no questions. She left it to him to make the running. He did his best to explain the attraction, own up to his weakness and admit guilt.

Sally's eyes were fixed to the floor. Ewan could feel the tension in her body and sense the force of the anger that was boiling up. If only she would say something. Maybe swear at him. Even hit him. But she did nothing.

The silence was excruciating. Excuses dribbled forth. They sounded pathetic. He willed himself to be more honest. He must tell Sally the real reason. He was scared, but a confession without the truth is no confession at all.

You've been distant, he heard his voice falter, since we had Lor…

…Don't you dare blame her, you pathetic excuse for a man, Sally screamed, running to the bathroom.

Sally please, Ewan begged through the locked door.

Get out of this house, Sally sobbed. Get out of my sight.

Your balls?

Do you understand women? Ewan was forever asking Paul over the takeaways that were their staple diet.

Paul was the music writer at the West. Like everyone else at the paper, he knew Ewan and Samantha had been an item. He seemed cool with the whole thing, offering Ewan his spare room until things sorted themselves out.

If I did, Paul said, mopping up the rogan josh he'd spilt on the coffee table, I wouldn't be eating a shit curry in a shit rental in Northbridge with a shit like you.

I suppose not, Ewan conceded, necking his beer. But, you're damned if you do and you're damned if you don't.

Who wrote that one? Was it Stock, Waterman and Aitken? Paul mocked.

Ewan smiled, but continued undeterred. What was I supposed to do? Lie about the affair?

Maybe.

How could that be the right thing to do?

There are some things people prefer not to know, Paul said.

Ewan gathered up the plates and dumped them in the sink in the open plan apartment.

Sally's not that type, Ewan said, extracting two more beers from the dark fridge. The light faded away the previous night like a dying star.

Obviously she is, Paul said, accepting the proffered stubbie. Sorry to say this, but you should've just broken up with Sam and kept your trap shut.

It's a no-win situation, Ewan mused. If I'd done that, I would've felt appallingly guilty. And there would have been this permanent wall of secrecy between us.

Ewan fell silent with his thoughts. And can you imagine what would've happened if she'd found out later? Ewan added.

It would've been ancient history by then.

You're not a great source of comfort.

At least I gave you a bed.

You did, mate. Thanks.

Paul took a call, leaving Ewan to ponder his fate. Paul unlocked the sliding glass door and stepped outside onto the balcony. A wall of noise from the traffic and the late night revellers burst into the room like a backdraft.

Ewan pounced when his host re-entered.

Do you know what hurts most? Ewan asked.

Your balls?

Sally is punishing me for telling her the truth. She's paying out on me for doing the right thing.

Correct me if I'm wrong, Gandhi. Wasn't it you who was nailing the boss?

Fuck off, Paul, Ewan said, not finding him particularly helpful.

Sobbing as she went

The tension was thicker than the rough cut slabs of toast that accompanied Ewan's 'big brekky'. Sally had chosen the healthy fruit salad option.

Ewan looked over to the grassy area adjacent to the redeveloped South Beach cafe. Lorna was chasing seagulls and menacing them when they landed.

Ewan was searching for a topic of conversation less emotional than the subject matter to date. Asking Sally how her practice was going had drawn a frosty response. That very cool reaction constituted a thaw compared with the ice that formed when he asked how Lorna was getting on at school.

The emergence of WikiLeaks had come at a great time for Ewan. Never before had his calling so perfectly coincided with what was trending in the news. While Julian Assange saw traditional media as the devil incarnate, he'd heard of Ewan's reputation for cause journalism. The planets aligned for Ewan. He'd secured an interview with Julian Assange to do a major feature.

Unsure of Sally's reaction, he thought he'd give this new line of conversation a run. You won't believe this, Ewan said, but I've secured an interview with Julian Assange.

How interesting, Sally responded as if the opposite were true.

Ewan resolved to push on. It's not for quite a while, but it's amazing even to get it.

That's wonderful, Sally said without feeling.

He's a fascinating guy, but he's strange.

How so?

How so fascinating or how so strange?

Why is he strange? It goes without saying that everyone you meet at work is fascinating.

Ewan could taste the acid, but steeled himself to swallow rather than bite. He's a contradiction. I'm with him one hundred per cent on government and corporate secrecy. Yet, he is guarded and defensive about himself and Wiki. Something doesn't gel.

He has a higher order purpose, Sally explained. Isn't that it?

I guess that's it, Ewan conceded.

Just like you, Sally added.

At that moment, Lorna skittered back. Can we go now?

Dad's taking you out this afternoon, remember? Sally said.

Do I have to go? Lorna whined, hunkering into Sally. Look, there's a dog, Lorna shouted, changing the subject and her mind, as she was wont to do.

Ewan willed himself to have one more crack at breaching Sally's defensive wall.

I was thinking, Sally...

...Don't Ewan.

Just hear me out! Let me come home. Don't be like Assange. You can find compassion for your clients, people you don't even know. Can't you bring yourself to find some for me? Someone who loves you and I think deep down you love.

Sally raced off in Lorna's direction, sobbing as she went.

You're amazing

In the months that elapsed following the breakfast at South Beach, Ewan felt Sally's resistance slowly weakening. He was invited to dinner quite regularly, joyfully picking Lorna up from school and helping her with her projects.

Once the date for the Assange interview was settled, Sally took an interest in Ewan's preparations. Ewan described the Julian Assange he'd got to know. Assange was never shy in talking up WikiLeaks. He was in his element exposing government secrecy. He teased the readers with promises of ongoing revelations that would blow people's minds. This showboating was par for the course for Julian Assange. He was a publicity junkie.

He's a narcissist, Sally announced one night, refilling Ewan's soup bowl.

Who is?

Julian Assange.

Is that it? Ewan said, blowing on his soupspoon. Don't they look at themselves in the mirror all the time?

Sally smiled at him. It warmed him. He felt sad, reflecting momentarily on the intimacy with Sally that he'd squandered.

Narcissistic personality disorder is a mental condition in which people have an inflated sense of their own importance, a deep need for admiration and a lack of empathy for others, Sally said with a self-satisfied smile.

Go girl! Ewan exclaimed, deeply impressed that his detailed description of Assange had revealed so much. He secretly hoped that none of that description was supposed to refer to him.

When you look more deeply into this personality type, you see that narcissists live behind a mask of ultra-confidence. But behind it lies a fragile self-esteem that's vulnerable to the slightest criticism.

That sounds exactly like him, Ewan said. Tell me more.

This personality disorder wreaks havoc on every facet of life, particularly intimate relationships, Sally said.

Ewan knew Sally better than anyone. These comments about Assange were also aimed at him.

These people get resentful when they're not given the special favours, the accolades and the attention they believe they deserve.

You're amazing, Ewan blurted out.

I'm glad you appreciate that, Sally said, making her eye contact felt.

I really do. Assange is a narcissist, you are amazing and I have been a bloody idiot.

One in a million

Ewan's 'Inside Assange' feature hit the spot. It was acclaimed for its in-depth analysis of the man, private as well as public. The feature broke new ground, penetrating the posturing to reveal the person. Ewan's feature exposed hitherto unknown aspects of Assange's personality, revealing inherent contradictions.

Ewan was buoyed by his article's reception. For some reason, the high he was getting from it sparked intense guilt about the Harolds. He'd been so self-obsessed over the last twelve months that he'd ignored them. He'd been allowed home for some time now. The separation from his family had been unbearable. It had been a time of reflection for Ewan. He'd reset his moral compass to where it used to point - towards meaningful relationships.

Ewan rushed his copy a little to make time for an outing, just a few doors up the road from his home. He parked up the street, outside the *Haroldic* homestead. He clambered from the driver's seat, juggling the pack of beers he'd picked up from the bottle shop round the corner, and skipped across the road.

The bench was where it should be, but there was no sign of man or beast. Ewan looked around, wondering what to do. He leant over the balustrade where he could get a good view up the paved pathway to the back garden. He did the same from the other side of the veranda. It seemed deserted.

Ewan feared the worst, but hoped for the best. Human Harold was so old he was on overtime. Maybe they had gone to stay with a relative? Perhaps Harold1 was having his blood pressure checked and Harold2 was asleep inside and deaf to the world? Ewan rapped on the front door. He admired the old-fashioned brass knocker shaped like a bloodhound.

He could feel the sound vibrations as he pounded the hound. Nothing stirred. Ewan tried again. Still nothing. He collapsed against the door. Tears welled up. Was he sad at the loss of his friends or ashamed of his selfish neglect?

Ewan wiped his eyes. He gave the knocker a final volley. Rat-tat-tat-tat-tat! The door creaked open.

Where's the bloody emergency? Harold1 protested.

Ewan was overjoyed at the unexpected sight of his friend, but dismayed to see him looking so old and sick. He was on double time not just overtime.

Thought you'd slung your hook, Harold said, standing in the doorway.

I brought some beers, Ewan said brightly, holding up his six-pack.

It's a bit early.

But, it's beer o'clock, Ewan countered, remembering one of Harold's own sayings.

Harold was still reluctant.

C'mon, Ewan urged him, for old time's sake.

Harold clumsily snibbed the lock before stiffly lowering himself onto the gnarled bench.

Here's cheers, Ewan said, handing Harold a beer and clinking it against his as he handed it over. I expected to find you out here in your usual spot.

Harold didn't respond.

Where's Harold2? Ewan asked.

The old man peered into the distance, braced against his walking stick.

The penny dropped. I'm so sorry, Ewan said. How long ago?

A couple of months back, I guess.

Ewan wanted to ask what had happened, but was unsure if he should. Would that show compassion or just condemn the old man to relive the raw emotion?

The two men sat in silence like they used to do. What had once been comfortable was now awkward.

Harold was a great dog, Ewan said in time, still staring into the distance.

One in a million, Harold mused.

Ewan cracked another beer. They drank without conversation. Ewan said nothing because he didn't know what to say. Harold was mute because there was nothing he wanted to say.

In due course, Ewan gathered up the empties. He put the remaining beers on the cushion he'd been sitting on. He bent down to grasp Harold's shoulder as he left.

As he walked home, Ewan determined to buy Harold a new dog. Once the front garden gate had clanked closed behind him, Ewan found himself tearful again. Harold wasn't a dog that could be replaced. Sally likewise.

The Walkleys

Ewan hit the jackpot with his feature on Julian Assange. On the strength of it, a lucrative job offer had been forthcoming from the Murdoch News Limited stable. Ewan's principles had rebelled at the prospect but had been overpowered by his ambition and his passion to effect change.

Tonight he was in Sydney for the announcement of the winner of the Walkleys, journalism's most prestigious award.

The time-honoured build-up to the announcement of the winner had frayed Ewan's nerves. His current colleagues from the West Australian, gathered around him at the lavish table, looked every bit as anxious as he did.

The win had come with a rush and was now a blur. He was standing alone in the foyer, catching his breath. He could no longer bring to mind the moment when his name was called out. He could barely remember what must have been a long, circuitous walk to the stage, manoeuvring around the tightly packed tables. He fingered the figurine that was still clutched in his hand. He really had won. But what did he say on the podium? Did he thank the right people? If only he'd prepared a speech. He'd been too superstitious to do so.

A penny for your thoughts?

Ewan looked up to see Samantha.

Outside of the office, Ewan didn't know what to say to Sam anymore.

She leant over and pecked him on the cheek. Congratulations, Ewan. It was a brilliant piece.

Ewan inclined his head to accept the accolade. He raised the trophy with an embarrassed smile.

It's a shame Sally isn't here with you, Samantha said.

Don't Sam, Ewan said.

I mean it. I realise how difficult it is for her. I mean would have been, sitting at the table with the rest of us.

It's OK, Ewan said, trying to change the subject. Really it is.

I'm just saying…

…I know. It's OK. It really is. I understand why Sally didn't come.

Have you told her yet? Sam asked, linking her elbow into Ewan's. Let me get a drink for the champ, she added.

I was just about to call her.

Great, Sam said. I'll get us a champagne and you convey the good news.

Thanks, Sam, Ewan said, pulling her to him for a hug.

I'm proud of you, Samantha said, heading for the bar. And so is Sally.

One child policy

The roaring fire was most welcoming in the bar at the Rottnest Lodge.

Ewan and Sally were enjoying a free weekend. Lorna was staying over with a child from school. Sally got cross that Ewan wouldn't go bike-riding with her. Other than that, everything was going swimmingly.

The Lodge reminded them of an old country pub on the Yorkshire Moors they'd frequented before leaving for Australia. The Moorshead, built in the fifteenth century, had a fair excuse for needing a makeover. The Lodge, a mere pup by comparison, needed a boot up the backside to get itself into shape.

Ewan and Sally cared little for its state of renovation. They were seeking something more fundamental than aesthetic appreciation. Rest and recreation was all that mattered.

An excellent Margaret River cabernet sauvignon compensated for their overdone steaks. Sally spoilt herself with her favourite lemon tart desert. Ewan sufficed with a black coffee.

Thank you for allowing me back, Ewan said, taking Sally's hand.

Sally looked down her nose at him. Thanks for coming back, she said, with a sly grin.

I suppose Lorna's pleased we're all together again? Ewan checked.

Of course, she is.

It's hard to tell.

I know she is.

Ewan changed tack. Is Lorna going to be OK?

Sally considered the question while scavenging the last crumbs from her tart. I honestly don't know, she answered.

She's socialising better, Ewan suggested hopefully.

Yes. When she's in the mood.

That's important, Ewan said thoughtfully.

Sally nodded. What's more, she said brightly, Lorna is a natural leader when she wants to mix. You should see her with the other kids.

What does she do?

She makes up the games. She's the one who bosses everyone around.

You worry, don't you? Ewan asked seriously.

All the time, Sally answered, raising her head from her plate. Every minute.

What exactly do you worry about?

Sally weighed her words carefully. It's what's going around in her head that worries me most. Sometimes she says the weirdest things.

Such as?

She comes out with the strangest things. I'm surprised she's even heard of them. I have no idea where she gets them from.

Now I am worried!

Let's not spoil our weekend, Sally said. Would it help to take your mind off things if I invited you to my bed?

Maybe it could, Ewan said. He pulled Sally up. Shall we make another baby?

Like China, we have a one-child policy, Sally replied.

Weird and wonderful

Six months had passed since their wonderful Rottnest weekend. Ewan walked home from spending some time with Harold. He took him a beer and a home-cooked meal once a week these days.

Ewan was the most settled he had ever been. He and Sally had put the past behind them. They were happy again together. Lorna's behaviour was worrying but manageable. Sally's private counselling practice was building. Ewan's journalistic star had never been brighter. As a Walkley winner, he had free rein to roam across the News Limited stable.

After CCTV and WikiLeaks, Ewan felt he had done government secrecy to death. Now he was homing in on the social impacts of new technology. It was an emerging field, full of analytical possibilities and rich in human interest. It was a topic that crossed over into Sally's family counselling work. It was a passion they could share.

There were many academics and commentators muscling in on the same space. Facebook. Twitter and Instagram were being dissected like laboratory rats. PhD students were researching the effect of screen use on the malleable minds of the young. They were examining the impacts of modern technology on interpersonal communications, family life, community development and every potential negative consequence no matter how tenuous the link.

While the field was crowded, Ewan continually elbowed himself to the front. He had some critical advantages over his rivals. He was a good writer. He had the clout to get his ideas out there, thanks to the Murdoch media empire. And, most importantly, he had an angle on it, many others lacked. Thanks to Sally's insights, he had a strong handle on the individual and group psychology at play.

Given the horror stories he'd been sharing with Sally, he was amazed when she bailed him up one evening for another discussion about Lorna's constant bleating about getting a mobile phone.

Not this again, he protested. We've been over it time and time again.

Sally delivered a glass of red to placate him before joining Ewan on the sofa.

Calm down. We need to discuss it because it seems all her friends are getting them

No way, Sally. This is the surest way to corrupt a young mind.

I agree, but we can't ignore peer pressure.

It's the parents. They don't think things through.

It's not just the phone issue, Sally persisted, remaining as calm as she could. Lorna is angry with me because I won't let her use the Internet when I'm not around.

Too bad. That's what I say, Ewan said, standing up to control his temper.

But, it's not easy, Sally reasoned with him. The teachers are telling the children to look things up on Google.

We have to hold the line here.

OK, OK, but don't be so dogmatic.

I'm not being dogmatic. I'm being sensible. Lorna has issues anyway. She doesn't need to be exposed at her age to the weird and wonderful screwballs brought to you courtesy of the World Wide Web.

It's OK, Sally said, standing up. I agree. I'm just telling you.

Hope is flooding my world in light like the rising sun on a frosty morning.

Feeling is returning below the waist and I have never felt happier. At long last, there is room in my heart to show Cassidy some compassion. She responds with warmth that has been absent for so long. We have heart to hearts. We apologise to each other and forgive ourselves.

I need to tell you something, Cassidy says.

I can hear the hesitancy in her voice.

It's about Lorna, she explains

Go on. You're making me nervous.

She's talking about going home.

Do you think she should? Is she ready? Has she told her parents? My questions gush forth.

I asked Lorna not to tell you, Cassidy confesses.

Why? Why would you want to keep this from me?

I'm not keeping anything from you. I'm telling you now. I'm letting you in on this now because the time is right.

O-kay. Why is it right now?

Because you are getting better and because you can consider Lorna's best interests now.

Couldn't I before? I venture. I raise my hand to prevent Cass from answering. It's OK. I understand where you're coming from.

Shall I talk to Lorna about it?

Yes. But be careful to try to understand and not judge, she counsels me

I thought I'd become a better person than that.

You did. I'm sure you will again, Cassidy says, rising painfully to kiss me.

How the bonds of friendship get stretched to the limit

One o'clock in the morning

The heart attack caved Randy's chest at the appointed time.

One a.m. is the hour of choice for cardiac arrest. We should set our alarms at one minute past one in the morning. If we wake up, we can celebrate or at least anticipate the prospect of another day on this planet.

I felt bad. I'd dissuaded Cassidy from answering the call. She was a switched on girl in every sense. Now and again I wanted her to turn off. Disconnect from the world. Especially in bed.

I'd succumbed to post-coital loss of consciousness. Then the suite's intercom sprung to life, announcing itself in that dreadful two-tone alert so beloved by airports. Cassidy did the honours, padding off to the console. Our plane was ready for boarding but this would be no joyride.

Cassidy was beside herself on the short limo trip to the emergency room at the Saint John's Health Centre. She shivered the whole way, clinging to me for body heat. Cass's default mode was confident and efficient. I'd never seen her like this - vulnerable and fearful.

We'd been hanging out together for the best part of a year. The product development, prototyping and testing had dragged on all that time. Cassidy was beautiful, smart and sassy. She was too much of a girlie girl for the classic feminists amongst us, but she was a powerful, high-achieving woman nonetheless.

She seemed to dig me. I'd distrusted her motives early on. I thought of myself as a business deal rather than the real deal. But she began to open up to me.

She told me about her awful childhood. She was one of five neglected children. There's an inverse relationship between fertility and intelligence, I remember her telling me. It was a funny line, delivered in deadly earnest. The kids were left to fend for themselves. The so-called parents used their welfare checks to fill their arms not their fridge.

After several long years in the dubious care of the authorities, she was rescued and adopted by the Steinbachers. Her eccentric adoptive parents provided the creature comforts unknown to her beforehand, but struggled to embrace her emotionally. Compared to their natural offspring, Cassidy felt accepted rather than loved.

When Cassidy spoke of such things, the words she chose were biblical, almost messianic. Her tale was one of abandonment and salvation. It was plain to see that early childhood adversity had forged in her a steely determination to succeed. At the same time, it had stripped her of the confidence to give trust.

I asked her what she saw in me. She was mockingly evasive as usual. I insisted a little longer than was customary. Why me when you can have any guy you want?

No reason, she explained.

What kind of reason is that?

No reason.

Randy's wife, Sonia, was pacing the waiting room. It was desolation row. Festering fast food containers and abandoned coffee cups mired the landscape. Sonia gushed into Cassidy's arms. Even in a crisis, I could sense Cass stiffen and pull away. Sonia was a mess, spraying the room with recriminations and regrets.

What happened to Randy? I asked in a stern tone.

Sonia wailed by way of reply, snivelling into her silk, monogrammed handkerchief.

Fortunately, a doctor in green hospital scrubs appeared. He was drawn and exhausted like a marathon runner who's hit the wall. His urgency to get down to business was evident. He demurred in deference to Sonia's overbearing grief. Just his luck after an eighteen-hour day.

Cassidy's composure had grown in response to Sonia's emotional disintegration. She motioned to me to tend to Randy's wife.

I'm Randolph's sister, she said, leading the surgeon away from the veil of tears.

I caught snippets of the conversation about Randy's condition. Ventricle, artery and stent cracked a mention. I couldn't discern the prognosis from Cassidy's demeanour. She'd clicked back into ice-queen mode. I scanned the room, rubbing Sonia's back to comfort her. She was my botoxed baby. Tribes of distressed relatives had set up camp in the four corners of the waiting room. It was a giant dock where the prisoners awaited the verdict of the medical jury. Sonia's blubbering was impressive by western standards, but she was no match for the keening and chest beating from the team from the Middle East.

The surgeon shook Cassidy's hand. Sonia and I rose as one as Cassidy approached.

Well? Sonia asked in a jarring tone. Aren't you going to share the news with Randy's wife?

Cassidy threw back her head, but composed herself.

It doesn't look good, she said, choking back her own tears, but he's in good hands.

Like a limpet

Randolph J. Steinbacher Jr. clung to life. Like a limpet. Like a jumper with second thoughts, grasping for the railing. Like spandex bike shorts around a sweaty crotch.

Randy peeked more than once into the valley of death. Not finding what he saw much to his liking, he rebuffed the grim reaper, rallying each time despite the diminishing odds.

If the man mountain wasn't exactly reduced to a molehill, he emerged from the ordeal not much bigger than a hillock. While a shadow of his former physical self, Randy's spirit was irrepressible. Invalidity suited him. It randified him. His strengths and weaknesses were magnified. His idiosyncrasies became more entrenched. Randy's passions burned brighter. His depressions were blacker and descended for longer. His quest for revenge on Zuckerberg verged on the maniacal. Despite stern medical warnings that he should not stress himself, Randy insisted on updates on Operation Shuck the Zuck.

He was eventually discharged to a sanatorium. This plush institution in Anaheim was no less luxurious than the suite at the Bel-Air, where I'd long since taken up residence. Even receiving the prescribed nursing care, his recuperation would be slow. Randy's cardiologist was solemnly insistent that his patient would go to the rest home or nowhere. I was unsure whether he was insightful about the raft of temptations bobbing around the hotel or determined to hoist another sale to Randy from his affiliate recovery centre.

Cassidy rebuffed Randy's attempt to take back the helm of the good ship Steinbacher Investments and Enterprises. I kept my counsel. I feared her motives were not entirely protective. For someone who had lived for so long below decks as Randy's first mate, this was an opportunity of a lifetime for her to secure the bridge and take command.

Cassidy and I sanitised the business updates we gave to Randy. We didn't dare tell him he wasn't the only one on life support. The fact was, after the campus trials, Frenzy was in the intensive care unit.

Cooking with gas

Zak Ryman was ex-Facebook. He had the intel on how they tested their products. Like so many, he couldn't find a kind word to say about Mark Zuckerberg. This made Zak the all-round perfect choice.

Zak was ridiculously handsome. He was the guy to avoid on a double date. He was also very smart. I wished he had bad body odour, just to even up the stakes. He didn't. He had no bad smell. But he did have bad news.

Miki and I listened for the best part of an hour while Zak expanded on the trial results. The Alabama campus had gained some early traction, but the other three student groups merely flirted with Frenzy before reverting to their gaming, snapchatting and youtubing.

Miki had the patience of a saint, but I'd had enough. Bottom line, Zak?

The bottom line is Frenzy belongs in a laboratory.

You mean it's too academic? Miki asked.

Zak hesitated. Then he came clean. It isn't fun. It's too scientific.

My exasperation showed. That's its winning point of difference, I observed.

I know, Zak replied. But, it's clunky. You know students participate in experiments to earn pocket money, right?

We nodded.

Well, that's how they see Frenzy. Do you know what the guy who won the MacBook said?

We didn't want to know.

He said, thanks for the machine, dude. Do I get paid for the experiment, too?

This was bad enough. I was wondering how bad it could get. Is it salvageable?

Of course, Zak responded with enthusiasm.

I heard Miki exclaim in relief.

I was more sceptical. It was in Zak's interests to try to right a sinking ship.

Are you sure? I asked.

Sure, I'm sure. Get rid of that mad professor of yours, hire a dozen more ICT students and you'll be cooking with gas.

Hell's hotbox

Rivulets of sweat cascaded from my every pore.

Why would any sane person subject himself to such torture? I asked.

Because it's good for you, Miki responded.

Do you Japs even sweat? I ruminated aloud.

It's good for you, Miki insisted.

Brussel sprouts are good for you, I responded, but I make a point of not eating them.

Stop complaining, Miki said, pouring water on the coals to make matters worse. It's a great place to think, Miki added.

I let it go. He was taut, tanned and terrific, sitting there with just a towel round his waist. I imagined him with Nina. Two perfect bodies entwined.

I've been thinking about Zak's report, Miki said.

I'm glad one of us can think straight in this tropical monsoon.

We have to switch it round.

Don't speak in riddles, I admonished him. My brain is steamed.

The relative pull of Jeremiah's theory and the market smarts of the kindergarten team need to be reversed.

I sucked on the Evian. That's the easy part, I said. The real problem lies with how Jerry is going to take this.

He won't like it, will he?

How can you nips be so damned cool even in a sweatbox? Dr. Jeremiah will go fucking ballistic.

He'll think we're on the marketers' side? Miki ruminated.

Not just that, I said. He'll accuse us of trashing his life's work.

It's a problem, Miki concluded, closing his eyes and pulling his knees beneath him Buddha-style.

I towelled myself yet again from head to foot.

I heard a sound emanate from the figure in the mystic trance. There's another problem.

I didn't want to know.

Miki told me anyway. The dynamics between Randy and Cass aren't helping.

You're telling me, I responded mournfully.

What's that all about? Miki asked.

I was in a quandary. Cassidy had issues with trust. It had taken her a long time to confide in me. I was reluctant to betray her. Nor did I want her to kick me out of bed. The trouble was I needed Miki as much as her. Frenzy was in deep trouble. I knew I couldn't bring it around alone.

My best defence was the coward's code - answer a question with a question. Maybe Miki already knew, or at least suspected, about the relationship issues. How do *you* read it, I asked?

I don't know what to make of it, Miki said. It's obvious that Cass is more than just Randy's assistant. Forgive my indiscretion, but I thought she night be his whore when I first met them. But, she's sweet on you. I can see that. I just don't get it. But this much I do know. It's the story of the quick and the dead. Cass leapt quick smart into the power vacuum when Randy nearly died.

You're right, I conceded to Miki, still trying to avoid disclosure.

And Randy's up and down like a yoyo these days, Miki added distractedly. His thing with Zuckerberg is getting worse. It's threatening the whole project.

I nodded. I went through another towel. For someone who has had so much practice, I lie really badly. It's got me beat, I said.

Miki reached over, grabbing my arm. This was not the Miki I knew. He looked sternly at me. This was the most direct I had ever seen him.

Level with me, he insisted.

I can't, I protested weakly.

You have to. The project is at stake.

Cass has told me things in confidence.

You can trust me, Miki said.

How would I put it? Straight out was best. Cassidy is Randy's sister.

No way.

It's true.

Next you'll be telling me they're identical twins.

She's adopted.

Is that so? Miki said, letting go of me. We were both disarmed.

I decided on a Randy ploy. I stood up and dropped my towel.

One shock at a time, Miki said, raising his hands in horror.

Get me out of hell's hotbox, I implored Miki, and I will tell you more.

Free pork

Not very subtle, I know. But, once I'd persuaded Jerry to fly down from San Fran, I chose Engel's bagel cafe off Beverly to break the bad news to him.

Miki got the Jewish angle with my strategy. He still had trouble leaping the cultural divide to grasp the tactical significance of a blast of chicken soup for Jerry should he need his heart restarted.

I'd briefed Miki on the full picture between Randy and Cassidy as far as I understood it. He listened as attentively as he could, but he was clearly distracted. Miki had problems of his own. Yukio was growing impatient with the apparent lack of progress, especially as we'd already drawn down heavily on his equity. He'd also heard of Randy's heart attack and wanted to know who was controlling Randy's stock. We didn't know how to respond to that question. We didn't think it a great idea to reveal to this *miso-gynist* that Cassidy was in charge. Nor did we think it highly reassuring if we told him Randy was calling the shots while receiving his own.

We delayed our meeting with Jerry for half an hour so Miki could hook up with Yukio and some of his associates via a conference call. I arrived early, at the original time, to herd my far-flung thoughts. I ordered a bagel with lox and cream cheese. How low was I prepared to stoop? Was anything off limits in the stakes of securing Jeremiah's ongoing participation? Was I prepared to resort to a tactic that even I found morally repugnant?

Unprepared to change the habits of a lifetime, I resolved to answer in the affirmative just in time for Miki to walk in.

How did it go? I asked Miki nervously.

Hard to say, he responded. Where's Jerry?

He's always late, I explained. Want to hear a Jewish joke? I added to lighten the mood.

Sure, Miki said, turning to pay attention.

What's the Jewish dilemma?

I don't know.

Free pork!

I laughed. Miki didn't.

I don't get it, he said.

Fortunately, Jeremiah walked in at that moment.

Miki offered to go to the counter. He kept returning to consult with Jeremiah. What size gefilte fish do we want? How many serves of cholent do we need? In the meantime, I made tiny talk with Jerry. To describe it as small talk would be an unwarranted exaggeration.

Miki returned in due course, a culturally enlightened man.

Don't keep me in suspense, Jerry said eagerly. I'm excited to hear the trial results.

Miki's heart must have sunk. Mine drowned.

Kiss Frenzy goodbye

Miki and I looked expectantly at each other. You tell him. No, you tell him. These words remained unspoken.

Is something wrong? Jerry asked, scanning our faces.

Yes and no, I stuttered.

It's nothing that can't be fixed, Miki added as much to reassure himself as anyone.

Jeremiah fiddled with his glasses, then produced a grubby tissue to wipe them.

Miki gestured silently to me. I knew what that signal meant. He's your friend. You brought him into this project. You have to be the one.

I looked around at my fellow bagel-munchers. There were no other candidates. It had to be me.

Jeremiah, Jerry, I stammered, you're a genius. You are. We go way back, don't we?

Jerry perched his smeared spectacles back on his nose. Sure we do.

Well, as critical as the psychosocial media element is to our product differentiation, the project prototype didn't fly.

What do you mean it didn't fly? It's an application not a fucking aircraft.

How can I explain this? I speculated aloud. Students in this day and age aren't academic. These days they don't go to college to study or learn. It's just something they do if they can't think of anything else. University is like childcare for big kids.

What are you saying? Jeremiah asked. I don't get you.

Fortunately Miki weighed in to help. Jerry, these kids see Apple and Instagram as the standard. They find them hip. These cool gadgets and this whole social media craze are about having fun.

But Instagram is shallow, Jerry protested. Facebook is worse. It is meaningless, futile activity.

We're not bailing on your psychosocial media, I said.

You're not?

Of course not, Miki reassured him.

Jerry ran his hands through his greasy hair. He was confused. He was keeping it together, but for how long?

We have to tweak it, Jerry, that's all, I said waving to the bus boy. Zak, the consultant, reckons he knows what's required. We need to rework the graphical interface. We need to make it brash, edgy, fun...

...You mean dumb it down, Jerry said bitterly.

Bring us three chicken soups, I commanded the kid.

Look at it this way, Miki expanded. Softly softly, catchee monkey, that's what it is.

Don't patronise me, Jerry snapped. I thought you guys were serious about the science.

We are, I said.

Of course, we are, Miki agreed. It's the science that will set us apart. But the psychological elements have to creep up on people. We have to lure them in first...

...By promising them more digital dross.

No, I protested, it's not that. It's bait, that's all. We have to draw them onto our hook. And then, once they're landed, they will be ours. They won't be captive. They will willingly stay to savour the experience. They will appreciate the depth of our product. They will crave the meaning of true friendship.

Three cartons of chicken soup were delivered with unprepossessing plastic spoons.

Guys, Jerry said in a threatening tone.

Drink your soup, Jerry, I urged. It'll calm you down.

I am calm, Jerry corrected me. I'll drink the soup because I like it. But then, he said mid-slurp, I will be on my way.

You can't, Miki and I said in unison.

Talk to him, Miki, I insisted, grabbing my phone to go outside and make a call.

Miki gave me a 'what the hell are you playing at?' look.

I motioned to him to cool it. Don't let him leave. Don't let Jerry do anything hasty, I said.

This was make or break. This was do or die. This was the moment for any cliché with a similar meaning. More than that, this was time to plumb the depths. To hit rock bottom. I dialled Cassidy's number. She'd better be there.

C'mon, c'mon, I urged the phone gods to make her answer.

At last, the line engaged. I don't remember how I put it. There was no delicate way. This was no time to make nice. Whatever I said to Cassidy, my message was clear.

Blow Jerry or kiss Frenzy goodbye.

Taking one for the team

Sinking into the plush leatherwork of the limo with Cass, I'd just re-qualified for handholding rights. Normally, I would have slipped my intertwined hand down between her legs. I didn't press my luck.

As we piloted noiselessly through the rough and tumble of the LA evening peak hour in our luxury metal cocoon, I relished the bodily comfort of being persona grata with Cass again.

It had been touch and go, so to speak. Arguably, my reference to 'taking one for the team' had not been the best approach. In my defence, I was stressed. Without Jerry, Frenzy would have been consigned to its app-less fate as a hopeless failure.

Since when have you been my pimp? Cass had screamed, having serviced Jerry in the limo not half an hour before.

Consider it taking one for the team.

When you let Yukio give you one up the ass, you can talk.

We retreated to our corners. Look I'm sorry, I said, inviting further punishment, once the bell sounded again. It was the only way.

Did you try very hard to come up with another plan? Cassidy screeched. My belting continued. Like negotiation? Maybe persuasion? Some kind of incentive?

Jerry isn't a normal person, I whimpered. You know that.

You brought him on board, she said, delivering another uppercut to the jaw.

I know, I know, I said, throwing in the towel. Jerry is a sex pervert. It's an a-dick-tion, I ventured in humorous defence.

Strangely, she wasn't in the mood for a laugh. Cassidy found a pack of cigarettes in one of the compartments. She lit one although she didn't smoke.

Did you even consider a hooker? She coughed.

He lusts after you, Cass.

The privacy screen rolled down. We have arrived.

Shall I wait here? Señor Flexistaff inquired?

Give us a minute, I barked back.

The screen rolled up in a more urgent fashion.

I don't need another lecture, Cassidy said.

This is not a lecture, I insisted. This is a statement of bottom-line fact.

OK, get it over with.

In ten minutes' time, Randy is going to be in this car with us, on his way home.

Get on with it.

So, as I've stressed a hundred times, you've done a brilliant job. You are even more competent and capable than you are beautiful, but Randy is head of the company and you have to step back.

Even if the stress kills him?

Let's make sure it doesn't, I said with more exasperation in my voice than I intended. Because if it does, the empire will collapse around us and you'll be turning tricks with guys who'll make Jerry look like Brad Pitt.

I cursed my parents. Why hadn't they taught me to keep my big trap shut?

The funhouse

I slumped into one of the multi-coloured beanbags that festooned the Frenzy funhouse, located with all the other digital asylums around San Jose. I helped myself to a decent brew from the fancy espresso machine that had cost us an arm and a leg.

The project was on a more even keel. Jerry had temporarily been 'sucked back' into the fold. Miki had sweet-talked Yukio into a six-month extension. Randy was getting stronger by the day and relishing being back at the helm. Cassidy was frustrated, but keeping the lid on it. The division of responsibilities between Miki and me was working. I was accountable for stakeholder relations, as it was known. This meant keeping Randy, Cassidy and above all, Dr. Jeremiah, sweet. Miki was heading up the product regeneration with Zak.

The funhouse was aptly named. I looked around the converted warehouse. The walls sported a rainbow of garish colours. The offices were ovoid metallic pods. The meeting rooms were glass cubes. The staff room, where I was lounging, was a wonderland of toys, table-tennis tables and techwaste. The sweet smell of weed and the bitter aroma of coffee beans invaded a nostril each.

I deliberately arrived early for my meeting with Zak. I liked to check the playground out for myself. It was hard to believe anything got done there. Meeting Axel, the head programmer, did nothing to assuage my concerns. I declined a toke. I was getting old. Since when did I consider a clear head a prerequisite for doing business?

How's it going, man? Axel asked, mid-puff.

How's it going here, more to the point?

Really well. We're cruising, actually.

I was on the point of asking him why 'cruising' was a KPI of good progress.

Did you see what was trending this morning, dude? Axel asked me.

No, it's daytime. I've been working.

I wet myself, Axel said, kicking his legs in the air. There's this guard dog…

Nothing further was forthcoming. I have heard of these animals, I responded.

This guard dog is deaf and blind.

A deaf and blind guard dog?

Yeah. And can you guess how he catches burglars?

I thought for a moment. Sniffs them out? I guessed.

You have heard the story, Axel giggled.

After this interlude, Zak's project supervision was firmly in my sights. It was lucky Randy hadn't visited this nuthouse yet.

At that moment, Zak walked in.

Axel sprung to his feet. Better leave you suits to your balance sheets and your action plans and whatever else you business dudes get off on.

He's off his face, I observed.

Relax, Zak advised, slumping down in Axel's vacated beanbag.

I can see why he's called the 'head' programmer, I added with acid on my tongue.

This is his free time, Zak explained. He works all night.

It's good to hear that he works at all, I replied sternly. Zak. Tell me straight how are things progressing here.

Really well, Zak said, with all the authority slouching at floor level allows.

Cruising? I suggested.

For sure.

You're not bullshitting me?

Not at all. The new guys I hired are ex-Facebook. They know the basic tricks. Better still, Dr. Jerry's associates are on board with the program. They're the right age group and, how can I put this? They don't have Jerry's ego, so they're cool with allowing the psychosocial media content to sit in the background.

What does that mean for the end product? I asked. Psychosocial media is our unique differentiator.

It still is, Zak reassured me. But, this time, Frenzy will present as cool and edgy. The kids will be into it because it's fun. Deep down, though, it will be amazing. It will revolutionise friendship as we know it.

We walked out into the California sunshine. I was thankful to be upright again.

Axel approached. Want that toke now, man?

Why not? I replied.

Zak's positive report had taken years off my life.

frenzship

Cassidy and I were ready and waiting in the foyer of the Hotel Bel-Air when Randy's limo pulled up. We were shocked to find a stunning redhead, dressed in full chauffeur's uniform, holding the rear door open for us.

I don't think you guys have met Miranda yet, Randy explained, craning round to see us settling into the back.

I shook my head.

Is Miguel on vacation? Cassidy asked.

Yep. On a permanent one, Randy confirmed, as the car drove away.

He's not dead, is he? I asked.

As good as, Randy concluded. Dead to me, anyways.

What happened? Cassidy asked. He's been with you forever.

The sonofabitch was diddling the maids.

Come on, Randy, Cassidy protested, you've known about that from way back.

It's not just that, Randy continued, shifting further round so he was almost facing us. He was stealing from me.

Never! Cassidy exploded.

He was. Truly. He was caught red-handed and not for the first time.

So you fired him? I surmised.

Sure as hell did, Randy roared. He turned to face the front again. Caught once too often with his cock in the till, Randy mused philosophically.

We cruised out to LAX. Miranda parked the limo illegally before heading off to collect the passengers.

Asian formalities were observed as Yukio and Loo joined us in the back of the black beauty.

This was Showtime. Somehow, I had delivered on my obligations. There had been some hairy moments, but my stakeholder management had worked out. Randy had kept himself busy sticking his fat fingers back into all the pies. Cassidy had started some strategic spot fires to distract his attention from Frenzy and the funhouse in particular. That way, she also got what she wanted, oversight of the Frenzy enterprise.

It's a poor choice of words I know, but I had to hand it to Cassidy for her dedication to duty in the jerking Jeremiah department. She had him wound around her little finger - literally and metaphorically. A harsh word from Cassidy was sufficient to bring Jerry's ego to heel and to command her lapdog to kneel at her feet.

Similarly, Zak, Miki and the team had worked wonders in the Frenzy funhouse. I'd had a prior demonstration of the new look and feel. And, like the Lord God, I gazed over what had been created and I saw that it was good.

We reassembled around the same board table in Randy's suite at the Bel-Air. It was Take Two. The demonstrations were made. The lawyers had their say. The marketing gurus showed their campaigns.

I looked for signs of trouble. Yukio seemed relaxed. Loo's nose was running. Cassidy had her hand in Jerry's lap. Only Randy looked concerned.

We were well prepared for this. It played out like clockwork.

You look troubled, Randy, I said. What's the problem?

He surveyed the people round the table. They were smiling benignly at him. Randy liked cutthroat business deals. He detested all this bowing and smiling. Sorry to jump on your joy, he rounded on the group, but I distinctly remember telling you, heart attack or no heart attack, that I didn't like the name, Frenzy.

Miki and I looked anxiously at each other, exactly as we rehearsed.

Miki cleared his throat. He waved to the marketing guys, who were still standing at the front. Randy isn't keen on Frenzy, he said. Could you run the fallback option round the track for us?

They demonstrated the alternative branding – FriendShip.

All eyes were on Randy.

He sneered. He reached into his breast pocket and popped a couple more heart pills. Is that the best you can do for the fortune we pay you? That name is as exciting as a Polaroid of Sonia in her underwear!

We had counted on that reaction, even if the mental image had taken us by surprise.

We have one last version, Miki announced. Then we're out.

Give it a burl, Randy commanded with a flourish.

The marketing team obliged.

Randy sat for a while. I like it! Randy announced.

Relieved applause rang out.

I nodded to the hospitality staff who had slimed their way silently into the back of the room. Let's drink a toast, I shouted.

Glasses were charged, as was Randy's account.

I give you, ladies and gentlemen, boys and girls, I added with a grin, I give you – frenzship!

I took a peek at your book.

When?

When you were at physical therapy.

Lorna! I'm disappointed in you.

I don't know why you need to be so secretive. Lorna is pouting. It's only a stupid book. That's what you say all the time.

It's OK, I say, trying to keep things in perspective.

I'm confused now. I was planning to talk to Lorna about her idea of going home, but I'm now uncertain whether I should. Lorna is avoiding eye contact by standing at the window looking out over the hospital campus. I keep my powder dry.

Why are you so keen to read the manuscript? I ask in even tones.

Because.

Come on. Why? I say, working hard to sound curious rather than censorious.

Lorna hesitates, then commits. I want to know what you think of me, I guess.

But why? Now I'm getting this wrong. I correct myself. I mean, you know how great I think you are.

Maybe, she says, returning to her old hair-twiddling habit when things get personal.

Has this got anything to do you with wanting to go home?

I instantly realise that I've blown it.

You always get everything mixed up! Lorna screams, running for the door.

How you can choose your friends, but you can't choose your relatives

Call me Tony

Once the time came for Lorna to graduate from the Montessori school, Ewan and Sally bucked the trend, sending Lorna to a State secondary school. This subject generated heated argument. Sally favoured a private school to provide Lorna with the more individualised attention she needed. Ewan acknowledged Sally's reasoning, but could not countenance such a compromise of his egalitarian principles. Lorna went to the Melville Senior High School.

The school's catchment was firmly working class. The children came from a rich variety of ethnic backgrounds. Ewan was surprised at how smoothly Lorna negotiated the transition. He admitted to Sally that the grounding provided by the Montessori system had prepared the pupils well for change in their lives.

Over time, the usual adolescent challenges emerged. Ewan would complain frequently to Sally about the lack of discipline exerted by the other parents. Sally would remind him that this school had been his choice.

This morning, Ewan hadn't exactly covered himself in glory. He was sitting outside the principal's office. He could but crack a smile. The passing students were eyeing him off suspiciously. He looked like a dumb kid who'd been held back in his class for the past twenty years.

He should have controlled himself more, especially in front of Lorna with her principal present. But Mr. Lancaster, call me Tony, was a sanctimonious prick. Any head teacher with the mantra – short hair and long skirts – was obviously a dinosaur. Ewan did not subscribe to the theory that doctors, lawyers and teachers were superior beings, founts of all knowledge, to dole out wisdom to the ignorant masses.

Sally and Ewan had been summoned to a meeting to discuss Lorna's non-compliance with the uniform policy. The school had a point. Its dress code, consisting of a polo shirt in green or red, black pants or a decent length skirt for girls, was hardly draconian. Sally tried reasoning with Lorna when the first letters were sent home. They were friendly in tone and advisory in nature. Ewan was dragooned to exert parental authority over their wayward daughter. Lorna endured these disciplinary tribunals stoically, but would find a way to hike her skirt skyward regardless.

Ewan recalled the last of these sessions some three weeks beforehand. Sally had fronted him in his home office for a post-mortem once Lorna had taken to her room.

That girl is exasperating! Sally wailed over her steaming coffee.

You're telling me.

You can't even call that a uniform. It's a shirt and a skirt.

I know, Ewan agreed, looking up from his computer. It's not a blazer and boater, is it?

Sally sat on his antique desk in a space between the newspapers and the computers. Of course, the uniform is irrelevant.

Completely. It's a compliance issue to her.

Lorna is basically anti-establishment, Sally said, looking pointedly at Ewan. She can't accept people telling her what to do.

And? Ewan asked, knowing perfectly well what was coming next.

And she gets that from you, Sally added, with a triumphant smile illuminating her face.

Ewan heard a loud double rap on the principal's office door. He looked up to see Lorna's teacher sweep inside. She shot him a curious look, no doubt wondering why he was sitting there.

They'd tried to broaden the nature of the discussion with Mr. Lancaster, call me Tony. Sally had been diplomatic in agreeing that the uniform policy was perfectly reasonable and that Lorna should abide by it. When asked her view on the matter, Lorna shrugged, apparently entranced by the sweeping geometric patterns on the carpet. Lorna's dismissive behaviour was nothing unusual. Tony was having none of it. His body language stiffened.

Drumming his feet on the floor sitting on the naughty bench, Ewan could recall the principal's words that got his goat.

We can't have one set of rules for you and another for every other student, can we, young lady?

Ewan was riled both by the message and its condescending tone. He sat forward to enter the fray. Sally responded calmly before Ewan could wade in.

To us, Lorna is not a student, she is an individual, she said.

Of course, the principal conceded.

Sally continued. Mr. Lancaster, Tony, we understand the necessity of rules and we have spoken to Lorna about it, but a skirt that's slightly too short is not a big deal in the scheme of things.

Mr. Lancaster shuffled in his seat. I'm sure you understand, he said, looking from Sally to Ewan in search of some non-verbal support, that I can't make an *individual* rule for your daughter.

Fuck your rules! Ewan interjected.

Sally flashed him a stern look. Excuse my husband, Sally continued. Surely the role of the education system is to recognise the individuality of its pupils and nurture that.

Of course, but...

Sally stuck to her guns. ...There are no buts, Mr. Lancaster, Lorna has come from the Montessori school environment where she was encouraged to be true to herself.

I understand, but I am charged with the responsibility of building a school community where all students can thrive.

Ewan could no longer hold back. A community? He blazed. Is cyberbullying part of your *thriving* community?

I don't know where you're coming from with this. In any event, you need to calm down.

Fucking hell, Tony, I'm talking about double standards and warped priorities. We've been hauled in here to deal with our daughter's heinous dress code violation, while her classmates, who for reasons best known to their parents are all allowed to bring fucking phones to school, are victimising some poor African student or some kid with a learning difficulty on Facebook from the playground!

Mr. Lancaster looked at Sally in the hope of a calming influence. Ewan noticed the exchange of looks. Sally was giving him the evil eye. He was out of line.

I'll wait outside, he said limply.

When Sally and Lorna emerged from the office, Ewan got the frosty reception he was expecting. They made to brush past him. He grabbed Lorna by the elbow.

I apologise for my behaviour, he said dolefully.

You're an embarrassment, Dad, Lorna said, wrenching herself free.

I was sticking up for you.

No you weren't, Sally growled. You were on your soapbox.

Ewan let them go. He had driven to the school in his own car. This state of affairs was all his doing. What had he expected from the State school system? They don't have the resources to deal individually with a thousand students. There's nothing they can practically do about Facebook if the parents don't accept responsibility.

Ewan cut a dejected figure, plodding towards the car park. He would apologise to Tony. In truth, he owed Sally an apology too. Lorna, even more so. He had pressured Sally into Melville High. Sally hadn't been opposed to it, but she'd wanted to consider more seriously a private school. Maybe he had sacrificed Lorna's individuality on the altar of his own ideology? His dad, Jamie, would be proud of him.

As the car beeped in response to his electronic key, Ewan didn't feel very proud of himself.

Demolished

Ewan and Sally had been making the usual preparations for the onset of puberty in Lorna, but still found themselves totally defenceless when the ferocity of the storm hit.

Lorna had been a sickly baby, a misfit toddler and a renegade young girl. Now she had emerged as a rebellious teenager. Ewan's anxiety level was high, but he took some perverse comfort that her hitherto deviant behaviour had finally converged with the norm for teenage waywardness. Lorna was just like all the other girls – staying out, drinking and shouting at her parents. Ewan considered Lorna typical of the spoiled-brat generation his parental peers had spawned. Out of ideas as to how to quell this rebellion, Ewan had been hatching a plan to create a parents' alliance.

Ewan picked at his marinara while Sally absentmindedly twirled her carbonara around the prongs of her fork. They sat there mute. To Ewan, they seemed like an old married couple. The only difference was they hadn't run out of things to say to each other. The prevailing mood was not boredom. Their silence was more like the sombre mood of a defeated dressing room.

It was true. They were demoralised. They were failing with their daughter. For all their intelligence, education and communication skills they had no answers.

What are we going to do with her? Ewan threw it out there.

As expected, it drew no response. He was in eggshell territory - Ewan's customary fragile terrain. He had to do something. He calculated his options. Say nothing of what he was thinking and try to make it through dinner? Signal his intentions, but let it rest? Go for it?

Ewan ordered two more glasses of wine. We have to change our approach.

I don't want to talk about it, Sally said. I'm too tired.

I don't want to talk about it either. I want to do something. I *need* to do something. *We* need to do something.

The waiter deposited the drinks in those trendy tumblers Ewan hated. He was dressed all in black, symbolising Ewan's funereal mood to a tee. He made to clear the half-eaten plates. Finished with these? He checked.

Yes, No, they responded at odds. Laughter broke through for a flickering second. This was a fleeting gap in the cloud through which the light might shine.

We have to intervene, Ewan said.

What do you mean, *intervene*?

Let's get the parents together.

What would that achieve?

A common front.

You can forget Jade's mum, Sally said. She's hopeless.

But maybe she won't be in a group. Peer pressure is a powerful thing. I don't have to tell you that.

You do realise that I've spoken to all the parents before, Sally said.

I do. And so have I. But we've never tried to get the group of parents working together before.

That's because it's impossible, Sally said.

Why is it impossible?

The other parents are different from us. If Lorna had gone to a private school...Sally held up her hand to stop Ewan interjecting... things would have been different.

But...

...No buts. They would have been different.

You agreed to send her to a State school! Ewan protested.

I did. I'm not denying that. Sally flashed Ewan one of her 'shut up' looks. If you didn't keep interrupting me...

...Sorry, he said, sitting back in his chair.

Things would have been different. That's all I'm saying. I'm not suggesting what we did was wrong. My point is that the other parents at a private school would be more like us. They would be more articulate and more strategic. They'd be just as indulgent. Probably worse. But they would be people we could talk to about a common stand.

We still have to try, Ewan insisted.

I'm not being negative, Sally said. We have to face facts.

I know it's a long shot. But we have to try something different.

That shrug again.

I'll do it, he said.

What do you mean? Sally asked.

I mean I'll put the time into this.

You don't have the time.

I will make the time. Just let me. Will you let me?

To be honest, I haven't got the energy to stop you.

By the bell

It seemed a good idea at the time. Right now, Ewan wasn't so sure.

Assembling the parents had been no easy task. It required the rat cunning of the POWs in the Great Escape. Ewan acquired the other parents' phone numbers by stealth. He then worked his way through the list, inviting them one by one. In terms of degree of difficulty, securing a workable date was comparable to a triple-twist dive with pike. Persuading the invitees not to tell their children about the meeting was akin to undertaking the leap into a freshly drained pool.

Sally remained sceptical that this gathering would do any good. She was going along with it for Ewan's sake. It was up to him to run the meeting. While Ewan waited for the right moment to get proceedings underway, Sally busied herself in the kitchen, arranging platters of cheese and biscuits and filling willow pattern bowls with crisps and peanuts.

Ewan called the group to order. Reluctantly, the guests took their places on the two sofas and the kitchen chairs conscripted to make up the numbers. Ewan surveyed the group like a general inspecting his troops.

Jim, tall and bald, sat stiffly. His wife, Margaret, round and cuddly, balanced a plate awkwardly in one hand and a wine glass precariously in the other. Maria, dark and beautiful, struggled to keep her short skirt decent on the sofa. Her husband, Gino, impressive guns rippling from his vest, sat cross-legged on the floor beneath her.

Wayne's massive bulk was testing the resolve of the upright chairs. His wife, Tamara, not quite as big, was setting a new standard for fast food, judging by the speed at which the nibbles were disappearing into her mouth.

Finally, Ewan registered Julie and Chen, the Asian couple seated together on the other couch. They smiled politely, sipping nervously at their soft drinks.

Wendy, Jade's mother, hadn't made it. Jade was the ringleader of the group of wayward girls, spurred on by her neglectful, equally immature mother. Sally had predicted this. Ewan's confidence sagged. It was hard to imagine much progress being made without Wendy coming on board.

Ewan cleared his throat. I guess you're all wondering why I called this meeting.

Ewan realised the stupidity of this attempt at humour. He wished he could recall that opening line like an ill-conceived email. Luckily, he was saved.

By the bell.

Whirlwind Wendy

Ewan was a study in frustration. He waited impatiently for the storm of whirlwind Wendy to abate.

Jade's mother lashed the group with excuses, smashed its decorum and scattered its members to the four corners of the house.

Ewan feared Sally was right. These people were unprepared to face the problem. They would prefer to ignore it rather than deal with it. In taxation terms, they sat somewhere between issue avoidance and issue evasion.

He re-herded the cats as best he could. Thanks for coming everyone.

Wendy hadn't quite blown herself out. She forced herself into a gap on the sofa, tipping Margaret's cheese and onion crinkle cuts down between the cushions.

Don't worry about it, Wendy, Sally chimed in to stop the fussing.

Ewan was relieved that Sally had got involved at last. He soldiered on. We thank you all for coming. This is not going to be an easy conversation. But, to get to the point, I think you'd all be concerned about how our girls are spending their time these days.

There was no reaction. Not a flicker of recognition. This was a tough audience. He'd expected a few nods of agreement. Julie and Chen smiled back at him, but he could hardly take comfort from that.

Ewan hesitated. Sally chipped in again to save him. We're very worried about our daughter.

Obviously we can't speak for you, Ewan resumed. But *we* feel this group of girls is a bad influence on each other.

Maria looked put out. In what way? She asked curtly.

Ewan motioned to Sally to let him respond. Some worrying things have been going down in our house lately and I can't imagine life is a bed of roses with your girls either.

He could sense he had overstepped the mark. A tense silence descended over the gathering. The guests shuffled awkwardly in their seats. They looked at each other, hoping someone else would say something.

Ewan and Sally exchanged glances. He was getting worked up. His wife looked sternly at him.

Gino stood up. The others relaxed.

You're right, this is awkward, Gino said. But there's no point in us going to all this trouble if we are going to sit here and waste time. He left the words hanging in the air.

Go on, Ewan said.

Please don't think me rude, Gino continued. I, we all, thank you for your kindness and hospitality in inviting us.

There were murmurs of agreement.

But someone has to call a spade a shovel. The group is not the problem, Gino said with an air of finality.

Ewan was surprised that Gino had left it at that. I don't get you exactly, Ewan said.

The group is not the problem, Gino repeated. He hesitated then continued. So if I must spell this out further, I'm sorry to say…it is your daughter who is the problem.

Two different things

Ewan snapped. So your daughter's a perfect angel led astray by our Jezebel!

Listen mate, Gina shouted, if you didn't want to hear the truth, you shouldn't have called this stupid meeting.

I called the meeting to get to the truth, not watch people bury their heads in the sand.

So what are you saying about our girl? Maria said feistily, standing up to join the fray.

For Christ's sake, I'm not saying anything about your daughter, or about our daughter for that matter. I'm talking about the group of them. They're a gang, can't you see that?

What started like a meeting of the Country Women's Association degenerated into parliamentary question time. It was on for young and old.

Ewan was deflated. Accusations filled the air. In another setting, he would have suspected collusion. Ewan spent his working life uncovering and exposing conspiracies. He could almost smell them. But there wasn't so much as a whiff here. These people were of one mind without caucusing or rehearsal.

Sally stepped forward to quell the mob. She appealed for calm. She begged them to speak one at a time. He could hear the emotion in her voice as the insults rained down on them, but Sally could maintain her professional cool as long as Lorna was nowhere to be seen.

A weary resignation descended on the group. Resentment bubbled beneath the surface. Acrimony was treading water for the moment.

Wendy broke the silence. She hadn't spoken yet.

I'm gagging for a smoke, so I'll make it quick. Wendy looked directly at Ewan. Things got out of hand when your daughter started bringing that Muzzo round.

Who's Muzzo? Ewan and Sally asked in unison.

As you know, Wendy continued, fiddling with her pack of Winfield Red, I keep an eye on these kids when they come round to my place and…

…Give me a break, Ewan interjected.

Give you a break for what? Wendy shot back.

You don't keep an eye on them at your place. They go to your place precisely because they know you let them do whatever they like.

How would you know anyway? Wendy asked.

Sally stepped in. Please everyone.

Wendy ploughed on. Your daughter meets all these boys like Muzzo on the Internet and that's where the trouble starts.

You talk such crap, Ewan said. Lorna is the only one of the whole lot of them who doesn't go on the Internet. She doesn't even have a phone!

Are you frigging serious? Wendy stared him down.

We don't allow it, he responded limply.

Well then, Wendy said, gathering her belongings, what you think you allow and what your daughter actually does are obviously two different things.

That went well

As the angry parents filed out the door, exchanging sad looks with each other, Sally found the composure to see them out. She thanked them individually for coming.

Ewan searched through the empty bottles to find some shiraz to drown his sorrows. He collapsed onto the crispy sofa, rubbing his tired eyes. As if things weren't bad enough, he was sure to cop a blast from Sally. The front door closed. Footsteps rang out along the corridor. Ewan braced himself. BOHICA came to mind. Bend over here it comes again.

Pour me one, Sally said, flopping down beside him.

Ewan leapt hopefully to his feet. Maybe he could avoid the rectal examination. He woke a slumbering red from the makeshift wine cellar in the hallway. He detoured via the kitchen to grab Sally's favourite wine glass bought on one distant holiday to Turkey.

That went well, Ewan said.

Sure did, Sally replied.

I thought you'd be mad at me, he said.

I did too. But I'm more sad than mad.

Sally lay down with her head on his lap. He stroked her blonde hair, noticing from that angle the depth of grey in the roots.

Is she leading a double life? Sally sobbed.

Ewan stroked Sally's hair. I don't know.

Sally sat up to drink some wine. It's ironic, isn't it? I was convinced Jade's mum was the cause of all this. She's just a big kid herself. And I still dread to think what goes on at her place. But it seems we're no better than my clients. We can't see what's right in front of us.

We don't know that yet, Ewan said.

With or without us

Ewan let the dinner party conversation wash over him. He swirled the red wine absentmindedly around his glass. He politely declined his hostess's offer of a second serve of Cointreau trifle.

The travails of parenting teenage children dominated the dinner party conversation. It was the same at every gathering these days. Ewan reflected on how every generation was the same. His dad occasionally took time out from Marxist orthodoxy to ear bash his cronies on the subject of his ingrate son.

This group of friends, formed mostly from Sally's work mates and parents they'd connected with from Montessori days, had once talked about sex and mortgages. Those days seemed free and easy compared to the group therapy that was the norm of late.

Having thought about his father, Ewan wondered what he would make of this group. He smiled at the thought. One of the dinner guests caught it.

First sign of madness, he said.

What's that? Ewan asked.

Laughing to yourself.

Oh, yes.

Care to explain?

Ewan hesitated. Actually, I was wondering what my dad would think of our friends. He is a committed socialist, Ewan added.

And?

He'd think we were appallingly self-obsessed and he'd marvel at how middle-class people like us invariably make fucking awful parents.

Sally drove home. She drank a lot less than Ewan when they went out. Ewan was quiet, still contemplating the next steps they needed to take with Lorna. She was becoming increasingly sullen and introspective. There was a lot going on inside her head to which her parents were not privy. Then there was the prospect of a secret life.

Our friends think we're too strict, Sally said, bringing Ewan back to the moment. They think we should give her a phone and be done with it.

Too strict compared with them?

Compared with every parent we know.

That's because all the people we mix with befriend their children rather than parent them.

As I've told you before, all the other kids have been given mobile phones and iPads. And now we find ourselves in a much worse situation – it seems Lorna has got a phone from somewhere and God knows what else!

We don't know that yet, Ewan protested. I really like our friends. But they are all bourgeois at heart. They send their kids to private schools. They indulge them rather than guide them.

What about the parents at our daughter's *State* school? They are not rich, but their children are not expected to live in a cave.

Ewan sighed and tried to compose himself. Do you honestly believe that Lorna's behaviour would improve if we indulged her more? Do you consider it appropriate to grant impressionable young minds unfettered access to the Internet, pornography and stranger danger?

I simply repeat, Sally said, with the irritation deliberately measured in her voice, that we are alienating our daughter by treating her differently from her peers, and it seems that she's going down the path of trouble with or without us.

There was a momentary lull. Ewan remembered something relevant he'd been meaning to tell Sally.

I discovered something interesting on the same subject the other day.

Go on, Sally said testily.

You know this new cult, frenzship?

I read something. I don't know a lot about it.

I've been looking into it. It's highly sophisticated with a deep grounding in human psychology.

Yes, that's what I read.

I bet you can't guess who's behind it.

Try me.

Ewan told her.

Truly? Your old friend?

Ewan nodded. Small world, isn't it?

Lorna hasn't stopped by for a few days. I'm worried. I want to contact her. Cassidy advises me to let things be. Reluctantly, I comply.

This morning is so important and I want Lorna there. I'm about to attempt my first unaided steps under the watchful eye of my physical therapist and with the safety net of the parallel bars within reach.

I eye off the clock nervously.

She'll be here, Cass reassures me.

It's time. I stumble. Cass reaches clumsily for me. My therapist merely nods encouragement. At that moment, Lorna rushes in, hot and bothered.

I smile broadly at her. There is no way I will let Lorna down. These steps will be taken on my own and with no support.

It will be done!

The reason why people toast absent friends

Reunion

We were through the worst. In terms of the marketing clichés, frenzship was knocking every pitch out of the ballpark. The concept of psychosocial media captured the public imagination. It was kooky and cool. People were intrigued at the prospect of being introduced to perfect friends. They strained our website capacity to the limit. They downloaded the free app faster than ITunes could deliver it. Jeremiah was basking in the academic glory. Cassidy was relieved to have Jerry's mind and hands elsewhere. Randy was pleased as punch that Facebook had taken such a hit.

I made the mistake of letting down my guard. I was relaxing in the green room, having tagged along with Randy to a TV interview. Randy loved the limelight and performed surprisingly well under its beam. He came across as a genial eccentric as opposed to the irascible tyrant we knew he could be.

I was reflecting with some self-satisfaction on how far we'd come. It had been a hard road. It had made me grow up and re-evaluate many things about myself. My fundamental values, or rather lack of them, were still in place. But I felt different. I couldn't quite put my finger on why.

My mother had been pestering me since frenzship was launched. She was proud of me, I guess. I had fallen into the habit of letting her frequent calls go through to voicemail.

I glanced at my phone. She had rung me three times in the last hour. I stepped outside to get some peace and quiet.

I rang my mother back. She picked up immediately. I was unprepared for her news. My father was dead.

After the long night flight, my mind was playing tricks on me. I thought I caught a glimpse of Ewan across the crowded arrivals hall at Heathrow. Could that be him? I called out. He couldn't hear me over the hum of chatter, public address calls and the distant revving of jet engines out on the tarmac. I chased after him, swerving my bags around the innocent bystanders.

I elbowed my way within earshot. Ewan, it's me!

We backslapped. So sorry, he said.

He sounded like an Aussie. I asked the stupid question. What are you doing here?

Your mum contacted me.

Of course. I should have told you myself. I guess I didn't want to bother you.

My dad died at one in the morning. Bang on time. He'd always been a stickler for punctuality. It was death by mismanagement rather than misadventure. Celestial records confused his number with someone else's. He'd been cruising through life. He had the check-ups and full body scans only the rich and wealthy can afford. He wasn't ill. Then he died. How stupid is that?

I was touched that Ewan was there for me. I needed a friend. We exchanged news and gossip in the cab. It was a relief to escape reality for a little while. I was dreading the moment of reunion with my poor widowed mother.

The burying and grieving process was dreadfully depressing. Mother was in denial. Magical thinking had the better of her. She imagined that Dad would walk back through the door if she ignored the need to bury him. It fell to me to do the heavy lifting, and I'm not just referring to the casket. Somehow I managed to arrange the funeral and organise the wake. It was some undertaking.

Ewan's company was a welcome distraction from the drudgery of demise. As soon as we could decently nick off, I hired an old Jag and we headed out on a road trip up memory lane to Oxford.

Do you remember 'skinhead'? Ewan asked, once we'd barely inched our way onto the M40.

Of course, I said in an offended tone. We come running.

We come running, Ewan agreed with a smile.

Is that what you're doing here? I asked.

In a way, he said thoughtfully, although it doesn't count without using the safe word.

Now that you're a professional wordsmith, have you worked out what a safe word is? I teased him.

Maybe.

We let the scenery zip by. It's amazing how old friends, once reunited, can drop into an easy silence. Ewan broke it. I knew there was something on his mind.

How'd you get into this frenzship caper? He asked.

Long story.

We've got plenty of time.

The short version is that I met these dudes in Paris who were all over the emerging new technologies and then I ran into this crazy venture capitalist in LA who could bankroll our little invention.

Ever the entrepreneur!

Are you still a commie?

Don't start that, Ewan said. I was enjoying our drive.

You're no fun.

If you want a classic argument, Ewan said putting his feet onto the dashboard, I think frenzship's dangerous.

I snorted. You think getting out of bed's dangerous!

Seriously…

…Actually, I interrupted him, for once in my life, call it my new maturity if you like, I don't want one of these debates.

There's a first time for everything.

I read your piece about Assange and I'm sure your typically Luddite views about social media would be illuminating, but, you know what, I just don't want to go there.

I thought you were just starting an argument, Ewan said, laughing.

No, no this time. We're here for my dad's funeral. Out of respect for the old man, can't we just be two old friends catching up?

Sure we can, Ewan said, relaxing back into his plush passenger's seat. Let's go to the King's Arms for a streak!

Ewan suggested taking the park and ride to avoid the perpetual grid-lock of cars navigating through narrow lanes built for the horse and cart. I was having none of that politically correct shit. Instead, we drove around for ages looking for a parking space. Eventually I dumped the car in a half hour space. When your dad has just died, there's not much more traffic wardens or the universe can do to you. We detoured down some of our old short cuts to meander our way into town. We stopped to stare at the buildings on Broad Street.

Look at this place, Ewan said.

It's incredible, I said, endorsing his vibe.

We didn't notice it when we were students, Ewan said, looking up in wonder at the streetscape.

We didn't really live here, I said. This was a movie set.

We walked on. It's eerie, Ewan said, but it feels like I've never seen this place before.

It's like Amazing Grace. I once was blind, but now I see.

We were fully internalised back then.

I smiled to encourage him to expand.

The young are captive to their hormones, emotions and insecurities to such an extent that they live inside the cocoon of their own minds and bodies. Do you know what I mean? Ewan said.

Kind of.

Ewan spoke with familiar passion. They are insulated from the out-side world. They are impervious to what is external to them. That can be another person's suffering or the breathtaking history of an old city. Youth is fully internalised.

I think I get you, comrade, I said, settling back into the familiarity of our old friendship.

Ewan put his arm round my shoulder. We walked like that all the way to the King's Arms.

We took the Jag for a spin to Headington, a few miles out of Oxford. We spent the next couple of days eating and carousing, ostensibly to drown my sorrows. We talked bullshit about the past and the present. We observed the ground rules. We bonded like we'd never been apart. That's the amazing thing about friendship. You can pick it up like a favourite sweater. When you put it on, it feels familiar and comfortable like you've been wearing it every day.

We braved the cold afternoon wind to sit in the garden of the White Hart. It was a classic rustic pub – genuine Tudor with 'Duck or Grouse' signs. Despite what Ewan dubbed shithouse English weather, the locals flocked to enjoy the great outdoors.

We were forced to share a table with two middle-aged ladies who said 'love-ly' in sing-song style every other word. The garden was love-ly, the food was love-ly, your sister's wedding was just love-ly and I reckon your hair looks love-ly like that.

We felt obliged to join in. The bench was love-ly, the fork was love-ly and when I described my last crap as love-ly, we fell about like nitrous oxide victims. The lovely ladies continued love-lying without drawing breath. They barely registered the mirth and mayhem they were creating for others in their table-lands.

We fought for self-control. I imagined my parents in the 69 position. I hovered on the threshold of sanity. Ewan and I had eschewed the L-word for a whole minute. Our faces were almost straight and we were studiously avoiding eye contact. Just when we thought it was safe to wade back into the conversational water, one of the love-ly ladies unreasonably changed tack on us. She returned to the subject of her friend's hairdo.

Do you know what? She asked.

Oh no. Please don't!

You're so lucky you can have your hair cut short like that…

Don't you dare!

…and not look like a lesbian!

It wasn't our fault. These women wouldn't play fair.

I spent much of that afternoon excusing myself to talk with Cassidy back in LA. She was venting about Sonia interfering in the business. She didn't seem herself. She accused me of dissing her and not missing her. Quite a few times I'd been on the verge of hanging up. My anti-conscience counselled against it. It called up the highlight reel of Cassidy and me in the sack. Trust me, she was no butch Cassidy, short haircut or not.

I returned to our rickety garden bench from a toilet trip timed for giggling recovery. Ewan had made himself useful. Two Wadsworth dark ales beckoned. The love-lies had deserted us for their own table.

Cassidy's breaking my balls, I moaned.

Try having a teenage daughter.

That would be worse, I conceded.

Having a kid hasn't exactly been a bed of roses, Ewan said sadly. Sally went through hell giving birth. Lorna was holed up in the ICU for months. Mother and child couldn't bond as they should.

You should've told me, I said.

You should've asked, he responded.

I shrugged the remark off.

Suffice to say, Ewan continued, Lorna is a challenging teenager to say the least.

Aren't they all? You were a total wanker as I recall.

Yes, yes, but Lorna is different. She's a really bright kid. She could be anything. We just don't get her.

I'm warming to her already.

Yes, you're still very amusing, Ewan said sarcastically, but I'm trying to find a way of telling you something else.

Encouraging him to explain was like extracting an entire transfusion from the proverbial igneous substance. After a long break, Ewan spoke.

Things are OK now. But I've been a total jerk.

So what's new?

Very funny, he said, not looking amused. I had an affair, he muttered under his breath.

When was this?

A few years back.

So why are you telling me now?

It's strange. I can't explain it but I feel I need to.

Ewan told me the story. He was too embarrassed to look at me. The words spluttered falteringly at first as if through a blocked pipe. Then they gushed forth, released by a verbal plumber.

It was my editor, he said.

Bonking the boss. Nice one!

Ewan ignored me. We liked each other and life was tough at home. One thing leads to another.

Go on, I said.

It lasted a year. It's over and done with now. Well and truly.

I absorbed the information for a moment. How are things now between you and Sally?

We're fine now. But there will always be an issue of trust.

It dawned on me what he'd done. You told her about it, didn't you?

I had to. I felt so fucking guilty.

It was still a stupid thing to do.

That's what everybody says, he conceded. But I had to.

I fetched in another round. Ewan still looked troubled. You OK? I asked.

Yeah, I'm OK, he replied, picking up his pint.

Why did you tell me all that? I asked

Because you're my oldest friend.

I pondered for a while. That's weird, I observed.

I know.

Ewan had a stopover in Hong Kong on his way back to Australia. On the spur of the moment, I decided to go with him and make my way back to LA that way round.

After our nostalgic trip to Oxford, I thought I'd maintain the theme by introducing Ewan to some of my old haunts in Honkers. I took him to my favourite bar just off the Mid-Levels escalator.

After a few beers, we careered like skateboarders down the moving staircases. We clambered aboard a steamer in the nick of time. They hauled up the rusty green gangplank and sounded the siren. We shot the breeze, gazing out across the water at the junks and the junk sloshing back and forth in our ferry floss.

Hong Kong had been my home from home. I loved it – the steamy heat, the pungent aromas of the hawker stalls and the endless hustle-bustle of humanity. The perfection of my island love affair had but one blemish. The car domination always got to me. You couldn't walk anywhere at street level. Overhead walkways sprouted like mushrooms, poisonous ones at that.

When I lived there, I would jaywalk in protest. I played what I called 'Hainanese chicken'. I would sashay across the road, mimicking the buses, trucks and motorbikes that changed lanes without warning. I would swoop and sway like a lion dance at Chinese New Year. My antics drew raucous support and foul-mouthed invective in equal measure from the hawkers in their grubby white singlets and the toothless old crones squatting by the kerb. They cheered or chivvied me, grateful for some fleeting distraction from the tedium of a life spent waiting.

I steered Ewan to my favourite yum cha joint. I led the way, initiating him into my cross-stressing. Within seconds, he fell *fowl* of a rusty bicycle, piloted by a man of venerable age but minimal body weight, laden precariously with a squawking tower of chickens. Ewan was shaken by his near-death experience, but regrettably not stirred to try again to traverse that vehicular valley of death.

No fucking way, he said, rebuffing my proposal that we have another go. Let's join the sane people up there.

You're as boring as ever, I responded regretfully, scaling the iron steps behind him to become just another Luke Skywalker.

This is a capitalist's paradise, Ewan observed, as we made our way through yet another shopping centre connected by walkways. You force the workers who make the goods to spend their leisure time walking past shops so they can buy the things they made, but at a fat profit. It's just like the company store.

I took him by the elbow, guiding him towards the exit we needed. All courtesy of your freedom loving People's Republic of commie mates over the water, I said.

We emerged from the arctic environment of the *Lucky Plaza* or *Happy Gardens* or whatever it was called into the steamy outdoors. We were greeted by a sight that took my buddy's breath away.

The walkways were full to the grilles with chattering girls. The army of Philippino maids conscripted for domestic duties in HK got Sundays off so the families could have their cramped apartments to themselves. The women had no place to go, save the pedestrian overpasses. They would congregate there in plague proportions to gossip, groom and play games high above the bustling city-state.

Holy Shit! Ewan exclaimed. This is fucking unbelievable!

I remember that lunch well. The food was magnificent. The dishes were served on a spectrum of plastic side plates, colour-coded for price. They towered above us by the time we were full. The bottles of Tiger beer had gone forth and multiplied too. Every now and again, one would roll off the table to be fielded by a dutiful young girl. I speculated that she'd been placed at fine leg to cut off the prospect of us sneaking a quick run from the restaurant without paying.

What are you doing living in Australia?

We love it.

It smacks of colonialism, I said to get a rise out of my old mate.

Ewan ignored the sarcasm, explaining the great lifestyle they enjoyed in Western Australia. We drank like the final days before Prohibition. Our capacity for abstinence dissipated. Like footballers in a nightclub, we felt powerless to resist. We said yes to the foulest-looking dishes - the bat brains, the gorilla gizzards, the duck dicks, the polecat pancreases or whatever the fuck they were. We egged each other on like we used to do as boys when we dared one another to eat a hot chili from my mother's fridge.

The lunch wasn't memorable just for the food. The conversation was equally enlightening. Ewan was fired up by the spectacle of the pretty maids all in a row. He railed again against the depravity and cruelty of the capitalist system. He seemed to have closed his mind to the fact that Honkers was under the control of the communist Chinese.

This discussion descended predictably into another heated ideological brawl. We brandished half-gnawed drumsticks at each other and clumsily sloshed our beers to make a point. An urgent call of nature put an end to it. I stood up to grope my way to the piss-house.

On my way out, I yelled at Ewan in a voice so loud that it could be heard above the cacophony of Chinese conversations. You're still such a sanctimonious prick. Lighten up already. Hong Kong is great. It's fun! You should try having some!

We slumped back in our chairs when I returned. I eventually broke the tension, taking a big swig from the depths of another near-extinct Tiger.

Don't go, I begged him. Not back to the cultural wasteland of sheep and Sheilas.

It is my destiny, he declared with an elaborate sweep of his arm.

I found myself on the verge of a drunken, 'You're the bestest friend I ever had' speech. I pulled up in the nick of time to arrest my impending descent into the sentimental and maudlin.

Do you know what those Philippino maids were saying to us? I asked, shifting gear as clumsily as an L-plate driver.

No. Pray tell.

They were offering to love us long time as they say in the classics.

Ewan shook his head, rousing himself from his drunken torpour.

That's not the half of it. What they had in mind for us, my friend, would make one of your precious stevedores blush.

Ewan sat back as if to contemplate the vicissitudes of life. Our distended stomachs weighed heavily on our energy stocks and the booze eventually dummed down our overactive brains. I settled the ridiculously cheap check, winking at the teenager as if to say your job's done now. I slipped her a couple of bills that were insignificant to me but potentially a life-saver for her.

As we staggered onto the bustling street, I grabbed my old mate's arm.

Care to join me on the passageways to *poontang*, my old china? I asked.

No, I don't think so, Ewan replied sadly. I'll head back to the hotel.

Really? I asked solicitously.

Yeah, I'm sure, he said. I don't want to go through that again.

I'm showing off, just a little bit. I'm shuffling from my bed to the upright chair that Cassidy has placed exactly ten steps away.

The bedside cabinet, the meals tray on wheels and the armchair have been distributed along the route in case I falter. I collapse back on my bed after two 'runs' as exhausted as if I'd just done a marathon.

Cassidy has taken herself off as we arranged to allow me to have the conversation with Lorna.

Hey, Lorna, we need to talk about you going home.

OK, she says, not looking up from the fashion magazine that has taken her fancy.

Lorna, you know I'm going to get this all wrong and muck this up.

Yes. I know you will.

Thanks for the vote of confidence. Anyway, here goes. I think you're amazing. You have helped me so much. I would never have got through the Nina thing and then this without you. How am I going?

OK, I suppose, Lorna says, looking up at me momentarily then avoiding my gaze.

And...Cassidy loves you too, and Miki, and even Randy in his own way, but I understand if you need to go home, and it's really OK. Can I stop now?

Lorna hugs me and the tears roll down our faces.

Why a friend is not a friend is not a friend

Doonesday

Doonesday could only truly be herself in her safe haven. Only there could she be free of the rules, demands and expectations.

Only deep in the night, did she dare to come and go the secret way. The rest of the time, she had to run the gauntlet. To survive, she'd take a deep breath, make her herself so small as to be invisible and focus so hard on the inner her that she barely existed in the outside world.

The sentries were on constant alert. Before them, she could never disappear. If she covered her ears or closed her eyes, it made them angry. She had no option but to endure all the questions, accusations and recriminations.

In the end, they would let her go. She would sprint along the corridor to freedom. She would collapse on the floor with her back jammed against the door. In time, her breathing would slow. The fear and anxiety would be drowned in a warm, soothing tide.

Her eyes would survey her kingdom, exploring the hiding places. The ones that hid her contraband. All those precious wonders the guards were too trusting to discover. Did they underestimate her so? Did they not suspect she would find a way around their rules? Maybe they didn't want to know.

She took heart and strength from gazing up at her heroes. Striking defiant poses, they inspired her from up high on the wall. She freed McTavish from his cage. She stroked him tenderly. McTavish, her guinea pig, had until recently been her only true friend. Sad.

Doonesday would soon access her lifeline. It was hidden where *they* would never think of looking. She shivered in anticipation of the excitement to come. She will connect with her truest friend. She will become one with the person who means more to her than anyone or anything - her soul mate.

She hadn't always been Doonesday. Life seemed so empty back then. She remembered imagining herself an atom pinging and firing in constant motion, belonging nowhere, adhering to nothing.

She was misunderstood. No, that didn't cut it. She felt like a creature from a parallel universe. Her parents and her so-called friends believed she was one of them. But she was merely living amongst them, observing their relationships and behaviours for a future time when life would make sense in a meaningful universe.

Were these thoughts pure fantasy? Perhaps she had once been born of aliens? Maybe she was one of the stolen children, but from another space-time paradigm.

Her parents claimed to be protecting her. They saw her as something fragile like an antique vase to be kept in their bubble wrap. They wanted to cocoon her from the world and all its dangers. They understood so little of the World Wide Web that they thought it possible to keep someone from it. Their attempts were futile. A young girl can find a way to get whatever she needs. Why did they even bother?

She had found a way, without their knowledge, to escape from her earthly being and fulfil her destiny. It had been ridiculously, laughably easy. After a few clicks of a button, she had found herself.

The revelation had been amazing. It made light of the effort of gathering the equipment, finding a way to connect, discovering the vital source and then answering the endless online quizzes and the personality and perception tests. She might not have persevered if it hadn't been the coolest thing to do.

Then it was like seeing God. Suddenly life's possibilities seemed endless. She had travelled through time and space to her own universe. Once the pieces of the jigsaw slotted into place, the total picture made perfect sense. The chances of finding just one kindred spirit in one tiny corner of the world were infinitesimally small. When the scope of the search was expanded to every corner of the globe (the galaxy?), when the pool included friends of every age from every culture and walk of life, the prospects of finding so-o many people just so-o unbelievably like you rose exponentially.

FireHeart1000 was mysterious and sophisticated. Her avatar was a flaming pink heart. She pretended to be older than she was, but Doonesday could sense she was close to her own age.

FireHeart1000 was her first true teacher. When Doonesday had been overcome with the novelty of it all, FireHeart1000 brought her back to earth. Sure, it's cool, cool as, but it's just computer science.

How can it know that you and I should be friends?

That's what it does, stupid!

How does it do that?

There's lots of clever shit built into it. Psychology. All those questions and patterns and all that boring stuff you have to do to sign in, that like sorts through people in a million different ways.

I just love it, Donnesday cooed.

It's just science.

FireHeart1000 had that deadpan, dismissive tone to her. It sent shivers through Doonesday every time. Doonesday wanted to be like Fire-Heart1000. So worldly. So confident. So epic. The thought of losing her was too much to bear.

Doonesday held back as long as she could, but that need for reassurance would win out in the end. Can we always be friends? She asked.

That depends.

Don't you like me?

I do now or we wouldn't even be connected. It only allows people to connect who should be friends. You know that.

I know, Doonesday agreed.

But still...the cursor pulsed endlessly...people change.

You're scaring me! Doonesday typed. What do you mean?

They're re-testing you all the time, even though you don't realise it.

OMG. I didn't know that.

Yes, with all their science and psychology voodoo. Every little thing you type is analysed a zillion times.

What for? Doonesday asked.

To validate us. That's the word.

'Validate'? What does that mean?

You know, the friendships have to be valid. Just like when we were chosen. People change, don't they?

I feel sick, Doonesday said.

And then there's the limit.

What limit? What do you mean?

FireHeart1000 explained. There has to be a limit. This isn't some sci-fi fantasy. You can only have so many friends. If our bond weakens or if our other relationships strengthen, it could spell the end for us.

Doonesday thought she might cry at the memory. To distract her mind, she checked the dumb clock on the wall. Only ten minutes to the best thing in her life - hooking up with Amity451.

In such a short time, she had encountered all these amazing people. It was incredible how, with everyone presented to her, she had made a meaningful connection. In the false world of home, school, concrete and trees, she felt like one of a kind. In the real world, she belonged to a true community of friends.

Amity451 was her best friend. Maybe even more? That familiar tingle zapped her as it always did when she thought of him in that way. Amity451 was the only one in her entire life who truly wanted to know her. He wanted to understand every little thing about her. He found her that interesting and compelling that every little detail had to be revealed. He made Doonesday feel unique. He made her feel special in a way no one had before.

Doonesday was sure Amity451 could read her mind. The bond felt so strong that they could have been identical twins, maybe even clones of each other. He seemed to read her thoughts and predict her every move. Was he her controller? Did she exist only in a video game? Was 'Doonesday' his creation, allowing him to predict her every thought and action?

Amity451 intrigued her from the very beginning. He was like the best present you ever had, hanging high on the Christmas tree. If you stood on tippy toes, you could reach it. You could almost feel its shape and form. You could almost tell what it was. But you could never grasp it. It remained enticing yet elusive.

That was Amity451. He was magical, brainy and witty. Above all, he was fun. Fun in a way she hadn't encountered before. He was challenging and provocative.

Amity451 helped her grow up. He was constantly stretching her, pushing her boundaries, asking that one extra thing of her that was making her a happier and better person.

Everyone noticed the difference in her, even her parents. For the first time in her life, she felt happy. Not all the time. Not like in those dumb magazines for girls her age where the gorgeous model-types with long blonde hair meet the football captain and hold hands on the way home from class.

Feeling happy for Doonesday wasn't like that. She was still down a lot. School still freaked her out. Her parents were just...yuk. But she had things to look forward to. She had true connections, real friends, at last.

'Nice to see a smile on your face', her dad would remark if they chanced to meet. She would grin inanely back. He was too busy to notice. The temptation to reveal the truth was so strong. How did she restrain herself from coming out of her own closet? She wanted to let on, own up, broadcast it, that she had found people from her own universe just clicks away over the Internet.

So she held it in. How long could she go on like this? The restrictions made her want to scream. She detested all the sneaking around and the faking of headaches and period pains just to get out of school. It was the only way to get some time for what actually mattered in her life - connecting with her friends. The folks were so yesterday. Get out and make some friends, they kept nagging her. Yet she had them. Real, true friends. She just couldn't acknowledge them.

Doonesday opened the window. She fanned the smoke from her spliff away from the house. She poked her head back inside. Unbelievable – still five minutes to go. Doonesday swept McTavish up from the floor. She tweaked his ears and kissed his pink twitching nose. He at least tried to understand her. She dangled him out of the window like Amity451 would – to give him a thrill and test his courage.

How she loved Amity451's challenges! She calmed her nerves by recalling them in order. Picking a daisy, learning hello in Chinese, sniffing pepper up her nose, stealing a garden gnome...no, that wasn't next…that's right, scratching her name into a bus stand, then stealing the garden gnome, flashing her knickers, what was next?...what's the time?...two more minutes…switching on the hydrant at the shopping centre, shoplifting the skirt, that was scary, running off with the baby in the pram…OMG, did I really do that?

She missed one out. She always did that. The memory was so precious she didn't dare spoil it. Still one minute to go. Just this once wouldn't do any harm. It was the time she had the worst stomach cramps. Her mum thought she was faking them and dragged her to school. Her dad was hopeless as usual, just agreeing with everything the witch said. Then the teachers made her do gym and Jade just laughed and laughed at her as she was doubled over in pain.

She went to the toilet then snuck out of school without telling anyone. She took the bus and then ran home crying. She was desperate. She had those thoughts, bad thoughts that she wouldn't remember now. As *they* weren't home, she retrieved what she needed from its hiding place and logged in. Sweet, darling Amity451 was there. She hadn't the slightest doubt that he'd sensed her troubles and had dropped everything to be there for her.

They must have chatted for a whole hour. Her tears dripped onto the keyboard. Her typing was so terrible. He made little jokes about it. Amity451 was so tender and caring. He was so understanding. He knew exactly the right things to say.

'That was the moment I understood for the first what it meant to have a friend'. Doonesday giggled that she'd just said that out loud without realising it. Then, even after spending all that time looking after Doonesday, he still cared enough to set her a task. It was such a beautiful one. He challenged her to sit her parents down and talk to them and tell them exactly how they were making her feel.

It was so hard. But she did it. She couldn't fail Amity451. The olds were gobsmacked. Instead of tearing strips off her for wagging school, they hugged her. They took her out to her favourite restaurant. It was the best night she could remember with her parents.

It was all thanks to beautiful Amity451. He knew her better than she knew herself. He showed her the meaning of friendship. She felt that electricity again. He had been the first to plant a seed of friendship inside her. She could feel it growing into something even more beautiful.

Hey! The words flashed across the screen at the appointed time
He was there.
Hey yourself! Guess what, Doonesday typed
You kissed a prince and it turned into a frog.
Almost.

What am I guessing then?

My guinea pig has been flying.

Without a parachute?

Not exactly.

Without a safety net?

I was holding him.

That's not flying.

You're right.

Did you miss me?

Of course.

Do I light up your life? Amity451 asked.

Her fingers paused to take courage. You are my life!

Doonesday's heart was racing. The screen flickered. The silence was deafening. Had she overstepped the mark?

She was saved. A new message appeared. Here, piggy, piggy, piggy.

Doonesday smiled. Amity451 warmed her universe.

Here piggy, piggy, piggy. Speak to me.

He can't type.

Then you must channel him.

Like a medium communicating with the dead?

With the nearly dead?

I don't follow.

You will.

Doonesday's cursor pulsed in time with the fast beat of her heart.

Are you ready for your challenge?

Always ready.

Have I ever done you wrong?

Never.

Never? Repeat that to me.

You have never done m wrong - never, ever.

Doonesday awaited her next command. As always, she was giddy with the expectation. At the same time, she felt her true life force pulse through her veins. She'd never felt so breathlessly alive.

Her orders arrived. Is piggy, piggy, piggy alive?

Dah, ye-es.

It shouldn't be.

Shouldn't it? Doonesday felt her fingers shaking.

No, no way.

But I love him.

Will you not do something for me?

Anything.

Wring its neck for me.

Doonesday recoiled. She looked away from the screen. Amity451 was just testing her. Her loyalty must be unquestionable. Her vitality returned. If it would please you, she responded, I would.

Another pause. I sense you doubt me.

Never, Doonesday replied instantly.

Then don't mess with me.

I wouldn't.

But you are. You say 'would'. To prove your allegiance, you must say 'will'.

I will, she typed.

Now repeat the whole sentence.

Doonesday hesitated again. This is a test. It's just a test. She mustn't waver. I will wring its neck.

Good.

Now? Doonesday's fingers trembled.

Of course not.

Doonesday relaxed. She skipped across the room to drop McTavish back into his cage. It was just a trial. She passed. What joy to meet the challenge.

Doonesday's screen burst back into life. Do you think about our connection sometimes?

Always, Doonesday confessed.

Can you put your finger on it?

I feel it. It's almost like you can read my mind. I find it hard to put it into words.

Shall I interpret it for you?

Yes. You are so clever at such things.

It's simple really. We are deeply compatible, you and I…

Doonesday felt the electricity.

…We are aliens in our so-called worlds, but we are true free spirits. We reject the false boundaries of convention. We are spontaneous creatures, free to do what we want and do it as we please.

Exactly. We are kindred free spirits.

Shall we exercise our freedom now?

You've lost me.

Will you accept my challenge?

As ever. You know I will.

It is time then.

Yes.

I don't want you to wring the piggy's neck.

Doonesday felt so relieved. I knew it. I knew it! Her fingers danced across the keyboard.

Make the piggy, piggy, piggy fly.

Doonesday hesitated. What?

I want McTavish to truly fly. I want you to give McTavish wings.

He cannot fly. She feared serious repercussions from her defiance.

Yes he can. We all can. Fling him as high as you possibly can from your window and he will defy gravity, the very laws of Newton, and you will see that pigs can fly.

A cold dread chilled Doonesday, freezing her to the spot.

What are you waiting for? The screen demanded to know.

Cassidy is absent this morning, having final checks before the moment of truth. Now that Lorna and I have broached the subject of her leaving, she seems like her normal self again.

It's time for me to explore a little more deeply. Tell me what you're thinking, Lorna. You know, about going home.

She fiddles with her hair. It reminds me so much of when I first met her back in Fremantle.

I understand if you want to, I continue. Maybe you're right. You probably should go home. You're a different person now. Try it out again to see what you think of it now.

I'm wondering if Lorna is going to respond. Then she says. I don't know if I should.

Go on.

I don't really want to. I kind of miss the olds, but I don't want to get back to that horrible old routine.

You've changed now. And so have they.

I know. I don't know. I don't know if I should.

It's OK to be confused. Just sit with it. I'm confused all the time.

OMG, I might end up like you! She teases me with that wicked grin I love.

How to win friends and influence people

Cometh the hour

Cometh the hour, cometh the app, I said. There lies the fundamental truth of the twenty-first century.

Even airbrushed at twice life size in cardboard, Dr. Jeremiah looked pretty average. Like a statue of Christopher Columbus searching for the Americas, his squinting eyes scanned the horizon. Jerry's dorky comb-over had been gelled back. His comfy pullovers had made way for designer threads. Miki and I stared up at him like dumbfounded natives sighting giant ships.

In the right place at the right time, Miki said. That's how I'd put it.

That's rather uncharitable, I objected, steering Miki towards the podium for the book launch.

The truth hurts, Miki continued. People were tiring of Facebook. We lucked in.

Maybe so, I said in no mood for negativity. To buoy the tone, I swiped two more vodka somethings from a passing waiter's tray. frenzship's meteoric rise is testament to visionary thinking and sheer hard work, I announced, toasting our success.

I never thought I'd hear you talk about hard work, Randy joked, emerging from a throng of admirers.

Once he'd cleared death's door, Randy discarded healthy habits like a depraved nun. Contrary to medical advice, he stacked the weight back on and reverted to his intemperate ways. Fat not fit was again the order of the day. Greenback not green leaf was his modus operandi.

I was in a coma after my heart attack, Randy said as we shuffled forwards so the frenzship crew would be loud and proud, front and centre.

Miki and I exchanged glances.

Being in a coma was hell good fun, he reflected, shaking his head. Amazing that. I got my revenge on Zuckerberg in that beautiful sleep and here we are today doing it for real, he added, clapping us aggressively on the back.

Dr. Jerry's editor stepped forward at that point, tapping the micro-phone and raising her hands to bring the chattering classes to order.

I tuned out during her extensive valedictory. Miki was right. The timing for frenzship couldn't have been better. But our cult status hadn't just been a matter of luck. We had taken social media to the next level. We had redefined relationships in the formative part of the new century. We had invented the new social science. We were re-writing the social media textbook.

Miki nudged me from my daydreaming. Dr. Jeremiah had been invited to the lectern. There was a second cardboard cut out on the stage. Jeremiah and his evil twin surveyed the masses.

Without further ado, ladies and gentleman, I give you the man of the moment, the Social Psycho himself, Dr. Jeremiah Levine.

Cassidy squeezed between Miki and me during the generous applause. I put my arm round her waist. She'd been under the weather for ages, but tonight she was fabulous again.

The frenzship team exchanged nervous glances. Jerry was a genius, but basic human skills, like speaking and reading, were not his strengths. 'Social Psycho' had been ghostwritten on the quiet by a veteran drunk author from Venice Beach. The local bars were thriving on account of his being paid twice - once for his prose and again for his silence. The publisher's PR team had written Jerry's speech for tonight. They'd coached him in minute detail like a spy going live in a John Le Carré potboiler.

Is he going to ad-lib? Cassidy whispered.

Let's hold hands and pray, I suggested.

Jeremiah read from the script. He followed the text word for word. His monotone delivery was as inspiring as the supreme leader of North Korea reading from an IKEA instructional leaflet. On this occasion boring was beautiful and dull, delightful.

Psychosocial media is a product of its time. It is not about now. It *is* now…[pause for applause]…frenzship has its detractors. However, unlike its precursors, its core is underpinned by science. frenzship is about welfare not wealth. It's about people not profits. Social media didn't destroy community as some people say. Social media didn't devalue our sense of community or trash our notions of friendship…

We smiled hopefully at each other. Stick to the script, stick to the script, we muttered.

…Globalisation and the march of technology transformed our way of life. Communities are no longer neighbourhoods. They have become more not less. The world has evolved into the global village. Likewise, the nature of friendship has evolved and its geographic scope has expanded beyond our wildest dreams. Thanks to MySpace, Facebook and other social media prototypes…

He even remembered the dismissive tone he was coached to use on the word 'prototypes'.

…our friendship opportunities have grown beyond our wildest expectations. But that was all that happened. They got bigger, not better. In fact, the prospects of a meaningful friendship declined. We sacrificed quality for quantity. Depth for the shallows…

I could kiss him, Randy enthused.

…Then I invented psychosocial media. I had developed it over many years at UCLA. All it lacked was a modern application. And then. In fact, now, we have brought psychosocial media to the world thanks to the funky and fun framework of frenzship…

We cheered.

Way to go, Jerry boy, Randy whooped.

…and we have true, deep friendship again within our grasp. Not just with a small circle. Not just with the people we happen to meet in our little lives by chance. Now there is no restriction on our friendships. We have brought you friendship with the world…

Give that man a blowjob, I proclaimed, hugging the group to me while shrugging off Cass's disapproving sneer.

…frenzship has conquered the world. The appetite for psychosocial media is insatiable. The pressure to explain it to the world is now irresistible. We, academics, shun the limelight…

Like hell we do, Miki mumbled.

…but my good friends at Simon and Schuster were very persuasive. And so here we are today, not twenty-four months from the low-key launch of frenzship, revealing to the world the inside story of the science of frenzship. Please join me in celebrating the publication of my book, my future bestseller… [pause for laughter]…Social Psycho.

We screamed in joy.

If there truly is a God, he will ensure that even desperate perverts get laid tonight! I screamed.

Amen to that! Randy nodded approvingly.

Mon amour

The email from Nina took me by surprise. I was scanning my inbox in the back of Randy's limo with Cass by my side. Randy was on speaker-phone in the front.

Off the chart, my friend, he was crowing to one of his rival venture guys. frenzship's swelling bigger than a porn star's dick.

Cassidy was cranky with me most of the time. By contrast, she and Randy were getting along better now. Randy's empire was bigger than Ben Hur and she was on one hell of a chariot ride. I suspected even that wasn't fast enough for her. Yet her resentment towards Randy seemed to be diminishing.

I reacted with a start at the unexpected contact of Cassidy cuddling into me. I closed Nina's email instinctively. That spoke volumes about something. Cassidy and Randy got out at the hacienda. I stayed put in the limo to head out to Santa Barbara to iron out some contract wrinkles.

Alone again, I returned to Nina's email. It was mostly small talk, but it got to me. I felt a longing. I snuggled into the comfort of that familiar sweater of friendship. But this was more than friendship. I'd shut Cassidy out from the email. I did it without thinking. Did I still want Nina? Yes. Did I still want Cassidy? Yes. Was I, to quote the song, just a jealous guy? No. Was I just a shallow guy? I decided not to answer that.

After the chit-chat, she told me how proud she was of 'her boys', Miki and me. Write and me tell me everything about mon cher Nippon, she insisted. Was I a jealous guy now? Perhaps.

She gushed over what we'd done with frenzship. She described it as super-cool. She deeply admired the science behind it. I felt an impulse to convey telepathically some acknowledgment of Jeremiah's contribution. Then the image of Nina with Jerry was called to mind. I felt sick. I moved on.

Finally, the true purpose for her email was revealed. J'ai une conte très belle et inspirationelle! I have a beautiful story to tell you.

I put my phone aside for a moment. I wiped my eyes. Why did I feel so emotional? It wasn't the same sweater. It looked like the original, but it wasn't identical. Something had changed with her. I couldn't put my finger on what it was.

Nina had eaten dinner at her mother's place as she did week in week out. In the cyclonic chaos that was Nina's life, her mother was an immovable object. She stabilised Nina midst the flying debris of her whims and passions.

I opened my iPad and showed maman frenzship. I told her proudly that mes mecs, my guys, had created it. I took some credit, naturel-lement, for bringing the two of you together! Quand même, Mummy was in a relaxed mood that night and she was interested in how it worked. Like most people these days, she has a Facebook account, but rarely looks at it. Isn't this just another Facebook? She asked. Mais non, I insisted, and I showed her how it was different. She was intrigued. I had to slip out for a while. I left my tablet open on the kitchen table. I felt sure maman would try out the psychological testing.

When I got back, Mummy had a smile on her beautiful wrinkled face. She proudly showed me her profile. She asked me what I thought. It was amazing. I recognised my mother in every detail.

I left it at that, but a day or two later, I remembered my mummy's *affaire* with frenzship. I know it was naughty of me, but I couldn't resist the urge to complete the process she'd started. Once I'd signed her in and attached her psychological profile, I found my finger hovering over the all-important befrenz key. Should I? I had to.

I confess I forgot about it for a while. The Sorbonne is cutting staff again and I had to let more of my doctorate students go. It was just too awful. Anyway, the next time I was at Mummy's for dinner, I remembered. I logged in on my iPad. You won't believe it. She had her first allocation of frenz! Incroyable! I felt the strongest impulse to show her. My heart was racing. I plucked up the courage.

Mais non! She scolded me. You had no right, she complained.

I didn't put up a fight. I know chère maman very well. Her protests were token. She has an inquiring mind. I knew curiosity would kill this cat. I'm sorry for this long story, mais, mon amour, thanks to you, my mummy has a gentleman friend after all these years. Maman has a lover and she doesn't even know who he is! She knows that they will always be frenz because the bond is so strong between them. I know that they will be together this way when I am not around.

The story blew me away. The meeting with the attorneys came and went in a blur. *Mon amour*. What did she mean by that? It raised my hopes. For what? Was Cassidy not enough for me? I brought myself back to earth.

What did she mean by '…when I am not around'?

Nina asked me to kiss Miki for her and to send him her bons baisers. When I told Miki Nina's story, I left that bit out.

Thursday

The subtle changes were unnerving me. Somehow, like the Incredible Hulk, I was slowly turning green. My cynicism was melting away like an ice cream on a summer's day. Nina's love story about her mother strangely moved me. Some of Nina's expressions worried me just as much.

It should have been a joyful time. I just didn't feel that way. frenzship was going gangbusters. It was lauded by high and low, prince and pauper, saint and villain. The Guardian, of all publications, hailed it the innovation of the year. They praised it as the 'genuine world café'. They called for Jerry to win the Nobel Prize for science as the man who had reinvented friendship for the twenty-first century. Being Toy Story fans, they added, '…and beyond'.

While I was hardly practising asceticism Tibetan-monk style, I wasn't partying like it was 1999 either. A sense of dread weighed upon me. The younger me would have celebrated such success as pure justice. The wimpy new age me feared fame and fortune might be undeserved.

And then that fateful day arrived. It happened on a Thursday. This was a statistical aberration. Disaster generally strikes on other days of the week. Newspapers have pre-prepared banner headlines screaming 'Mad

Monday', 'Ash Wednesday', 'Black Saturday' and 'Bloody Sunday'. Quite possibly they have 'Fucking Friday' ready to go as well. But Thursday? No way bad things happen on that day. Until now. Those that predicted a hard rain was gonna fall did not don their gumboots in vain.

Cassidy had been picking fights with me continuously over dinner. She'd been so cantankerous of late that I let it go. She'd been mostly down, but sometimes up. Like a yo-yo.

You don't get it, do you? She accused me, stabbing at a recalcitrant crouton in her caesar salad.

Such questions from women are dangerous. You're in trouble if you answer 'yes'. You will be corrected and told you don't. The answer 'no' is an admission of guilt. It is tempting to ask 'what?' That's the worst of the three options. It implies not only guilt but indifference.

I resorted instinctively to, really?

That baffled her for an instant, but it did no more than buy me time.

Haven't you noticed how emotional I've been?

This question was nearly as dangerous, but I had to opt in. Of course I have.

And?

I presume it's women's troubles.

Oh! Women's troubles. You could say that.

I've been worried about you, you know that.

That's comforting because I had a miscarriage three months ago.

There was a lot to process in that. Fortunately, I had a night flight to New York to give me time and space to think. At first I was indignant. She told me she was on the pill! So what is she playing at? In time, the new caring me kicked in. Poor Cass. That must have been awful for her. How could I be so insensitive as not to notice? If she'd only shared this with me, I could have helped her.

I succumbed to the bottomless beverages available in first-class. I managed a few hours of fitful shut-eye. I felt less than average waiting for my bag at JFK. I checked my messages in the limo on the way to Randy's apartment on Fifth Avenue. Then I felt far worse.

It was Miki. He was hesitant, obviously choosing his words with care. I think we have a problem.

That's not a great way to finish a voice message, is it?

Your average kid

The emergency hook-up was to start in five minutes.

The frenzship executive team was assembling in Randy's business suite at the Bel-Air. Cass and I had taken the leisurely stroll from our bedroom to the meeting room. Cassidy had been insatiable that morning, taxing my capacity to perform under duress. Her recent revelation had unsettled me. You know what they say about pregnant women. Me no daddy I hoped.

Randy had stayed the night rather than head back to the hacienda. Sonia joined him. That was most unusual. I put my blue helmet on to keep the peace between the women. Miki had just texted in. He and Zak were a couple of minutes away, having consulted with the oracles of spin.

Dr. Jerry was resplendent in Full HD glory on the giant screen. He was unaware that we could see him preening. His ongoing makeovers had reached the point of total reconstruction. It was hard to reconcile the cool dude on the screen with the lecherous professor all of us knew and none loved. His skin had been moistened, his hair had been straightened and his teeth whitened. His clothes were designer retro. He looked every inch like Starsky. Or was the dark-haired guy Hutch?

Jeremiah was sitting in the communications room at the Westin Venice. His Social Psycho world tour had taken Europe by storm. He'd advanced faster than Hitler's tanks in 1941.

Once Miki and Zak arrived, Jerry was hooked in. We exchanged pleasantries with him while we waited for Randy to get off the phone. Jerry name-dropped as if, like his clothes, it was going out of fashion. In due course, Randy deigned to join us. Fucking asshole! He thundered. None of us cared nor dared to ask.

Miki brought the meeting to order. In his usual organised fashion, he got straight to business. Zak and I have just met with the Good Oil. Zak will share their advice with you, but let me first background you on the problem.

A fifteen year old boy in the Mid-West has committed suicide.

He must have lived in Cleveland, Randy quipped, anticipating grins on our faces.

As none of us was in the mood for jokes, Randy raised his palms in apology and slumped back into his chair.

This young man, Miki persevered, who didn't live in Cleveland, he added looking sideways at Randy, had a troubled life.

There you go, Randy interjected.

For Christ's sake, Randy, put a sock in it, Cassidy protested.

Miki surveyed the group to ensure he wasn't going to be further interrupted. He checked the screen for good measure. Jerry was filing his cuticles.

As I was saying, this kid was mixed up. He was acting out like most teenagers do. You know the score. Drinking, smoking weed, staying out late, not going to school - the usual stuff. This boy also had some issues - anxiety, depression…

…Your average kid, I observed.

Yes and no, Miki responded. Your average kid doesn't put a 22 in his mouth and pull the trigger.

The mental image dampened even Randy's exuberance.

Jerry interjected with a fractional time delay. While suicide is not statistically the norm amongst this age group, it may be a logical, and in that sense an *average* response, to his particular circumstances.

We looked at each other around the room. Before he became famous, Jerry had been a jerk. Now he was an alien.

Jerry's absurd interjection restored Randy's mojo. What the hell has one sick kid brain-painting his bedroom got to do with us? Randy demanded to know.

Maybe this will answer Randy's question, Miki said, losing his customary Mount Fuji cool. He flashed a slide onto a plasma screen, next to the one where Jeremiah was polishing his designer spectacles with the blue lenses.

It was a banner headline from the Dayton Daily News.

FRENZSHIP KILLED MY SON!

Jellybeans or Jihad

Zak reported on the meeting with the Good Oil. They'd stressed the need for damage control. They recommended communications that, while expressing appropriate regret and sympathy for the boy and his family, served to distance frenzship from the incident and accentuate all its positives.

Cassidy supported Zak's commendation of the Good Oil's approach.

Jerry thought we should wash our hands of the whole affair. He argued that there were so many contributing factors that it was absurd to link this boy's suicide to frenzship.

Randy agreed with Jerry in a strange axis of evil. In two days, no one will remember this kid's name.

Miki kept his head down. In the midst of this skirmish, he was wary of getting caught in the crossfire. Initially, I joined Miki on the sidelines. I was confused. This boy was fucked up already. He was renting himself out on the streets. He was a prime candidate to come to no good with or without the intervention of social media.

In an earlier life, I would have clung to these rationalisations like a drowning man hugs a rubber ring. I had good cause. Whatever happened to parental responsibility? If your child is hawking himself to pillow-biters round town, you damned well ought to know. And what about the boy? Who was he to mouth off at his mother? What right did he have to sneak out at night without permission? He could have done his home-work and helped around the house. Instead he took the easy option and he paid for the pleasure with his life.

In the here and now, I was feeling uncomfortable. The Dayton Daily News was alleging that this kid was groomed on frenzship by a predatory homosexual. They claimed that the perpetrator befrenzed him and then manipulated him Svengali-style to engage in degrading acts of prostitu-tion. The newspaper suggested that these unnamed practices were so lewd and disgusting that this wretched boy blew his brains out rather than live with the shame. If this were all true, could we justifiably blame the family or the boy alone and could our only acceptable response be to spin this drier than the best German washing machine?

I took my opportunity to weigh into the verbal fisticuffs. We need to think this through. We've got a lot riding on the success of frenzship. I agree we need to protect its reputation. But, we can't just sweep the bad stuff under the carpet.

Cassidy responded. That's not what I'm suggesting. We need to square the ledger, that's all. frenzship improves billions of lives every day. We can't trash its reputation because some weirdo allegedly misused it. In any event, we don't even know if he really did use frenzship.

Zak agreed. All Cass and I are saying is that we should go along with what our communications consultants have suggested. Let's get our positive story out there alongside our regrets and sympathy.

I say we just ignore the pissant Dayton Bugle or whatever the fuck it's called, Randy argued. Who gives a flying fuck what some schoolma'am editor thinks in some Mid-Western hellhole?

Randy, please don't take offence, Zak responded politely, but in this day and age, it matters what some hobo says on the sidewalk.

You've lost me, Randy said dismissively.

Cassidy weighed in to support Zak. Randy, what we're saying here is that what's printed in the Dayton Daily News is not just read by the God-fearing citizens of Dayton.

Jesus H. Christ, Randy screamed. His fuse was getting shorter and shorter. This is a two-bit story from a hick town and it will be staler than Sonia's home-made sourdough in a few days' time.

I nudged Miki. It was time for the voice of reason. Let's hear from Miki, I suggested.

You his ventriloquist now? Randy snapped.

Miki raised his hands. He was composed again. Please, everyone, take a step back. Let's stop arguing. Randy, with all due respect, what's published anywhere is read everywhere these days. Everything appears online. There are whole news agencies relaying every story published anywhere in the world to armies of followers on any theme you can name.

That's right, Zak agreed. Media is God and people prey to its garbage.

Miki continued. It doesn't matter what your passion is. It can be Plato or pornography. Jellybeans or Jihad. You subscribe to the newsfeeds of your choice. So this article is bad news for us and it…

…needs to be neutralised, Cassidy interjected firmly.

…cauterised before the cancer spreads, Jerry butted in.

Please, everyone, let's think not argue, Miki counselled.

A fragile peace was declared, momentarily.

We soothe

He nosed the rented BMW through rows of identical streets on the outskirts of Dayton.

It was a depressing neighbourhood. Was this a maintenance-free zone? Paint flaked off the old wooden structures and weeds flourished through the cracks in the crumbling concrete of the driveways.

He squinted into the pale, wintery sun. Is that 1276? This is it. He grabbed the documents from the passenger's seat. He was struck by an icy gust on opening the car door. The wind chill factor here was extreme. He pulled his coat collar up round his neck. He should turn the car heater down on the way back.

He jumped up onto the stoop. There was no bell or knocker. He peered through the frosted glass panel of the front door. Not seeing anyone or anything, he rapped loudly. After a few moments, the door creaked open. An obese middle-aged woman looked out at him. Her shy face was recessed into thick jowls and multiple chins. Round spectacles perched apologetically on a proud, bulbous nose. The woman wore a faded purple tracksuit, from which folds of skin protruded.

I think you're expecting me.

The woman nodded. Won't you come in?

Coffee was served. He accepted it to be polite. He declined the offer of cream and sugar shouted through the servery hatch.

The woman settled into the threadbare, maroon couch opposite. Their cups rattled nervously in their saucers.

I'm very sorry for your loss.

The woman nodded, choking back tears.

Do you have a photo of your boy? This was his standard practice. Don't let them sink into grief. Move to celebration of the life lived.

The boy's mother rested her teacup on a chipped glass coffee table, raised herself painfully from the sofa and then waddled across the room. She surveyed the photographs lined up in their matching wooden frames on the dresser. She made her selection.

Fine looking boy!

The woman nodded.

I can tell that he brought you great joy.

He did, she nodded, wiping at her weeping left eye. He sure did.

Alas, nothing can bring your boy back, he said, clearing his throat.

The woman looked up. Where did you say you were from again?

Our company is called the Good Oil.

The Good Oil? She said, pondering the meaning. Not for cooking, I guess. The hint of a smile on her face.

Not exactly, he said, seizing on the break in the tension. No, the good oil is for soothing. You know the phrase, oil on troubled waters?

I guess.

Well, that's what we do. We ease the pain.

I pray to the Lord for my boy's soul, the woman sobbed.

This next step was delicate. It required a steady hand. Your tragedy has moved people so much. We want to help you…recover.

The woman blew her nose in an overused Kleenex. Come with me, she said.

She held out her hand so the man could help her up. She shuffled along a narrow corridor. She hesitated outside a door adorned with a Lou Reed, Walk on the Wildside poster. She turned the handle and led the way in.

An astringent blast assaulted his nostrils. It felt like chemical warfare. It was ammonia or chlorine. He recoiled a step. Covering his nose and mouth, he ventured on. It was a teenager's bedroom with posters on the wall and beer cans on the shelves. He studied the posters more closely. Where he'd routinely expected to find scantily clad girls, ripped, bare-chested males strutted their stuff.

Sorry about the smell, the woman apologised. It's a little overpowering at first.

It's fine, he said, trying to breathe normally through the funk.

He didn't keep his room real tidy like this, she explained. They came and cleaned up. Out of respect.

The man nodded. The woman beckoned him over to the cheap, melamine desk, positioned next to the window that overlooked the neighbour's trashcans. There was a pile of electronics equipment and a spaghetti junction of twisted wires and cables.

The woman fished another ragged Kleenex from her tracksuit pants pocket. She sobbed out loud. This is the where the accident happened. This is the scene of the *crime*.

The choice of word silently wounded him. He was trained not to show emotion. He nodded sympathetically, as was appropriate.

My beautiful boy was lured here.

Silence seemed the best response.

She was wailing now. This faggot, this scum, killed my son. Just as sure as if he'd pushed him over a cliff, stuck a knife in his ribs or blowed his brains out himself.

He thought she might fall. He put his arms around her. Once steadied, he guided her back to the sitting room. He lowered her onto the couch. He found his way to the kitchen and opened cupboard doors at random to find a glass for some water.

The woman's keening ebbed away as she drank from the 'Mid-West is Best' emblazoned tumbler. She mopped her mouth with the back of her hand.

We cannot know the mind of the good Lord, he said. However, I truly believe he sent us to you, to ease your pain. I have a small check here to support you in your recovery.

The woman accepted it from his outstretched hand. She scanned it slowly as if reading the name of the bank and every word and serial number on it. She mouthed the words, 'Twenty-thousand dollars'.

She folded the slip of paper and looked up. Is this from frenzship?

No. It is from us - The Good Oil. We soothe people's troubles.

He closed the car door behind him. He slumped back in the driver's seat and let the relief wash over him. He could barely breathe in that house. The woman's emotions were choking him. The smell of the clean-up made him want to puke.

He fired the car to life. Let's get out of here. As he drove to the airport, one question haunted his thoughts.

When she signed the form, did she really not know the cash was coming from frenzship? Didn't she know or didn't she care?

Black ops

Miki deplored sport. For him, sitting through a game of any code was agony on steroids. Dragging him to watch the Lakers was fitting revenge for the saunathon. Miki was determined to talk shop. I shushed him until a time-out was called.

Have you seen the latest figures? He asked.

Nope, I said, focused on my hot-dog.

Our frenz numbers have climbed through all this.

Any publicity is good publicity?

In a way. But that's not the full story.

Go on.

The scandal's still hurting us. Have a look at this.

I glanced at Miki's iPad.

See what I mean? He said.

Shhh, the game's starting. Needling Miki was so much fun.

Well? Miki said, at the next break. The home team was 18 points down. The arena was like a morgue. Miki's question drifted to the bleachers opposite, drawing silent rebukes.

These are disastrous, I sadly acknowledged.

Absolutely. Our trust rating has plummeted.

Miki cheered when the final klaxon sounded. I glared at him. The home team had been thrashed. No one had seen a belting like that since the Germans invaded Poland. Fearing for Miki's safety, I ushered him under crowd cover towards the beer tent.

Miki managed to keep his mouth shut and stay alive. I arrived with two plastic beakers of Bud.

Don't you love going to a game? I asked.

I wasn't expecting an answer.

The spin's not working, Miki said.

I know.

Of course, Randy's happy. We've got more frenz than ever – that's all he cares about.

I nodded.

What about Cassidy?

What about Cassidy?

What's her take on this?

An errant elbow knocked me forwards, spilling half my beer. I looked around for the culprit. He was big, and drunk. I wiped myself down. I noted Miki's amusement.

Cass is not very talkative right now, I said. I was cautious about heading into anything private. I kept it on the work level. I think she still believes the PR line will work out. You know, the all compassion and no responsibility routine.

I showed her these figures earlier, Miki explained.

Then you know what she thinks.

I thought you might know different. Cassidy seems distant when I talk to her.

To get the subject changed and assuage Miki's suffering, I let him take me to a bar on Rodeo.

Miki ordered a cocktail. I stuck to the beers.

When Miki returned, I raised an issue that was troubling me.

Have you noticed how the dead boy's mother has gone quiet?

I have. That's been a stroke of luck for us.

I don't think it's luck.

Miki looked at me. His head was very still. He looked more alarmed than surprised.

I continued. It's black ops.

Black ops? I don't get you.

The Good Oil. They're black ops.

Miki was narrow-eyed, even for a Jap. OK. What are you saying here? He asked.

I'm saying that frenzship has the backing of a black ops team. The Good Oil are fixers. They have a legitimate arm that provides the spin and the PR...

...And?

They have a covert arm.

Why do you say that?

I'm pretty sure that poor woman was paid for her silence.

Come on, Miki protested.

Or worse? I added.

You mean threatened?

Yep.

I'm having trouble with this, dude. Miki said, shaking his head. I need a whizz.

I had no concrete evidence. But I recited a series of circumstantial events. Once the thought had occurred to me, I'd been able to recall numerous occasions when seemingly insurmountable problems had melted away.

I can't prove it, I concluded. But you have to admit it. That woman accused frenzship of murdering her only son. She was out for revenge. And then suddenly, miraculously, the cat got her tongue and all was forgiven.

Miki sat back to take it all in. His expression was pained.

If, Miki said, pointing his cocktail umbrella at me. If, I stress, you are right about this, who is behind it?

I shrugged my shoulders.

Come on. You've put two and two together. You must have a theory.

I don't.

Zak? Miki asked.

Nah. I dismissed the suggestion. He wouldn't dare.

Cassidy? Miki ventured reluctantly.

No way. She's not like that.

Randy, then. It has to be Randy.

I nodded.

When all's said and done, we don't know much about him, do we? Miki said thoughtfully.

We know nothing, I agreed.

I summoned Uber to get us two drunks home. We dropped Miki off at his apartment. He seemed reluctant to get out of the car.

What's the matter? I asked

We need to change tack, Miki said.

Go on.

It's no good telling people we're good guys. We have to prove it.

How do we do that?

We have to catalogue for the adoring public all the good that frenzship does, and has done. Give them chapter and verse.

I nodded. It was simple, but it sounded right.

And how do we do *that*? I asked.

I have an idea, Miki said, leaning on the handle before stumbling from the car.

Essentially foolproof

Life had been torrid at frenzship. Water finds the tiniest crack in a vessel. The suicide pressure wasn't easing up and we were all feeling it. As is often the case, teamwork is the first casualty. When frenzship was flavour of the month, we lapped up the accolades. We did team hugs. Now things were tense, we were splintering under the weight of the axe.

Miki, Zak and I organised a video conference call with Dr. Levine to explore concerns we had with the system's backbone.

I started with the usual cautionary opening gambit one had to use with Jeremiah. Jerry, don't get me wrong, we're not questioning the scientific rigour...

That meant, Jerry, we do want to question the science, but we don't want you taking offence and responding like a meth addict in the emergency room.

…but can you please explain how something that we understood to be foolproof in terms of (a) the matching process and (b) the assurance of anonymity seems prone to exploitation by some unscrupulous…

Miki interrupted me as I was making a hash of it. …Jerry, if frenzship can only match people who ought to be friends and if it's impossible to identify yourself or someone else, how could that sicko get to that boy in Ohio?

Jerry fiddled with his glasses to help keep his emotions in check. Gentlemen, he began in that tone of his adopted for addressing complete morons, let us assume that an intervention via frenzship did have some influence on this boy's behaviour, which I don't accept for one moment. However, making this assumption for argument's sake, I can confirm that the platform for our psychosocial media product is virtually flawless. Indeed it is statistically as close to perfection as humans can imagine. In addition, its encryption rivals the block chain so that its numeric combinations are changed millions of times per second. This renders it virtually unhackable.

Go on, Zak urged Jerry. This explanation seemed to be making sense to him at least.

As I was saying, Jerry continued, frenzship is essentially foolproof. However, he added, rolling the final 'r' and pausing for effect, I fear I heard my old friend use the term 'foolproof' in an unqualified manner. Nothing is 'foolproof'. Scientists play God, but they are not God, ignoring the fact that God doesn't exist. Nothing in the universe is or can be 'foolproof'. That very notion denies the natural order of things, the laws of physics.

Our LA trio looked at each other. This was impressive stuff even if two thirds of us had no idea what Jeremiah was talking about.

In summary, Dr. Jeremiah concluded, frenzship is 99.1% accurately predictive of true friendship and 97.8% securely preventative of identification. It is therefore not 'foolproof'.

In other words, Zak said by way of interpretation, given the millions of people signing up to be frenz, once in a blue moon, someone somewhere sometime will get frenzed with a raging psycho and despite the sophistication of the AI someone is going to manage to identify themselves or someone else.

In addition to our anxieties about the scientific platform we raised with Jerry, I shared my suspicions with Cassidy about the black ops. It took some uncharacteristic courage. She was as prickly as a cactus.

What do you think, Cass? Could this be true?

Sure it could, she said as if it wasn't a big deal.

You weren't in on this were you? I regretted the comment as soon as it left my mouth.

Of course not, she shot back. How can you think that?

If looks could kill. I crossed the room to where she was standing, surveying the famous twinkling lights of the city below. I put my arms around her. She stiffened, but let me cuddle her.

I didn't think that for a minute, I said. The truth is I don't know what to think these days.

Cassidy softened. She turned to embrace me, nuzzling my neck. You think you're worldly and smart, she said. But you don't know these people. They are capable of anything.

Which people, Cass?

Randy for one. I love him like a real brother. But he will do anything to have his way.

To fuck the Zuck?

Especially that, she said.

What about the Good Oil? Who are they really?

I honestly don't know. I've tried to dig into it. I trust Tyson and Maria. I'm confident they are straight up and down spin merchants. Beyond them, we don't really know who's behind the Good Oil, let alone what they do.

A soft kiss

I rustled up two coffees with Krispy Kremes at the arrivals gate. There were dozens of incoming flights. I couldn't even hazard a guess as to where Miki's anonymous visitor was coming from.

I nudged Miki to look at a cardboard sign an Asian guy was holding up to identify the passenger he was meeting. DR. FANG was written in large black texta. Miki laughed.

I had a dentist called Dr. Fang, I told him.

Bullshit!

A soft kiss on the cheek brought me back to reality.

It was Nina.

The three of us hugged for the longest time.

Miki and Nina jabbered away as we headed out to find the car. I trudged along behind like their porter, rattling Nina's huge suitcases across the uneven surface of the airbridge. I was grateful for the distance. Nina was not herself. I registered that immediately. She looked pale, but no more so than the other weary travellers. Something was not right.

Akin to the impossible feat of packing twenty students into a telephone box, Miki somehow crunched Nina's luggage and two passengers into his sports car. I gallantly sat in the back with the bags. I wasn't sure what I was dealing with so I was happy to stay out of it.

This nip *salaud* didn't tell me you were coming, I shouted from the backseat.

Miki wanted you to have a lovely surprise, Nina responded. Didn't you, cheri?

I did, Miki agreed, smiling with exaggerated smugness so I wouldn't fail to notice in the rear-view mirror.

My phone beeped. It was Cassidy. How's your old girlfriend? She asked

You knew?

Miki told me.

It's a nice surprise, I said neutrally.

I've got a surprise for you too, Cassidy said and then hung up.

It seems everyone knew about you coming but me, I shouted.

Didn't I used to tell you not to sulk? Nina teased me.

We chatted for a while. Nina seemed tense. She seized upon a break in the conversation.

Mes très chers mecs, she said. I need to tell you something.

I felt a deathly chill. A similar expression played on Miki's handsome face.

Nina swallowed deeply. Mes amours… I have MS.

These cruel initials pierced my flesh like nails driven into hands on the cross.

Oh, Nina, Miki exclaimed.

I couldn't think of anything sensible to say. So I said, why didn't you tell me?

Why didn't you ask? Nina replied playfully to break the tension.

I fleetingly wondered why everyone said that to me. Then I tried to make sense of such terrible news. At that point, my phone burst into life again. It was Cass. I answered it for some relief.

I didn't get any.

I'm pregnant, she said.

Lost for anything else to say, I replied, really?

Lorna and I are a team again. We are building on my momentum. Every day I take more steps with my chief coach and cheerleader.

Cassidy is resting. Every communication, be it call, text, the sound of footsteps approaching my room, can only mean one thing – Cassidy has gone into labour.

I can actually talk and walk at the same time now.

Lorna, what have your parents got to say about you thoughts on going home?

Nothing much.

Really?

I haven't told them.

Why?

Because I don't know if I want to go home.

That's not the point. You can do whatever you want, but you should at least ask them what they think.

OK.

Will you do it?

Maybe, Lorna says with her wicked smile.

Why people deserve the friends they've got

Not friends

Are you smashed? Her dad barked down the line to her.

Sorry Dad.

Stay where you are. I'll come and get you, he said. Where the hell are you?

As if he didn't know. Lorna was at Jade's house. Wendy, Jade's mum, was all right. She still remembered what it was like to be young. Lorna's parents had tried to get Wendy on their side, but she thought they were stuck up. Lorna smiled at how Wendy pushed her nose in the air when she mentioned her mum.

Lorna stumbled to the front of the house to show willing when her dad arrived. She steadied herself against the old station wagon parked in the driveway. Finally, she'd given Muzzo the slip.

Lorna settled onto the low brick wall out the front. She felt really ill, but at least she could feel sick out there alone. Her head dropped into her hands. She closed her eyes, desperate to get her world level again. Just as she was drifting off, she felt a presence beside her. Had her dad got there already?

Take one of these. It will make you feel better. It was Muzzo again.

Lorna shook her head dismissively. Thankfully, the lights of her dad's car came into view. She could feel the blowtorch of his disapproval blasting through the car window. Her mind wandered to the cruelty of his remarks when he'd last picked up her.

You were once my beautiful little girl, he said. Look at you now, with your hair shaved like that.

Lorna sat rooted to the spot. She couldn't get up. Her father got out of the car. He looked from her to Muzzo, who had pulled his red hoodie over his face.

This is Muzzo, Lorna explained to smooth things over.

Muzzo nodded to acknowledge the older man's presence, but didn't look up.

I've heard of you before, Muzzo, Lorna's dad said. Are you at the school?

Nah, Muzzo grunted, raising his head a fraction. I'm looking for a job.

Where do you live?

Not far from here.

Can I give you a lift?

Nah, don't worry. I'll find my way.

Lorna forced herself to get up.

Let's go, her father said. I'm getting cold standing around here.

Lorna got unsteadily to her feet, wobbled and then groped her way to the car. Catch ya, she said to Muzzo without turning round.

Yeah. Sick, he replied.

They settled into the drive. Lorna wondered how she could make the twenty minutes bearable. She felt bad about dragging her dad out of bed again. She didn't set out to cause trouble. She said no to the piercings the others got done and got only the one secret ink. All she wanted was an occasional night of freedom.

Her dad was sullen and angry. What could she say that wouldn't make things worse? She couldn't think straight. She was nodding off to the motion of the car. She didn't want to fall asleep. It would make him crankier still.

Who's Muzzo?

Don't start, Dad, Lorna said. It didn't come out the way she meant it. She thought to apologise, but the sick welled up in the throat. She clapped her hand to her mouth and screamed, Stop the car!

Lorna opened the door before the car had come to a full stop. She spilled her insides into the gutter.

Are you OK? He asked once she'd swivelled back into her seat.

Do I look OK? She replied. Wrong tone again. Just fouling things up.

What have you taken? He demanded

An E or two, Lorna replied wearily

Don't you know how many?

Everything she said came out bad. Don't worry, Dad. I'm OK.

Lorna could read her dad like a book - a boring one, right now. Keep going or let it lie, he was thinking to himself. But he could never leave things alone.

Who's Muzzo?

No one.

Her father took his eyes off the road to glare at her. I was told he was your friend.

He's not. He hangs out at Jade's, that's all, Lorna responded to placate him.

That's not what I heard, her dad grunted.

At that moment, an unmarked police car pulled them over. Her father wound down his window. The policeman shone his torch full onto Lorna, slumped in the passenger seat.

That's my daughter, her dad said.

Have you been drinking, sir?

No, of course not. I've just got out of bed to pick her up.

Would you mind giving me a breath sample?

If I must.

The testing took a matter of seconds.

Thank you, sir. I hope your daughter is OK.

They were minutes from home. Lorna felt doubly sick now. No matter how many times they went through this, it was always the same with her mum. She'd be waiting at the door, ready to pounce. Bursting to scream at her.

We're here. Wake up, she heard her dad say.

Leave me alone.

You have to get out of the car.

O-kay, O-kay. She wanted to move. She wasn't doing it on purpose.

He walked round to the passenger door and opened it. Her head jerked sideways.

What the fuck? Lorna said. She tried to apologise.

Get out of the car now! He yelled.

You don't have to be so rough, she protested.

The front door opened as they walked up the three entrance steps. True to form, her mum was standing there in the doorway. She took Lorna by the elbow and escorted her to her bedroom.

Then it started. The inevitable screaming match. Lorna covered her ears. She couldn't bear it again. She just wanted to sleep.

Those people are not friends! Her mother shrieked.

Secretly Lorna agreed. She registered the door to McTavish's cage gaping open. As she vomited again, she hoped the terrible images floating in the head were just an hallucination.

Dripping with sweat

Lorna woke dripping with sweat. She kicked off the remaining sheet to seek some relief. She was numb all over. If she hadn't just moved her foot, she might have feared herself paralysed.

Thoughts were a familiar jumble in her head. Where am I? What was I on last night? Is there any water here? Is it a school day? Am I still at school? Where's McTavish? Will *they* be home now or at work? Can I lift my head?

Lorna sat up. Nausea overwhelmed her. She slumped back against the pillow. She sensed she was in her own bedroom. She needed the bathroom. Somehow her legs responded. Lorna covered her mouth. She searched the room with her eyes. Which way was her toilet? Unable to recall these familiar surroundings, she panicked. Falling to her knees, she used every scrap of her failing energy to contain the vomit in her mouth.

She sobbed. It was spontaneous. Involuntary. At that moment, she could have called for her mum like she used to as a child. The urge was strong but unacceptable. She was not a child. She was her own person. She had to be strong and lead her own life.

The flow of tears eased. Her head cleared a little. She made a run for the bowl. She retched revolting bile. She wanted her mum again, to mop the sweat from her forehead. The earthquake subsided. She reached clumsily for the toilet roll, unspooling a cascade of floral tissue.

Recovery set in. Was it time? Lorna remembered the ugly red clock on the wall. There were just a few exhilarating minutes to go. She'd almost forgotten the only thing that mattered in her life. She staggered through the open door, stumbling her way to the bed. If only the world would stay still. She dragged herself upright. She willed herself to get through it. It was time to transform herself into someone to be proud of - Doonesday.

She felt for her laptop from behind the books in the cabinet where she'd hidden it. She wasn't thinking straight. She liberated the correct device from the place even professional thieves would never find it. It lit up. She'd be just in time. The signal to the neighbour's Wi-Fi conned from the boy next door was good enough. No need to resort to the laptop and use the 4G card Muzzo had stolen from his aunt.

The anticipation thrilled her. At the moment of her choosing, she would enact the touch of life. She held back to savour the joy of expectation. This time, there was no apprehension. This was an arrangement, not a random checking in.

Doonesday pressed at the screen with a theatrical flourish. It took a fraction longer than she wanted. Then Amity451 appeared.

I love you

What's bugging you, Doodoo?

I'm feeling sick.

A sick chick, huh?

You're so clever.

Yes, I am. Speak to me! Amity451 insisted.

I am.

You're not. Tell me how good it felt to liberate yourself.

Doonesday flinched. The terrifying vision of her guinea pig came flooding back.

Pigs can fly!

Not real pigs, Doonesbury typed to shake her mental image. Her stomach churned. Was that too provocative a thing to say?

That could be your next challenge! Amity451 wrote.

Was he angry? She must placate him. You're so cool, you really are.

I'm hot, actually. Maybe for you.

Doonesday's heart leapt. She typed the special words, but didn't press enter.

TELL ME THAT YOU'RE READY FOR YOUR NEXT LABOUR OF LOVE, Amity451 demanded in strident capitals.

Doonesday's heart was pounding now. Had he read her mind again? She had to commit to this. It was so scary! It could spoil it all, but she had no resistance.

Speak to me, Doodoo.

Doonesday hit return. I LOVE YOU.

Loop Pedal

Her mum had stepped on the loop pedal. Lorna tuned out from the endless repetition of those accusations framed as questions. What were you thinking? How could you be so cruel? Have you no feelings? Lorna made them into a rap chorus to drown out the noise.

Lorna was sorry. If they could see sense, they would back off. They wouldn't come down so hard on her. They would give her some time and space to breathe and try to explain. If they gave her the opportunity, she would try to help them understand that she had no choice but to do it.

She lowered her eyes unwaveringly to the floor. She'd caught an earlier glimpse of the scene laid out on the kitchen table. It was gruesome. It was cruel of her parents to confront her with this. Her poor guinea pig was battered and broken from the fall. She was sorry. She was suffering too. Couldn't they see that?

The reading of her charge sheet continued unabated in the background. She wanted to apologise. If only there was a way to express her remorse without giving into her parents' false reality. Her cruelty to McTavish was very wrong in this universe. But it was different in the real world.

If only they could comprehend.

I'm massaging Cassidy's swollen ankles. Her legs are propped on my knees. The sensation of her weight pressing on me is a secret source of joy after those endless insentient months.

Any minute now, I say, smiling broadly at my girl.

I want it to happen and at the same time I don't, Cass says dreamily.

Don't you want it over and out?

I do, more than anything. But I'm scared.

I nod. Can I change the subject?

Anything. Please.

Lorna said something interesting to me this morning.

Is that unusual?

No, but what she said took me back.

Go on.

She said one of the reasons she was thinking of going home was because you were really going to have this baby.

Didn't you know that?

No, I didn't. Explain it to me. Doesn't she want to be in the way?

No, Cass laughed. You're a man so you don't understand people.

Thanks.

She loves you.

I looked askance at Cassidy.

Not in that way. She does. You're her hero.

Poor kid.

You saved her. She loves you for that. And, Cass paused, she doesn't want to compete for your affection.

With the baby?

Yes. With the baby.

People are way too complicated for me, I sigh, returning to my role as masseur

How people come to make friends their own age

Cool Hand Luke

What we have here is a failure to communicate. The scene from Cool Hand Luke ran through Ewan's head.

Sally was fuming. The lid on the pressure cooker was ready to blow. Lorna was applying extra heat with the 'no comment' game she was playing like a seasoned politician. Lorna sat there, avoiding eye contact, lips sealed, steadfastly maintaining her silence.

Ewan was frustrated with both of them. He begged Sally to let him handle this himself. Sally wouldn't hear of it. Ever the detached professional with strangers, Sally was quite the opposite when confronting her own daughter.

Ewan knew that nothing would be achieved with all three of them sitting round the kitchen table like that. If Lorna persisted in invoking the Fifth Amendment, Sally would eventually lose it. There would be a slanging match. Resentment would be the only winner. Neither of them was of a mind to listen to him. So there was nothing for it but to go back to square one and get lost on that familiar road to nowhere.

Lorna was refusing to accept responsibility. She wouldn't explain what happened to that poor innocent pet. A moment's silence might provide space for her to open up. At times she seemed poised to unburden herself. Then Sally would browbeat her again and the opportunity would be missed.

At that moment, Ewan felt ashamed of his daughter. It was humiliating even to think that. Sally wouldn't admit to such a thing, but he knew she felt the same way. Yet it wasn't entirely Lorna's fault. They were bad parents. They'd done everything for the best. They'd been true to their own beliefs. They hadn't agreed every word of the parenting script, but they'd been very much on the same page. All they wanted was a childhood for their daughter - one where she could grow up at her own pace. They wanted their daughter to find her own path, free from the corruption of rampant commercialism and graphic sexual images. They wanted her to play outside and create her own fun.

This terrible incident with the guinea pig followed by Lorna staying out to some ridiculous hour had ambushed him and Sally before they'd worked out what to about Wendy's allegations. They'd been over it time and time again. Should we confront her about Wendy's claims or would that make things worse? Should we search her room and see if we can find anything or would that just breach her trust? Should we buy her a smartphone? Ewan remained resolute against that. Or would it be better to do nothing?

Ewan shut out the inquisition unfolding next to him. Was he to blame for overprotecting his daughter? Had it alienated Lorna? She *had* been treated differently. The other kids had TVs, laptops and phones provided for them. The other parents indulged their children in a way he couldn't fathom or accept. He couldn't understand what made these people feel so guilty. Why did they have to placate their children all the time? Why did they give into them at the first hint of conflict? In that laissez-faire environment, he and Sally had fought a losing battle to stick to their guns. Yet it seemed that she had found her own way of joining the crowd.

His confidence in their parenting had taken a beating, but deep down, despite this soul searching, his conviction wasn't shaken. A teenage girl shouldn't be free to browse the Internet or have an endless line of telephone credit to rack up massive phone bills. Maybe they *had* stoked the fire of rebellion by being too strict? But how might their strong-willed daughter have turned out, if they had gone along with the pack?

Ewan wished they could find the right balance. He and Sally continually fluffed it. When they should've been tough, they were tender. When they used the rod, they actually spoiled the child. The intensity of Sally's love for her daughter often clouded her judgment. Ewan's selfish aspirations for Lorna's future placed undue pressure upon her.

The disgusting raw egg-eating scene from Cool Hand Luke popped back into his head. It took his mind off the household train wreck running off the rails at a station near him. Thinking distracting thoughts was called a displacement activity. Sally had told him that. Way back when, in happier times.

The time had come

The guinea pig incident forced their hand. Ewan and Sally could not agree on the best thing to do. They settled for what they considered the least worst option.

The time had come to change tack to discover the truth. Even so, Ewan felt embarrassed loitering suspiciously outside his own house. He was relieved to see Sally's Holden Barina pull up. They opened the front door carefully, checking the hallway to make sure they had no company. Lorna had work experience on a Thursday afternoon. Her weekly trip to the music store was one appointment they could count on her keeping.

As Ewan stood at the door to his daughter's bedroom, he realised he hadn't been inside the room for a very long time. He recalled happier days when she would beg him – pretty please, Daddy – to read her a bedtime story. The memory warmed his insides. His wife jerked him to reality.

Are you going in? Sally asked impatiently

I was thinking that I haven't been in there for ages.

I guess that's the problem, Sally reacted.

Don't make it about me! There's been many a time when you've told me to keep out.

Sally softened. I know, she said, touching his arm. I'm antsy, that's all.

There was nothing for it. Ewan turned the handle. The door was locked.

Since when has there been a lock on her bedroom door? Ewan raged.

Calm down, Sally said. It's been there forever.

How come I've never noticed it?

Because she never used to lock it.

That comment hung in the air. It said it all.

Let's not stand here like a pair of robbers, Ewan said, trudging off towards the kitchen.

He helped himself to some water putting his head under the tap.

I hate you doing that, she said.

I know. It hardly matters right now, does it? Ewan snapped back.

Sally stomped through to the back veranda to enjoy the last strands of afternoon sun before it disappeared behind the neighbour's gum tree.

What will we do now? She asked curtly.

I feel like breaking the door down, Ewan said.

Do you think we should?

It would make a point. He said. Isn't it time for that?

It is. But it seems too sudden.

Sudden?

Yes, it's like lurching from one extreme to the other, Sally said. Throughout her childhood, we've respected her rights. We've bent over backwards to allow her privacy. And now, one afternoon, we sneak home and break into her room.

It's hardly like that, Ewan protested.

I know it's not. But, to her, it will seem like the Gestapo bought out the Salvos.

Ewan slumped down onto the timber deck, resting his back against a veranda post. What to do? What's for the best? He wondered. We can't back down now. We can't give in, he said.

I agree.

It's taken us all this time to screw up the courage to take a stand. We can't baulk at a locked door.

Wait a minute, Sally said, with a smile playing across her face. Of course!

Of course, what?

That door can only be locked from the inside.

Ewan perked up. Then a nasty thought struck him. She's not in there, is she?

No, she's not in there. There's no way she'd miss the music store.

Sally set off round the side of the house. C'mon, she shouted.

Earthquake victim

They were thankful that there was some way in, even if the slope of the block necessitated access via a ladder.

Now there was no turning back. Ewan looked at Sally for encouragement. She looked tense. She seemed older when she frowned like that. He wanted to tell her, but he focused on the job at hand – breaking into his daughter's bedroom.

Ewan wrestled the flyscreen aside and then muscled the window open. Why isn't the window locked? He asked.

It's never locked, Sally informed him.

We'll get burgled, Ewan replied absentmindedly before realising how absurd that comment seemed at that moment. The stepladder wobbled alarmingly. You have to see the funny side, he insisted. If you don't right now, you soon will when I fall off.

Sally stepped forward to support the ladder.

How does she get in and out? He called down. There's nothing around to stand on.

She was a bit of a gymnast when she was younger, Sally reminded him, and you clearly are not.

Ewan hauled himself onto the window ledge and then jumped down onto the floor. Fucking hell!

He picked his way across the room to open the door for Sally. He felt like an earthquake victim inspecting the devastation of what was once his home and possessions.

I've never seen anything like it, Ewan said. I thought guys were bad.

It's got much worse of late, Sally said. This is what I was confronted with on McTavish night, she added, instinctively picking things up from the floor.

Don't, Ewan shouted. Don't touch anything. She mustn't know we've been here. If we'd wanted her to know, I would've put my shoulder against the door and busted the damn lock.

OK, but get on with it, Sally replied, dropping the underwear back in a heap.

Ewan sifted aimlessly through the mass of papers on the desk. He lifted clothes and bags and the varied detritus draped over chairs and spilling onto the carpet.

What about under the mattress? Sally suggested.

You've watched too many detective movies, Ewan said.

The mattress was heavy and hard to budge. It was wedged firmly against the wooden bed base. He gradually worked his way around the perimeter.

Hello, he said.

What is it?

I'm not sure. Here we go. He looked up, red-faced. Weed and papers, he said.

Sally didn't dare catch his eye.

And there's more, he said. Just need to reach in a bit further. What's this? A student card. A fake one, he added, brandishing it in Sally's direction. Would anyone really believe she was eighteen?

Sally shook her head, too dispirited to answer. Shall we go now? She asked.

Not yet, Ewan said, we need to find what we came for. He fiddled around, sifting through her personal effects, searching under the bed, working his way through the bathroom cabinet.

There's a load of pills in here, he called through the open doorway. Does she have current prescriptions?

I don't think so, Sally said. Mind you, she could be on the pill for all we know. Doctors don't tell parents anything these days.

I know there's more, Ewan repeated to himself, re-emerging into the bedroom.

His eyes fixed upon the heavy wooden bookcase that had drawers and glass-fronted shelving to hide things in. He sorted carefully through the books, magazines and maps that were piled haphazardly onto the shelves. He had trouble sliding one of the panels open. It eventually shifted. He shook his head.

What is it? Sally asked in that timid manner reserved for those who don't really want to know.

Ewan produced a laptop. The other parents were right, he said ruefully.

Sally made to respond, but had clearly lost the power of speech.

Ewan set about replacing the computer.

What are you doing now?

I'm putting everything back where we found it.

So why did we bother?

We bothered… he said, shuffling the other found objects back under the mattress…to establish some control.

And how are we going to do that?

Well, for a start, we need to keep our options open about what we do next. Come on, he said, gesturing to his wife. Go round and support the ladder for me so I can get through this alive.

Ewan locked the door behind Sally, checked that the room was as much of a bombsite as he'd found it and rewound the tape to find himself back on the ground with the window closed behind him and the fly screen slotted back home.

Sally replaced the steps under the back porch.

What are we going to do? She asked.

I need a drink, he responded, and a think.

2308

Ewan and Sally were depressed to have found the laptop in Lorna's room. Not only was she not supposed to have one, but they feared for how she might have come by it. Finding the grass and the fake ID card filled in some of the blanks as to what she was getting up to when she stayed out late. Yet they were missing vital clues. Wendy had explicitly referred to a smartphone. They realised that she wouldn't have left that in her room. But how was it possible that they had never seen one lying around or stashed in her bag that she left all over the place?

Ewan suggested they work with what they knew rather than speculate on what they didn't know. This entailed reprising the routine the following Thursday. They tried the door just in case. It was locked. They worked in tandem to organise the ladder, gain entry to Lorna's bedroom and remove the computer that was still hidden in the same spot.

Time was of the essence. Ewan left Sally to backtrack through the relocking process while he scampered out to his car to get on the move. Ewan laid the laptop carefully on the seat beside him. He drove up the Stirling Highway, which was more like the Stirling Carpark these days. He tapped his fingers impatiently on the steering wheel while he crawled his way through the Claremont bottleneck.

He got lost in the light industrial area near the cemetery but then saw the sign he was looking for. Ewan grabbed the gear from the car. He followed the sign past the mechanics' workshop and tracked round the back to a weed-infested car park.

Ewan found a lanky youth in a Dockers beanie smoking by the back door.

Yeah, mate?

It was probably a question.

I'm here to see Shane.

I don't think Shano's here.

I've got an appointment.

Oh, OK. Wait here then.

Ewan peered into the cramped office. The desk and chair had seen better days. The pinboards groaned under the weight of generations of oil-stained timesheets and dog-eared safety posters. By contrast, the lever-arch files on the shelf were arranged in chronological order. It was untidy but nothing compared with his daughter's bedroom. There could be some order in the chaos.

Hey dude! Shane greeted him.

You *are* here.

Course I am, Shane said, wiping the oil and grease from his fingers with a filthy rag. Come in.

Shane sat at the desk, indicating where he wanted the hardware placed. He could see Ewan looking at him suspiciously.

Don't worry mate, he said, I can fix all kinds of things. He passed the laptop to him. Who put you onto me again? Shane asked.

It was Jake. You know, John Marsh's son who's the genius at the Apple Store.

Haven't seen Johnno Marsh for yonks, Shane said. You want me to jailbreak these? He added.

I think that's the term. Ewan felt stupid and pompous for responding that way.

Nothing illegal going on, is there? Shane asked with a grin.

No, nothing illegal. Maybe something immoral.

Immoral? I don't get you.

Don't worry. It's not important. It's our daughter.

Oh, Shane said, now completely engrossed in the task at hand. You know these Macs are a cinch, don't you?

Not to me, they're not.

Shane pressed keys on the laptop at lightning speed. You see, on a Mac, he explained, you can restart, hold 'option' until two icons appear, choose 'recovery', choose 'language', click 'utilities' in the menu bar along the top, open 'terminal', type 'resetpassword', choose 'Macintosh HD' and select the user you want to change the password for.

Ewan couldn't follow all that and he didn't much care. How long will this take?

Oh, not long, Shane said, not long at all. You see then you enter a new password, then restart, don't hold 'option', it will go back to the normal log in screen and the password you just created will now be the new password for that user.

That simple!

Shane wasn't one for irony. Yes, and you don't need to know the original password to do this.

Jake didn't make it sound that easy.

Well, he wouldn't, would he? Shane said

Why not? Ewan asked naively.

Cos they don't get trained to repair things at Apple.

I thought he was a genius.

Yeah, a fucking genius, Shane scoffed. They don't bother fixing things at Apple, Shane continued. Then he looked up at Ewan in a scholarly fashion. It's cheaper to give the punters a new one, isn't it?

I suppose so, Ewan replied. How long did you say it would take?

Enter the password and it's done.

Ewan selected his mum's birthday, 2308. He listened carefully to the explanation of how to access the computer without his daughter knowing there was another user.

A hundred bucks was daylight robbery for five minutes' work. Ewan considered it money well spent to gain some understanding of the double life Lorna seemed to be leading.

The Stirling Carpark was up to its tricks again. The private schools spat brats into their mothers' Range Rovers that were now crawling in convoy towards the safety of their mansions. Ewan met Sally at Van's in Cottesloe. Over a quick coffee, they scanned through the files and history. They found nothing to raise alarm.

Although the suspense nearly killed them, Ewan and Sally endured the wait until the following Thursday. This time Ewan headed to the Apple store in the CBD. Ewan forced himself to relax into the drive. He'd been pleasantly surprised that Jake had agreed to help. As a young person, Ewan thought Jake would baulk at helping a parent access his child's computer. Ewan told Jake about the sad fate of the pet guinea pig. That had been a good tactic. He could understand why Lorna's parents were worried.

Ewan made it to the Apple store just in time. It was pandemonium in there. It looked like a crowded basketball court. The blue-shirted Apple staff were standing the customers one on one. He strode up to the genius bar at the back. A serious-looking Asian boy approached him. Then Jake appeared from behind the counter and beckoned for Ewan to join him.

Thanks for doing this, Jake, Ewan said.

Put in your password please, Jake said. He seemed very different at work.

Ewan typed in the numbers 2-3-0-8. We've looked at this ourselves, he explained, but we weren't confident that we understood how to scan the whole picture of what she's up to.

Jake set to work. Ewan chatted away nervously. Jake was concentrating and not responding. It felt like a doctor's appointment. Ewan's x-rays were being examined. The physician had a serious look on his face. Was that from concentration or out of concern?

Jake looked up.

This is it. This is the verdict, Ewan thought.

There's varied use overall. You know, the net, Facebook, YouTube, soft porn, fantasy, and the like

And... guess what, Jake added theatrically.

Yes?

Your daughter is a typical teenager.

I'm mastering walking on crutches for long distances so I can go home.

My fingers are bruised, I moan to Cassidy and Lorna, from the weight bearing down on my hands.

Poor baby, Cassidy coos.

Poor baby if it ever comes out, I mutter, with a heartless pair like you two around it.

Then I realise Lorna might not be around. Do you know what your plans are yet, Lorna?

I thought I'd stick around for this baby to be born.

Cassidy now takes my breath away. We want you to be the godmother?

I shoot a look at Cass. She never discussed that with me.

Wow! Cool! Lorna exclaims.

Lorna leaps into Cassidy's arms, nearly forcing the baby out.

I smile. What a fantastic idea! What a great way to make the baby part of Lorna's life too.

How friends don't have to work out who they're gonna call.

Guilt-edged

Ewan felt guilty every time he used the Nespresso machine Sally had given him for his birthday. He loved the convenience and the coffee. He hated himself for supporting the multinational that fed adulterated milk powder to Chinese babies. He was disgusted that the used pods had to go to landfill.

Ewan and Sally were having trouble sleeping. Last night was no exception. They had agreed to have the issue out with Lorna as soon as they could catch her in a reasonable mood. Meanwhile, they tossed and turned in bed wondering whether Lorna was actually asleep or had snuck out silently through her bedroom window.

Ewan scraped peanut butter onto his toast, flipping the same old issues over in his head like some distasteful pancake. Were they making too much of it? All teenage girls rebel. Maybe acquiring her own laptop was only to be expected. How did she get it, though? At least the analysis of her Internet use didn't through up anything alarming. But did she also have a smartphone? Should he fall in with Sally over giving Lorna a mobile and be done with it? He could feel his resistance eroding like rock in a riverbed.

Ewan fired up his laptop. It was ironic that he was writing about the relationship between connectedness with technology and the disconnected nature of modern family life.

He squeezed another guilt-edged coffee through the machine. The themes of his home and working life were strangely converging. He was gaining traction in exposing the way global corporations were exploiting connective technology to corrupt the impressionable minds of the young. He'd quoted Leonard Cohen in the article he'd just submitted. 'The rich have got their channels in the bedrooms of the poor'.

Their trials and tribulations with Lorna typified family relationships everywhere. And yet, they had controlled the intrusion of technology and social media into their own household. Had their attempts to shield and insulate their daughter made any difference? Not appreciably. This was nothing new. Parents had been refusing to buy toy guns for their sons for decades, only to find that a tree branch made an excellent rifle. It had always been a struggle to keep the big, bad world at bay. In the modern era where mass communications surround you everywhere, repelling the invaders from your home and your castle was virtually impossible.

Ewan returned to the kitchen table, replenished coffee and additional serve of toast in hand. First he checked reactions to his article from the previous day. His search revealed multiple clicks on his syndicated feature, but not as many as he would have liked. Next he checked the various newsfeeds. He yawned his way through the numerous entries. Then one well and truly caught his eye.

It was from an obscure US print media source. It read:

FRENZSHIP KILLED MY SON!

Inside his head

Ewan had never heard of Dayton, let alone its Daily News.

He googled Dayton. It was a defence town in the Mid-West. He clicked on Wikipedia to find out more about the lifestyle there. It boasted of its environment, parks and rivers. But there was a less salubrious side to it judging by the numerous references to its rust bucket past.

He re-read the piece from the local paper. It was poorly written and therefore hard to understand. The focus was on the distraught mother's grief. Then there was her accusation. frenzship killed my son. Why was she asserting that? Why blame frenzship in particular when the boy had a checkered online history?

Ewan put the story aside temporarily. Research was easier in the office, especially now that he had a graduate assisting him. He showered quickly and hurriedly stacked his breakfast things into the dishwasher. He called Jessica from his car so she could track down the latest on the story.

Sure enough, this juicy suicide combined with the incendiary accusation was getting plenty of airplay. The ever-efficient Jessica briefed Ewan extensively at the office on coverage by the US network news programs, online magazines and print media. It was trending strongly on Twitter and going viral on Facebook.

Facebook will be breathing germs all over this one, Ewan said to Jessica.

She looked puzzled.

Going viral, get it? He teased her.

Jessica shook her head in pity, connecting Ewan to the New York desk, where an old friend of his was posted.

G'day, Gordon. Ewan greeted him. I'm surprised you're even awake at this hour.

Ever dutiful, you know me. Hangover or not.

You haven't changed.

Not like you. You're sounding more Aussie every day.

Listen, mate…Ewan ventured

…Very well, thank you, and how are you?

Sorry, Gordon, I confess this is not a social call. Have you picked up on this Ohio suicide?

I hadn't until young Jessica got on the blower. By the way, does she look as good as she sounds?

Let's not go there.

Still sensitive are we? Gordon mocked.

Gimme a break. This story is an important one for me.

Yes. Bashing the twenty-first century is your forte, isn't it?

Gordon, give it a rest. Tell me what you know.

Gordon rang back an hour later. Ewan contemplated the potential of the story. A troubled kid, dabbling in things he shouldn't, hooks up with some guy over an Internet site, gets in too deep for one of such tender years and ends up taking his own life.

Ewan took a break for lunch. He turned the issues over in his mind as he walked to the local café. His thoughts kept returning to Lorna. Could she be mixed up with anything like this? He comforted himself with Jake's assessment that her Internet usage was benign. But what else was she up to that they didn't know about?

Over his favourite chicken and salad sandwich, Ewan contemplated how to cover the story. It was trending strongly so clean air would be hard to find. The newshounds would be sniffing all around it, but his value proposition was to be the only one to pick up some different scent. His challenge was to find a unique angle on the story. He doodled in the margin of the West Australian, open at his table. What is it about frenzship? Why has it been so successful? A smiling waitress with the falsest of eyelashes cleared his plate. Then a thought struck him from left field. What did the mother say exactly? Or at least, what was she quoted as saying? He punched the password into his phone and hooked back into the link.

'The scum got inside my boy's head. Literally'.

Ewan smiled at the use of 'literally'. The scum got inside my boy's head. There was something in that. Is that why frenzship is different? It gets inside people's heads. How exactly does it do that? He wondered.

He needed to examine frenzship in more depth and to understand the science better. Then another snippet of news came back to him that could help him do both. Ewan raced to his car and navigated past the big box retail showrooms and fast food outlets until the shopping centre came into view. Parking was easy there in the middle of the day. He found a spot close to the escalators that accessed the retail floors. He was disorientated. All shopping centres looked the same and every floor was identical. He consulted the store directory. If he could read the map correctly, the shop was round the next corner at this level.

Once he got to the bookstore, he had no trouble locating what he was looking for. There was a life-size, cardboard cut out of Dr. Jeremiah Levine beckoning would-be readers to a head high stack of copies of The Social Psycho. Ewan read the jacket as he waited at the cash register. It proclaimed Dr. Levine as the reinventor of friendship in the twenty-first century.

Was this friendship or foeship? Ewan pondered.

Wrong reasons

As he yawned his way to the breakfast table the next morning, Ewan found Sally reading the copy of Social Psycho he'd left on the kitchen bench when he'd got home late from work.

Did you hear about that suicide in the US? Ewan asked Sally as he began to nespress his guilt.

A little bit.

The mother blamed it on frenzship.

I know. Is that why you bought the book?

Partly, Ewan said, sliding his bread into the toaster. And partly because it occurred to me that Lorna could be mixed up with this.

Do you really think so? Sally responded in an alarmed tone.

Not really, Ewan responded bringing his breakfast to the table, but we don't know for sure what she's up to.

Sally took her cup and cereal bowl to the dishwasher.

What do you make of it? Ewan asked, pointing to the book. Is it more than pop psych?

Definitely. This guy is extremely well researched. If this social media website is as soundly based as he claims, it truly would set it apart from the rest.

Have they stolen this concept of psychosocial media from someone else?

Not that I know of.

Is it academically rigorous?

Extremely, Sally replied without hesitation.

I think it's plain dangerous, Ewan concluded, heading for the dishwasher, and I think I'm going after it.

What about your old friend?

That's the point.

That makes it tough, Sally agreed.

No, it's not that. The problem is...I suspect I don't only want to get frenzship.

What then?

I think I want to get him.

You want revenge?

I want to get even.

For what?

I don't really know.

That's a bit sad, Sally said. Have you been waiting for an opportunity?

Like Sun Tzu, Ewan responded.

What do you mean?

You know his adage surely.

Remind me.

If you wait by the river long enough, the bodies of your enemies will float by.

I'm late for work, Sally said, heading for the bathroom. Then she popped her head back into the kitchen. Why don't you interview Levine?

I could try, Ewan agreed, but he's got an army of minders.

On his world tour? Sally said sarcastically on her way out.

Ewan checked his phone to start his day. He read a new email from Gordon. Ewan rushed up the corridor to find Sally.

Guess what! Gordon came up trumps for once.

Sally raised her eyebrows. Gordon was not her favourite person.

Yes, Gordon! He has heard a whisper about the boy's mother.

The boy who shot himself?

Yes. It seems frenzship paid that poor woman to keep quiet.

That's terrible, Sally said sternly.

Yes, but great for my expose. This is dynamite.

Whatever happened to journalistic ethics? Sally pondered aloud.

Santayana

Ewan was convinced young Jessica was flirting with him.

They were spending a lot of time in close proximity, peering at computer screens and poring over papers spread across the desk to nail this frenzship story.

It was one of those stinking hot days in Perth. You can cook your eggs on the asphalt. The Fremantle Doctor hadn't made house calls for the last three nights. Working back in the office with the air conditioning on full blast wasn't such a bad option.

Ewan had bitten into the forbidden apple before. Unlike Adam, he had made his way back into the Garden of Eden. Ironically, his dad, Comrade Jamie, was wont to quote Santayana. Those who fail to learn from history are doomed to repeat it. Ewan had learned this lesson, and off by heart.

Let's call it a day, Jessica, he said, rubbing his eyes. Thanks so much for working back.

No worries, she said brightly. I like to help.

We've uncovered a few useful leads, don't you think?

Yes. I will follow up the Spanish case and the one from Copenhagen tomorrow.

That Danish judgment is revealing, Ewan said. Chief Justices don't cast aspersions lightly.

Absolutely, Jessica agreed, gathering up her belongings and stowing them into her shoulder bag. She hovered before leaving Ewan's office. Can I tempt you to a quick drink? She asked.

Santayana. Santayana, Ewan muttered to himself. Sorry, Jessica. I must get home... to my wife and daughter, he added so the message was not lost on either of them.

OK, no worries, she said, waving goodbye.

Jessica's alluring frame reappeared in the doorway.

Not even time for one? She asked in a pretty please fashion.

Santayana, Santayana. Sorry, Jessica, not even time for a taste.

After that interlude, Ewan took no chances. He kept out of Jessica's way. He felt bad about how he was treating her, but he needed to be strong. Or was he just being weak and pathetic like those men who blame women for leading them on?

Jessica was a brilliant intern. She would make a great journalist one day. She was hard working and smart. Best of all, she was tenacious. When she was chasing down a story, she was a terrier. She had her jaws around frenzship and she was not letting go.

Ewan needed to get glasses. He was spending so much screen time these days. Once he'd finished reading Jessica's paper in his home office, he stood up for a stretch. He was finding it difficult to concentrate. Lorna had missed her curfew again. Sally was ringing round the other parents. In the short-term, he wasn't worried. Lorna would turn up. The long-term was a different story.

He got his mind back to the task at hand. Jessica's report was explosive. It required careful handling. If she had her facts straight, he could light the fuse and retire to admire the firework display that would illuminate the sky like Australia Day over the Swan River. If there was a miscalculation or a stray match was thrown his way, this affair could blow up in his face, disfiguring him and those around him.

Jessica had chronicled five or six instances where frenzship had been cited as a potential factor in serious crimes. These ranged from stalking at the lower end up to suicide and murder. In four of those, there were plausible alternative explanations for the course of events. These instances could be valuable as circumstantial evidence, but they would not stack up in the court of public opinion, let alone a court of law.

The two remaining cases were different. frenzship featured prominently in criminal trials. In Barcelona, a prosecution for grooming a minor and illegal penetration made much of the influence of frenzship on the behaviour of an underage girl who became prey to fleshtraders. The case in Copenhagen was more interesting again. A young boy was allegedly recruited by a motorcycle gang, addicted to crack cocaine and ultimately executed for breaking club protocols. In this case, frenzship was not only raised by the prosecution in proceedings but also featured prominently in the written judgment handed down by the Chief Justice of the Criminal Court.

Ewan returned to his desk. His coffee was cold. He scrolled back through Jessica's report to find the attachment containing the Danish court record. The Ministry of Justice website helpfully carried transcripts in Danish and English. Ewan re-read the passages Jessica had highlighted in yellow. He cut and pasted an extract into a separate document.

...It is arguable that frenzship should not be categorised as a social media product. This market segment is differentiated, as the name implies, by activities that are social in nature, conducted via modern digital communications.

In the expert testimony provided by Professor Lars Johannesson from the Psychology faculty at the University of Copenhagen, it was suggested that the classification applied by frenzship to itself, i.e. psychosocial media, was apt in that its core methodology revolves around psychological testing and interpersonal relationship development.

As such, products such as frenzship present risks and opportunities to society distinct from pure social media. The connections that are made are significantly deeper than those experienced in the social media environment and the influence exerted over the behaviours of others can be profound. This warrants review by government(s) to determine the extent to which control and regulation may be warranted. Put in lay terms, frenzship has the potential to 'get into the head' and impact the decision-making of participants and as such warrants specific investigation from a legislative standpoint.

Ewan typed the headline for his emerging article. 'frenzship or foezship? - should this dangerous site be banned?' He searched his electronic file to find the references to the Ohio suicide boy's mother. His recollection was accurate. She had used the same phrase as the Chief Justice - getting inside people's heads. Ewan's conviction was growing stronger. Psychosocial media was dangerous.

He mulled over the word 'dangerous'. He opened Gordon's summary of the investigation into frenzship's alleged standover tactics. He'd turned up several instances where vocal critics of the psychosocial media site had buttoned their lips for no apparent reason. People who change their minds so suddenly have usually been paid or warned off. None of these likely brown bag recipients would talk anymore. This was testimony to the amounts of cash involved or the severity of the threats issued. Gordon had put the allegations to frenzship's PR machine, the Good Oil. They had laughed it off, flatly denying any wrongdoing.

Ewan smiled at a sentence Gordon had written in code. In the good old days, we would have 'made inquiries' of the banking system. These days, we don't do that sort of thing. Ewan knew exactly what that meant. After all the phone-tapping scandals, his fellow journalists were keeping their noses clean.

Ewan began the slow process of compiling his feature. The tone would be important. It would need to cause a stir. The copywriters and sub-editors would take care of that, sensationalising the story whether he liked it or not. While his colleagues just wanted to sell newspapers, Ewan had a higher order purpose than that. He wanted his expose to make a difference.

To achieve that, his research would need to be impeccable, his writing incisive and his message clear and compelling. This was the biggest test of his life. Compared to this, his finals exams paled into insignificance.

Ewan paced the room again. Was his handle on the psychology good enough? There will be pushback. They will break his article down sentence by sentence, word by word and pick it apart. They won't just have their lawyers crawl all over it. Dr. Levine will roll out the big guns from every respected faculty of psychology from the world's most prestigious universities. He would need some experts on his side. Maybe that psychology professor from Melbourne University Sally collaborated with from time to time?

At that moment, the front door violently slammed. The impact shook the weatherboards. Ewan ran to check on the commotion. He followed the footsteps. He searched frantically around. There was no one there.

Sally ran towards him from the bedroom.

Lorna? Is that you? He called through the closed door.

He repeated the question. No response.

Ewan banged louder on the door. Lorna, open the door. He was shouting now and rattling the door handle.

Open the door, this minute!

Not now, Dad. Lorna's plaintiff tone surprised and unnerved him.

Vortex

Nothing changed. Lorna hadn't come home for several days this time. Just when they were poised to confront her on what was going on, she went AWOL.

Ewan's neck hurt like crazy. Someone had stuck his head in a vice and wrenched it sideways. He wriggled himself upright. He'd fallen asleep on the couch. His head was fuzzy. His brain was in some strange vortex of excitement and fear where frenzship and Lorna were spinning together out of control.

In her sleep-deprived fractious state, Sally had alienated the authorities. From the outset, the police were disinclined to take missing teenage girls seriously. Ewan could see their point. To them, teenage rebellion was the norm. All young girls run away at some point. Ninety nine point nine per cent of them come home. Ewan took comfort from that.

Sally insisted on her rights. She lectured the police on their responsibilities. Ewan watched nervously. Sally's legendary professional detachment ran for the hills when she was personally involved. He played an unfamiliar mediation role. He gently escorted her from the Fremantle police station. He reassured Sally that Lorna would come home. The statistics proved it.

Ewan and Sally each took time off work to search for their daughter. They exhausted her likely haunts and the patience of their friends and parents from school. Sally's confrontation with Jade's mother, Wendy, had been a lowlight. A slanging match in Wendy's driveway was nothing new for Wendy's neighbours. Listening to a family counsellor screaming at the top of her voice, 'This is a drug den, not a home', probably occurred less frequently. Despite Sally's tirade, Wendy stood her ground, insisting that she hadn't seen Lorna for a couple of weeks.

Ewan massaged the offending tight muscles before standing up. He snuck along the hallway, as usual avoiding the creaky floorboards like a kid on the footpath stepping around the cracks. The bedroom door was ajar. Sally was sleeping at last. Just as dreamers check their lottery numbers every week, Ewan pushed Lorna's bedroom door open. It didn't close anymore. He'd wrecked his shoulder and wounded his pride two nights ago splintering the door from its frame. There was no jackpot. Lorna hadn't come home.

Ewan was wide awake now and desperate for coffee. He thought better of a guilt press as the whirring of the machine might wake Sally. He settled for the relative peace of the electric kettle. At that moment, the phone rang. It took Ewan a moment to register where the sound was coming from. It was the police.

Some thirty minutes later, Ewan and Sally started at the sound of a key turning the lock. Sally rushed towards the front door. Ewan tentatively raised himself from the bar stool at the kitchen bench. He looked down the hallway to see Lorna brush past his wife and hustle towards her bedroom.

Hey, you! Sally shouted, bristling with anger.

Only then did they notice a silhouetted figure hovering in the doorway.

This may not be the best time, the policewoman counselled, looking sympathetically at Sally.

They regrouped around the kitchen table. Ewan wondered at the old adage. WPC Angela Heslop looked about sixteen.

Where did you find her? Sally asked, eyes fixed on the floor.

There was an incident with a car, WPC Heslop explained. A group of four girls was involved. One of them, Jade, borrowed the keys to her mother's car. She collected the other girls from a pre-arranged spot. She didn't have a driver's licence, but she still took them for a joyride around the local suburbs.

Unbelievable, Ewan muttered.

The car collided with a row of wheelie bins on Canning Highway in East Fremantle. A passing patrol car observed the incident. The police found three of the four girls hiding in the local park.

Sally and Ewan exchanged looks.

They saw a fourth girl but couldn't catch her. There was a strong smell of alcohol in the car. A bottle of vodka and several cans of alcopop drinks were found.

Ewan struggled to make sense of it. I'm assuming no one was hurt, he said.

That's correct.

What about damage?

The car's grille is a bit mangled but otherwise nothing serious.

That's a relief, Ewan said, searching for a positive.

There was an awkward silence. Sally broke in. I'm a social worker. You've probably seen all this before.

All too often, Sally said, but I didn't expect to be so directly involved. It can happen to anyone.

Will any charges be laid? Sally asked fearfully.

The policewoman thought carefully. It's not up to me, she said cautiously, but I seriously doubt it. The girls weren't caught in the driver's seat and the car was borrowed rather than stolen.

Sally looked relieved. That annoyed Ewan. So they will get off scot-free?

Basically.

I'd like Lorna to be charged, Ewan said.

Don't be ridiculous, Sally shot back.

If I could say something here, the WPC intervened, the important thing for now is that your daughter is home and appears to be in pretty good shape.

Ewan stood to round up the coffee cups. If there are no consequences for these children, how the hell are they going to learn anything? He wondered aloud.

Ewan! Sally rebuked him. Do you know where she's been these last few nights? Sally asked the policewoman.

Not for sure. But I'd suggest she's been with Jade at her house.

Jesus Christ! Ewan shouted. I knew it.

Wendy lied to me, Sally snivelled.

Hypocrite

They grounded Lorna yet again. Lorna wordlessly retreated to her bedroom. She seemed exhausted.

A handyman came to repair her bedroom door and for good measure secured her window. Ewan and Sally left her alone, but watched the room round the clock.

Ewan called to see Wendy again, without letting on to Sally. She took her time coming to the door. She took long enough for Ewan to speculate about what might be going on. Sex or drugs? Probably not rock and roll.

Wendy was horrified to see him. Ewan bit his lip. He maintained his calm and did not react to provocative references to his wife as 'that stuck-up cow'. His mission was to locate Muzzo. Just as Ewan was convincing himself that frenzship was somehow connected to Lorna's deteriorating behaviour, so Ewan was certain that the mysterious Muzzo had something to do with Lorna procuring her computer and suspected phone. It couldn't be a coincidence that Lorna had hurtled downhill like an out of control go-cart from the time the frenzship craze started and Muzzo had also slimed his way onto the scene.

Ewan's problem was that he was head-smart not street-smart. He could sniff out a corporate fraud from a mile away and turn the screws on the board and management until the truth squeezed through a gap in the undergrowth and slithered across the front page. By contrast, Wendy, who was right there in front of him, was like a shadowy underworld figure hidden behind a team of corporate lawyers and media managers. She stared back at him with her surprisingly clear blue eyes. He concluded sex rather than drugs. She had only met that boy Muzzo a handful of times. They hadn't said more than half a dozen words to each other. She had no idea where he lived or how to contact him. She had asked Jade, she said, maintaining Ewan's eye contact while defiantly folding her arms. Jade 'didn't know nothing, neither'.

Ewan's tea was terminally stewed. He'd forgotten about it with so much on his mind. As he added more milk than usual to counteract the bitter taste, the hint of a smile broke through his permanent frown. It was like sunlight on a stormy day. 'Jade don't know nothing, neither'. Grammatically and practically, did that mean she did or didn't know something?

Ewan was determined to dig deeper. He clicked onto Google and searched for frenzship. He navigated to the website. He understood it chapter and verse, perhaps better than anyone unconnected to the vile enterprise. But he had never registered. Jessica and his interns before her had variously been signed-up frenz, but he had never done so himself.

He plugged in a hotmail account he used as a journalistic pseudonym and pondered a suitable password. An obvious candidate occurred to him. 'Skinhead' was taken. Skinhead12 did the trick.

His mission was to befrenz Lorna. He knew she would be there. He would do so anonymously. He would try to engage her. Then he would have a better understanding of the extent to which this make believe fantasy world was polluting her mind.

He set about searching for his wayward daughter. He had to guess what her avatar would be. In his spare time, he had been jotting down names, places, books and other titles that had resonated with her in the past. He assumed it worked like his previous pet hate, Facebook. He floundered around, looking for the search mechanism. He googled 'how do I find frenz?'

He didn't fully understand the answers from the user community. He returned to the site. There was no search mechanism. He banged his fist into the desk, rattling his empty cup against his crumb-strewn plate.

It was obvious. That was the defining factor of frenzship. That's what set it apart from pure social media. You can't find or choose your frenz. With psychosocial media, the system makes frenz of you. Not for the first time, the Orwellian essence of this monster made him shiver.

Ewan willed himself to succeed. Like a marathon runner with just five kilometres to go or an author nearing the end of his manuscript, he would push on. He gave himself a silent pep talk. I am an eminent, world-respected journalist. I have been to places and seen things very few others have. I have a first-class degree from the world's finest university.

Ewan opened the psychosocial media testing environment. If anyone knew his daughter, he did. He knew her as she was and as she wanted to be. He would take his time, plenty of time. He would consider carefully the ramifications of every question and every test. He would make himself compatible with Lorna and befrenz her, thereby thwarting the high and mighty Dr. Jeremiah Levine.

Ewan got down to business. It was complicated and required his full attention. His concentration was intense.

Ewan failed to notice someone creeping up behind him. At the last moment, he sensed something, turning sharply around. He found Lorna looking over his shoulder. Her faint smile was knowing.

You're such a hypocrite, Dad.

A solitary word

Ewan's mind remained shrouded in fog. He sat at the lights, phone illegally in hand, poised to do something both desperate and embarrassing.

Sending this text was preposterous. He was descending into some escapist fantasy. His estranged ally, now his arch-nemesis, would renounce evil and ride like the wind through the jaws of hell to defend the innocent and protect the weak. Yeah, sure.

It was ludicrous. But doing nothing wasn't an option. To hell with it. Type one solitary word.

Not yet. He had unfinished business first.

I didn't answer my phone. That's the way these things go. I was heading for the PT room when it rang. I had a head of steam up and turning round didn't seem an option. There had been so many false alarms that I no longer expected there to be a labour mayday call at all.

I make it back to my room. I towel off the sweat from my exertion. I check my pulse. It's coming down nicely. I look for my phone.

Thunderbirds are go. That's the message.

OMG, she's in labour.

I struggle into my clothes. Where is Miki? It's prearranged for him to escort me to the maternity wing.

Where the hell is he? My brain paces out the nervous father's walk.

Hey dude, I hear Miki's voice as his head appears in the doorway. For once in your life, try not to be late!

How friendship demands sacrifice of us all

You don't understand

I was being punished, and deservedly so. It takes a shallow man to say this. I couldn't cope with having the love of my life and the other love of my life in the same room.

I wanted them both and I wanted neither of them. They were each perfect and equally flawed. I howled at the moon. How could any god be so cruel as to inflict such a horrendous debilitating disease on someone as beautiful and precious as Nina? And how divinely sick was the joke to let Cassidy get pregnant at the same time?

Miki was holding things together better than me. It was easy for him. He hadn't got Cassidy pregnant. At least not to my knowledge.

We took Nina to the Alfred Coffee and Kitchen for some West Melrose cool. Miki was antsy to get down to business. He pulled me aside while Nina was on a toilet break.

I need you to get a grip, he said.

It's not easy, I whined.

Deal with it, Miki responded unkindly. Here she comes. Let's get down to work.

Nina heard the last part. Before we get started, Nina said with a sigh, please hear me out.

We sat back to listen as she popped a heady cocktail of multicoloured pills.

I'm neither so strong that I want to spend every living hour contemplating my disease nor so weak that no one can mention it. So, mon cher Miki, stop checking on my welfare every minute and, you, stop walking on eggs.

Eggshells, I corrected her.

Nina was right. I wasn't coping with her being sick. I felt this overpowering need to protect her. I felt guilty about my undeserved good health and I also didn't want her dirtying her hands helping us muck out our frenzship pigsty.

She leaned over and kissed each of us in turn on both cheeks. We wiped away tears. Friendship had clubbed us like unsuspecting seals.

Miki set the scene midst the flurry of cups and plates coming and going. It's obvious that our current messaging isn't working. Whether the other members of our team accept that or not, we have to find a way to restore frenzship's standing.

I nodded.

Miki continued, now looking at me. When you told me how positive Nina's email about frenzship was, a light globe switched on in my thick skull. It seemed obvious to turn to her for help.

You could have told me, I said resentfully. It felt good to get that out.

I wanted to surprise you, dude! He protested.

Nina looked anxiously between us. I caught her eye. I backed off, for her sake. The secrecy still rankled with me, but I let it go.

I guess it doesn't matter now, I conceded.

We need Nina to help us reset our communications. She is famous now, he added.

Nina looked bashful. To tell you the truth, she said, I feel bad about that. You know, profiting from the Arab Spring.

Nina had been the first commentator to understand the significance of that ghastly act of self-immolation committed by an obscure Tunisian fruiterer, Mohamad Bouazizi, that momentous December day.

Be that as it may, Miki continued, Nina is now a recognised authority on the status of social media as a source for good and as a tool to free the oppressed.

The prospect of Nina entangling herself with frenzship angered me. This was a time to care for her not expose her.

I'm not comfortable with this, I said in a faltering voice.

They fell silent, awaiting an explanation.

Nina, Miki is a great guy, but he shouldn't have asked you to do this. It's not fair on you.

Miki shook his head. You don't understand…

…I *do* understand, I insisted. It's a brilliant strategy. But we can't ask Nina to sell out.

You really don't understand, Miki repeated sadly.

Shhh, Nina said, putting a finger to her lips. I appreciate your concern for me, mon amour, but there is no academic purity anymore. Let me ask you a question. Do you know who pays my salary?

The Sorbonne?

Not anymore. Citroën sponsors my program.

That's immaterial, I countered. If you speak out for frenzship you will associate yourself with a communications tool developed purely and simply for profit. And worse than that, bad things have happened.

That's not the point, Miki said. The petticoat of his frustration was showing.

He's right, Nina agreed. It isn't the point. Do you remember my story about maman meeting the man of her dreams via frenzship?

Of course, I nodded.

That's why I'm here to help you. Not because of my mother. But because this brilliant piece of science allied to the power of modern communications is a powerful force for good.

And evil, I added.

Of course, Nina conceded. But that is not unique to frenzship. It is true for every new piece of technology. It's true for all change for that matter. Nuclear science cures cancer and fries people. It has the power to destroy the world. The Internet connects people, gives them access to limitless information and exposes children to disgusting paedophiles.

Exactly, Miki agreed.

Does frenzship bear no responsibility for that poor kid blowing his brains out? I asked.

Nina considered her response. As difficult as this issue is, she said, entrancing me with her big brown eyes, my answer is no. frenzship cannot be blamed for what people do with it.

Did you get that line from the gun lobby? I asked with a more scornful tone than I intended. I was sounding more like Ewan every day.

Miki paid the bill and we walked arm in arm, just like that day at the Sorbonne.

Can I explain to you why you really don't understand? Miki asked me.

If you must, I replied ungraciously.

I asked Nina for advice. I didn't ask her to get involved. I just want you to know that.

I shrugged my shoulders. Nina hugged me.

I volunteered, cheri. I want to help.

O-kay, I said. Are you doing this for friendship or frenzship?

Miki got it.

Nina didn't. Je ne comprends pas, she said.

It's quite a show. Cassidy is resting on the bed. I'm sitting in the armchair alongside. Randy, Miki, Zak and the crew are drinking the best French bubbly, strictly against hospital rules.

The weirdest part of the tableau is Lorna cradling her goddaughter, Charlotte Tabetha, tentatively in her arms, anxiously scanning the faces around the room to check she's holding the newborn right.

You should get one of your own, Randy chirps.

For God's sake, Randy, Cassidy rebukes him. If you weren't my brother...

Observing this strange nativity scene, I see clearly what I need to do. I heave myself up onto my crutches and shuffle and puff my way swiftly into the corridor. There is something I need to do in secret. I lean on the doorpost of an adjoining empty hospital room.

I feel for my phone in my pocket.

With friends like these, who needs enemies?

The birds and the bees

The old man intimidated him.

Ewan had often daydreamed of finding himself in this position. Sinking into the plush leather armchair, face to face with the media mogul, the kingmaker himself. He had imagined himself confident and forthright. It pained him that when fantasy became reality, he found himself cowed.

The magnate's voice was strangely soothing. His accent was lost in the Pacific, somewhere closer to the States than home. Sitting there in the gentleman's club, listening politely, Ewan accepted that he was not his father's son. Comrade Jamie would have told the mogul exactly what he thought of him and to hell with the consequences.

Ewan registered his editor-in-chief sweating freely. He was no doubt worried about how Ewan would answer this particular question.

I appreciate the commercial reality, sir. Ewan's expression was slow and deliberate. He despised himself for referring to the man as 'sir'. Even if all the others did, he did not need to kow-tow in this way. Ewan glanced around the room. His respectful tone had calmed his bosses.

I don't for a moment underestimate the market power of our advertisers and backers, let alone Google and Facebook. Call me old-fashioned, sir, but I can't put a value on the truth.

There was a long pause. Cigar smoke was puffed into the atmosphere. Don't get me wrong, son, I'm not scared of these people.

Ewan and his boss shook their heads in unison. Of course not.

And...

Ewan was unsure whether the patriarch was pausing for effect or had lost his thread.

And, he continued, I think your expose is superlative. You read at Oxford, did you not?

That's right.

Politics and economics wasn't it?

Ewan's boss mopped his brow.

And philosophy, Ewan added as reassurance.

The old man nodded in respect. Don't get me wrong. We're going to run this.

Thank you, sir, Ewan said, looking across to his editor in triumph.

I just want to be sure someone in your position knows the facts of life.

The facts of life?

That's right. The birds and the bees of the global media business.

Ewan inclined his head to indicate that he was ready to listen.

The media man waved his empty brandy tumbler in the direction of a black-suited waiter. In this business, he said, dripping gravitas, when you hurt someone, they hurt you.

Ewan nodded.

It's like the basic law of physics. For every action, there is an equal and opposite reaction. Except...

Ewan resented this man's ability to command his attention.

...the reaction in the media business is never equal. If I can speak in the vernacular, these guys will shit on us from a great height.

I appreciate...Ewan stammered.

The figurehead raised his hand to interrupt. You don't have to respond. So long as you understand.

I understand.

A refreshed brandy was gratefully acknowledged. Tell me about your time at Oxford.

frenzship or foezship?

The intercom made an airport announcement at some ungodly hour.

My mind flashed back to Randy. In my semi-unconscious state, I concluded that he'd been rushed back to hospital. I didn't want Cassidy to hear the bad news first-hand so I headed off to the front door. I checked my phone on the way. I had four messages. There were two each from Miki and Nina. There was nothing from Randy or about Randy.

Nina and Miki were at the door. They looked anxious. I waved them in.

Where's the fire? I asked.

Right here, Nina replied, opening her iPad.

I scanned the headline emblazoned across the screen. frenzship or foezship – Should this dangerous site be banned? I shook my head. I knew who would be responsible for this.

With friends like yours, who needs enemies? Miki asked.

It's wonderful

Sally read intently. Ewan's article ran across six pages. Pride welled up. Tears choked her. She was so proud of him. At that moment, she was so much in love with this man, who was committed to changing the world, or at least what he could.

It's wonderful, darling, she said.

Friends like these

Woken by the noise, Cassidy made her way to the kitchen. She was surprised to find this particular gathering. I felt my heart rate elevate as it always did when she and Nina were together. Neither of them gave me cause. It was a reflection of my confused state of mind.

Who died? Cass asked, picking up on the funereal mood.

I handed Cass a mug of black coffee. frenzship probably, I said.

This is your so-called fucking friend again! Cassidy shouted, glaring at me.

I nodded regretfully.

My piece is virtually ready, Nina said to lift our spirits.

We'd better go with it, Miki said, like now.

I return to the impromptu baby shower. I observe Randy nervously as he takes his turn to nurse Charlotte.

I sit beside Cassidy on the bed. She looks exhausted, but serenely happy. We did this, I whisper.

We? Cassidy questions me.

Lorna is lapping up the attention from the handsome Zak. I feel good about what I just did. It probably is time for Lorna to pursue the next phase of her life. Without some external intervention, I imagine her stuck between the floors of her decision-making, frantically pressing the alarm bell to summon an elevator company that has long since gone out of business.

I feel the warmth of Cassidy's hand in mine. Lorna is nothing like the girl I first met nor could she possibly yet be the woman she is destined to become.

When friendship determines that a man's gotta do what a man's gotta do

Disrupting disruption

As soon as you let your guard down, they know you're weak. When you're strutting your stuff and puffing out your chest, they steer clear. But no sooner have you staggered into the ropes, steadied your wobbles with a glove on the padded corner post, than they smell the blood and come in for the kill.

The snag was I was becoming a SNAG. I wasn't yet a card-carrying bleeding heart, but my feminine side was coming to the fore in an unwelcome manner. I'd fought hard to prevent Nina from getting involved with frenzship, but she was determined to take her chances. She wrote her article and then returned to Paris as suddenly as she arrived.

Nina's timely intervention had blunted the attack on frenzship and had shifted the debate. We used the contacts that she had with Le Monde to get her article published in the New York Times and syndicated round the world. She called it, 'frenzship – Disrupting Disruption'.

I re-read her article online. Nina's writing was a little stilted and her arguments couched in language that was rather too academic. For all that, her reasoning was lucid and her message compelling. Her thesis was simple. For the first time in history, new technology had made it possible to disrupt the disruption. Throughout time, the world has been rocked by seismic shifts, literally in the form of natural disasters and metaphorically through cataclysmic man-made phenomena wrought by pandemics, warfare and geopolitical revolution. Fundamental change of this kind is referred to in the modern world as 'disruption'.

Irrespective of the genesis of such disruptive change, whether it was natural or caused by human intervention, the social order has been devastated and relationships in families, tribes and nations have been destroyed. The speed of change has accelerated with time. Technology is transforming the world before people's eyes. Economic and social structures are now so fluid that they offer hope and opportunity at the same time as they destroy confidence and certainty. The glass is both half-full and half-empty.

Nina argued that the world was now spinning so fast that there was no prospect of its momentum being reversed. Life could end, but it couldn't go back. In this context, the basic human values – hope, compassion, love and friendship – had to be reinvented to survive.

Nina argued that frenzship had offered the world a pathway to developing relationships for the new order. She recounted heart-warming, good news stories illustrating how psychosocial media had transformed lives and enriched experience. She acknowledged that frenzship could be, and had been, used by evil people to do evil.

For her conclusion, Nina quoted John Mayer's song lyric, 'Love is a verb, it ain't a thing'. She extrapolated this to friendship. The world has changed forever and so has friendship. It is pointless to hark back to the good old days of friendship. 'Friend' is no longer a noun. It has become a verb. We cannot have friends as constant objects to keep. 'To friend' is dynamic. It is about now not then. BeFrenz is a verb. It is synonymous with making friends in the twenty-first century.

I was proud of Nina's intellect and happy that she had helped us right the ship. We were now back on course. The hull had been damaged and the sails were patched but we were sailing ahead again and the skies were turning blue.

And yet, I still felt at sea. I lacked the academic conviction that drove Nina's thinking. When I first met her, I didn't care whether something was right or wrong, I just wanted it to work, and of course to make money. When she argued that all information should be freely available and that technology was value-free, I found it quirky and interesting. Now, I wasn't so sure. Did frenzship carry no responsibility for evil done in its name?

Shakespeare was right. Conscience doth make cowards of us all. Mine kept creeping up on me. It scared the bejesus out of me. It was like your least favourite older cousin when you were a kid. He would leap out from a dark doorway with a Dracula mask on. That's what was happening to me.

I blamed my two women for unnerving me. They were awakening guilty feelings that had previously slept like a baby. These were once strong and sexy women. They were the type that excited and scared me at the same time. They fucked your body and fucked with your mind.

Now they were struck asunder. Cassidy was prostrate with morning sickness. If she'd been renting the suite, she could have sub-let everything but the bathroom. Her silky blonde mane was tied back and matted. Her sexy tight clothes sat impatiently on the designer shelving. These days, a night out for Cassidy was a sortie beyond the ensuite.

Nina's condition was less predictable. While Cassidy was continuously laid low, Nina was up and down like IT equities. Her body had become a mystery to her. It belonged to someone else. Waking up was a lottery. If she was lucky, she would feel good and she could look forward to a normal day where disease was far from her mind. On less propitious mornings, she would rouse herself to find free-floating malaise. It was the weirdest feeling. She could not describe it. She had no choice but to accept it. For that day, she would be an invalid. Her disease would dominate her thoughts. Worse still, her mind would obsess about the degenerative nature of her condition. She was under siege. She was under no illusions that one day the bad days would breach the walls of resistance and would overrun the good.

I was ensconced in LA with Cassidy, at least, physically. But, half of my soul was in Paris with Nina. Just as Nina didn't know what any day would hold, I couldn't predict on any day, or at any moment, how I would feel. About life. About them. About me.

I looked at my dishevelled appearance in the hallway mirror. I longed to be myself again. Arrogant. Selfish. Happy.

A text jolted me back to reality. It was just one word.

Skinhead.

Dumping?

There should be a how-to guide for this sort of thing. How do you dump someone whose head is over the toilet bowl? Dumping for Dummies? Maybe Dumping while Dumping?

I wasn't intending to dump Cassidy, as such. I just needed some breathing space. I craved lebensraum, if I can put it that way without giving the wrong impression.

Cassidy was a mess. Having reinvented myself as some sort of human being, I wanted to help her. She wouldn't let me. The harder I tried, the nastier she got. I consulted with Miki.

It's a tough one, he said, shaking his head.

I hadn't pulled another basketball stunt for this assignation. I wanted his help and co-operation. We strolled from Santa Monica along the promenade to Venice Beach.

What about a termination?

What about it?

Have you discussed it?

I took a deep breath, distracting myself with the views on display at Muscle Beach. Are you here to help or get me killed?

O-kay, Miki said, setting off again. Don't bite my head off, but why do you think she got pregnant?

I sat on a metal bench. I couldn't take my eyes of this amazon of a woman with biceps on biceps, racks on racks and mane on mane.

The sixty-four million dollar question, I conceded. I don't know why. Did you know she had a miscarriage?

Miki shook his head.

She did. It must be six or nine months back. She didn't tell me.

What do you mean?

She only told me later. I was horrified. Sort of flattered, too. I thought maybe she loved me. You know, wanted me as the father of her child.

Don't get soppy on me. It's creepy coming from you.

I smiled, pausing to think. Things changed when Randy had his heart attack. She loves her bro, don't get me wrong, but I think she saw his illness as an opportunity for her to take centre stage, for her to shine.

Miki nodded for me to continue.

It's horrible to say this. When Randy recovered, it was a blow to Cassidy. Randy is such a jerk. I love him to pieces, everybody does. I don't think it's ever occurred to him that Cassidy would like to step out from his shadow.

But she's been running frenzship with us. She's been given that opportunity, Miki said.

It's not enough. It's a country not an empire.

Miki stood up. I knew he was short of time. We started walking back.

So you're telling me that Cassidy wants a baby to have something of her very own, Miki remarked.

Is that what I'm telling you? I asked, stopping to think more clearly. I don't know. Maybe. The problem is that Cass is confused. I'm confused. The foetus is definitely confused.

Miki smiled.

Cass is mixed up, and guilty about it, I continued. She takes it out on me.

You need a break, my friend, Miki concluded as we approached his car.

I wanted to tell him what I was planning to do. I willed myself to man up. I couldn't bring myself to do it. Somehow rivalry endured over all those years. He was now my friend and my only confidant, yet I couldn't share this with him.

Miki climbed into his car. Have I helped at all? He asked.

Not really.

Didn't think so, he said, waving as he drove away.

Without the manual, I didn't make a good fist of it.

Cass, I'm going to Paris for a little while.

You can go to hell as far as I'm concerned.

It's hard to explain yourself to someone who is dry reaching. I wanted to tell her that I was worried about Nina. I had planned to reassure her that I wouldn't be gone long. The fact was I was simply checking on a friend. I wanted to reassure Cassidy that I did want to be with her and support her and the baby. But, most of all, I was desperate for her to understand that we needed a break before we killed each other, at which time all these other commitments I was prepared to make would be rendered redundant. Instead, I turned around and walked away. There were so many reasons why I didn't tell Cassidy any of those things. I didn't know how. I didn't think she'd listen. I didn't know whether any of it was true.

At the graveside

I slept like a baby on the plane. I dreamt of my brother. I hadn't seen him for thirty years.

He was standing at the graveside during my father's funeral. He hadn't attended the real thing. I presumed no one knew where to contact him. Perhaps my mother had just forgotten about him.

The eerie thing was that my father was there too. It was raining in my dream. My dad stood next to my brother, sheltering him under an outsize black umbrella. They looked across at me from time to time. I tried to cross to their side of the unfilled plot. I jostled past the other mourners. Then I found myself winding my way through endless corridors in an institution. It was clinical and cold like an old-fashioned hospital.

It took me ages to make it to where they'd been standing. By then, the coffin had been interred. The soft, wet earth was mounded high on the burial plot. Big drips of rain splattered on the paved pathways. My father was gone. Underground, I assumed. And my brother had disappeared.

The dream was disturbing, but heart-warming in its own way. My father was protecting and comforting my long lost brother. Was my brother dead and buried by now? It seemed best not to know.

I lifted the window blind. The sun was rising, bathing the horizon in crimson and orange light. The stewards were busy at work in the galley. I guessed we might be an hour out of Charles de Gaulle. I reconstructed my bed into a seat in time to receive the warmed wet towel. I refreshed myself. Gratefully, I accepted a freshly-squeezed orange juice in return for the used flannel.

I felt anxious. I had good cause. The situation with Cassidy was more than a train wreck. My locomotive had ploughed through the buffers, hurtled along a crowded platform and taken out the majestic station concourse. I hadn't contacted Nina about my visit. I had no idea of the reception I would get. Back in the day, she may not have let me up into her apartment. She might have mocked me from the upper window as being needy and pathetic. I wondered in passing if the key was still suspended on elastic inside the letterbox. It was a stupid thought. It occurred to me that I hadn't even checked if Nina lived in the same place.

Over breakfast, I rehearsed my announcement to Nina that I was in Paris. Even in my own show, I was a terrible actor. My performance was wooden and unbelievable. Did I really propose to claim that I was passing by? Would she really believe I was in Paris on frenzship business? She might have if I'd contacted her and told her I was coming over. But I didn't. Now, she would know that I was there because she was sick. She would hate me for that. She was fiercely independent before she was diseased. Now she would be doubly so. I could sleep in the airport and get the next plane home. Home to what? To Cassidy? I groaned so loud that my fellow passengers turned to check me out.

Once the A380 had cruised to a halt on the greasy tarmac, I reached for my phone. I dreaded what I might find. To my great relief, and considerable shame, there was nothing from Cassidy. There was just one text.

We come running?

I don't know

History does repeat itself.

I took the airport train to the Gare du Nord and consigned my bag to the tender loving care of the left luggage office. The French love a uniform. The attendant looked magnificent. In his full regalia, resplendent with brocade and epaulettes, he looked for all the world like the self-appointed dictator of an obscure African nation renowned for its poor dress sense. Possibly Cameroon.

For all his finery, the attendant had the manners of a sewer rat.

Seulement une?

Une quoi?

Une valise?

Oui.

Une, six ou vingt-quatre?

Valises?

Heures.

Six.

Vingt.

Valises?

Euros.

I wondered if please and thank you had recently been banned by the word secretariat of the EEC. Having conducted what business I rightfully had in Paris, I resolved to promenade along the banks of the Seine and crunch along the deserted towpaths to reprise my lovelorn Parisian past.

I detoured to lose myself amongst the teeming tourists. The magnificent views of the Tuileries, Sacré Coeur and Notre-Dame may have inspired the renaissance, but they did little to lift my spirits or resolve my inner turmoil. I still had no idea how to present myself to Nina.

I stopped for a coffee in one of my old haunts. As stupid as it was, I half expected to find someone I knew. I stood to drink my coffee as is the local custom. My command of French had deteriorated. I grasped but a few bars of the everyday concerto playing out around me.

It was just as well. I needed to think. My problem was that I didn't know why I had come to Paris. I ordered encore un coup from the pony-tailed, unshaven barman. Did I come to care for Nina? Did I run to escape from Cassidy? Did I love Nina? Did I hate Cassidy? Was I embracing responsibility? Or was I running from it?

My blood pumped faster from the caffeine but my neurons processed at the same sluggish rate. I let my body transport me to the Sorbonne. It was around the time when the afternoon lectures would finish. Students filed past me, shouting, laughing and holding hands. Peter Pan was alive and well. Just like in the Rodriguez song, these were different individuals but the same people that I remembered from long ago.

Nina shuffled uncomfortably down the staircase. She squinted into the sunlight. Her expression gave nothing away. I stood limply, smiling feebly in her direction.

She approached me. C'est toi.

Oui, c'est moi.

What are you doing here?

I don't know.

Mutual Incomprehension

It was a wet, wintry afternoon. This was hardly the weather you associate with the south of France. Nina agreed to take a few days off. I drove the whole way while she dozed in the passenger's seat. I remembered how impossible driving on the Continent had seemed before I lived in a left-hand drive, right-hand side of the road country. Nina would wake up from time to time and smile at me indulgently. I could tell it was one of those days when she didn't feel too well. She seemed happy to have me around.

Nina's aunt's house was a classic stone cottage in a picturesque village with la mairie and l'église facing off across the town square. The oppositional status of church and state in even the smallest village was not lost on me.

The old blacksmith's house had slate floors, heavy window frames and low ceilings with sturdy beams. The main rooms gave onto a delightful inner courtyard that had been the waiting room for horses needing new shoes.

I brought Nina some wine as she lay on the rug in front of the roaring open fire. We'd buddy-fucked. Poised to reacquaint myself with the buried treasure, she manoeuvred me to take her the other way. I resisted. She insisted. She climaxed within seconds. She held me inside until I pulsed weakly, apologetically into her anus.

I lay beside her. Why? I asked.

Because I'm dying.

I escaped to take some exercise, and to be alone. Nina was feeling weak so I knew she wouldn't join me. I hiked to the top of a nearby hill. You could see for miles over lush pasture. The extended carpet of green was woven in a recurring pattern of ploughed furrows, unmortared stone walls and rustic farmhouses. The smoke billowing from the chimneys layered the painting with a band of grey.

The beauty contrasted violently with the ugliness playing out around me. I'd leapt from Cassidy's frying pan headlong into Nina's fire. Nina was in physical, mental and emotional decline. I cried into the wind. I cursed bad luck. Mine as much as hers.

The sharp, cold wind took my breath away. It blew the cobwebs from my mind. I would go to Ewan. He needed me. I needed to be needed by my old friend. Ewan was someone who knew me. He was under no illusions about what a shit I was, am and would yet be. He was someone who loved and hated me.

I took the long way back. The path wound its way to the other side of the village. I wasn't sure how to get back to the central square. It didn't matter. It wasn't a big place and I was in ho hurry. I stopped for a coffee. I sat outside at a chrome table with matching chairs. The white-aproned patron arrived. I changed my mind in favour of something a little stronger.

Un anis, s'il vous plaît.

I slugged down the pastis in one shot. I gasped as the firewater burned my throat. What did Ewan want of me? Did he expect me to shut frenzship down on the strength of one of his emotional, commie rants? Was he so naïve as to think that I would have the power and authority to stop the psychosocial media juggernaut like one of his heroic protesters lying down on the train tracks?

Monsieur, encore un, I shouted, motioning to the waiter.

I drank with more circumspection this time. I poured the liquid over the refreshed ice, relishing the aniseed scent and enjoying the slow metamorphosis from clear sky liquid to cloud and fog.

Ewan wouldn't invoke the so-called safe word for something like that. I smiled at his bloodied face when my quick thinking saved us both from a much worse pounding at the hands of those bovver boys. I mused that it would be something personal. Not leading with his dick again? Not likely with him. That boring bastard would stray no more.

After my third Ricard, I concluded that it didn't matter. I would head off to rescue my friend. I would save him like I always did. In doing so, I would once again demonstrate my absolute superiority. He had done his best to destroy everything I'd worked for. He'd pulled out all the stops to trash my legacy. But I would still be there for him. Regardless, I would honour our schoolboy pact.

I readied my mobile, flicking onto the text screen. I scrolled down to his latest SMS. We come running? Typical Ewan, he would misunderstand my motives. He would assume that I was responding to help him.

I set off to check on Nina. I left twenty Euros on the table.

Before I left I got my response away.

We come running? I was running in more ways than one.

We come running.

We are back at the Bel-Air. We are just like any ordinary family. Yeah right!

Charlotte is a beautiful little girl and everyone coos over her, so that's pretty normal. But beyond that...

Cassidy is obsessed with recovering her figure. Our Mexican nanny watches the sleeping babe, while Cass ups her workload in the gym. I accompany her there, strengthening my legs from atrophied jelly to something approaching muscle.

Uncle Randy smokes his cigars over the precious offspring and Sonia sneaks a cuddle when Cassidy isn't around. The only truly stable figure in Charlotte's early life is Lorna. The godmother is devoted to her.

Lorna and I spend more time together now that I'm out of hospital. We take the baby for a walk and we talk.

Lorna is more confused than ever about what to do. She does and she doesn't want to go home. She does and she doesn't want to see her parents.

I haven't told Lorna what I did. I encourage her just to go for a month. She says she'll think about it.

Charlotte's status in the whole thing has changed. Before she was born, she was a solid reason for Lorna to go to avoid the competition for affection. Now that Charlotte is here and there is no competition as everyone is fully focused on the baby, my daughter has confused Lorna even further.

Distracted by my thoughts, I don't notice the text pinging on my phone.

How you distinguish an acquaintance from a friend.

Up, up and away

Lorna was up, up and away again. Ewan and Sally were barely holding it together. They would take turns to trawl the usual haunts. They waited down the street from Jade's house, but all to no avail.

Ewan had initially taken heart from the belated response to his two texts. But there had been a deafening silence since. He was disappointed but not surprised. All those years ago, back in the laneway near Cardiff House, his feelings hadn't lied. Would he really come running?

He knew that he could rely on no one else. He would have to put an end to this chaos himself, and alone. Careful not to raise Sally's hopes, Ewan pulled some strings in the background. Eventually, one of them jerked a figure to life.

As much as he detested the guy, Ewan reconciled himself to asking Marcus, the senior crime reporter at the West Australian, for a favour. This required him to confide in someone devoid of compassion or discretion. He knew it would cost him. The inevitable price with someone like that would be to have your family drama bandied around every water cooler in the building despite the fact that he no longer worked there.

Marcus was better placed than anyone Ewan knew to use the grapevine to get some intel on where the homeless youth hung out in the Hamilton Hill and Spearwood areas. Ewan had taken a punt that Muzzo would live in a squat. He could still be living with his parents or be sharing a house with some other kids. However, from what Ewan had seen that night, his clothes were just dirty enough and his look sufficiently wild-eyed to suggest that he lived on the street or at least was a transient.

Ewan had been back at work for most of the day. His concentration was poor and his judgment fuzzy. He was on the verge of giving this pretence away when a text from Marcus arrived suggesting a meeting at a pub in the city. Ewan bought a round and steeled himself to put up with the ceremonial humiliation that was inevitable. Nothing had changed. He still detested Marcus. He still hated the way he flicked his hair from his eyes in that annoyingly flamboyant manner of his. He held a folded piece of paper theatrically between the thumb and forefinger of his right hand.

I have something for you, Marcus said.

Instinctively, Ewan reached for it.

Now, now, Marcus scolded him. Let's not forget our manners.

For fuck's sake, Marcus, this is not a game.

Did I say it was? Marcus asked, keeping the information out of Ewan's reach. I have put myself out to gather some intelligence for you.

OK, you win, Ewan said. Marcus, thank you for helping me. May I please have the note you are holding in your hand?

You may, Marcus said, dropping the paper so it floated like a parachute. It spiralled into Ewan's beer.

Ewan fished the now blank piece of paper from his ale. What was on it?

Some places for you to check out. No guarantees, of course.

Ewan could see Marcus weighing up the possibility of telling Ewan that sadly the information had been erased. Ewan knew he would have to beg. Do you have another copy?

Of course, Marcus said, scrolling around on his phone. I've texted the info to you.

Marcus, thank you, Ewan said. I've got to find this guy, so please excuse me.

Ewan jumped into his car and inched his way through the freeway traffic until he could turn off at South Street. The first two addresses were in Coolbellup. Someone had told Ewan recently that Coolbi was the new Subi. He hardly thought so. The streetscape shocked him. It was Perth's pale imitation of East Harlem or the Bronx. The brick veneer houses were locked down tight with metal shutters over all the windows. The front yards were concreted and littered with rusting cars, old washing machines and piles of magazines. The occasional pensioner struggled under the weight of laden plastic shopping bags. Two under-employed men leant on a wall smoking. They eyed Ewan with suspicion. It occurred to him they thought he was a policeman.

That wasn't a bad guess as it turned out. He found the first two addresses. They were across the road from each other. He snooped around the front gardens and walked up the side pathways to the back. He peered through the windows that weren't barred or shuttered, but he could see little other than his own reflection. He found no signs of life.

The same went for the final two locations on the list. These were in Hamilton Hill. It was same old, same old - dilapidated houses that were boarded up with overgrown gardens strewn with rubbish. Ewan pushed aside a fence post that was coming away so he could explore the back yard. As he climbed through, he found himself face to face with a middle-aged Aboriginal man wearing a grubby orange hi-vis jacket. His eyes were as wild as his unkempt grey hair. They sized each other up for a moment. Suddenly the man's demeanour changed for no apparent reason. Ewan saw fear in his eyes. The man turned and hurried on his way. Ewan strode after him. He easily overhauled him, restraining him by the elbow.

I'm not a cop, Ewan reassured him.

You look like one.

I know, Ewan conceded. I'm looking for my daughter. She's run away.

You can't lend me a cigarette, can you?

I'm sorry I don't smoke, Ewan said, all too conscious of how rich and condescending he must appear to the other guy.

Can you lend me a couple of bucks for food?

Sure, Ewan said, fishing in his pocket. He produced a ten-dollar note.

The man's mood improved. He eyed the money expectantly.

I'm very worried about my daughter, Ewan said, handing over the cash.

The man looked at the ground. He shuffled nervously from foot to foot. No girls living here, he said.

Actually, I'm looking for a guy, a friend of hers. You might know him.

The man shook his head, fingering his treasure.

Ewan persevered. His name's Muzzo.

The guy turned to escape inside via the side door.

Please, Ewan begged. He's not in trouble. He might be able to help me find my little girl.

The Aboriginal man turned back to face him. You sure you're not the filth.

I'm not.

That Muzzo comes round sometimes. You know, sleeps here and that.

Mustapha

Ewan was nervous about fibbing to Sally. She would never trust him again. Not completely. Not implicitly, like she once did.

In their current distressed state, nothing was normal. They would drive around the streets aimlessly hoping to catch sight of Lorna. Ewan told Sally he was going out to look for her again. She nodded. This was the new normal.

Ewan felt faintly ridiculous cutting the car's headlamps and shuffling down in the driver's seat. He was hardly James Bond, although his number plate did end in 007. He had nodded off in the car the previous night. He willed himself to stay awake this time. He wasn't confident that he would recognise Muzzo again if he appeared. He'd just seen him the once at Wendy's house. He'd been furious with Lorna at the time and hadn't exactly been preparing to pick the boy out in an identity parade. He recalled long, curly black hair peeking from his hoody. There was adolescent stubble on his chin. He remembered the round prominent nose he'd seen in profile. Ewan knew he couldn't pick Muzzo out in a crowded room, but the cues he had should be enough to identify a lone youth rocking up to a particular house.

After another endless wait, a guy and a girl appeared from a laneway. There was a commotion in front of the house. The figures were in shadow but Ewan fancied the girl could be Lorna. Ewan burst from the car without thinking and raced across the road. The girl had already scarpered. Ewan saw no sign of her, but a gate to the house next door was creaking against its hinges.

Ewan was in two minds. Should he chase the girl or confront the guy? The boy stepped forward, his face now illuminated on one side by a spliff.

Muzzo?

Who wants him?

Ironically, Muzzo didn't recognise Ewan.

Muzzo, it's Ewan, Lorna's dad.

Muzzo set off towards the side door of the house.

Ewan trotted after him, grabbing Muzzo by the shoulder.

What do you want? He growled.

Was that Lorna with you just then?

No, mate. Leave me alone.

I need to find Lorna. Where is she?

I don't know, man. Why are you asking me?

Ewan pushed his way in front, blocking the youth's path. Look, Muzzo, I don't know who you are or anything about you, and I don't want to know. Lorna has been missing for days. We need to find her.

She's not here, if that's what you're asking.

Ewan pushed Muzzo against the wall. Look here. This is not a game. This is not a joke. I will get the police involved if that's the way you want to play this.

Muzzo pushed Ewan away, fumbling along the dark path towards the back of the house. I haven't seen her for a few days.

So, you've seen her since she left home.

I don't know anything about her leaving home.

Where did you see her?

Nowhere, Muzzo said, rattling the handle of the back door.

Ewan grabbed him again. I don't want any trouble. Just tell me where you saw her.

Muzzo was reluctant. Ewan fiddled in his right trouser pocket. He fished out a note. To Ewan's relief, it was a fifty-dollar bill. Ewan waved the note. Tell me where Lorna was.

At the power station, Muzzo said, reaching for the money.

Jesus Christ!

I'm not joking, man. Give me the money, I just told you what you wanted to know.

Ewan fiddled in his pockets again, producing more notes and a business card. Help me, Muzzo, and I will make it worth your while.

O-kay, he said. We don't hang out much. I don't think she likes me.

Ewan was in no mood for relationship counselling. Where should I look for her?

Here and there, you know.

I don't know.

I'll tell you what, Muzzo said, relighting his joint. If you make that a down payment, I'll ask around.

You'd better not be bullshitting me.

No BS, man. Not if you give me a grand to track her down.

Ewan was furious. He needed to stay in control. He hated the idea of giving into blackmail from a shit like Muzzo. But, in the circumstances, it seemed like the best deal he was going to get.

Ewan allowed Muzzo to grasp the bill, but did not release it. He poked his business card in Muzzo's shirt pocket. If we're to be partners, he said, I want to know one more thing.

Muzzo tried to wrench the note free. What's that?

Tell me about frenzship.

What about it?

I think it's connected to Lorna's disappearance.

Muzzo shrugged.

Well, is it?

How would I know, man?

Because you acquired a laptop and a phone for her, didn't you?

Muzzo freed the note. He folded and unfolded it.

You got her connected, didn't you?

That's not a crime, is it?

Stealing is, Ewan snarled, instantly regretting the tone in his voice. He needed Muzzo sweet.

Do we have a deal then? Muzzo asked.

OK.

For a grand?

Before Ewan could answer, a blow struck him across the neck. Then a knee crashed into his thigh, crumpling him instantly. Fists battered him round the head, while fingers expertly plundered his pockets.

Ewan felt blood pouring from his nose and seeping into his shirt and pants. His assailants stood by, rifling through his wallet. They shared out the credit cards and the hundred dollar notes he kept for an emergency.

In the half light, he could make out a grubby hi-vis jacket. Ewan could see Muzzo, standing there, looking as shocked as he was.

You just cost me a grand, you cunts, Muzzo shouted after the fleeing assailants. Stupid fuckers, he mumbled.

Love you too, Mustapha, don't wait up! The laughter gradually peeled away.

Punching bag

Nespressoguilt was the least of Ewan's problems at that moment. He pressed another mug full and sat down to clear some emails. He rang Jessica and steered her towards a new study reporting that juveniles in the US convicted of violent crime were ten times heavier consumers of violent video games than the normal population of youths without criminal records.

Once his urgent work was out of the way, Ewan settled down to his real business of the morning. He lifted his shirt and inspected the bruising. It was turning from aggressive black to sickly yellow. He had played down his mugging for Sally's sake. It could happen to anyone roaming the streets like that. He was OK, that was the main thing. He had put a stop on his credit cards. They could be replaced. He inspected the cuts on his face. They were healing nicely. He resisted the temptation to pick at the scabs.

He hadn't reported the mugging to the police. Even if it had been a random attack on a passer-by, there would have been no point in getting the cops involved. If they wouldn't look for a vulnerable girl who repeatedly went missing, they would hardly pull out the stops for a reckless middle-aged man wandering the streets at night. Beyond that, it would have been a bad idea to complicate the missing person's case with an assault on a family member. The constabulary might have put two and two together and made five. Then they might have taken some misguided interest in a non-existent but more complicated case.

The unexpected attack in the back garden might have queered his pitch with Muzzo. Mustapha was his actual name – was that of interest? Ewan nevertheless remained confident that Muzzo would make contact with him. Muzzo had more or less confirmed that frenzship was connected to Lorna's disappearance. Did he actually say that? It was so difficult to recall someone's precise words delivered in the heat of the moment, especially when you're being kicked like a football and pummelled like a punching bag.

Lorna stares intently at our baby girl, who, just as I predicted, is already being called Charlie.

She still looks blue to me, Lorna insists.

It's OK, I respond. It's my favourite colour.

I can stand without support now so I take turns with Lorna caring for the bub while Cassidy rests.

I've got this idea, I venture.

Oh, no!

It's a good one.

Try me.

Let's write the end of the book together.

Lorna is elated. Can we? For real?

I think we should. In a way, the next part is our story. It's about you and me.

I guess so. I couldn't write it. You have to write it.

O-kay, but I do want you to read this bit. I want you to critique it.

Like a teacher, you mean? Cool.

No, not like that. It's about you. It's about what your life was like and what you were thinking and doing, and why.

I get you, old man, she nods. I really do need to help you with this as I don't think an old like you would have a clue.

How when friends come running, they know not what they do

So

I recall three jet-lagged thoughts from my arrival in Perth, the most remote capital city in the world. Are the rest of the passport officers on strike? That dog looks too cute to be a drug hound. This airport looks like a disused airstrip in Hicksville, Arizona.

I'd delayed telling Ewan of my arrival. I trusted myself possibly less than he trusted me. My emotions were in such turmoil that it had become an even bet whether I returned to Cass, flew back to Nina or did my skinhead duty and came running for Ewan.

Ewan was waiting for me. I was relieved he'd come alone. We stood a few feet apart, sizing each other up. He looked exhausted with thick black rings traced below his eyes. I figured I was less tired than him despite the jetlag.

His dad was coming out in him more since I saw him at the funeral. His black hair was now more flecked with grey. His grey beard was less flecked with black. He looked in reasonable shape. A bit podgy perhaps. He was dressed smartly for him. His clothes were classic rather than fashionable. He was a Ralph Lauren polo man from the tower block in central London. I had to laugh

He drove a Toyota Prius. It was a hybrid, naturally. The journey from the airport past the warehouses, showrooms, fast food outlets and cheap motels was tense. We chatted amiably but superficially. We were would-be lovers too scared to make the first move. We were prize-fighters waiting for the opportune moment to strike. We were kids in the sweetshop eyeing off the liquorice straps.

Ewan proposed a tour. He pointed out a few of the sites of Fremantle – the port, the original prison built by convicts for convicts, the ornate facades from the turn of the twentieth century. Then he drove up a narrow bitumen path onto Monument Hill. It sported an elaborate obelisk that was converted for the purpose of honouring the locals claimed by the two world wars. We inspected the mounted torpedo erected as a tribute to the US submariners lost in the vicinity of their WWII Fremantle base.

Ewan oriented me to the panoramic features of the 360-degree view. He indicated the port, Cottesloe beach, the Swan River and the suburban inlands that had housed tent cities at the time of the goldrush similar to the canvas town once established on the mound where we were standing.

You could have a future as a tour guide, I complimented Ewan,

But? Ewan knew there would be a sting in the tale.

A man could get thirsty seeing the sights.

Let's go, Ewan said, breaking for his car. I know just the place.

We headed for a micro-brewery called Little Creatures. I admired the warehouse conversion in glass and stainless steel that revealed the underbelly of the brewing process.

This used to be a crocodile farm, Ewan observed.

Really? I responded. I let myself get away with that one. It was hard to imagine trainee handbags skulking ready to pounce behind the vats and the taps.

I imagine you've had six breakfasts since yesterday, Ewan said, producing two lurid salmon coloured notes to pay for our pale ales.

Are you being a cheapskate already?

OK. I'll get two large pizzas. Then I can watch you throw up.

We settled on wooden stools at a long bench out the back. We supped in silence, observing the fishing boat action across the frothing, messy water of the harbour. The stink-boat trawlers were manoeuvring into their narrow berths to unload the catch.

That's a nasty bruise, I observed.

I walked into a door, Ewan responded with a smirk.

It was time to get serious. How's Sally? I asked.

So-so.

That's no good, I said. And Lorna?

Ewan smiled at me in a knowing way. I thought it best to leave that subject alone.

We sank back into our beers, still searching for the right things to say. I've travelled a long way, I said.

I appreciate it.

Thanks for coming to my dad's funeral, by the way.

No worries, mate, Ewan said.

You are a right fucking Aussie.

You sound like one of the Beach Boys.

We laughed like we used to in his bedroom with the cricket ball. I reminded him of the love-lies. We felt the warmth of friendship. It was more intense than the midday sun, even in Australia.

I had to go after frenzship, Ewan said. It blurted out. He wanted to get past this awkwardness.

No, you didn't.

It's dangerous, you know that.

Getting out of bed is dangerous, I snarled.

We'd been chatting for no more than five minutes. We hadn't seen each other for a while. I could sense us dropping into the familiar groove. A set piece argument was unavoidable.

Own your actions, Ewan, for Christ's sake. Don't tell me you had to do it. You chose to. Just be honest.

Ewan hesitated before responding. Be that as it may, my actions pale into insignificance compared with inciting rape and murder.

Don't insult me with such twaddle. You got a first-class degree, didn't you?

frenzship *is* dangerous, Ewan insisted. It's a vehicle for the depraved to mess with people's heads.

A waiter, wearing a green bowler hat festooned with glitter, interrupted our slanging match. Two pizzas, guys?

We nodded.

I returned to my theme. Stalin wasn't so bad, comrade. Mao was a regular guy. These mates of yours brainwashed generations and sent dissenters to the salt mines. The poor bastards in Russia and China had no choice and no liberty. With frenzship, you have the ultimate freedom. No one forces you to sign up.

I checked on Ewan's reaction. He was frowning and shaking his head.

And then you get options at every step, I persisted. People are recommended to you as frenz. They're not totalitarian police frenz who follow you around whether you like it or not. In frenzship, no one stands over you and forces you to make new frenz.

Ewan wiped his greasy fingers on a napkin he'd trapped before it blew away. Let's be rational, please. As your old girlfriend said in her article, psychosocial media itself is neutral…

…So you accept that, I chimed in.

Of course I do. That's not rocket science. Your lady friend was also right that many inventions, splitting the atom, for example, have applications that are good and bad…

There you go! Argument over, get me another beer.

I will, but just listen for once. Responsible governments, institutions and corporations need to evaluate the potential for products to be used for good or evil. In the case of radiation, for example, some sort of balance is there. The wonderful stares down the unthinkable. With frenzship and psychosocial media, the spurious goodies, like making meaningful friends in the digital age, are insignificant compared to what the bad guys do with it. They use psychosocial profiling to corrupt children.

Do you know the probability of someone being able to do that? I retorted. It was one of those moments when I wished I had a better head for statistics.

What I'm saying, Ewan insisted, is that the good frenzship can do is not worth the risk of the proven damage it has done. Now I'll buy another drink, he announced, setting off for the bar inside the warehouse building.

I acknowledged the refreshed ale Ewan plonked onto our table. He waited for me to respond.

Your problem always has been and obviously still is, I said, scoffing the last pizza slice, that you are a card–carrying communist who wants the State to poke its snotty nose into every corner of our lives. Your solution to all evils is to have the State tell people what's good for them. Well, I've got news for you. I am an individual, even if you're not. I don't want the fucking government making decisions for me because (a) they have their own best interests at heart, not mine (b) I'm more than capable of making my own decisions and…(c) there is no fucking c.

Ewan looked unimpressed. You don't think there's a smidgeon of self-interest poking through here?

What do you mean?

Don't you have a major stake in frenzship?

Yes. What of it?

And aren't you minting money from it?

Yes, I'm making money.

Well, then, Ewan said, raising his palms in a gesture of finality.

Well, nothing, comrade. You have no idea about business. You've never even sniffed its bum. In business, you take risk and you hope for reward. Risk equates to reward. The greater the risk, the greater the reward. I can tell you, without fear of contradiction, that we worked our balls off for years on end and risked more than you can imagine to get to where we are now.

And that's all that matters?

I didn't say that.

We drank our beers and licked our wounds.

I was offended by your personal attacks on me, I said, looking up at Ewan. How could you do that to a friend?

Ewan blazed back. They weren't personal. I don't think I ever mentioned you.

You didn't. You must have realised what frenzship would mean to me. But you still did your best to sabotage my life's work. Some kind of friend you are!

Ewan swirled the frothy remnants of his beer around the bottom of his glass. I don't resile from my actions, he said, making eye contact. I don't regret what I did for one minute. But, I will admit that I was worried I was focusing on frenzship for the wrong reasons.

I bit my lip. Such as?

I told Sally that part of it was to get even with you.

I leant back to contemplate Ewan's message. Fair enough, I said. As we are now playing true confessions, the misuse of frenzship by the sick bastards of the world concerns me greatly

That's love-ly, Ewan said.

I laughed. Lend me your silly, plastic money, I said.

Ewan handed me a big yellow note. It was fifty dollars. I returned with four beers.

In case the price goes up, I explained.

So, Ewan said.

So, I repeated.

You came running.

I came running.

The blubber factory

I thought I was back in LA. The light streaming through the paper-thin blinds stuffed my chances of sleeping off the jetlag. I stumbled from bed to bathroom to have a wake-up piss. I found the remote that worked the window shades. I had an awesome view over the rolling sea. The vista was clearest blue. I concluded I was not in LA.

I'd booked this apartment over the Internet. It was,'…a premium unit with king size bed, vibrant, modern furnishings and a dreamy balcony overlooking the fishing boat harbour'. I looked out to where Ewan told me the America's Cup defence was raced. I saw no sailing ships. Curiously, a US battle group was steaming towards Fremantle. I hoped that wasn't an omen.

I'd expected to encounter some resistance to my staying in a hotel rather than sleeping in their spare room. Ewan confessed that Sally didn't know I was coming. I wasn't sure how to interpret that, but I was happy enough that my accommodation freedom wouldn't be a source of contention.

I promised to contact Ewan as soon as I was upright. I didn't feel like it. I needed some alone time to think about what the hell was going on with my life. I settled on a stroll around the seafront before seeking out some breakfast. The fishing trawlers were chugging back to port to unload their overnight catch. The seagulls formed a raucous guard of honour to welcome home the fleet. The seafood restaurants and fish and chip shops were coming to life. Circular table tops were rolled into place for lifting onto their bases. Red and white gingham tablecloths flapped at the edges until the place settings weighted them down.

I took pity on a lonely proprietor scanning the faces of the passers-by in the hope of some business. I ordered a strong black coffee with bacon and eggs. I needed some fortification. I tried to focus on Ewan and the here and now. I still didn't know what I was doing on the other side of the world. Beyond running away, that is. But my thoughts dragged me back like a team of huskies to the ice and snow I'd left behind.

Nina accepted my departure with equanimity as she had all those years before. Chatting and fucking with her in the farmhouse had given me some deeper insights. Her father's unexpected and untimely death shaped her early life. Her mother was left with no choice but to cope independently. Nina inherited this quality in spades. The two women established a sisterhood based on strength and independence. It made sense to me that Nina despised dependency, which she equated with weakness. That's how she'd seen me in the past. And now, when others would quake with fear at the thought of their looming, progressive dependence, Nina spat in its face. For herself, Nina despised my mercy run. But she acquiesced graciously to my need to do it. We drove back to Paris, heading straight to the airport. We kissed a passionate goodbye.

Cassidy wasn't returning my texts or calls. I missed her and I wanted to tell her so. I wanted to find out how she was feeling. I wanted to explain myself to her. I wasn't a deserter. I was missing in action. I was lost somewhere in the impenetrable jungle of my life. I would emerge in due course and put things to right.

The breakfast was greasy and disgusting. The waiter asked me how it was.

Greasy and disgusting, I said.

I'll tell the chef.

Judging from his checked trousers and the grubby tea towel draped over his shoulder, I assumed he held that august role too.

I proffered my Visa card.

We're cash only.

I'm credit card only, I said, walking off.

I skirted the water's edge in the direction of the old prison. It was called the Round House. I inspected the Whalers' Tunnel through which the whale carcasses were once hauled from the sea to the blubber factory. I smiled at the apt metaphor for my life. Friendship had dragged me across the sea and was now propelling me through a tunnel to I didn't know what.

I walked up the hollowed stone steps onto the circular prison parade ground. The wind was fresh, exposed up there. I stopped to text Miki to ask him how Cassidy was faring. I felt better for having done that, token gesture that it was.

I dialled Ewan's cell phone. It didn't work. I could never master the international dialling codes. An SMS from the local carrier advised me on the combination of a plus followed by digits that I needed to use. I gave it a try. It seemed to be working.

Hello, Ewan Mackenzie speaking.

You better have a fucking good reason to have used the safe word.

The voice said

Are you serious? Sally glared back at Ewan, sitting outside at Gino's café.

Yes, he's in town. He's staying at the Quest.

Why didn't you tell me? She asked, rummaging in her handbag for a tissue to dry her eyes.

I'm not sure.

That's a cop out.

Hear me out. I'm not sure because there were several reasons. But, above everything else, I didn't want you to talk me out of it.

Well, I don't want to see him, Sally snapped.

Ewan had expected this reaction. He'd been thankful that his guest hadn't counted on a bed.

I can't understand why you would do this, Sally wailed.

Let me explain. I hold him and his cronies accountable for what has happened to Lorna. You know that. I think he should put things right.

How is he going to do that?

We need to find out who she's hooked up with on frenzship. He will know how to do that. If we knew who was poisoning her mind, we could do something to counteract that influence.

And what if he can't? Or more likely won't?

If he can't do that, there will be something he can do. Hopefully, he can arrange for me to befrenz her like I tried to do. Then we could put positive messages into her mind.

You know there are simpler ways of controlling a child, don't you!

Sally, we've been over this. You know how it works – you're the behavioural psychologist. If we clamp down on her when she comes home, she will disappear for longer next time.

What makes you so sure?

Because I talk to her.

And I don't? Sally snuffled, ripping open a new pack of tissues.

You can't. Not right now. She just won't talk to you.

And what gems does our daughter impart to you in your father-daughter tête-à-têtes when she honours us with her presence at home?

Not much, to be honest. She's hanging in by a thread. We mustn't cut that cord, however inadvertently.

Ewan hadn't explained everything to Sally yet. He was unsure how Sally would react, but it had to be done.

There's another reason I asked him to come.

Ewan's solemn tone made Sally look up.

This is going to sound stupid.

Everything you say is stupid, Sally said with a slightly lighter edge.

True. But here goes. I need my old friend around.

He's still your friend?

He'll always be my friend.

Ewan fetched some magazines and the local paper. They tried to take their minds off their troubles, just while they ate their breakfast. Ewan's mobile rang.

Hello, Ewan Mackenzie speaking.

You'd better have a fucking good reason to have used the safe word, the voice said.

I know what you're like

Ewan swung by the Quest. Then he drove us around the coast, past the cranes and the container loading stations hugging the sea and sand on the left and the swanky new apartments on the right. Then we headed left towards the Indiana Tearooms.

These are real beaches, Ewan bragged.

A bit narrow, I countered. Have you been to Mission Beach? I asked.

Not lately, Ewan responded as he parked the car.

We ordered some of those infernal share plates that are all the rage and a couple of imported beers. I told Ewan about my breakfast adventure and speculated that the police might be after me. Ewan was distracted. He was in no mood for chitchat.

Spit it out, I said. Here I am. I have come running. We have Corona beer and tapas just over the border in Mexico. Why the fuck is it skinhead time?

Ewan's tale of woe with his daughter poured out. He spilled his guts. His emotions spewed forth like puss from an oversized boil. He explained about finding her stolen computer gear. He told me about hacking into it and his suspicions she had a smartphone she used to connect into frenzship. He stressed that when his major article came out, he didn't even know Lorna was on it. He had pieced together the timing of the deterioration of her behaviour. frenzship was clearly at the heart of it.

By the time our Cajun chicken wings and arancini balls arrived, I was feeling as bad as him.

I feel like Jesus innocently sawing wood in the carpentry shop, I said.

What is that supposed to mean? Ewan responded wearily.

Why me? I'm asking myself. What do you expect me to do? Get the hammer and nails and extend my palms?

Put things right.

How?

Find out who's poisoning her mind.

I took a deep breath. I was there to help, but I was unwilling to be branded as the villain of the piece.

I'm not sure what you imagine I can do, I said. I will make some calls. I will ask my Japanese associate, Miki, to see if we can access her account, as it's an *emergency.*

I looked at Ewan in stressing that word. I need to warn you. frenzship is not some DIY kit that I, or anyone else for that matter, can pull apart. But, leaving that aside, I have come running to help my old friend. Before we get started on this, let me get this straight. I am not your whipping boy.

Ewan was slumped forward over the table. I could almost feel the unbearable weight on his shoulders. I didn't want to add to it, but I couldn't stay and help him without getting some things straight.

I soldiered on. We will beat this. You and I. Together. Just like old times. I promise we will. But, I won't help you on the terms you are offering.

Ewan looked sullen. Defeated.

You and Sally are Lorna's parents. Whatever else happens in the world and whatever other influences impact on children, the parents carry the major responsibility.

Ewan picked at his food. I wanted him to argue with me. I felt uncomfortable delivering Hamlet's soliloquy.

I'd been too blunt. I needed to be more conciliatory. I know I'm not qualified to speak on this subject. I don't have kids of my own. I thought of Cass. It spooked me for a moment. I don't have kids, but I know it must be hell these days with them bombarded from every angle, in every room of the house, with celebrity shit and pornography. frenzship is wonderful and terrible. I accept that. But I can't do this with you if I'm here to cop the blame.

You *are* to blame, Ewan said solemnly. But Sally and I are more so.

That was what I needed to hear. I nodded in recognition.

Actually, he stammered on, it's me who has been the bad parent.

Don't do this, Ewan, I urged him. I've said my piece. I'm happy.

No, this is important. I let Lorna down.

Come on, everybody fucks around. Men are weak.

I'm not talking about that, he corrected me. I shielded Lorna from all of these bad influences.

I don't get you, comrade.

I persuaded Sally that Lorna shouldn't have mobile phones and computers and grow up glued to electronic images. That hopeless little screen, I think Leonard Cohen called it.

But that's impossible in this day and age.

I know. I made her an outcast with her peers. I see that now. But you know what I'm like.

Yes, I know what you're like. Ideology first, people second. Remember those Soviet posters you had on your bedroom wall?

Ewan looked sheepish. He nodded.

I think you live life in some poster-land yourself. You're one of those heroes, wielding a hammer or a sickle, to save the people.

Ewan sat slumped in his chair, depressed and defenceless.

All I'm saying, trying to say, is there's a real world out there, beyond the posters and the glorious images of virtue that you consistently deny.

Ewan peered out to sea for the longest time. That world is not one I particularly like.

But it's there. It's real.

It needs to change. We need to change it.

We can't. You can't.

I'm not like you. I can't accept injustices. I can't live it up while others suffer.

I'm a shallow prick. You know what I'm like.

I know what you're like.

Cordial but cold

I emailed Miki about accessing the kid's account. I did it to keep faith with Ewan. I remembered Jerry's explanation about the dark web, the block chain and all that shit. I knew frenzship didn't work like that.

Then Ewan and I set out to look for Lorna. We did a tour of Perth's southern suburbs checking on the places she was known to frequent. Ewan was agitated. He didn't understand why Lorna had run away again. He and Sally had been taking great care not to pressure or aggravate her.

I suppose it was the family meeting, he speculated, as we sat at yet another interminably long red traffic light.

The family what?

We all agreed to meet once a week as a family to assess how things were going.

And you can't work out why she ran away? I observed unhelpfully.

Our first stop was at the house where one of Lorna's best friends lived. It was a bleak area. I'd never seen houses like these before. They were modest brick structures but had carved lions guarding the front gates like the porn palaces in Malibu. The front yards were concreted over. Some had a circle cut out of them. They looked like holes in the ice carved by Inuit fishermen.

Italians, Ewan explained.

Wasn't Michelangelo an Italian? I asked.

Ewan ignored me, outlining his plan instead.

I'm not doing that, I protested.

You have to.

Why me?

Because they don't know you.

Have it your way, I said, climbing out of the passenger's seat. I walked up the driveway. I rang the bell. I couldn't hear a ring. Unsure if it was working, I knocked on the door. I looked back to the car for guidance. Ewan had driven off. What the hell was going on? I persevered by walking round the side of the house. I saw a teenager through the window smoking at the kitchen table. Maybe I'd found Lorna.

I knocked on the window. The girl looked up. Her blonde hair was piled on her head in a topknot. She was pretty, but with too much make-up for my liking. She ignored me. I knocked again. She pouted and raised herself with such reluctance that you'd think I was dragging her away from the right hand of God.

She spoke to me through the glass. Yeah?

Lorna?

What?

Are you Lorna?

No. Who are you?

This was clearly a question I should have prepared myself for. Unsurprisingly for me, only stupid answers proposed themselves. Such as Lorna's pimp or David Beckham. Those wouldn't do.

I'm Lorna's uncle.

The girl weighed up my credentials.

Who are *you*? I added.

I'm Jade. Lorna's not here.

Has she been here?

Yes.

This was promising. When?

She's been here loads of times.

I was warming to this girl, but I wasn't making any progress. I racked my brains to remember the other name Ewan instructed me to ask about.

Have you seen the other guy? Muzza? Is that his name?

Muzz-o, she corrected me.

Yes, Muzzo. Have you seen him?

Yes.

Hundreds of times, too?

That's right.

I nodded to my new friend, Jade, and repaired to the front of the house. I walked to the kerbside and saw Ewan's car parked a fair way down the hill. I briefed Ewan on my failed mission.

Next, we look for this guy, Muzzo, Ewan said, pulling away.

Ewan told me about his mugging. I tried not to laugh. We staked the joint out for an hour or so. Nobody came or went.

Let's go home, Ewan announced.

I didn't want my yawning and complaining to be the reason why we left.

It's OK, Ewan said. We'll come back later.

Ewan drove surprisingly fast for him. It was like being in a getaway car.

Slow down, comrade, you'll get me killed.

Sorry. I just wanted to get out of there.

Where to now? I asked, willing the answer 'pub'.

Home. To see Sally.

Does she know I'm here yet?

Yes.

Does she want to see me?

No.

Great.

I was on the point of protesting when my cell phone vibrated in my jacket pocket. It was Miki. I wished I hadn't answered it. I didn't want to be the bearer of any more bad news.

What's happening? Miki asked.

You wouldn't believe me if I told you.

I don't believe you anyway.

OK, cut the wisecracks. How did you go?

No can do, Miki said. frenzship doesn't work like that.

I know. I shook my head at Ewan. Did you speak to Jerry?

No, he's still globetrotting. But I spoke to one of his team. He told me with pride that the system is watertight. That means everyone's privacy is protected and it is virtually unhackable.

Yeah, I think I get that now, I acknowledged. But it's not foolproof, is it?

No, but even our own guys can't get into it.

Ewan looked at me expectantly. I shook my head more emphatically.

What about Cass? I asked, full of apprehension

She's OK, but she's not wonderful.

She won't speak to me?

Not yet. I'll talk her round. By the way, that's not all.

Go on. It can't get any worse.

Maybe, maybe not. Randy's playing protective big brother now so keep your head down.

Great. That's all I need.

We drove on in sombre fashion. Ewan had unreasonably pinned his hopes on cracking frenzship. I wanted to bemoan my fate with Cassidy, but I didn't think Ewan was in any state to lend a sympathetic ear.

By the time I'd bearded Sally in her den, I was desperate for the comfort and solitude of my apartment. Sally had been like an iced syrup - cordial but cold. When I left, I hugged her to me. She stiffly complied.

It's going to be OK, I reassured her. I realised it was a hollow promise coming from the likes of me. I am Ewan's oldest friend. I won't let him down.

Sally then hugged me back. She kissed me on the cheek. Thank you, she whispered.

I raided the mini-bar for a scotch on the rocks. I thought about calling Nina, but was unsure of the time difference. Then my phone lit up with a text. It was Ewan.

Muzzo has made contact.

Rockingham Road

I groaned aloud. I needed my bed. I'd earned my bed. I made suggestive faces at it. It solicited me with a crooked finger like Marilyn Monroe in Diamonds Are A Girl's Best Friend. We could have made beautiful music together. Instead, Ewan would be here in ten minutes.

If I couldn't make long, lingering love with the linen, I resolved to have a quickie with the shower. I pulled my smelly clothes over my head, waited for the eco-massage spray to turn to warm and lathered up with the sampler shampoo. No sooner had I done so than the apartment buzzer grated on my ears. Don't you hate that? Why does the toilet roll have to run out when you're in a public convenience and at risk of pooing your pants? I was trying to be a good friend. What more did the universe want?

Ewan informed me that Muzzo wasn't responding or answering texts from the number.

He probably stole the phone, I suggested to Ewan.

The look on his face told me that he hadn't reckoned on that.

Anyway, what did this Muzzo guy say? I asked.

He said it would cost me a grand and to wait for him to contact me again.

What could possibly set you back that much? I asked. Is he a dentist? I added as an afterthought.

Help to find Lorna.

There was nothing for it but to wait. I started working my way through the mini-bar. Ewan's frown got increasingly dark. He needed his wingman sober.

I resorted to the plunger coffee. Then the call came. Ewan responded 'yes' several times.

Let's go, Ewan announced.

Where are we going?

I'm to meet him at Fremantle station.

We buckled up and headed off.

Is it a set-up? I asked.

Now who's the nervous Nelly? Ewan asked, keeping his eyes fixed on the road.

We stopped at an ATM. Ewan returned cursing. The limit on one day was $500. I reluctantly fished around in my jeans pocket. I produced five green notes.

Don't you still owe me five quid? I asked, reluctantly parting with the cash

Ewan smiled through gritted teeth.

I'll get out of the car and get in the back, I said to Ewan. Make him sit in the front. It's safer.

Ewan pulled into the car park next to the station that is reserved parking for commuters catching the train. It was dark, but we had a good line of sight all around. A text came through at one o'clock. Ewan directed Muzzo to the bays nearest the station. I got out and stood by the car, with the two car doors open. Eventually, a figure did a rapper walk across the car park from the station. I could make out thin legs in tight black jeans and a figure huddled into a dark red hoody.

Who are you? The boy asked me.

I'm Ewan's best friend, I answered.

Besty eh? He sniggered.

Get in, Ewan shouted across from the driver's seat.

Muzzo was reluctant to comply. He hesitated, assessing the situation.

Scared of two old blokes, are you? I sneered.

Shut up! Ewan rebuked me. Muzzo, get in for Christ's sake. I want to find Lorna. I don't care about the money.

He sat down. I closed the front passenger door, then climbed in behind him.

Where's the coin?

It's notes, I said.

Will you shut up? Ewan was very testy. It was understandable.

Ewan laid the money on the console between him and the boy. Take us to Lorna and it's yours.

Muzzo was scratching and wiping his nose between his fingers. He was high on something. He looked at the money. Then looked away. He was contemplating a grab and go. I slid my hand into the door lock so I could make a quick exit behind him. It was cat and mouse and I wasn't sure which side we were on. I felt Muzzo was poised to try it on. Ewan obviously felt the same. My mate snatched the money and jerked the car forwards. Instinctively, I reached round, grabbing a generous handful of Muzzo's parka.

What the fuck? Muzzo shouted.

Ewan put his foot down.

Don't you want to know where Lorna is?

Of course I do, Ewan snarled. Just tell me the address.

How do I know you'll pay me?

Because I don't want to have to kill you, I said, wrenching his jacket backwards into a choker hold.

OK, OK, Muzzo said. Take it easy. She's on Rockingham Road. I'll show you.

What are friends for?

The boy seemed to have lost the will to take the money and run. I relaxed my grip on his jacket. He slumped forward, banging his head on the dashboard as his seat belt wasn't engaged. Ewan kept one hand on the wheel, while pulling Muzzo back into his seat.

I restrained him again from falling forwards. You don't think he's overdosed? I asked.

God, I hope not, Ewan responded, poking Muzzo. Wake up, come on, wake up.

Muzzo returned to consciousness momentarily.

What's the address, Muzzo?

What address? What are you talking about, dude?

Where Lorna is. What number Rockingham Road?

His head lurched forward again. I grabbed his collar. I slapped his face. Once, twice, three times. Do you want the money or not? I asked him.

He righted himself. Yeah, the money. Cool, he said, wiping his runny nose.

What number, Rockingham Road? Ewan pleaded.

It's along here. Turn left over there.

Now where?

Round the back. You see that factory there. Round the back.

Ewan steered the car between commercial waste bins and parked forklifts. He looked round at me.

I know, I said. Go really slowly. I'll look out this side.

Ewan pulled up next to a corrugated fence. There were houses backing onto this industrial complex. I slapped the back of Muzzo's head a few times.

He came to again. Cut it out, he protested.

Is this the place? Ewan asked.

Money first, Muzzo said.

Listen you junkie shit, I said, climbing out of the car and opening the passenger door.

Cool it! Ewan warned me. Is - Lorna - in - there? Ewan asked very slowly and very deliberately, holding up the wad of cash.

I already told you, didn't I?

I dragged the sniveller out of the car.

Give me the cash, Muzzo grunted.

Ewan handed it over. I looked at Ewan in disbelief. How could he be so stupid?

Muzzo grabbed the money and stumbled away. I could have caught up with him and reclaimed our cash, but Ewan had already set off towards the house. He'd left the engine running and his car door open. Was he planning a quick get away or was his mind elsewhere?

I trotted after him. Stop and think a second, I shouted.

Ewan was through the unhinged back gate and sprinting towards the dimly lit house. I had no choice but to chase after him. After all, what are friends for?

Pompeii

Ewan didn't wait for me to rush inside.

I was only seconds behind. I found him stopped dead in his tracks inside the kitchen. You could see down the hall from there. My heart rate slowed. This place was depressing rather than dangerous.

It was like the aftermath of the eruption of Mount Vesuvius. Just like in Pompeii, people lay where they fell. Beer bottles, bongs and other drug paraphernalia were strewn around. The snoring ranged from light staccato to heavy bellowing. We stepped over bodies like victorious soldiers with bayonets at the ready to finish off the wounded.

I stood back, waiting for Ewan to claim an ossified figure as his daughter. We searched through other rooms that looked tidy by comparison. I guessed these might be where the actual tenants stayed. I could sense Ewan's anxiety rising as we cleared the various rooms with no result.

What about in there? I shouted to Ewan, pointing to a lean-to off to the side of the house.

Ewan trotted in that direction. Lorna, Lorna, wake up, it's me. I heard Ewan's voice across the hard stand.

The girl looked very pale. She was fully clothed, which was a relief.

Are these her things? I asked, shining my iPhone light into the shed.

Yes, that's her backpack over there.

Ewan gathered up the sleeping girl in his arms while I stuffed clothes, make-up and anything else I could find into the empty pack.

I stopped Ewan before he could exit the shed. Wait a minute, I said, rolling up Lorna's sleeves. I checked her arms under torchlight. Clean, I said.

Ewan sighed in relief and headed out. He weaved his way around the comatose figures. I cleared the fallen gate from his path and then helped him arrange the girl onto his back seat. I slid in beside her to support her.

Her breathing's even, I said to encourage Ewan.

Ewan started the car, circled it around and navigated his way back to the main road. He came to a stop rather than pull out.

Ewan turned around. I don't know where to take her. Do you think we should go to the emergency department?

I checked her pulse and listened to her breathing like I'd seen it done on the hospital soaps. She seems OK, I said. They'll ask a lot of questions.

I know. I want to avoid that.

Don't you want to take her home?

That's the problem, Ewan said. If you think they'd give her and us the third degree at accident and emergency, that would be nothing compared with Sally's interrogation.

There was only one other solution. I wasn't sure if Ewan was angling towards it or whether he just wasn't thinking straight under the pressure.

I went for it. Let's take Lorna to my apartment.

Do you think so? Ewan asked.

I still wasn't sure if he was playing me. It's the best option, I reassured him. Get going.

Ewan pulled out onto Rockingham Road. Here, take my mobile, he said. Text Sally.

I figured she would appear on his message screen. What do you want me to say?

Ewan paused. I've got no idea, he said. You're the bullshit artist. Work something out.

Hi Sally. I've found Lorna. She is OK. Contact soon. Love Ewan. I read the proposed message to him.

Put Ewanx, he said.

I made the change and sent the text. She'll be relieved, I said.

It's amazing what banal comments you make in a crisis. He didn't respond.

We didn't want to arouse suspicion at the Quest apartments. To the casual observer what we were about to do would look like an abduction. I directed Ewan to park the car near my unit under a street light that wasn't working. I let Ewan sweep Lorna up while I played look-out and skipped ahead to open up the apartment.

We made it undetected. I directed Ewan to the bedroom. I watched him lay Lorna down on her side as a precaution. He stroked her hair and kissed her cheek. He left the door open so we would keep an eye on her.

He joined me on the sofa. We looked at each other.

Thank you, he said.

Just an average night out in LA.

He smiled. He rubbed his eyes and stretched his back. What do we do now? Ewan asked.

I told him the truth. I have absolutely no fucking idea.

I'm glad I did

Over a couple of beers, we prepared Ewan for the moment of truth. Sally would be overjoyed that he'd found Lorna, but she would be confused and angry that he hadn't brought her home. He would need to stay calm and rational under the onslaught.

Just tell her truth, I advised him. I observed myself spouting these moralistic platitudes when all I did was cheat and lie myself.

As soon as Ewan's key turned in the lock, he heard Sally rushing up the hallway to meet him. Ewan hugged her to him. He held her tight and kissed her neck. She's OK. She's going to be OK, he whispered.

He turned his wife round and walked her towards the kitchen. Everything will turn out fine.

He sat Sally down at the kitchen table. She asked the inevitable question. Where is Lorna now? She's not in hospital, is she?

No. She's safe. She's fine.

Where is she?

Ewan braced. He told Sally where she was and who she was with. He told her that a safe haven was best for everyone in the circumstances. He said that she needed some space to recover. He said that he and Sally needed to re-set now that the emergency was over.

Sally was passive. She fiddled nervously with her wedding ring.

It is for the best, Ewan continued. You do see that, don't you?

Sally's response astounded him. Yes, I do, she said.

Ewan took Sally's hand. They sat in silence for a while. He was relieved. She was probably just exhausted.

I'm glad you called on your friend for help, Sally said.

Me too, Ewan said. I still don't really know why I did it. But I'm glad I did.

Cass looks fabulous already and Charlie (ugh!) is just as beautiful.

Charlotte will thank me one day for the recessive genes on my side. Babe and mother are both babes.

Lorna has just announced that she has made up her mind to go home, to give it a try.

Are you sure, like totally sure, that I can come back here if it doesn't work out? Lorna pleads with Cassidy and me.

Don't go with that attitude, I suggest.

Shush! Ignore him, Lorna, Cass interjects. You can always come back. This is your home, I add to make amends.

Your second home, Cassidy corrects me.

I get her point. I change the subject. Tell me Lorna, what did you really think when you woke up that morning in my hotel apartment.

I thought you were a pervert.

No, really. I need to know.

I thought you were a pervert.

How acts of friendship can leave you fumbling around in the dark

Better qualified

The responsibility weighed heavily upon me. I was dog-tired. The delayed jetlag was playing tricks with my mind. I felt disoriented for a while. I worked out where I was and eventually figured out why a teenage girl was sleeping in my bed.

I was desperate for some shut-eye but shit-scared Lorna would chuck a rock-star on me and choke on her own vomit while I slept. I settled for a cat-nap in the armchair in the bedroom. I hoped she wouldn't wake until the morning. She was bound to freak out, waking up in a complete stranger's bedroom in the middle of the night.

My own snoring woke me from time to time. My head lurched forward and I would sit up anxiously. I repositioned Lorna onto her side a couple of times and replaced the blankets on top of her.

I heard the double beep of my phone. I came to. It was light. I panicked. Lorna was lying on her back, but her breathing was rhythmic. I tiptoed into the living room. The text was from Ewan asking for an update. I told him all was fine and that I would call him.

I scratched and farted and went for a piss. I felt like death, or worse. I wondered how Ewan had gone facing his Waterloo. I had my own challenge squarely in front of me. What on earth was I going to say to Lorna? What would I do if she started screaming?

I pondered whether I should ask Ewan to come over to handle this. Or maybe Ewan and Sally together? I felt disinclined to do so. I had an inkling that a third party might manage the confrontation better. Arrogantly, I also considered myself better qualified for the task. While Ewan and Sally spent their youth building orphanages, I was busy whoring and scoring. I felt this gave me the upper hand in relating to a kid who was testing her boundaries.

I was starving. I couldn't remember when I'd last eaten. It seemed as good an approach as any to call room service and order a slap-up breakfast for two. I may as well get hung for a sheep as a lamb. If a teenage girl is to wake up in an unfamiliar apartment with a middle-aged man who is a complete stranger, she might as well scream for help on a full stomach.

A long story

I put the groaning tray down on the bedside table. I hesitated. Lorna was still sound asleep. But Ewan was texting me. He would rock up soon and my opportunity would be gone. To do what? Play the hero? Prove myself to Sally? Do some good? I wasn't sure.

This was it. I gently kneaded her shoulders. No response. I shook her a little more forcefully. She groaned. There was no turning back. I slapped her face gently. Lorna, wake up. You need to wake up. Come on.

Lorna's eyes opened. She was terrified. Instinctively, I put my hand over her mouth to stop her screaming. It was a silly thing to do, but it did buy me time to explain.

Lorna, it's OK. I'm a friend of your parents. I'm your dad's oldest mate.

I removed my hand. You look like an old pervert to me, Lorna sneered.

She was probably right. I must have looked awful. I hadn't been to bed, washed my face or cleaned my teeth.

Are you a pervert then? Lorna asked, raising her knees to her chest to assume a defensive position.

I scanned her face. Hidden deep somewhere, I could see Sally in her. Sally's English rose complexion was masked by kohl that had run around Lorna's eyes and thick black make-up that was caked to her skin. Dirty blonde hair was streaked with purple and red and shaved to the roots on one side.

Not anymore, I answered.

She tried to sit upright. I moved to help her.

Don't touch me, pervert, she said, shrugging me off.

Are you hungry? I asked, pointing to the breakfast tray.

What's the catch?

I helped myself to a croissant and some coffee. Don't do me any favours, I said.

I've gotta pee.

Through there, I said, nodding in the direction of the ensuite.

She climbed back into bed, sitting up with the covers wrapped around her. She cast longing glances at the spread.

Do you want to eat or fight? I asked.

I could kill some toast and vegemite.

I positioned the tray over her lap so she could help herself. She fiddled with the plastic container of the single serve.

Here, let me, I said, peeling the flap back for her. What were you on last night?

Nothing really. Just Es, Lorna said, clumsily scraping the spread onto the toast. And booze.

I checked your arms, I said.

She looked at me at me in a way that asked what right I had to do that. But she ate her toast and said nothing.

Why am I here? Lorna asked. Truthfully.

I refilled my coffee, wondering how best to respond.

You're not going to rape me then? She added while I was rehearsing the story mentally.

No, I'm not, I said firmly.

Aren't I your type?

No, you're not. Besides, I am in enough trouble with women without adding an under age sex charge to my problems.

Lorna cracked half a smile. Clearly ravenous, she devoured a croissant next, spraying the crumbs to the four winds. OK, if you're not a pervert, Lorna mumbled with her mouth full, why am I here?

It's complicated, I said. My guts told me not to mention the girl's parents. I felt I was establishing some sort of rapport with her. I suspected the reference to parental authority might lead her to clam up. It's best, that's all.

For you?

For *you*, I think. For everyone. For me also, I added.

Why for you if you're not a pervert?

That's a long story, I said. I tell you what. If you shower and clean yourself up, I'll tell you all about it.

Over a drink?

Over an ice-cream, maybe, I replied.

Are you sure you're not going to perve on me in the shower?

I'm sure, I said, taking myself and my coffee cup out into the lounge room.

Breaking up

I left her at Simmo's, the ice cream joint at the fishing boat harbour.

Don't go anywhere, I said.

Lorna rolled her eyes. She was intent on her sundae, at least for now.

I walked away to ring Ewan, keeping her in sight the whole time. She'd scrubbed up to some extent after her shower. Her crumpled clothes were goth or punk. Possibly gunk? She looked better au naturel.

Where the fuck have you been? Ewan demanded on answering the phone.

I'm your skinhead friend, remember? I came running.

OK. We're worried sick. What's going on?

She's OK. She's had a hearty breakfast, then a shower and is now having a healthy walk.

Yes, sure. Tell me what's going on.

She has eaten a good breakfast. She has had a shower. I may have exaggerated a tad about the constitutional, but we are outdoors.

Hang on, Ewan said. I heard him relaying my news to Sally.

I was keeping my eyes peeled on Lorna. She was concentrating on her mobile phone. The one she didn't have, I surmised. She looked up momentarily. I waved.

Ewan came back on the line. Sally wants to know when you're bringing her home.

Now I was in trouble. I wasn't taking her back. I would kidnap her if I had to.

Later, I said. Give her time.

Sally wants to speak to you, Ewan said.

I'm sorry. I can't hear you, I said. You're breaking up.

What a shame. I accidently pushed the 'end call' button.

Spyman

Come on, we're going, I shouted to Lorna.

I haven't finished, she complained.

A taxi was stationed at the rank over the road.

Hurry up, I shouted. There's our cab.

She shuffled over under sufferance.

Get in, I instructed.

She threw her cardboard ice cream carton into the kerb. That annoyed me. Now wasn't the time.

Where to? The driver asked in a thick African accent. He turned round, towering over me.

That was a good question. I didn't know anywhere in this strange city that was worth visiting. Then an idea came to me. Ask the young lady, I suggested.

Where to, Miss?

Lorna grinned at me. She looked good when she smiled. Fraser's.

The destination registered with the driver. He turned around and got the car underway.

Why Fraser's? I asked.

Mum and Dad took me there once for my birthday. It's swanky. It's in King's Park.

Is that a good place?

Yes, it's a big park. It's got specy views.

I nodded.

Are you a yank?

No! I tried to sound offended.

You sound like one.

I went to school with your dad in London.

Oh.

We disappeared into our own thoughts. I knew nothing about her. I had no idea what she would be thinking about. Did she have a boyfriend? Was she an addict? If not to a needle, then maybe to pills? What did she think of me? Why was she acquiescing to this outing?

I had just as little insight into my own expectations and motivations. Was I playing the hero? Maybe. What if she ran off again? It was a chance I felt like taking. Did I think I could help her? I convinced myself I did. I really thought I could. She's a rebel. She's much more like me than Ewan. She's nothing like Sally at all. Her parents wouldn't understand a free spirit. It wasn't in their make-up.

I texted Ewan. Lorna was glued to her mobile. I covered my screen. Ewan, don't freak out. Trust me. For once.

His reply was instantaneous. This had better work out. Sally is issuing threats to your testicles.

Forty-five dollars, the driver said.

Jesus, I don't want to buy the cab.

Fraser's was very posh. It took me back to LA. What was going on with Cassidy? Maybe I should clear the air with Randy and then see if he would help me connect back with Cass?

I needed to stop daydreaming. As we walked into the restaurant, I wondered what the staff and customers thought of me with this young punk girl. Father? Pusher? Pimp?

Can we sit over there? Lorna asked, pointing to a table with an uninterrupted view over the city.

I didn't dare tell her what a pathetic excuse for a capital city skyline we were looking at. I'll order, I said.

No fish, Lorna replied. Vodka and tonic, though.

No fish and no alcohol.

She pouted. Bored.com, she muttered.

We had an upmarket spring roll each. She still seemed hungry. I followed that with a Cajun chicken breast and some fancy salads. She tucked into that too.

I've decided you're not a pervert, Lorna announced right out of the blue.

Excellent. I'm glad we've cleared that up.

But I still don't understand why you're being nice to me.

Because I'm a friend of your parents. I told you that already.

We ate in silence for a while.

You don't ask me lots of questions, Lorna said. Not like my olds.

I'm not the curious type.

I bet you are, she countered. I bet you're just dying to ask me things. You don't want me to run off.

I was enjoying this interlude. This girl really did remind me of me.

Do you *want* me to ask you things?

She focused her gaze on her food. She looked up, bright-eyed. Maybe.

OK. Why did you leave home? This time.

She was reluctant to answer. Perhaps she didn't know why. Perhaps she didn't want to tell me.

I didn't leave home…Lorna wrapped her tongue around the words that she might or might not utter…I escaped.

Do you mean home is like a prison?

Like a prison? It is a prison.

I felt I should protest to defend Ewan and Sally and to be true to the adults' union. I resisted. I needed to be a friend to Lorna rather another oppressive 'old' as she liked to call us.

You don't like rules and regulations, do you? I said.

Lorna slurped on a smoothie that really didn't complement her meal. Do you? She countered.

No, I hate them.

Me too.

I signalled to the waiter. Bring me the desserts menu and a draught beer.

Make that two, Lorna chirped.

The waiter looked to me. One beer, thanks.

Lorna slurped at the bottom of her milkshake.

Your dad and I go way back. We were at school together and then went up to Oxford. Except for your mum, I know him better than anyone else in the whole wide world.

Lucky you.

I am lucky. Because I have an old friend, a great friend.

Her eyes locked onto me. I've got friends, great friends, actually.

I almost slipped up and degenerated into being an 'old'. I wanted to tell her that, at her age, she couldn't have a great friend. Friendship takes time to mature. Again I resisted.

I'm glad to hear that, I said. The funny thing is that I nearly didn't come.

Why *did* you come?

Because your dad asked me for help.

Help with what?

I don't know exactly. Help with you, I guess.

Lorna stiffened. So that's why you're here. You're a spy.

I'm not a spy, I protested. I answered your dad's plea for help even though I didn't know what he wanted from me.

I don't believe you, she said.

This was a show of defiance. I decided to ignore it. As I was saying, I nearly didn't come. Not even to help my oldest friend.

OK, why? You want me to ask. Why did you nearly not come?

Because he had been attacking me in the newspapers. Condemning everything I'd be working for.

Such as what?

frenzship.

Lorna looked down. She sensed a trap.

I own frenzship, I explained.

No way! That's def not true.

I do. I do own frenzship. Well, to be accurate, I invented it, and own part of it.

Lorna looked up at me. Is that for real?

I nodded.

That's ridiculous!

I smiled.

Is that why you're here? She asked.

I don't know. Partly, I guess.

Are Mum and Dad going to cruise by any minute, Mr. Spyman?

Not unless you told them where we are.

Insanity

Just give me a night, I pleaded with Ewan.

I held the phone away from my ear. He was getting hysterical. Don't get hysterical, I said.

Ewan spoke more slowly. I could see his point, or rather Sally's. A middle-aged man consorting with a vulnerable, teenage girl was not a good look. Sally was going to call the police and I could be up for deprivation of liberty.

I get all that, I said to Ewan, anxiously scanning the restaurant for a sign of Lorna returning from the bathroom. But what have you got to lose?

Our daughter.

You'd not so much be losing a daughter as gaining a son-in-law…

…This is not a game.

OK, OK, I'm sorry. But, I'm being serious now. You and Sally have nothing to lose. If I bring Lorna back right now to home and hearth and the loving bosom of her family, she'll be gone again in a few days.

You don't know that, Ewan said resentfully.

No, I don't know that. But I'd bet the Godwin Johns prize, which I hold if you haven't forgotten, that she'll do a runner again.

Ewan was silent. He knew it was true.

You know the definition of insanity? I continued. Doing the same thing and expecting a different result.

Where will you go? Ewan asked in a quiet voice.

To a different hotel.

Which one?

I didn't know where we were going. So I couldn't tell him. It wasn't a good idea anyway. It's best if you don't know, I said confidently.

I don't know, Ewan mumbled. This is making me very uneasy.

Do you think I'm some kind of pervert too?

What do you mean 'too'? No, of course not.

Have some faith, my old mate. Give me a chance to do some good. Wasn't that the point of skinhead?

What am I going to tell Sally?

The truth.

She'll alert the police.

So be it, I said.

I hung up. I trotted anxiously into the restaurant. I scanned the balconies and the parkland below. I returned to the bathrooms. I hovered outside. There was no sign of Lorna.

I might be calling the police myself.

I'm OK

An ageing beauty of a waitress took pity on me. At another time, I might have kidded myself that she fancied me. On this occasion, I just wanted to avoid the humiliation of being run away from.

Do you need some help? High cheekbones asked, pointing towards the ladies.

I nodded gratefully.

Wife or daughter?

Time to think. Niece, I corrected her.

Yes, the punk.

Goth, I suggested.

Wait a minute.

I shuffled from foot to foot. I checked for texts.

I watched the door swing open. My saviour shook her head. I downgraded her on my messiah scale.

I returned to my table. It was as good a place as any to wait. I closed my eyes and tried to think happy thoughts. Nina then Cassidy visited me. I thought of my childhood. My MIA brother appeared and then my poor father. I was on the verge of a policy change to contemplating ritual disembowelment and horrendous acid scarring, when a cheery voice overtook that impulse.

Here she is, it said. Your uncle was worried about you.

I looked up. My lady friend was steering Lorna towards the table. This humble waitress was now Jesus and the Prophet Mohammed rolled into one.

Don't do that to me, I moaned to Lorna.

YOLO, old man, she said. I was just like scabbing a ciggie.

Let's go, I said, grabbing my stuff in one hand and Lorna in the other.

Where to this time?

Name a hotel.

Observation City.

OK, let's go there.

Sick.

I paid the bill and searched for the taxi rank. I found it opposite an elaborate war memorial. I took in the view. At least the river in this city was impressive.

Observation City, I said to the driver.

Do you mean the Rendezvous at Scarborough Beach?

That's the one, I answered, having no idea where Scarborough Beach was but liking the sound of the name.

Lorna made to climb in the back seat. I held her up.

Speak to your mum first. I said.

No way, Lorna replied, backing away.

Text your dad, then. Or no hotel.

Lorna stopped to consider. I started her text. 'Hi, Lorna here…'

I handed my phone to her. Tell them you're OK.

'…I'm OK', she added.

Don't put yourself out, I said with all the sarcasm I could muster. Anyway, get in.

A real way

It occurred to me that by some marvel of modern technology the police could be waiting for us. They weren't. The hotel was pretty dated but there were signs of an effort being made to introduce it to the twenty-first century.

I stay in hotels all the time. I swagger up to the reception counter and they greet me by name like a long-lost soul mate. I don't need to hand over a credit card. Everything is arranged.

I eventually made it to the front of the queue. The young Indian man, dressed like the proverbial pox doctor's clerk, looked at me and I looked at him. He didn't seem to recognise me nor I him. Then I realised I needed to book a room, from scratch. What room, or rooms? If I got one room, Lorna might think me a pervert and I might get arrested for corrupting a young girl. If I booked separate rooms, she might eat and drink her way through the mini-bar and then do a runner. My habit of stealing the shampoo and the shower cap seemed innocuous by comparison.

Raj broke the silence. I inferred his name from his silver-rimmed name badge. How can I help you? He asked.

What do you suggest as accommodation for me and my niece?

Raj took one look at my 'niece'. 'Underage hooker' was the phrase on his lips. I suggest an adjoining room for you, sir, and…your niece.

Excellent suggestion, I encouraged Raj.

Lorna was happier than a pig in shit. Instead of faeces, she had a whole hotel room to herself without parental supervision. I laid down a few simple rules to protect my bank balance. Lorna waved me away, closing the adjoining door behind her.

Dinner at seven, I shouted through the door. Meet me in the lobby.

I realised that I had no clean clothes. Nor did Lorna. Never mind. I took off my shoes. I lay down for a little nap. I fantasised about how I would spend my prison term. Could I jag the role of librarian or would I be condemned to boil soiled linen for the term of my natural life? I wondered whether my feminine side would come to the fore when I was sharing a cell.

I woke with a start. I worked out where I was. Shit! What's the time? Seven twenty-two. Fuck. I scrambled to attention. I fiddled with my shoes. Surely I was old enough by now to undo my laces when I took them off? I shuffled on one foot to bang on Lorna's door. I banged louder. I shouted. Not again. Please God, not again.

I bit the end of my recalcitrant knotted shoelace and sprinted for the lift. At ground level, I searched expectantly for Lorna and…there she was!

She pointed to her wrist.

Good girl, I said. Sorry to be late.

I'm hungry, she announced.

Great. Me too. Gourmet or burger?

Burger.

OK, down the escalator, I suggested with the confidence that a big laminated poster that reads, 'The Burger Joint – down the escalator' gives you.

Lorna ordered with aplomb. The twelve-year-old waitress turned to me.

The same, I said, hoping it didn't have beetroot.

Lorna returned to the subject that must have been preying on her mind. Is it true what you said about owning frenzship?

Scout's honour, I replied.

What? She looked puzzled.

Totally, I said, trying to select more intelligible language. I totally own it. Well, not 'totally' in that sense.

I get you. That's cray-cray. I love frenzship.

Great. Why?

I've made frenz. They're awesome.

Better than real friends? School friends?

Lorna fiddled with the straggly strands of hair on the non-shaven side. I don't have any other friends. Not really.

The waitress brought us the apple juices Lorna ordered. I was grateful for the interruption. I didn't know where our conversation was headed nor whether the direction was somewhere I should be going.

Lorna looked at me sideways. Are you sure you're not a pervert?

Why do you keep asking me this?

Because it makes you squirm.

Thanks very much! I told you before. I'm doing this out of friendship for your dad. I scanned Lorna's pretty face. Are you sure you don't have friends, you seem cool to me?

She fiddled with her straw to avoid showing her embarrassment at my compliment. I'm sure, she whispered.

I know you *do* have them. I went calling on their parents with your dad.

Yeah, that would be right. She looked me directly in the eyes in that manner of hers that belied her years. Do you even know what a friend is?

OK, I hear you. Why don't you have 'friends' then? I asked, framing the quotation marks with my fingers in that way I despise.

Lorna scratched her head on the short side. Because I'm different.

That explanation blindsided me for a moment. It showed impressive insight for a girl her age. Is that why you don't get along with your parents? I asked.

Sort of.

Two plates piled high, each with a massive burger, fries, salad and, you guessed it, beetroot, arrived. Lorna's jaws opened wider then the average crocodile to accommodate the bristling bun.

I was suddenly not hungry. I needed a beer, but resisted.

Can I tell you the skinhead story? I asked.

Knock yourself out, Lorna mumbled through a full-of-mince mouth.

You know how it goes, so I won't repeat it. Lorna's eyes widened as it went on. She wiped the beef juice and tomato sauce from her mouth with the back of her hand. I resisted the temptation to pass her a serviette. It was a long time since I'd been a teenager. I'd never been a girl. I hadn't spent any time over the last decade with anyone that age. But I could interpret the way she was reacting. At least I thought so. She'd never thought about her father as a kid. She hadn't considered him as once having been a silly, vulnerable, immature human being.

I was out of my depth with this experience. I had to play the game, whatever it was, on instinct. Has your dad told you about when he was a boy?

I don't think he ever was one, Lorna said sharply.

Bingo! I knew it. He's a great man, I added.

Yeah, yeah, Lorna yawned.

He is, but he's also a boring bastard.

That's more like it. Can I have another sundae?

Why not? You've got your own bathroom to throw up in.

Sweet!

Lorna ordered something disgusting. Abstinence wasn't making my heart grow fonder. I defiantly ordered a beer.

Your dad gave me the shits at school. He still does actually.

Lorna smiled. It was like I was farting in church.

He's always so serious. I found him very hard work. I've got to tell you about when we got him to streak.

Lorna had no idea what streaking was. I told her the story. I embellished it, naturally. She laughed out loud. She looked so good with a smile on her face.

I thought I'd been talking too much. I got up to go for a piss. You're not going to disappear on me, are you?

Probs not.

Please don't, I said, pleading with my hands clasped together. I will be in so much trouble if you do.

I was relieved to find her face full of cream and strawberries when I got back. I ordered another beer.

This time Lorna used the serviette. If Dad's so gay, why are you friends with him?

That was a fucking good question. If I'd been a politician, I would have spun a suitable answer that would have left her none the wiser. Being me, I shot from the lip.

I love your father and I hate him. I'm sure he feels the same way about me. I guess you know about his media attacks on frenzship?

No. I know he hates the Internet. Did he really do that?

What planet do you live on, Lorna?

Not your dead star, old man. Mine's a young planet.

Thanks again. I playfully reached for the sundae as if to take it back. Anyway, he hates frenzship. He hates modern communications. He hates capitalism. Do you know what that is?

No, Lorna said, licking her spoon. He hates everything.

I was getting this wrong. Rubbishing Ewan was not going to help. I'm not explaining myself very well. I said. In fact, I'm not making any sense at all. But, what I'm trying to say is…that's what friendship's like. You can't explain it. You love people. You hate them. You want to help them. You want to get one over on them. Sorry. That's the best I can do.

I understand, Lorna said sympathetically.

You do?

Yeah, I think so. My frenz are like that. Some of them.

Do you want to tell me more?

Maybe. It's, like, love I guess. I don't know. But I feel that my frenz really get me. They think about the same things as me. They don't find me strange.

Are you saying your schoolmates do?

Shit yeah! Everyone does. The olds think I'm an alien.

I'm sure they don't.

They do.

I was on autopilot again. I was flying somewhere without the controls.

Can I ask you something adult? Something difficult?

If you let me sip your beer.

OK, a sip, but you have to answer first. Are your frenz less real than, say, normal friends? Are they more like imaginary friends you might have had when you were a little girl?

Lorna stared me down. Did you really invent frenzship?

Yes. I told you. We had a mad professor who did all the science bits.

Then you should know. But maybe you're just an old. Frenz are real friends. That's what friendship is these days, old man. We don't become mates because we get into a fight and strip naked and run around poking our willies at girls. We really communicate. In a deep way. A real way.

Three in the morning

I managed to hit the sack around three in the morning. My head was whirring in several directions. Some hours before, when I still had some presence of mind, I texted Ewan. I promised that Lorna would come home in the morning.

Lorna and I chatted for hours in the lobby bar. It closed around one a.m.. We didn't notice. Our relationship was elastic. At times, I felt close to her. I thought I could become the 'bloke down the road' – the friendly adult every teenager needs – recognising that the road from Fremantle to LA was a fairly long one. At others, I suspected she saw me as just another 'old'. One with deep pockets to reach into.

I found various ways of asking Lorna the same question. Why did she run away?

Finally she responded. Our house is like a concentration camp.

I allowed the expression on my face to convey my disapproval. I didn't allow it to distract me. Why is it so bad? I asked.

She considered the question. It just is.

She didn't want to go there. I'll answer for you, I said, muddling through. I know what it would be like. I know your dad. And your mum. They'd be strict. They'd have things they reckon are good for their daughter and things that aren't. They'd be old-fashioned. They'd want you to eat fruit and get fresh air and not watch TV and not have a phone or the Internet or anything!

She smiled at me hamming it up.

Is that right? I asked.

Yeah!

But they'd talk to you about all this. They'd explain everything to you. I know them.

Lorna got animated. Yeah, they do that. We have these gross family meetings that make me want to stick my fingers down my throat, but they never listen to me.

Isn't that normal? Don't all parents do that?

No. The other olds from school live in the modern world. They let their daughters have phones, go out, wear make-up, everything, basically.

For once, I knew how to proceed. Remember when I was telling you stories about your dad when he was a boy?

I'm not a retard! It was only an hour ago.

Well, I noticed something about you. Something important.

Lorna stopped twiddling her hair and looked up at me.

You'd never thought of Ewan, your dad, as a boy, I continued. I could tell. And, because your parents emigrated to the other side of the world, you don't have grandparents around or family friends from back in the day to fill in the gaps.

Like you, you mean?

Yes. So, there's something really important you don't know.

She found an old piece of chewing gum wrapped in silver paper deep in her pocket. Her eyes lit up.

We are all a product of our own childhood.

Yeah? I hope that's not true for me.

But it is! It will be, anyway. What I'm saying here is that your parents are bringing you up in the best way they know how.

Oh my God!

They are. The best way. It is in fact the only way they can, given their own childhood and their own experiences.

Lorna had never met her grandparents. I explained what comrade Jamie was like when Ewan was a boy. He was an amazing guy, but a control freak as far as parenting went. I told her what I knew about Sally's parents. Your mum was raised by a God-botherer – I think Lorna got the point.

You look tired, I said. Do you want to go to bed?

Nah, I'm OK.

Am I boring you?

A bit.

Am I lecturing you?

Yes.

But you understand what I'm saying?

Yes. My parents can't help themselves.

I laughed out loud. I guess so.

Lorna took the chewie out of her mouth to inspect it. She stretched it out like a snail appearing from its shell then rolled it home again. I like people better online than I do in real life, she said, putting the tasteless, colourless ball of rubber back in her mouth.

I nodded for her to continue.

You think that's sad, don't you? All olds do.

Maybe. Is it?

Lorna's face lightened. It isn't. It's much better. You can do other things when you're talking. You can be alone as soon as you press one key. And you meet such epics on frenzship. You end up frenz with people from all over the world instead of boring bogan kids from up the street.

I had a vague idea what 'bogan' meant. Ewan had described our good friend Muzzo like that. It was as good a segue as any so I threw it out there. Like Muzzo?

Yeah. Him.

I was curious to dig deeper into how she felt about the boy. Lorna foreclosed on the option.

I had a lover on frenzship, she said, pulling her knees under herself to get comfortable.

I felt anxious. I tried not to show it. Tell me about him, I said.

Amity451.

That's clever.

Why?

Amity means friendship.

Does it? Sick!

Who is he?

An arsehole.

Oh. That's a shame.

He got me to do stuff. Like kill my pet. That sent the olds ballistic.

What else?

Other stuff. Lorna hesitated. You know.

I felt like I was to blame. I tried to hang in the conversation. You fell out with him?

Yeah. He's an old, for sure. Not who he said he was.

A pervert?

Yeah, like you, she said bursting into giggles.

I'm sorry, I said.

Why?

I started it. frenzship. Your dad holds me responsible. For it and for what happened to you.

He told you about that?

No! I protested. It was obvious something bad happened to you that involved frenzship.

It wasn't bad, Lorna said. It was great for the longest time. Amity451 was a creep. That's all.

Perhaps.

Anyway, I've got great frenz too. They help me cope with the olds and everything.

A king wave of fatigue crashed over me. I was physically and emotionally drained. I'm going to fall over soon, I declared. Jetlag, I explained to Lorna.

I'd like to go overseas, Lorna enthused. We were going to Bali last year. I got my passport and everything. Then they grounded me.

Well, you never know, I said.

What do you mean?

I didn't want to share the idea that had just entered my head. I will take you somewhere tomorrow, I said.

Awesome. Where?

Home.

Lorna's face switched to sad. She shook her head.

You know you have to, I insisted, standing up to go. I'll come with you.

Big deal, she moaned.

Let's go, amigo, I said.

We headed for the lifts. Raj gave me a knowing smile.

The Ten Commandments

I woke up with a start. It was very light. I fearfully checked my phone. 5.53.

I had messages. I didn't want to look. There was one from Randolph J. Steinbacher Jr.. Not a perfect way to start the day. It was the broadside Miki warned me about.

Randy accused me of dereliction of my post at frenzship, emotional abuse of his sister, extortion, arson and general crimes against humanity. I may have exaggerated with the last three. Suffice to say he was pissed.

I turned to Miki's message. He'd made no progress with Cass. Randy was on the warpath. I was expecting those two tidings of joy. The third upset me. He told me he'd FaceTimed with Nina and she was not in a good place.

I closed my eyes to rest. The bad news did laps around my mental velodrome, urging my imminent arrest to join the peloton of my problems. I found it hard to sleep. I gave up. Then I must have dozed off. It was suddenly eight o'clock.

The world-weary cynics amongst you will like the next bit. I knocked on Lorna's door. I shouted loud enough to wake the whole floor. She'd vamoosed! What a surprise! I was amazed to find Raj still on duty. He reluctantly let me into Lorna's room. I felt his judgmental eyes boring into me.

She really is my niece, I said. It was a stupid thing to say as it wasn't true. It was, however, closer to the truth than what he was obviously imagining.

The mini-bar was empty. Funny she didn't take the shampoo and the shower cap.

I ruefully paid the bill, including for the mini-bar. I called a cab to take me to Ewan's house. The last guy to see storm clouds brewing like this built an ark. I wondered if a hasty covenant with God could help me too. To assess the prospects of the Almighty affixing the divine seal to such an agreement, I did a quick self-assessment against the Ten

Commandments as best I could remember them. I had coveted my neighbour's wife, although never his ass. Her ass, yes, but never his. I had borne false witness to both Nina and Cassidy. Yet, it wasn't all bad. To the best of my knowledge, I hadn't carved any graven images, but that was quite possibly because I didn't know what they were. I ran out at three of ten. I might need to forego the rainbow side of this bargain to get it across the line.

The cab arrived. To say I was not looking forward to what I had to do next is to think of myself as an English noblewoman called Anne or Jane meeting some fat guy called Henry in the sixteenth century. I tipped the driver generously so as to feel someone's love. Their gate creaked ominously. Like a victim dangling from the gallows, I took my last walk along their path. I rang the bell. I heard footsteps rushing to the front door. Sally opened it.

Where's Lorna?

Talking to camera

The first thing I did in the safe haven of the Quest was to book myself an air ticket.

How can I put this? Ewan and Sally made it clear to me that my mission had failed. They didn't exactly put it in those gentle terms. Sally was sullen and bitter. She could barely hide her contempt for me. Ewan was angry and frustrated. To him, I had proved that nothing changes. My mock-kidnap routine was classic self-indulgence. I would have done the same thirty years ago. He restrained himself from speaking his mind. Out of friendship? Perhaps in recognition that I had at least come running.

I owed them an explanation. I gave them justification. I resorted to my tried and true habit of over-promising and under-delivering. I claimed to have established a meaningful relationship with Lorna. I got the chance to explain some things to her that are important. I educated her about her background. As a consequence, she is more understanding about her mum and dad and the beliefs and expectations that guide their parenting.

I continued in this vein as if Ewan and Lorna weren't there. I was speaking to camera. The expression on Ewan's face was a familiar one - incredulity. Sally wouldn't look at me. Her body language betrayed her growing hostility.

Lorna and I talked at length about friendship and frenzship, I continued. I rolled the z to emphasise the difference.

Sally finally met my eye. Contempt had escalated to hatred. Ewan sensed the danger of an eruption. He restrained her with a hard pressed against hers.

I ploughed on. Lorna and I debated what it meant to have a true friend and whether physical friends met in traditional fashion at school, work or over the garden fence were more real than relationships forged through technology. Lorna doesn't believe she has any flesh and blood friends. Obviously, I'm not telling you anything you don't already know. She also considers tech-friends to be just as real as others. That's a view held by many or most Gen Y, Z, A, B etc. I'm sure you know that too.

I was on a roll. I was like a stand-up comic, firing despite the deafening absence of laughter. The show must go on. I added over-reaching to the sin of over-promising. The time we spent together will be a watershed. You'll see. Lorna will come home. You won't need to look for her. When she does, things will be different. Life will be better.

It was a ludicrous speech, even to me. I had tried living in the skin of a human being. I answered the call and I came running. I took a risk in engaging Lorna the way I did. I did it for the right reasons. I thought it was worth a shot. I backed myself to pull it off. I failed. I also failed the test of personal transformation. I could now add failing Lorna to letting down Ewan and Sally and disappointing Cassidy and Nina. I was free now to return to type. I was an asshole after all.

I stood up. The wooden chair grated angrily against the solid floorboards.

I'll see myself out, I said, heading towards the front door.

My hand was on the doorknob when I heard movement in my direction. I kept going. Ewan caught up with me as I opened the rickety gate.

He hugged me. Despite everything.

I could get drunk

I had twelve hours to kill before my flight.

I considered my options. I could go for a long walk. I was too tired. I could go to a beautiful beach. I've got those at home. I could go shopping. I had no one to buy for. I could go to an art gallery. Too boring. I could go to a movie. Too depressing. I could get drunk. Good idea.

I strolled aimlessly from Ewan's house. I found myself on the Cappuccino Strip. The crowd was busily breakfasting in the colourful footpath cafes. I couldn't stomach such public parading of bonhomie. I crossed the road to the Newport Hotel. It was just the place. There were two fellow drinkers. They looked the worse for wear. Beer o'clock had arrived early for them. I climbed onto a bar stool, politely leaving a gap between us. My neighbour glanced in my direction, nodding just a fraction. I reciprocated, hoping that he wouldn't take that as a friendly act. It occurred to me that I'd met Randy in circumstances like this. Somewhat like this. I didn't want to go into business with my new friend.

Time flies when you're having fun. I racked up a fair tally of beers. I watched a variety of sporting contests on the big screen until the codes melted into one. Australian Rules football was wrestling in gaudy underwear. Basketball was soccer for tall people. Hockey was a cruel trick played by chiropractors on an unsuspecting populace.

The hotel was getting too crowded. Our numbers had trebled. The stool immediately next to me was taken by a cheerful Maori wearing an All Blacks rugby shirt.

Cheer up, bro! My new companion chirped.

I realised he was talking to me. I smiled limply.

Someone just die? He asked, picking up on my cheery mood.

Yes, I answered cruelly. My wife went down in a plane crash.

My Kiwi pal was disinclined to believe me, but the depth of my misery unnerved him. Sorry, bro, he said, dismounting from his stool to find better company.

I gathered up my loose change from the bar to set sail for the Quest. I attempted a fond farewell, but it seemed my fellow drinkers could cope without me. I staggered around the port city in a historical reference to its past as a drinking hole for the waterside workers. I spied the Round House. This helped me gain my bearings. I stumbled through the market stalls festooned with local arts and crafts weighted down against the rippling breeze. I lurched past the lunching layabouts nestled amongst the fishing boats. I looked up to see that my quest for the Quest had been fulfilled.

After a moment's angst, I recalled that this mini-bar was intact. I attacked it with gusto. The mixed nuts would suffice to accompany this liquid lunch. I got the remote to work. I avoided the sport. Soaps. Yes, I would cleanse myself this way. Days Of Our Lives. Now there's a subject worth considering. What have I done with my grains of sand? Have I impacted on this universe in a way that will live on after me for infinity or close to it?

There was a loud banging on the door. I assumed this was a distraught lover begging his married girlfriend to open up for him so he could say his last goodbye. I could do without that scene. The knocking persisted. She was determined to hide from him. Bang, bang, bang. My flight. What time was my flight? What time is it now? Oh, no. Better get up. Better try. God, my head hurts.

OK, OK, I'm coming. I opened the door. Yes, what is it?

Ewan was standing there, with Lorna.

Thanks

I apologised for my condition. I apologised for the state of the room. I apologised for the erosion of the ozone layer. Lorna was amused. Ewan was not.

Even in my befuddled state, I knew what I had to do. I must back myself again.

I invited my guests to sit down. I cleared the drinking detritus from the sofa and the coffee table. Lorna plonked herself happily onto an armchair. Ewan eyed the grubby surroundings for somewhere safe and clean to sit.

We looked at each other. It was awkward.

Lorna broke the silence. She produced an iPhone. Mum and Dad gave it to me, she said.

Really? I said, falling back into bad habits.

I'm sorry about running off, Lorna said.

It's OK.

I had to sort something out.

OK.

Then I went home. Do you know why?

No. I don't think so.

Because you promised them I would.

I looked at Ewan like I used to all those years ago. I wanted him to acknowledge how clever I was. Old habits die hard.

Thank you, I said to Lorna. That means a lot.

Ewan sat forward. I knew what was coming. So did Lorna. He was about to pontificate.

Lighten up, comrade, I warned him.

Ewan brushed my comment off as he always had. We all have to change. That's obvious. Mostly me. I have to. Lorna has to. Sally too.

Ewan turned to Lorna. He paused. She looked up from her screen.

I was so proud of you, darling, he said. You made your mum so happy when you hugged her. It was just like when you were a little girl. Thank you.

Lorna was embarrassed. She returned her gaze to the screen.

I just needed to say that, Ewan continued.

He was about to spoil everything. No one knows you like an old friend does. Not even your lover. I couldn't let him stuff everything up. Not when we were on the cusp of something. Change? Renewal? My head wasn't clear enough for this. I just had to stop him.

Ewan, can I talk to you please?

He looked angry. I'd stopped him in his tracks. He was about to say something of significance.

Outside?

Ewan raised his arms in frustration. He shot me one of his WTF expressions. He looked across at Lorna in expectation that she would protest at being excluded from whatever it was that I felt I had to say. Lorna was immersed in her new toy. She couldn't have cared less.

Come on, I said, levering Ewan out of his seat and escorting him onto the balcony outside my apartment door.

If Lorna had lifted her eyes, she would have seen two middle-aged men, silhouetted against the powerful lights illuminating the harbour, gesticulating wildly to each other. She would have observed wild disagreement followed by accusations leading to pleas and exhortations and concluding with victory and resignation.

A good twenty minutes had passed before we returned inside. My arm was round Ewan's shoulder in the manner of a coach with his protégé.

What's going on? Lorna asked, eyes fixed on a YouTube video.

I'll fill you in on the way home, Ewan said.

Do we have to go? Lorna moaned.

Yes, come on, Ewan urged her.

Reluctantly, she roused herself, without breaking her concentration on her mobile. She turned to me in passing.

Will I see you soon?

Yes, you will, I reassured her.

She turned back, all the while remaining focused on the video. She kissed me on the cheek.

By the way, Ewan called back as he closed the door. Sally says thanks.

Hypnotic Hold-Up

I felt surprisingly sober. Ewan's text arrived as requested. I went about my business on the Qatar Airways website.

Amazingly enough, I still had three hours up my sleeve before I needed to head off for the local excuse for an airport. I could go to an art gallery or a movie. I could get drunk. Maybe not. I elected for the walk instead.

The sea breeze had picked up. I pulled my shirt collar up for warmth. Groups of seagulls fought over lonely, discarded chips. But for watching a recent re-run of The Birds, I might have entered the fray. The thought of food came to mind. I would outspend the hapless flock and buy myself a whole bucket of fries.

I munched on them as I braved it out to the end of the South Moll. I was feeling better about myself. I had responded to the cry for help. And I had helped. I needed now to help myself. I had to find the courage to face the litany of home truths that awaited me.

Replenished and somewhat refreshed, I set about packing. It had always struck me as a strange term. It implied filling something very full. My bag was cavernously empty. When I left, I'd chucked my toothbrush, deodorant and a few clothes into it along with my laptop and charger cord.

Accordingly, after ten seconds, I was officially packed. I did a last check for errant belongings like a SWAT team systematically clearing a terrorist hideout. I pulled the apartment door closed behind me and trailed down the stairs to reception. I was relieved not to find Raj moonlighting at the Quest. I settled the bill with the friendly lady. She called me a cab.

Compared to the snorting and snarling traffic on the freeway to LAX, the trip was like an excursion to a country fair. The driver had disconcertingly thick lenses. He was the talkative type. I let the monologue wash over me.

Say again. I realised he'd asked me a question.

What's the worst trip you ever had?

I was tempted to tell him it was with a legally blind cab-driver who wouldn't shut up. I didn't get a chance to reply before he told me about a bus trip he went on in his native Kenya.

This is the honest truth, he continued.

That sounded ominous.

I was travelling from our village to Dar-Es-Salaam. It was at night. An old man and a younger fellow got on at a remote village. The young boy was big and strong. We hadn't ventured on more than a few miles, when the young hooligan stood over the driver and made him stop. My fellow travellers and I were very anxious. Some of the ladies started to weep. The older man raised his hands and called for silence. And then you will never believe what happened…

I came to. Really?

No, you won't believe it. The old man hypnotised the entire busload. He sent every man, woman and child into a trance, including the bus driver. And then we most willingly handed over as much as we could afford to the boy who came round with a hat, as if giving to a deserving charity. The man and the boy alighted some miles down the road. As he was descending, the old man released us from our befuddled state and told us that we would be happy to have donated our savings. What do you think of that?

I was ready this time. Amazing!

Yes it was. And do you know, that it was reported in the Kenya Times, no less. And can you guess the headline? The driver asked excitedly.

I'm afraid I can't.

Hypnotic Hold-Up. That's what they called it, the man said, relishing the memory. Hypnotic Hold-Up. Can you believe it?

Are you fishing for compliments? Lorna asks.

It wouldn't be the first time, Cass interjects.

Come on, ladies, be nice. It's important that I understand this. Why did you let me help you? I need to get this part right.

I don't know.

What is it with people your age? Why are you so intellectually lazy?

Take no notice of him, Lorns, Cassidy says.

You're supposed to be helping me finish the book, I say, appealing to a different emotion.

Amazingly, Lorna puts her cell down like someone about to make a statement of note. I was scared, she explains. I was afraid of what I was getting myself into with Muzzo and those shitheads and I was terrified that I would suffocate slowly if I went back home.

That makes sense. But why did you let me help?

Lorna weighs her answer. Because you were the only person around, I guess.

Cassidy smiles at me triumphantly.

Why does everyone enjoy my comeuppance so much?

How from the barren soil of youth, the harvest of friendship is somehow reaped

Anything for a friend

I was paged in the business class lounge. I went to the front desk. Ewan was there.

You shouldn't have bothered to see me off, I said.

I'm not seeing *you* off.

Lorna appeared, brandishing magazines bought with Dad's money. She looked a tad more respectable, no doubt following a lecture on the dangers of appearing too way out.

I organised their entry with me as guests. Lorna was beside herself. She surveyed the food counters, the snacks and the drinks. This is all free!

Yes, it's free, I confirmed. No alcohol, I warned.

Lorna headed off to consume the freebies.

See what a responsible uncle I am?

That remains to be seen, Ewan responded in a serious tone.

How did it go? With Sally.

She took some persuading.

I can imagine, I said. I'll get us some beers.

On my return, Lorna was scoffing doughnuts and ice cream while she played video games.

Who would have thought it? Ewan said.

Exactly, comrade.

We both knew what we were talking about.

It's a funny thing, friendship, Ewan said. I hated you so much for the exploitation by frenzship. And then when I realised Lorna was caught up with it herself, I could have bought a gun and shot you.

You would have missed.

Ewan laughed, grudgingly. But I still loved you even when I hated you.

I know.

I felt like killing you, but if someone else tried, I would have taken the bullet for you.

Someone else might not have missed.

Come on, be serious. Don't make a joke out of everything.

I'm sorry. I'm immature.

You are.

And you're a self-righteous prick.

I am.

And a complete idiot.

Why?

Because you're letting me take your daughter with me.

Our flight was announced. Ewan and I stood up. Lorna was oblivious. We hugged.

Thanks for coming, Ewan said to the back of my neck.

You did say 'skinhead'.

You could have ignored it.

I couldn't. You know that.

I suppose. And thanks for what you're doing.

Anything for a friend.

Sally thanks you too. You know, despite...

...I know.

We stepped apart and looked at each other. Just as we had when I first arrived at this tin shed of an airport. Lorna had gathered her things and was focused on us.

I'm still going after frenzship, Ewan stressed.

Of course, I conceded. You're a boring troglodyte. What more could I expect?

As long as you know, he said, turning to Lorna. Come on, Lorna Doone, let's get you on your way.

We settled into our business class seats. Lorna's eyes were like saucers. She looped her arm into mine, as Nina had done all those years ago.

Thanks for doing this for me, she said.

I'm not doing it for you.

OK, for Dad, then.

It's not for your dad, either.

Who for then? Lorna asked, gripping me for a straight answer. It's for me. I'm doing this for me.

Distraction or a shield

Despite the luxurious circumstances of our travel, Lorna complained a lot once the novelty wore off. I patiently explained the length of each leg of our trip. Her body language drifted to the bottom when it sank in that, after we landed and changed planes, we had the same amount of time to go on the second leg.

I was grateful for the stopover in Doha. It provided some new scenery for Lorna. In my unfamiliar supervisory role, I realised for the first time the range of temptations that are rolled out to entice weary travellers. I imagined what Ewan would do in this situation. I resolved to do the opposite.

I made Lorna follow me to the Al Mourjan Business Lounge so she knew where it was. Then I set her free. Make sure you're back here by eight ten at the latest, I instructed her.

Cool, Lorna shrieked. She stared around her, uncertain which way to go to explore the untold delights.

I requested an Asahi. I tried to look like an infidel so the waiter wouldn't scowl at me for partaking of alcohol. I settled into an absurdly comfortable armchair to contemplate my standing in the world, life and everything. Lorna was uppermost on my mind. Should I have warned her to keep her boarding pass safe? I probably should have. This trip was going to have its moments. Not only because of what I had to do. Those exams would be tough enough. Now I had thrown Lorna into the mix. The papers would be set in Hindi.

Was it true what I said to Lorna? That I was doing this for me. It was and it wasn't. I needed a friend by my side. That much was gospel. Lorna grounded me. Taking some responsibility for her was helping me face my own reality. But I was also helping my friend. As misguided as my judgment might ultimately prove to be, I thought I could relate to Lorna at this stage of her life more meaningfully than her parents could. I wanted to act out the fantasy of rescuing her to return her in a better state. Ewan had called me on the arrogance and the selfishness inherent in my actions. I knew I was guilty as charged. But I was innocent too. Lorna thanked me for helping her. I should have acknowledged the truth in that. My motives in that regard were both selfless and selfish. She needed help and I wanted to provide it. Why? Simple. She was so much like me. In saving her, I would save myself.

After the third and most strident PA announcement appealing for some miscreant to come forward, it occurred to me that the peculiar name in question could be mine if mispronounced by someone whose Arabic was vastly superior to their English. I summoned the energy to check it out. I was horrified to find Lorna at the reception desk with two security guards in tow.

Are you this girl's uncle? The big-breasted female demanded.

Ye-es. I am. What's the problem?

Can I see your boarding card? She asked.

It's nothing special, I warned her, reluctantly fishing it from my back pocket.

She grudgingly returned it.

I thought you might be disappointed, I said with a friendly smile.

This was another of those occasions when my attempts at humour seemed to pass unappreciated.

I advise you to keep your niece with you if you wish to board this flight. The advice came from the thin man who was holding the girl by the elbow.

I gave Lorna the stare.

What? She glared at me. I was just looking at some random jacket.

Fortunately, we both slept through the second leg. We said little as we inched our way through the tortuous arrivals process. The taxi queue was mercifully short. I'd organised international roaming for Lorna. She promised me she had texted her mum and dad.

The cab was stuck in the morning peak hour traffic. Nothing had changed. Lorna was too spaced out to take in the sights. I stopped nudging her. There would be plenty of time for that. I closed my eyes and tried to relax. I had texts and phone messages waiting for me. I resolved to ignore them for the time being. I wanted to act on instinct rather than work from some calculation or to a plan. Lorna's presence gave me courage. As a source of strength or as a distraction or a shield? I wasn't sure.

It was surprisingly cold as we unloaded the bags from the taxi. The usual surcharge was added for use of the credit card. How do these merchants get away with that? Everyone pays by card these days. What happened when cash was first introduced? Did the farmer hold back two carrots when you stopped paying him with eggs?

Lorna waited with the bags. There was no sign of life downstairs. I fumbled in the familiar place. There was nothing. That was strange. I looked up to the top floor. There was no sign of life.

I promise

I had Lorna with me. I needed to change tack and get her sorted out. I took her to the accommodation. She was tired and irritable. I saw to it as best I could that she was OK. My guess was that she would sleep through until nighttime. I was safe to go out.

I took my third taxi. Again to no avail. This was a predictable fate for those who don't call ahead to warn of their impending arrival.

I made some calls.

I eventually got someone. You'd better come over, he said.

The old place?

Yes, the same place.

My taxi driver was reading the newspaper in the same spot where he dropped me. I tapped on the window. He was reluctant. I wasn't in the mood for an argument. I climbed in beside him with an expectant look on my face.

After another struggle with the one-way streets and a broken down bus that had disgorged its disgruntled passengers onto the sidewalk, we arrived at our destination. I made my way to the familiar door and signalled my presence.

Jacques shook my hand and guided me into the living room. He gathered up two brandies from the drinks trolley. He handed me one and saluted me.

I hate to be the one.

The one for what? I asked anxiously.

The one to tell you.

What? What are you saying?

Nina is dead. Elle est morte. Je suis désolé. Nous sommes tous désolés.

Shock does amazing things. It registered with me that Jacques was dyeing his hair. His short, tight curls were hennaed in contrast to his whiskers of grey consciously shaved to stubble length. The Curvoisier tasted like crisped biscuit. Jacques' wife, Marie-Claire, was framed in the window seat like a still life portrait.

Excusez-moi, I stuttered. I fumbled in my coat breast pocket for my phone. I had ten messages from Miki. I scanned them, not really taking in their meaning. Each was more desperate than its predecessor. In the fog that was my brain, I noticed texts from Randy and Dr. Jeremiah in the mix.

I felt a delicate touch on my elbow. Marie-Claire led me to the elegant sofa. She sat me down, lowering herself next to me. She held my right hand in her left, gently stroking me with the other. Jacques refreshed my tumbler, placing it on the carved occasional table in front of me.

What happened?

A car.

How?

Jacques shrugged, puckering his lips.

Please tell me.

On ne sait pas, Jacques said. We don't know.

When did this happen?

She was found three days ago.

That was a strange thing to say. What do you mean by 'found'?

The husband and wife looked at each other. The unflappable Jacques shuffled in his armchair.

We don't have all the details, he explained. Then he hesitated.

Go on. Please.

The police aren't saying much. Nina's car hit a tree.

An accident then?

A tree way off the main road. En pleine campagne. In the middle of nowhere. Do you know what I'm saying here?

No, I don't!

What my husband is trying to say, Marie-Claire spoke in that deliberate fashion of hers, is that the police have not ruled anything out.

I looked from one to the other. What are you saying? You're confusing me.

Suicide, Jacques whispered as if he didn't want to hear the word himself. It could have been deliberate. There were no skid marks and no other tyre tracks around to indicate another car.

I extricated myself from the sofa situation. I walked robotically to the bay window. The sound of the ice clinking against the side of my glass was deafening. Jacques' secret garden was still magnificent. Nina used to love it there.

When is the funeral? I asked without turning from the view.

Tomorrow, Jacques replied. Your Japanese associate is flying in tonight.

I felt a warm touch on my shoulder. You will stay with us, of course, Marie-Claire said.

I can't, I stammered. It sounded ungrateful. I would but…

…Nonsense, Jacques insisted, I will cancel your hotel reservation.

No, it's not that. Thank you, really. It's just that I'm travelling with my…niece.

A niece? Jacques was rightly surprised.

Well, she must come too, Marie-Claire declared with a note of finality.

No, I said equally firmly. Then I looked around to soften the impact. Seriously, you are most generous, but things will work out best if Lorna and I stay at the hotel.

I made my excuses. I needed to get away. Jacques insisted that his driver take me back to my hotel. In my dazed state, time was distorted. The car pulled up outside in what seemed like a matter of seconds. Jacques patted me on the back as I ducked my head to slide into the back seat. Marie-Claire cut a pathetic figure, waving feebly in the background.

A demain, Jacques said sadly through my open window. See you tomorrow.

I deleted Miki's messages. I couldn't face the sadness of the unfolding drama. Instead I rang him. I'd forgotten he was supposed to be in the air. The ongoing ringing was strangely soothing. My reverie was interrupted when Miki picked up.

At last, he said.

I'm sorry.

Where are you?

Paris.

So you knew. Why the devil didn't you answer my messages?

It's a long story, I said. Where are you?

I'm still on the plane. We landed two minutes ago. Where are you staying?

I told him.

OK, I haven't made a booking. I'll try to get in there too.

No. Don't, I said as an afterthought.

Why? You sound really weird.

I know. I'm in shock.

Don't worry. I'll fix the reservation.

Don't. Really. Don't stay there.

Why not? You're scaring me.

Because my niece is with me.

Your niece?

Yes. She's Australian.

I didn't know you had a niece.

I know. I don't.

I realised this botched narrative sounded suss.

Miki, why don't you stay with Jacques?

Do you think I could?

Definitely. They invited me. But, you know, what with my niece.

Will you call them for me?

Yes, I'll fix it. Remember the address? I asked.

Of course.

OK, then. I'll call you later.

I don't trust you, Miki said.

I will. I promise.

A blur

Lorna was a godsend. She'd slept right through my trauma save for an hour in the hotel restaurant before she collapsed again.

This morning she was as excited as anyone could be. Lorna demolished a gargantuan breakfast of savoury pancakes followed by syrupy-sweet waffles that would have made a truckie chuck. She'd woken up early and done her research on the tourist sites she wanted to hit.

It was apparent that my energy didn't match hers.

You seem sad, Lorna observed. Have I done something?

No, I reassured her. You've been asleep!

She laughed. Then she jumped up. Let's go.

It was warm for the time of year and the weather was fine. Perfect for sightseeing. And burying. I recalled the bedraggled throng at my father's consignment. If you'd swapped their black suits for yellow wet weather gear, the moistened mourners would have looked the part. And then there was the phantom funeral attended by my wraithlike brother. I could picture those huge droplets splattering down from my father's umbrella.

Lorna had her heart set on the metro. I persuaded her that the sights were best tackled on foot.

But it's so far.

And it's so good. You won't even notice.

We walked the Champs-Elysees past the Arc de Triomphe then took in the Tuileries.

Unreal! Sick! Lorna exclaimed at intervals.

I doubled back along the Seine to the Ile de la Cité. I pointed to Notre-Dame cathedral.

The Hunchback lived in there, I said, pointing up at the bell tower.

Which hunchback?

Don't you know anything? Haven't you heard of the Hunchback of Notre-Dame.

Yes, I have actually, Lorna said in a hoity-toity accent. It's a cartoon. I saw it as a kid.

We stopped for un chocolat chaud. I'd forgotten how expensive Paris was. Two hot chocolates and a bun cost me even more than it did in Perth. Lorna's enthusiasm was infectious. Whenever my mind strayed to the tragedy of Nina and more specifically to how badly I'd failed her, Lorna would prattle away, insisting that I pay attention.

The geography and layout of Paris remained familiar. It was as if I'd never left. I successfully wove my way through side streets so I could serve up the most dramatic effect. We turned the corner and then I waited for it.

Oh my God! Lorna shrieked as the Eiffel Tower came into view in the distance across the sweeping approach. She snapped away on her phone camera. As we got closer, she racked up the selfies. Then she busied herself posting the results. Was she using Facebook, Instagram, Snapchat or Frenzyfoto? That was the first I'd thought of business for quite some time.

The queues to ascend the tower were horrendous. Greek pensioners seeking essential medicines wait less time than this. I got progressively anxious in the line. The time until the funeral was ticking away. I hadn't told Lorna about what happened. I didn't want to burden her. Now I would have to lie to her. I still had an uncanny knack of bearing false witness.

Lorna opened up an opportunity. Why are checking your watch, old man? Do you have a date?

I faltered for a moment, weak at the knees. That phrase undid me. A date? I had so many. Before. And now, did I have a date? I did. A date with death. A date with destiny, actually. A date worse than death?

Are you OK? Lorna asked. You don't look well.

I snapped myself back. I needed to hold firm. I'm fine. The jetlag just hit me.

You should have slept longer.

What? Yes. Hey listen. There's something I have to do this afternoon.

A date?

Not a date. I will have to leave at two-thirty.

We'd better get in by then, Lorna pouted.

The innocent self-obsession of youth.

We made it just in time. Lorna was blown away. I bundled her into a taxi and looked at her sternly.

Don't worry, she said. I won't disappear on you. I've already demolished the mini-bar.

I glared at her.

Just kidding, she giggled as the cab pulled away.

I can't describe the funeral. It barely registered. Familiar faces and complete strangers crossed my field of vision.

I realised with horror on arriving at Père Lachaise that I was dressed in casual clothes for a funeral in the heart of bourgeois Paris. I momentarily turned tail. Then I thought of Nina. What would Nina say? She held these conventions in contempt. Dressed in jeans and a casual shirt, I would be honouring the memory and free spirit of my gorgeous girl.

The same could not be said for the officiating priest. Miki and I stood aloof from the rest of the mourners. We leant on each other. I barely heard the curate's prayers and eulogy. His mere presence offended me. Nina detested the Catholic Church. Her mother was a religious type. But she was Jewish. Why this? To keep up appearances. That was it. It was for the friends and family, not for Nina. Nina doesn't care now. She was stone cold dead. In a box. Soon in the ground. I sobbed. Miki comforted me.

Miki and I shook hands with the others politely. Jacques and Marie-Claire invited us back for a drink. Miki looked at me.

My niece, I explained.

D'accord, Jacques said, shaking my hand vigorously in both of his. Next time, hein?

Absolument.

Promis?

C'est promis?

Miki reassured his hosts that he would take a taxi to their house later.

We trudged away. At the height of grief, you can read another's thoughts.

Ali Bar Bar? Miki checked.

Ali Bar Bar, I confirmed.

For another time

It's quieter than I remember, Miki observed, laying down the two lagers with tequila chasers.

We were never here at five o'clock, I observed.

Not in the afternoon, anyway, Miki joked.

I checked the incoming text. It was from Lorna. All good. Watching a hundred TV channels.

I smiled.

From your niece? Miki said sarcastically.

Yes.

Trouble really is your middle name. One girl in the club and now one in the ground. Isn't that enough?

It's not a girl.

Niece? Miki said, raising an eyebrow.

Well, it is a girl obviously. But not the sort you think.

Well, why the 'niece' line? Or did your brother reappear?

No, nothing like that. Lorna's like a niece.

Who is she then?

Ewan's daughter.

Ewan Mackenzie's daughter?

Yes.

The Ewan Mackenzie, the anti-frenzship crusader's daughter.

Yes.

Holy Christ.

Him as well.

Why didn't you respond to my texts about Nina? Miki asked, changing tack.

It's complicated, I said, downing my mescal in one.

It always is with you. I was worried about her. I told you. I was trying to reach you.

I sidestepped. I needed his opinion on something different.

Do you think she killed herself? I asked fast like a stomach punch.

Miki exhaled deeply. He didn't answer.

I asked you a question, Miki.

Yes I do.

That rocked me. I protested. Why? How can you say that?

It's not a judgment. It's an answer. You asked me the question.

I calmed myself. Do you really think so?

I'm sorry, but I do.

The emotion was raw. For both of us. We stepped back from the fire for a moment.

Why would she do that? It was a rhetorical question more than anything.

Miki responded anyway. You know why.

Because she couldn't face it?

Miki nodded.

Something odd happened when I visited her recently, I said, shaking my head.

Miki looked puzzled.

When I was with Nina a month or so ago, she made me do something.

Miki waited for me to explain. It was personal. It was speaking ill of the dead.

Are you going to tell me? Miki asked.

I swallowed. Nina made me fuck her up the ass.

She *made* you.

Yes. I didn't want to.

Miki was angry that I brought this up. Why are you telling me this? It's tasteless.

I shrugged his irritation off. I asked her why.

And?

She said, 'Because I'm dying'.

I don't get you. What does that even mean?

I took a deep breath before speaking. I assembled my thoughts carefully. It was symbolic. Of her decline. She was degraded. And she degraded me. That was her fear. Do you see now?

Yes, I think so.

You do?

I think so. That's why I think it was suicide. That's why she put an end to it.

Because she would drag us all down with her?

Exactly.

I got in another round. This will need to be my last, I declared.

Miki smirked at me. He looked very Asian once in a while. Because of your *niece*?

Yes.

She's a good influence on you.

She is actually, I observed, feeling a pleasant flush of emotion.

I dragged myself back to grim reality. I'm sorry about your texts. I should have done more.

Me too.

I mean for Nina.

I know. Me too. Miki paused. What would you have done, if you had your time again?

I don't know. That was a reflex answer. I should've stayed with Nina instead of going to Australia.

Miki seemed miles away, reflecting on things done and not done, like I was. Would you have helped her?

I was confused. That's why I should have stayed, I explained. To help her.

I should have come myself, Miki said sadly. Not when it's too late, like now.

Belatedly I got Miki's drift. At least I thought I did. What did you mean by 'help her'? I asked.

You know, he said, fearing the words on the tip of his tongue, help her.

Do it?

Yes. You know, in a better way. A gentler way.

We drank in silence for what seemed an eternity. We were stuck halfway in the dark tunnel of our thoughts. We didn't dare go forwards and we couldn't go back.

My instinct as ever was to flee. I've got to go, I announced, standing up and gathering my things.

OK, Miki nodded. I can't face Jacques and Marie-Claire right now. I think I'll drown my sorrows here.

See you Stateside, I said, extending the palm of my hand for him to clasp.

Sure, he said, making contact.

I set off, but stopped in my tracks. I returned to the table. Miki looked up.

I couldn't have done it, I said.

He nodded in acknowledgment.

Not that. That would hardly be love.

What about friendship? Miki asked. Wouldn't that be the ultimate act of friendship?

I left that comment hanging in the air. For another time, perhaps.

Avoid the pain?

We'd passed through passport control and French customs. It was a standing joke between us. Lorna struck before I could.

No, I won't run off. No I won't shoplift. Yes I will return here in good time.

I took refuge in the business lounge, smiling as Lorna skipped off into the crowd. She was a good girl, deep down. Smart, sassy and rebellious. She had Ewan and Sally in there too. She'd taken to caring for me in my grief.

I tried to keep the tragedy from Lorna, but I'm not a great actor. If I had a heart, I would wear it on my sleeve. Lorna caught me sobbing once too often.

Why are you sad? She asked. You can tell me.

I forced a laugh through my tears. It was such an adult thing to say. How old are you? Fifty?

I'm old enough.

That was fair comment. My friend died. A very close friend.

Is that why we came to Paris rather than go straight to where you live?

Not exactly. I wanted to see my friend. She was sick.

What with? Lorna sensed she had overstepped the mark. You don't have to answer that, she said.

Lorna had been keeping an eye out for me over the remaining few days we had in Paris. I took her to all the fun spots and I made her trudge around the museums and the Louvre. Ewan would have been proud of me for forcing Lorna to eat her cultural greens.

We stood in front of the Mona Lisa. I'd told her about the fake one in my living room with the wandering eyes. She peered between the admiring bodies in front of her.

It's not very big, is it? Lorna observed.

I told you that.

Cute smile, but.

She looks like you, I teased.

No way, she protested. Not with that daggy haircut.

Lorna plonked herself next to me. She was only five minutes late. I was about to break the news to her that our plane had been delayed.

Do you know the first thing I'm going to do in super-cool LA? Lorna asked me.

Sleep?

No. I'm going to get another tattoo.

No, you're not, I shot back.

Why not? Don't be so boring, Lorna sneered.

You've already got one?

Want to see it, pervert?

Don't start that again. Do your parents know? I asked.

Hardly.com.

Anyway, I said in a firm tone, I am returning your body to the tender care of your parents exactly as they left it.

What if I have a haircut?

Don't be a smartass.

When Lorna was up, her brain was like a will-o'-the-wisp. She would cut and run from subject to subject.

You know your friend, she said cautiously. The one who died…

I nodded.

…was she your girlfriend?

Yes. And then she was my friend.

I don't get you.

After we stopped being boyfriend and girlfriend, we just became friends.

Lorna pondered the answer. Do you think you could have been frenz?

What do you mean? We were friends, I just told you.

Frenz, she stressed. Do you think what you had would have been up to the standard of true frenzship?

Out of the mouths of babes. That was an incredible question. Only someone of Lorna's age, a child of the digital era, could have come up with that. It floored me. I really don't know, I stammered.

It would have been better that way, Lorna said so blandly that she could have been commenting on the weather.

What do you mean by that?

Lorna seemed reluctant to expand. The comment had slipped out and she seemed to regret it.

It's OK, I reassured her. I'm not offended. You don't have to answer.

She looked up from the spooning of her hot chocolate. Frenz don't die on you.

I looked blankly at her.

They sometimes disappear, which is cruel and sad. It's not the same, that's all I'm saying.

You mean the emotion? The feelings?

Yes. Losing someone doesn't hurt as much as…you know,

Like Amity541? I asked.

451. No, not like him. Other frenz, I mean. They move on from you

or you from them. And then there's the frenzship limit.

I saw the light. Through one of Leonard Cohen's cracks that let it in. Is that why you keep your flesh and blood friends at a distance? To avoid the pain?

Lorna returned to her video. Now you sound just like my mum.

Enough said, I conceded. By the way, I've got some bad news.

Yeah, I heard you. No tattoos.

Not that. The plane's delayed.

Fuck.

Don't swear.

Now you sound like my dad.

Over time

I did a double-take. Cassidy met our plane. She was clearly showing. Miki told me that the morning sickness had passed. She looked healthy. Dammit, she looked beautiful!

We kissed. It had longing.

Welcome to LA, Lorna, Cassidy said, formally holding out her hand.

Lorna shot me an angry glance. I had omitted to brief her on the complexities of my life back home. I figured sudden death in Europe was enough for a teenager to have to cope with.

Look at you, I remarked to Cassidy. Someone knocked you up.

Yes, someone did.

Randy's latest factotum was on hand. Mitchell had a rugged face and long dark eyelashes. I assumed Cass had chosen this one. Lorna couldn't take her eyes off him. She was lapping up the attention.

Cassidy and I hung back, walking slowly, arms threaded around each other's waist.

I didn't expect you, I said, kissing her tenderly.

I wasn't sure if I would come.

Miki has filled you in?

Yes. I'm so sorry. About Nina.

I was too choked up to respond.

What a tragedy, Cassidy said. You must be devastated.

I steered Cass out of the way of two daredevil toddlers on ripsticks. Only in LA.

I treated you badly, I said. I'm sorry.

I'm the one who should be sorry.

Really?

Cassidy laughed. You're back! Truly, I *am* sorry.

Don't, Cass. You don't have to.

I do, she said, bringing me to a stop and turning me to face her. I wanted this, she said, running both hands over the swelling belly, so much that even I didn't acknowledge it. I was scared to, I suppose. I didn't know what I wanted.

Who does?

I was really confused. I'd had that taste of running Steinbacher. I imagined myself one day as the Queen of frenzship. And then my dear, sweet stepbrother went and recovered on me. All along, I wanted a baby, but I didn't realise it. And then there was you.

Then there was me.

Yes there was you - a selfish asshole.

Thanks.

A selfish asshole I came to love. A selfish asshole who still loved someone else.

I kissed Cassidy and led her on towards the carpark. Lorna and Mitchell had disappeared from view.

I don't know if that's true, Cass. The bit about me still loving Nina, I mean. The part about me being an asshole is pretty undeniable.

Cassidy cuddled into me.

If I'm honest, I continued. I'm just selfish. That's the long and short of it. I wanted you both.

That's OK, Cassidy said.

No, it's not! I reacted angrily. It's not OK.

I was a bitch, too. Let's face it.

Why?

I should have let you go to Nina.

I shrugged.

More than that, I should have shoved you out the door to go to her when she needed you.

I squeezed Cassidy's hand to indicate she was forgiven.

And now look what happened.

Cass, I said, conjuring up a smile, if you're going to blame yourself too, you'll need to get to the back of the queue.

She laughed.

What now? Cassidy asked. Are you staying in LA?

Yes, I intend to.

Will you stay with me?

I'd like to.

I won't ask you for how long, Cassidy whispered.

How about this? I said, turning her to face me again. How about for as long as we're friends?

That suits me.

That suits me too.

We walked on. Mitchell was loading the bags into the limo. I could see Lorna beaming from ear to ear. I thought the conveyance might please her.

Hey, I've got a question for you. Inspired by Lorna.

OK, but you're not getting the other nineteen!

Do you think we would be frenz?

Frenz?

Yes, would our friendship qualify as frenzship?

That's asking a lot, Cassidy smirked.

Maybe over time, I suggested. By the way, I added, is Randy still after me?

I threw away the key to his gun closet if that answers your question.

Harold3

Lorna handed me back my iPad. Ewan looked less than comfortable embracing the modern world of FaceTime.

She seems happy, Ewan said.

She's got LA at her fingertips. What is there not to like?

Well, the Lorna of old would have found something, he observed. And not just one thing.

I laughed. She's still a handful, don't get me wrong. To be honest, I'd struggle without Cass.

Lorna idolises Cassidy, Ewan said. And who is this guy, Mitchell?

Don't worry about him, I said, he's the chauffeur who's doing her when we go out.

Ewan glared back at me.

Sorry, I said, raising my hands in apology. Tasteless joke. On a more serious note, I continued, what did you think of Lorna's nose ring?

What? He thundered.

It's very discreet.

You're so fucking irresponsible, he shrieked.

And you're still so gullible, I said, falling about laughing.

Hey, Ewan said, looking serious again. Thanks for helping us.

She's helping me too.

You're a true friend, mate.

I came running.

You did. Ewan raised his hand. I've got another friend I want you to meet. If I can make this technology work, you need to come with me. It won't take a minute

The video picture pitched and rolled like the tablet was in a big swell and then it broke up and froze.

Lorna appeared at my side. Are you still talking to Dad?

I was, I said. He wants me to meet someone.

Oh no, Lorna said, shaking her head.

The picture cleared and Ewan's scratchy voice could be heard again. Can you hear me now?

Yes.

Have you got picture?

Yes, I said as a very old man seated on a wooden bench came into shot.

This is Harold, Ewan said.

Howdy Harold, I said with a cheery wave.

Is that him there? Harold said in a scratchy voice, pointing a gnarly finger in the direction of Ewan's screen.

Howdy Harold, I repeated.

G'day, he grumbled. New fangled nonsense, he muttered.

And now may I present someone else to you? Ewan said theatrically.

Go on.

Ewan paused for a second. You'll find this guy interesting. He has an intrinsic understanding of friendship. It's in his DNA.

Can't wait, I enthused.

The shaky camera settled on a thin, brown dog sleeping at the old man's feet.

Who's this? I asked.

Harold 3. He's Harold's best friend.

Epilogue

I just met Ewan at LAX. Lorna wasn't expecting him. When he made it to the Bel-Air, they hugged like it was a minute until the bomb was to go off.

I'm watching them now out on the veranda, overlooking the lights of LA. In the background, Cass is playing Sally's role. She hasn't forgiven Ewan for his attacks on frenzship just as Sally can never truly let bygones be bygones over the terrible influence I've had on Ewan's life.

Am I still fascinated by the concept of friendship? Yes, I am. Am I much the wiser having written this book and after playing my part in redefining the very concept in the age of disruption? No, I'm not.

If you press me now to define what friendship is, I have to resort to the central premise of frenzship. Our technology sorts through billions of people in the world and reduces the list to a handful of people with whom you should be friends.

Some like Ewan say it dehumanizes friendship. I understand why they say that, but they are wrong. frenzship opens up the possibilities and refines your search. In so-called 'normal' friendships, we do that, but in a very clumsy way.

I've come full circle now. In stealing the word 'friend', Facebook has done us all a favour. It has made some of us review what the term really means. The bond Ewan and I have is the real thing. It is a true friendship, not an example of that overused word. He and I are lucky, I guess. We both met someone who, despite our cavernous differences, really should be our friend.

FRIENDSHIP

is a mirror to presence and a testament to forgiveness. Friendship not only helps us to see ourselves through another's eyes, but can be sustained over the years only with someone who has repeatedly forgiven us for our trespasses as we must find it in ourselves to forgive them in turn. A friend knows our difficulties and shadows and remains in sight, a companion to our vulnerabilities more than our triumphs, when we are under the strange illusion we do not need them. An undercurrent of real friendship is a blessing exactly because its elemental form is rediscovered again and again through understanding and mercy. All friendships of any length are based on a continued, mutual forgiveness. Without tolerance and mercy friendships die.

In the course of the years a close friendship will always reveal the shadow in the other as much as ourselves, to remain friends we must know the other and their difficulties and even their sins and encourage the best in them, not through critique but through addressing the better part of them, the leading creative edge of their incarnation, thus subtly discouraging what makes them smaller, less generous, less of themselves...

Friendship is the great hidden transmuter of all relationship: it can transform a troubled marriage, make honorable a professional rivalry, make sense of heartbreak and unrequited love and become the newly discovered ground for a mature parent-child relationship.

The dynamic of friendship is almost always underestimated as a constant force in human life: a diminishing circle of friends is the first terrible diagnostic of a life in deep trouble: of overwork, of too much emphasis on a professional identity, of forgetting who will be there when our armored personalities run into the inevitable natural disasters and vulnerabilities found in even the most average existence...

Friendship transcends disappearance: an enduring friendship goes on after death, the exchange only transmuted by absence, the relationship advancing and maturing in a silent internal conversational way even after one half of the bond has passed on.

But no matter the medicinal virtues of being a true friend or sustaining a long close relationship with another, the ultimate touchstone of friendship is not improvement, neither of the other nor of the self, the ultimate touchstone is witness, the privilege of having been seen by someone and the equal privilege of being granted the sight of the essence of another, to have walked with them and to have believed in them, and sometimes just to have accompanied them for however brief a span, on a journey impossible to accomplish alone.

From 'FRIENDSHIP' in CONSOLATIONS:
The Solace, Nourishment and Underlying Meaning of Everyday Words.
© David Whyte & Many Rivers Press

Acknowledgements

My thanks go out to all my friends for putting up with me, not abandoning me despite my neglect and for providing the inspiration for this book. They will recognise themselves here for what they really did and what they should have done that I made up.

Above all of them, I thank my darling Carol for her encouragement, patience and faith in me that I can carry out what I set myself to do.

I acknowledge also the contribution of my publication facilitator, Ian Andrew, for his sage advice, professionalism and good humour.

Finally, I recall with great fondness my recently departed friend and mentor, 'Umpire John Simmons' to whom this book is dedicated. The look of regret he would give me from 22 yards away when raising his finger to give me out LBW taught me everything I needed to know about friendship.

About the Author

Ray is a business leader, presenter, social media commentator and author.

Ray has a background and Master's degrees in philosophy, psychology, business and social work. Ray runs his own management consulting business, From Left Field. He is in demand as a non-executive director, serving on writingWA, the peak body for writers and readers in Western Australia, amongst other boards, is a Fellow of the Australian Institute of Management and of the Australian Institute of Company Directors.

Ray Glickman has presented at numerous conferences around Australia in recent years in his own humorous and provocative style.

As a lifelong student of individual and group behaviour, Ray writes about the impact of the modern world on traditional values and morality.

Ray's first novel, Reality, published by the Fremantle Press in 2014 is a darkly entertaining thriller about manipulation in the twenty-first century. It was shortlisted for the WA Premier's Awards in 2016.

Enjoyed the Book?
Leave a review

Follow Ray at:

Web: rayglickman.com

Blog: rayglickman.com

Twitter: @RayGlickman

Facebook: www.facebook.com/realitybyrayglickman

Email: glicko@bigpond.net.au

Reality

Six people have been chosen at random. Without their knowledge, Kathy, Mario, Garry, Hannah, Robert and Julia are about to participate in the ultimate game of manipulation.

A stranger brings them together, but can this ruthless puppeteer really be held responsible for the choices they make? In the end, who is to blame for their actions: for their deceit, infidelity and crime?

At the heart of this thought-provoking novel lie questions of fate and self-determination.

PRAISE FOR THE BOOK

"... Glickman crafts an ensemble of varied and distinct characters for his lucky six, but his greatest trick is making the reader complicit in the Master Plan of his narrator — while you know full well that this expert manipulator is a high-functioning sociopath you ought to loathe, you'll be just as keen as he is to see how his plan pans out."
Scoop Magazine

"... a fast paced, well structured and utterly compelling narrative. Reality is a darkly entertaining novel."
writingWA

"... is hard to put down once you start reading."
Roger Hanson, The Mercury Newspaper

"... thought provoking and darkly funny."
Sarah McNeill, Timeout

"... Fast paced, punchy and in your face... a book that you can't put down."
Villages.com

Lightning Source UK Ltd.
Milton Keynes UK
UKOW03f0637120417
298942UK00004B/291/P